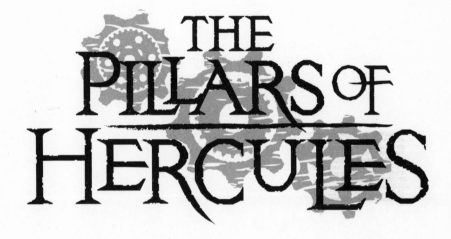

THE PILLARS OF HERCULES

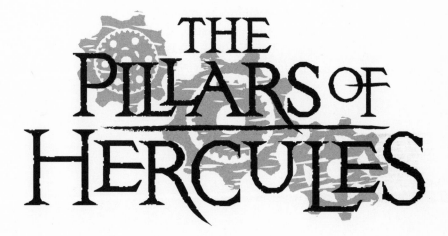

THE PILLARS OF HERCULES

DAVID CONSTANTINE

NIGHT SHADE BOOKS
SAN FRANCISCO

First Edition

ISBN: 978-1-59780-397-7

Night Shade Books
http://www.nightshadebooks.com

For my parents

Alexander the Great's conquest of the Persian Empire took a mere five years, after which he turned West again. Athens, which had expected to enjoy her vast Mediterranean possessions while Alexander became embroiled in endless Eastern wars, was suddenly faced with a battle-tested Macedonian army. For even as Alexander declined to become mired in a perpetual campaign in Afghanistan, his sorcerer-spies were unearthing ancient magicks from beyond the Hindu Kush... magicks with which he intended to crush the Athenian Empire and rule the known world. It was to be the ultimate conflict, and it began when Alexander unleashed his full might on Athens' most vulnerable province: Egypt.

—Hieronymous of Cardia, *The War of Athens and Macedonia*

Nine thousand was the sum of the years which had elapsed since the war which was said to have taken place between those who dwelt outside the Pillars of Hercules... commanded by the lords of Atlantis, an island greater in extent than Libya and Asia... and afterwards sunk by an earthquake the likes of which had never been seen...

—Plato, *The Dialogue of Critias*

Above all else, it was the uncovering of the secrets of the elder races that forever changed the destiny of the younger ones.

—Aristotle, *On Machinery and Magicks*

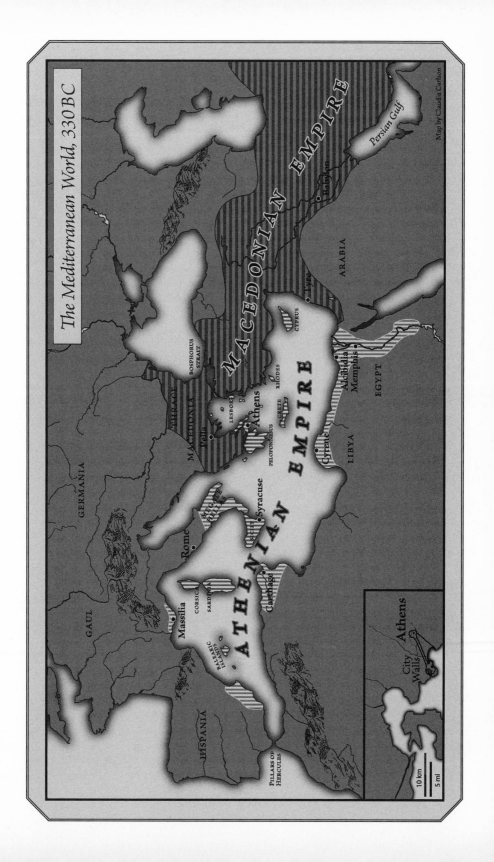

The Mediterranean World, 330 BC

MACEDONIAN EMPIRE

ATHENIAN EMPIRE

GERMANIA

GAUL

HISPANIA

PILLARS OF
HERCULES

BALEARIC
ISLANDS

Massilia

CORSICA

SARDINIA

Rome

Carthage

Syracuse

PELOPONNESUS

CRETE

LESBOS

Athens

Pella

MACEDONIA

THRACE

BOSPHORUS
STRAIT

RHODES

CYPRUS

Tyre

Alexandria
Memphis

EGYPT

LIBYA

Cyrene

ARABIA

Babylon

Persian Gulf

Athens

City
Walls

10 km

5 mi

Map by Claudia Carlson

CHAPTER ONE

The bar he was in had a name, but Lugorix was too drunk to remember it. And right now he was intent on getting even drunker. So far his plan was working.

Everything had gone blurry a while back. The other mercenaries, the assorted whores, the drinks being passed around like they were going out of style—all of it was starting to swirl around his head. And the bedlam taking place outside the bar had long since subsided as the party inside got ever louder.

Which didn't mean that news wasn't still reaching those within.

"He's across the Nile," said Matthias suddenly.

Lugorix turned blearily toward the smaller man who sat across the table from him. His best comrade in all the world, but right now he was just a fuzzy haze. Lugorix tried to focus on that grinning face, but found himself distracted instead by the patterns on the cloak that Matthias wore over his archer's armor. Lugorix wondered how he had never noticed that the cloth was made up of no less than three different shades of grey. He was starting to think there was actually a fourth when...

"Did you hear what I just said?"

"Heard you," replied Lugorix. Greek wasn't his strong point. "Didn't realize you needed a response."

"There *is* no response," said Matthias, his grin widening still further. "We're all fucked. So drink up."

"That's what I've been doing, friend."

The Dryad's Tits. That was the name of the bar. It wasn't one of the classier ones. The smell of sweat and puke mingled with the aroma of a particularly rancid roast mutton that only became remotely edible when one had downed several drinks. Lugorix and Matthias had been in the place for more than an hour, though it seemed like much longer than that. Various lowlifes—even on home-ground a scout had to have his contacts!—kept bringing Matthias news. But all the reports trended in the same direction. All orders had ceased. The city's commanders had fled, and the defenses of the Nile delta had collapsed. It was every man for himself now.

Problem was, there was nowhere to go.

"You say he's crossed the Nile?" asked the bartender.

"In several locations," replied Matthias. "Sliced the spine of Egypt, is what I'm hearing. Elephants and cavalry and Zeus only knows how much infantry—"

"Never mind all that," said the bartender. "What about *him?*"

And for a moment, the conversation immediately around Matthias faltered. Nothing too overt—just ears perking up here and there, keying on his response. Even through the haze of booze, Lugorix was feeling the same way too.

But Matthias only shook his head.

"No idea," he muttered. "But it can't be long now."

"He didn't spare any mercs in Asia," said someone. "No reason he should spare us now."

"So what the hell went *wrong,*" said the bartender.

"Magick," said Lugorix suddenly.

"And gold," said Matthias. "Way too much of it. The whole Persian treasury's his to dispose of, right? Reckon everybody above the rank of captain got bought off. And the generals got top billing. They'll be living in villas on the Tigris for the rest of their lives."

"At least they sold out for a good price," said someone.

"Speaking of," said the bartender, "you guys owe me half a drachma for that latest round."

Matthias reached down beside the daggers along his belt, opened up a pouch—tossed coins onto the bar. "Better spend that quickly," he said.

"Not like I'm the one who's forfeit," said the bartender. Lugorix started laughing. The bartender glanced at him.

"What the hell's your problem, Gaul?"

"Not just *my* problem," said Lugorix. "Yours too. The Macks will burn this whole city to the ground. Same way they burnt the fleet."

"No," interjected Matthias. "Not the same way at all. Sacking this city is just going to be business as usual. The fleet, now that was the—"

"Magick," said the bartender.

Another quick pause in the conversation. Matthias glanced around at some of the watching faces.

"So what?" he asked. "You all know he's gained access to whole new types of sorcery. What's going on outside is proof of that."

"Can't fight magick," said the bartender.

"Sure you can," said Matthias. He started re-stringing his bow. "You just need sorcerers to do it. And all the ones we had to hold the Delta are either bribed or dead by now."

"Your arrows won't help you anymore," said Lugorix—a tad vindictively, but he was tired of Matthias acting like he knew it all. Especially when they were all waiting to sell their lives in one final stand. Which would probably occur on the roof of the bar, perhaps within the hour, and certainly before morning.

"Neither will your axe," replied Matthias evenly.

"Don't be so sure," said Lugorix, patting the axe, which he'd christened Skullseeker for reasons that were obvious enough to those who'd had the misfortune to face it. It was intended for two hands, though he was strong enough to wield it with one if he had to. The weapon was primitive but effective—its double-headed blade made entirely of stone, except for the bronze that lined its razor-sharp edge. He had a sword as well, but generally preferred the axe.

"Bartender," said Matthais, "another round here."

"Man's final hours shouldn't just be about alcohol," Lugorix said.

"What else would you have them be about?" said Matthias.

"Women."

Matthias laughed. "Well, that's why we came to this bar. Couldn't help but notice you've been sucked off at least five times in the last hour."

Six, actually…but Lugorix wasn't going to quibble. This bar was easy pickings to begin with, and his long blond hair, fulsome beard and yard-wide chest made it even easier. That, and his trousers—something that no self-respecting Greek would wear, thereby making Lugorix the proud owner of a truly exotic fashion. No doubt about it, Greek women had a thing for barbarians. But as usual Matthias had misunderstood him—

"Not talking about my dick," said Lugorix. "Talking about yours."

"What about it? You so plastered you want a piece?"

"I'm saying you should *get* a piece. So far you've had nothing."

"Ah. That's because I'm saving myself."

"For what?"

"The right girl."

"Riiiight—" Lugorix turned as the door of the bar opened.

It was a woman, alright.

The oldest he'd ever seen.

She looked like she was native Egyptian, too—dark wizened skin and white hair that must have once been as black as her eyes. Now she scanned the room with those eyes, and all who regarded her looked away. It was as though with the crone's arrival, an apparition had stepped into the bar—a physical harbinger of the fate that awaited them all before the night was through. The only ones who weren't intimidated were far too drunk for common sense.

"*That's* your girl," said Lugorix, nudging Matthias.

"Shut up," hissed Matthias. But the woman's eyes had already turned in his direction—and gone wide with recognition.

"She's coming this way," whispered Lugorix.

"I can see that, idiot."

"You know her?"

"Not that I know of," said Matthias.

"Looks like she knows you."

"Will you *shut the fuck up?*"

The crone reached them. Lugorix realized she was wearing a headband of some kind—almost like a tiara, though bereft of jewels. She was toothless, too, and he was tempted to make some joke about how that might aid her in whatever she might do to Matthias. But then she looked directly at him, and all his alcohol-fueled levity vanished. Her eyes up close were the realest thing he'd seen all night—the realest thing he'd seen in years, the realest thing since that night in the Pyrenees on the eve of his banishment, when the shaman of the thunder-god Taranis had bid him look within the fire and behold his fate and in those fires he saw his future: the flames of burning Egypt, though it was only now that he remembered them. The woman reached out, stroked his beard. Chills shot up and down his spine, and he seemed to look down into abyss.

"Old mother," he said, "enough. Mercy. I beg you."

She stopped. Reached out to Matthias, ran a hand through the ringlets of his black hair. The gesture was almost playful, but the expression on her face was anything but.

"You're the ones," she said in accented Greek.

Matthias and Lugorix looked at one another.

"I'm sorry?" said Matthias.

"You heard me," she said. "My mistress needs you to come with me." The words echoed through Lugorix's skull in a way that made him realize that he and Matthias were the only ones who could hear this witch—for such was what Lugorix was now assuming this woman was. No one else was even paying attention anymore. The party had resumed around them. He felt his legs start to move of their own volition—felt himself get up. But Matthias seemed to be putting up more resistance.

"Why should we?" he asked.

"Because otherwise you'll die," said the woman.

"Ah," said Matthias. "We're going to do that anyway."

"True. Such is the fate of all mortals, no? But not necessarily this night, at the hands of Macedonian soldiers."

Lugorix was too far gone to even process this. Matthias mulled it over, then pulled on his linothorax cuirass and donned his helmet. Lugorix disdained both, but the two had long since agreed to disagree on the matter. The crone led them to the door, opened it on a sight that was anything but pretty.

The buildings of Alcibiadia towered all around them—a vast city on its way to becoming mausoleum. Flames licked from some of the upper windows. Screams were coming from all directions. But over all those screams, they could hear something far more chilling—a myriad voices of anger and rage, all fused into one, all of it far too close.

"The mob," said Lugorix.

The crone nodded. She led them through alleys and back roads, keeping to the south of Canopus Way, where it sounded like a full-on riot was in progress. Most of the street-lamps had been broken, but that was all to the good. Especially since the moon and flames were making things a little too bright for comfort. Lugorix carried Skullseeker, and Matthias had nocked an arrow, but the crone was clearly intent on avoiding trouble. They heard the breaking of pottery a few streets away as looters found some intact shopfronts.

"And the Macedonians haven't even arrived yet," said Matthias.

"They will soon," said the crone.

Stairs, ramps, sloped gardens—Lugorix could see they were climbing into the city-heights now. The aristocratic district, though there didn't seem to be that many aristocrats left. Everyone had fled or else they were hiding. Lugorix looked at the houses and mansions as they passed—wondered at how many secrets they'd held, how many lives they'd concealed behind their walls—how many they still concealed. In the months since the Athenian recruiters at Massilia had offered him gold in exchange for his axe, he'd seen more of the world then he'd ever dreamt existed. But ultimately he was sworn to return to his village. Honor demanded it. He couldn't end his journey here. He hoped against hope this crone really *did* have a way out of this mess. They were leaving the houses of the wealthy behind now, entering one of the many hilled parks that dotted this section of the city. For the next few minutes they followed the crone through tree-decked trails, climbing ever further. Until—

"Taranis save us," said Lugorix.

Straight between two trees, they could look out across the entirety of the portside city. All of Alcibiadia had been plunged into total chaos—the mob was pouring across the ramps and through the plazas. But that was nothing compared to what was happening out to sea.

"The fleet," breathed Matthias.

"You knew this was happening," said the crone. "Why act so surprised now you see it?"

"We only *heard* about it," said Lugorix.

"Hadn't intended to lay eyes on it," said Matthias.

But neither of them could turn away. At least two hundred Athenian warships were burning out there, dots of fire sprinkled through the night, all the way out to the Mediterranean's horizon. And the flame atop the colossus that was Pharos Lighthouse was sufficiently bright as to potentially obscure other stricken boats, still closer.

"How the hell did he do it?" said Lugorix.

"That's how," replied Matthias—gesturing at one of the nearer ships. As they watched, jets of flame gouted across it, broadening from out of a narrow stream, flung by a source almost immediately adjacent to the boat.

"Sneak attack," said a voice.

They whirled.

A woman had stepped out of the shadows. She was tall and willowy—taller than Matthias, though Lugorix still loomed over her. Dark as her skin was, the skin immediately under her pale green eyes was even darker from exhaustion. The nose beneath that was delicate, poised above a strange half-smile. With a start, Lugorix realized how young she was—that she couldn't be past her late teens. But her expression held a wisdom beyond her years.

"Incendiary weapon," she said in perfect Greek. "Devised by Alexander's sorcerers. His mechanists found a way to contain it, project it through bronze tubes. Not that far, but they made good use of it all the same. Some of the Macedonians crept up on the fleet using fishing skiffs, but I'll wager his forces hit most of those ships from points along the shore. To which the admiral had hewn a little too closely."

"He was paid off," said Matthias.

"Of course," said the girl. "Same way the Macedonians were able to infiltrate the docks in the first place. Everyone's been bought. And now Alexander's bearing down on the city founded by the man who gave Athens her empire a century ago."

"So where do we fit in?" said Matthias.

"You don't," said the crone.

"None of us do," added the girl. "That's why we need to leave this place."

"I hope you're not looking for us to provide you with the means of exit."

The girl shook her head. "All that's required are your swords."

"I'm sorry?" said Matthias.

"You're the ones I've seen in visions," cackled the crone. "True of spirit. Blessed of the whore Fortune. Uncorrupted by the stink of Alexander's gold."

"The man didn't *offer* us any gold," said Lugorix.

"Because we weren't worth it," said Matthias dryly. Then, to the women—"So what are *you* offering us?"

"A way out of this city," the girl replied. She glanced at the crone: "They're not too swift, are they?"

"What do you expect," replied the crone. "They're men."

"You really can get us out of here?" said Matthias.

"Told you we had a path that'd preserve your lives," said the crone, and she sounded as gone as Lugorix was starting to feel. "You run escort duty for my lady. You follow our lead as we steer clear of this deathtrap. All you need to do is kill anyone who gets in our way."

"Who's going to do that?" said Lugorix.

"Who isn't," said the girl.

"And who exactly are *you?*" asked Matthias.

"My name's Barsine," said the girl. She gestured toward the crone: "This is my servant, Damitra."

"Barsine," said Lugorix. "That's Persian, no?"

"One more reason we're on the same side," said Barsine. "It's time to move."

The other side of the park bordered one of the aqueducts, the hill sloping down to where a bit of judicious scrambling allowed them to climb into the channel in that structure's upper-tier. Water sloshed up to their knees, pumped up from the Nile to keep the gardens of the rich in bloom—Lugorix could only imagine at what expense. Barsine began to lead the way.

"Wait a second," said Matthias.

She turned. "Yes?"

"You're going downriver. Deeper into the city."

"So?

"So I thought you were trying to get us out of here."

"I know what I'm doing."

"Doesn't look it."

Her face reddened. "Don't question my orders."

"You're giving us orders?"

Lugorix realized this was going nowhere. He looked at Barsine. "You want us to run escort, this is the wrong way to do it."

"Meaning what?" asked Barsine.

"This isn't a proper formation. I'll take the lead, Matthias brings up the rear. The two of you in the middle."

"The Gaul speaks wisdom," said the crone. "His friend, not so much."

Matthias blanched. "I'm just trying to understand—"

"You heard the lady," said Lugorix. Matthias threw up his hands, admitting defeat. He mock-bowed to Barsine. She didn't smile.

"We need to make haste," she said.

They did just that, moving out across the city. Below them the shouting was getting louder, the screams more frequent. Smoke drifted past as more fires kept breaking out. Occasionally the aqueduct they were on intersected with others; each time, Barsine gave directions unhesitatingly, always taking them further downhill. Lugorix realized that his suggestion for their deployment had a big disadvantage—he couldn't ask Matthias what the hell they'd gotten themselves into. The cool night air outside the tavern had made him feel more sober; but now that he was moving across the city's roof, it seemed that all the alcohol had rushed back into his brain. He figured that was as much a function of the weirdness of the situation as anything. And the way Matthias had looked at Barsine made him uneasy. He knew his friend well enough to know that the man's arguments were really just a means of flirting. But these women had enough of a hold on them without Matthias playing into their hands. A Persian noble, accompanied by her very own witch... Lugorix knew when he was out of his element, and sneaking over an aqueduct in a stricken city with that kind of company certainly qualified.

As they neared the place where aqueduct became tunnel, the noise around them rose up a notch in intensity. The screams increased in number; the shouting got louder, was interspersed with the galloping of hooves—and the clash of steel on steel, as well as commands bellowed in a Greek dialect so harsh it was barely Greek...

"They're here," whispered the crone.

"Macedonians," muttered Barsine. For just a moment, Lugorix realized how scared she was—how much of a façade she was putting up. She was practically running now, slipping and sliding through the water, and everybody was keeping pace. The sack of the city was beginning all around them. Lugorix wondered if anyone was still alive back at the *Dryad's Tits*. Presumably they were selling their lives dearly. Not like they had a choice. The Macedonian soldiers clearly had orders for slaughter, and they were carrying out their instructions with alacrity. And high above the city—

"Look at the Pharos," said Matthias.

He might have saved his breath. It was impossible to miss. The fire atop Pharos Lighthouse had suddenly blossomed toward inferno—perhaps triggered by Alexander's sorcerers, perhaps the function of his sabotage of the fuel within the lighthouse. But someone had obviously managed to coat the upper portion with incendiary, and now that substance was blazing into full fury with a light that sent ghastly shadows roiling across the top of the aqueduct. The four of them splashed onward, picking up the pace still further. The water was getting deeper, and from the smell of the tunnel just ahead, they were crossing into the city's sewers. Lugorix led the way inside—and slowed down almost immediately, holding out his arms to stop the rest of them in their headlong flight.

"We need light," he said.

"Damitra," replied Barsine.

"M'lady," said the crone. There was the sound of her pulling aside cloth—fumbling for something—and then a dim bluish glow suffused the rocky walls around them, radiating outward from an amulet the crone was holding. Lugorix was impressed.

But then he felt the ground shift beneath his feet.

At first he thought it was some byproduct of the crone's magick. But then he realized that what he was standing on was *alive*—and twisting with a suddenness that sent him flying. From the corner of his eyes he saw a gigantic pair of jaws rising from the water, snapping straight at Barsine—who was knocked out of the way by Matthias.

"Crocodile," he yelled.

"I noticed," said the crone. She thrust her amulet at the thrashing reptile. There was a flash as the glow went white-hot, followed by a sizzling. Lugorix smelt burnt flesh, but the beast seemed unphased. It leapt at the crone, but she dodged aside with a surprising nimbleness. Lugorix raised Skullseeker, and brought it down in a sweeping arc onto the creature's neck. If he was hoping for a decapitation, he was disappointed—the axe made it a few inches in and then stuck fast beneath the hardened scales—but Lugorix used the purchase to leap onto the back of the crocodile, holding on and trying to work the axe deeper while the animal bucked and writhed in a frantic effort to throw him off. Matthias had his bow out—

"Close-quarters," snarled Lugorix.

Matthias nodded, tossing the bow back over his shoulder and drawing his *xiphos* short-sword as he raced in at the crocodile, somehow dodging past its teeth and slotting the blade straight through the roof of its mouth. The beast convulsed, but Lugorix held on, barely avoiding being smashed into the tunnel ceiling while his axe finally started to hit paydirt. Blood gouted up at him as he cut into the animal's brain—he leapt off as it flopped over and went into further convulsions. Matthias turned to

Barsine, who was standing as though petrified.

"Are you alright?" he asked.

"I'm fine," she said in a tone of voice that made his question sound like an insult.

"Wait," said Lugorix as the animal's death-throes ceased.

"Wait for what?" asked Damitra.

"No noise," he said, gesturing at the tunnel mouth.

Sure enough, most of the noise in the immediate vicinity outside had died away. They looked at one another.

"Probably because we just made so much of it," hissed Barsine.

"There," said Lugorix—pointing back at the tunnel mouth, as a Macedonian soldier scrambled over the side of the aqueduct and into view.

"Get him," said Barsine.

"On it," said Matthias—there was a twang as an arrow leapt from his bow, shot through the air, and smacked straight through the soldier's face. He fell without a sound into the water.

"There'll be more of them," said Matthias as he nocked another arrow. Sure enough, even as they waded deeper into the tunnel they could hear a hue and cry being raised behind them. The shouting sounded like it was at least an entire squad, the Macedonians in hot pursuit of the four fugitives racing into what was evidently a whole labyrinth of sewers. At the behest of Barsine, they turned left, then right, then left again. Damitra had dimmed her amulet to the point where it was just barely visible.

"I hope you know where you're going," said Matthias.

"Just stay alert for more crocs," said Barsine.

Lugorix was working on it, but he was somewhat distracted by the Macedonians behind them. Their yells and shouts echoed through the catacombs, and it was impossible to tell whether or not they were gaining.

"Lugorix," said Matthias.

Lugorix turned—realized that the others had stopped. Barsine and Damitra were studying a section of the wall while Matthias studied Barsine.

"What are you doing?" said Lugorix.

"Quiet," said Barsine.

"And keep an eye out," said Damitra. She fumbled her hands along the wall.

"It's right here, somewhere," said Barsine. The shouting was coming closer, along with torchlight...

"They're coming this way," said Matthias.

"I didn't hire you for your tactical analysis," said Barsine.

"Didn't realize you'd hired me," said Matthias.

"Can we talk about this later?" said Lugorix.

"Both of you shut up," said Barsine. She twisted something in the stone. A section of the wall slide aside.

"Gods preserve us," said Matthias.

"We need to do that ourselves," said Barsine. She scrambled through. Everybody followed, to find themselves in a narrow passage. Barsine shut the slab behind them while Damitra re-intensified the glow. They heard the muffled shouting of the Macedonians somewhere behind them. Barsine led the way forward, leaving them all trying to keep up in more ways than one.

"Where in Hades are we?" asked Lugorix.

"Near the harbor," replied Barsine.

"Wouldn't we rather be *at* the harbor?" said Matthias. "That's where the boats are, right?"

"They've all been burnt to the waterline by now," said Barsine. She opened another door, looked out at the room beyond.

"Except that one," she added.

CHAPTER TWO

The ship that sat at the underground jetty wasn't like any ship Lugorix had ever seen. At first he wasn't even sure it *was* a ship. It had no mast, rode low in the water, and was a combination of both metal and wood, lacking towers aft and rear, instead sporting a lower, raised platform which ran along its center. A strange cylinder was positioned just behind that platform—and now as Lugorix looked, he realized there *was* in fact a mast, but that it was lying along the deck, fastened horizontally into place along with its sail. The entire vessel was no more than thirty feet from end to end. Damitra helped Barsine down onto the platform, whereupon Barsine opened up a hatch. Both women looked up at the men.

"What are you waiting for?" said Barsine.

"Is this a magick ship?" asked Lugorix.

"Not at all," said Barsine.

"Persian," said Matthias, suddenly understanding. "You're Persian spies."

"You forget," said Barsine. *"We* ruled Egypt first."

"Before Athens took it from you," muttered Matthias as Barsine climbed through the hatch and disappeared within.

Damitra grinned toothlessly. "Like my lady said: we're all on the same side now." She unfastened the ropes and the ship started to drift away. Lugorix and Matthias leapt aboard.

"Welcome to the *Xerxes*," said Damitra. She tossed her amulet down to Barsine, who caught it—and then shoved it into a strange copper lattice framework set against one of the walls in the compact room below. Sparks flew across that copper and Lugorix felt a rumbling grip the boat. The water behind them started churning and smoke began pouring from the cylinder.

"We're on fire!" screamed Matthias. Lugorix wasn't wasting any time on words—he was about to jump into the water when Damitra yelled at him to stop.

"We're not on fire!" she shouted in his ear. "This ship moves by burning!"

"I see," said Lugorix, not seeing at all. The boat was surging away from the jetty, out into the hidden harbor. Matthias shrugged, started to climb down through the hatch when—

"No," said Damitra. "You need to stay on top till we get clear."

"Of what?" said Lugorix—and then he ducked his head as the roof dipped toward him and the ship churned through a narrow cave-mouth and out into the open ocean. And it *was* the open ocean, he quickly realized—the tunnel entrance was situated well beyond the Great Harbor, out on the northern edge of the main city-island, which was now on fire in multiple places. Even as Lugorix watched, a series of explosions rocked that receding island; pillars and towers began toppling into one another, causing a chain-reaction of deafening booms and crashes. But then all that noise was drowned out by a larger explosion from above. Lugorix looked upward to see the—

"Pharos," breathed Matthias.

The enormous lighthouse was shaking as though it was in the throes of earthquake—shaking and swaying from side to side. Lugorix thought for a brief moment of all he'd heard about that lighthouse—of how it could its light could be seen by ships for scores of miles, of how its operators could stand at its base and use a series of lenses to gain a telescopic view from the top, of how the giant ballistae at its top could punch straight through the sides of enemy ships. But those who were destroying the Pharos had never given it a chance to deploy such measures. For a moment, the lighthouse's swaying slowed its oscillations—it seemed to Lugorix for just the briefest of instants that the structure would hold against whatever infernal sorcery the Macedonians had unleashed upon it.

Then it started to topple.

Right toward the boat. Lugorix heard himself muttering prayers to Taranis. As if in a dream, he watched that lighthouse blot out the sky as it crashed down toward them. Neither he nor Matthias nor Damitra said a word—he wondered if they as transfixed as he was. Or perhaps they had all already reached the afterlife. Barsine was the only one to react—she stopped the boat entirely, threw the engine into reverse as the lighthouse crashed down toward them, long arcs of fire trailing in its wake. Lugorix's eye was rooted to the statue of Poseidon that adorned the Pharos' summit—the trident that the god held had come loose and sailed like a missile over the boat and into the water. And then the lighthouse itself impacted, a huge wall crashing into the ocean, sending up a vast spray of water even as a colossal wave rolled across them, almost capsizing them entirely. Damitra lost her grip; Lugorix grabbed her with one hand while he held fast to the rails with the other. Barsine stopped reversing, sent the boat forward through swells that rocked them as the ship picked up speed, plowing over the final resting place of the Pharos and out into the deeper ocean. Damitra drew herself from Lugorix's grasp.

"I owe you for your quickness," she said.

Lugorix was too rattled to reply. They were reaching the edge of the burning Athenian fleet; the *Xerxes* zigged and zagged as Barsine maneuvered it through wreckage. Lugorix gaped as they headed straight at what was left of a trireme, more than a hundred feet long, but now almost burnt to the waterline.

"Those are the smallest of 'em," muttered Matthias.

"What?"

"Look past it," hissed Matthias.

Lugorix nodded, his eyes wide in disbelief. Triremes may have been the most numerous of the ships in the Athenian navy but they only had three decks of oars. Teteres ("fours") and penteres ("fives") formed the middle types of dreadnaught, while the largest were the octeres and the deceres, though not much was left of those now. Lugorix remembered seeing a decere once—it seemed like it went on forever, bedecked with flags, held upright in the water by long catamaran-outriggers, and sprouting so many oars as to look like the needles covering a hedgehog, while a whole array of ballistae and catapults lined the decks. Such ships were the mainstay of Athenian naval power. But now a whole fleet had been reduced to a holocaust of flame and wreckage. And as Barsine steered her strange vessel ever deeper into the maelstrom, it became clear that parts of the ocean itself were on fire—that Alexander's incendiary somehow burnt on the surface of the water. Damitra was muttering something in Persian that Lugorix figured to be a prayer. She was gazing at intently at one spot in particular. Lugorix stared.

And then he realized what she was looking at.

"People," he said slowly.

Sailors adrift in the water had noticed them, were swimming toward them, screaming for help. But their boat simply accelerated, the paddle-wheels within turning ever faster as it churned past. Matthias looked aghast.

"What in Athena's name are we doing?" he asked.

"Not picking up survivors," said Damitra.

"Why not?"

"Too great a risk."

"According to Barsine?"

"She gives the orders."

Matthias' face darkened. The yelling was growing louder as stricken sailors realized their last chance was passing them by. Matthias turned to the hatch but—

"No," said Damitra. "Don't go down."

"I need to talk to her."

"You mean you need to force her."

"Try and stop me, witch."

"*I'll* stop you," said Lugorix suddenly. Matthias whirled toward him.

"What's *your* problem? Those sailors are—"

"Already dead," said Lugorix. "Most of them are badly burnt. We stop for any, the rest will swamp us. And even if they don't, the pursuit has that much more time to catch us."

"I haven't *seen* any pursuit yet."

"We should keep it that way. If anyone climbs aboard, be sure to throw them back in."

"*What?*"

"That why we're up here," said Lugorix. And then, to Damitra: "True?"

She nodded gravely. "And once we get out of here, you'll be keeping watch."

They were leaving the fleet in their wake now, heading out into the swells of open ocean. Spray lit by the glow of the burning boats behind them splashed across their faces. Lugorix grasped the railing, looked at his friend's bemused expression.

"So where *are* we going?" Matthias asked Damitra.

"Athens," she replied.

"Why?"

"Mistress has friends there."

"That's just fine," said Lugorix. "Best place to hire out for more merc duty."

"You're already hired," said Damitra.

"You keep saying that," said Matthias. "But every time I ask for details, Barsine tells me to shut up."

"That's because she noble."

"Nobles abandon sailors to drown?"

"Nobles don't negotiate with servants," said Damitra.

Matthias' laugh was more of a bark. *"You're* her servant. We're just along for the ride."

"She'll need your help in Athens."

"For what?"

"Bodyguards."

"To protect her from who?"

"Mistress has many enemies. Macedonian spies everywhere."

"Don't you have powers that help you beat them? That allow you to see 'em?"

"I see them closing in. And you saw what they did to Egypt."

"But Egypt is just one province," said Lugorix. "Athens is the capital. Biggest fortress in the world. Impossible to take by storm—"

"They may not need to take it by storm."

There was a long pause.

"But you need to help mistress," she added.

"She'll need to pay," replied Matthias."

"She will."

"Will she?"

"She's very rich."

"Now we're talking."

"Now keep watch."

"What?"

But Damitra was already climbing below. Matthias watched her go, then turned to Lugorix.

"You believe any of that?"

Lugorix pondered this. "What part of it don't you?" he asked.

"The part about her being so damn rich."

"She owns this boat, doesn't she?"

"Doesn't mean she has gold somewhere."

"She's noble."

"Are you some kind of parrot? *Once* she was noble. Persian Empire doesn't mean shit now. Not since Alexander got through with it."

"Well," said Lugorix thoughtfully, "looks like the Persians still got some kind of operation going. And anyone with a boat like this might have a hefty payday waiting for us."

"Are you crazy? This bitch is trouble."

"That's what you say about anyone you have a crush on."

Matthias snorted. *"I* have a crush on *her?* Zeus man! *She's* the one with the crush on *me."*

"She does an excellent job disguising it."

"She's an aristo. They're good at playing hard to get."

"You need to quit while you're ahead, Greek." Lugorix sensed he wasn't getting through to him, but figured it was worth a shot. "She already got us out of that Mack-infested hellhole. If she can get us gold, so much the better. But I doubt you'll get a slice of her into the bargain."

"Remember how I told you I was saving myself?"

"Get ready to wait a long time."

Matthias nodded ruefully. "Waiting's all we can do right now anyway."

Lugorix knew that Matthias was right. The hours slid by and the water washed across them and gradually the glow behind them disappeared into the night. Stars shone above them, sprinkling illumination across the waves. Lugorix felt like those stars were hauling him up into the sky—like that water was dragging him under. The last few hours seemed like one big crazy dream. He realized dimly that he was beyond exhausted.

"Time for sleep," said a voice.

He whirled. Damitra stood there. Matthias stretched and started for the hatch.

"Not you," she said, gesturing at Lugorix. "Him."

"What about me?"

"You stand guard till dawn."

"That's still hours off!"

"If you see anything—anything at all—call down."

Matthias nodded slowly. Lugorix climbed down into the cramped control-room of the strange craft, Damitra following him. In addition to that humming copper lattice, there were levers and gears all around, and he didn't understand any of it. He expected to see Barsine at the helm, peering through one of the viewing slits. But instead she was asleep in a cot in the corner, curled up, her knees against her stomach. Damitra had taken her place at the helm—and now she pointed to a hatch aft-side.

"Sleep there," she said.

"What *is* this ship?" he asked.

She seemed about to tell him to get stuffed. But then her face softened. "Long-range explorer," she said.

"What's that mean?"

"Commissioned by the now-deceased Great King Artaxerxes to find the edges of the Earth."

"The Earth has edges?"

"Of course. It's flat."

Lugorix remembered the mercenaries debating this very issue around the campfire one night. Some had said it was flat, others claimed it was round. Others had used the word *sphere*. Lugorix had gotten bored and wandered off to look for whores. "And so you want to reach the edges?"

"Artaxerxes wanted the chroniclers to tell the story of the edges of his dominions. But his jealous vizier Bagoas had him poisoned. Then purged his court. Among those who perished was Barsine's father, the satrap Artabazus."

"I'm sorry to hear it," said Lugorix.

"Indeed. But he was the man who Artaxerxes had put in charge of the building of the *Xerxes*. Before he was executed, he told his daughter the location, in what used to be our secret docks in province of Egypt. Which by now belonged to Athens. And shortly thereafter, Bagoas himself was poisoned by the Great King Darius III. So fugitive Barsine was summoned back to court. She went. But a few years later, Alexander came. Now she's trying to escape all over again."

Lugorix's eyes had glazed over halfway through this. History wasn't something he gave a shit about. "Interesting," he said.

She looked amused. "Get some sleep," she said. He climbed through into an even more confined space, found another cot, passed out before he even knew it.

He dreamt again of home, dreamt of his family's funeral pyre on that day so long ago—dreamt anew of Athens. Images of Egypt tore through him like wounds. Barsine's face danced in front of him, but he knew far more fear than he did desire. He saw Matthias shoving past him and chasing her, antlers on his head and a donkey's tail on his behind. And then—

"Wake now," said Damitra.

Lugorix opened his eyes. It felt like he'd just closed them. He staggered through into the engine-room; Barsine was still asleep. Damitra gestured at the hatch above them. He climbed through to find that dawn had just broken, the sun scattering the ocean with dappled light. Matthias was staring at that sun, looking like utter shit, but still awake. He turned to regard Lugorix, his eyes red with whatever stimulant he'd taken.

"So soon," he muttered.

"Try not to dream of Egypt," said Lugorix.

Matthias nodded, shoved past him while Lugorix settled down to watch the Mediterranean.

There wasn't much left of the city from which they had departed. The Macedonian forces had razed most of Alcibiadia to the ground. All that was left of Pharos Lighthouse was a smoking stump. The bodies of thousands of Athenian sailors littered the beaches, but that was nothing compared to the tens of thousands of soldiers and civilians lying dead in the streets. Only native Egyptians had been spared. Fresh from their triumphant sack of the city, the bulk of the Macedonian army had moved on to the base of the Nile delta—the ancient Egyptian capital of Memphis, from which the Athenian garrison had already fled. Alexander was now entering the city in triumph and the whole population had turned out to welcome him as liberator, lining the roads, watching from the rooftops, straining to get a glimpse of the man himself. The cheering was deafening as row upon row of troops from the Macedonian phalanx paraded down the Azure Way, their massed *sarissae* extending upward in an endless field of spears, a procession of armor-clad elephants pacing after them. It seemed no wonder that Persia had fallen so quickly, that Athens' hold on Egypt had crumbled overnight. Sun glistened on the bronze armor of the young conqueror, and those who could see the face beneath the ram horns that adorned his helmet marveled at his beauty—like a god, they said. Still others said that he *was* a god—the divine Pharaoh reborn, returned to claim his rightful heritage.

All of which was causing Eumenes no little anxiety. From his position toward the rear of Alexander's cavalry entourage, the chief of staff watched his prince bask in a tidal wave of adulation far beyond anything anybody had expected. Certainly it blotted out the specter the Macedonian high command had been living with these last few months—Alexander's chagrin at ceasing his eastward advance, his outrage at his father's orders to garrison Persia and return to Macedonia. Alexander had indeed turned west, but not back to Macedonia—instead he'd struck suddenly at Egypt and met with utter success. Yet Eumenes knew all too well that when it came to Alexander, success could be even more dangerous than failure. And those stories his damn mother used to wind him up with... if the man *really* started to think that he was a god, then only the gods knew what would happen.

Ahead, the cheering grew still louder. They were coming out into the city's central plaza, which lay in the shadow of the mammoth Temple of Ptah. Officers barked orders; men spread out as the marching phalanx seamlessly doubled its width, herding back the crowd and ensuring that much more space for Alexander. The phalanx then parted down the middle, allowing Alexander and his officers to ride straight up the marbled steps that led over the temple moat to Ptah's main gate. Crocodiles filled that moat; Eumenes could see them sunning themselves like nothing out of the ordinary was taking place. At the topmost step, Alexander gave the order to dismount. He turned to acknowledge the crowds as his bodyguards stood around him.

Then he raised a single hand for silence. As though he had pulled a lever, the crowd noise suddenly began to die down. *He has them in the palm of his hand,* Eumenes realized. He could tell them to do anything, follow him anywhere—and they would. Even so, the bodyguards were anxiously scanning the crowd, looking for that lone Athenian assassin who could turn the whole world on its head with a single blow. He wouldn't survive the casting of his dart or dagger—but if he was accurate in its throw, his name would assuredly live forever. But Alexander was as heedless of danger as he had been when he'd led the charge that broke the Persian center at Gaugemela—and Eumenes couldn't help but notice that his face was flushed with the same barely restrained excitement. A temple interpreter stepped up beside Alexander, and translated as Alexander started speaking:

"People of Memphis. People of Egypt!" That set them cheering again, but this time he kept talking, projecting his voice in the marvelous stentorian tones that his tutor Aristotle had taught him back when he was a mere boy instead of a man with the face of one. "People of Egypt! I congratulate you on once more claiming your status as a free people! The curse of Athens has been lifted! No longer will they take the fruit of your labors, no longer will they own what belongs to you! Instead, now it is *you* that will own *them*. What would you do with your new possessions?"

The crowd's cheering subsided into a bewildered burbling. No one knew where he was going with this, least of all Eumenes. But he knew Alexander well enough to know that this was merely part of the his ruler's rhetorical style—drawing his audience in, leading them on. Other orators became bogged down when their audience floundered in confusion. Alexander simply used it to his advantage.

"What would you do with them?" he repeated. And suddenly Eumenes realized what was to take place. Macedonian soldiers were leading a score or so of bedraggled men from out of the mass of the army and up the stairs—Athenian soldiers, officials, and mercenaries. Some still wore their armor. Some were wounded. All looked scared.

"These men came from over the sea to plunder you," said Alexander. "Do any of you know any reason why they should receive clemency for it?"

The crowd bayed like wolves. They understood their role now, and yelled for blood with the alacrity of those who know they are going to get it. One of the prisoners began begging for mercy, but his guard cuffed him hard on the head, sending him stumbling to his knees.

"I didn't think so," said Alexander, though only those close to him could hear him now. "Throw them in." This last to the soldiers who held the Athenians. They began to scream as they realized the manner of their death—and then they were shoved off the steps and into the temple moat as the crowd bellowed with delight. Most of that crowd couldn't see what was going on in the moat—but Eumenes could, and his horror was only amplified by the fact that he had to pretend that he was enjoying this. The crocodiles thrashed about the hapless Athenians, pulling off limbs like they were made of wet clay, turning the water red with blood. Other crocodiles seized their prey and dragged them down to the bottom, still struggling, until more crocodiles tore the victims piecemeal from their captors' jaws. Eumenes had no idea the moat contained so many of the animals. He found the sight of that writhing carpet of reptiles to be little short of obscene—found it hard to believe anyone could worship anything so repulsive, save as a talisman of horror, and in that moment he hated Egypt with all his heart. With a start, he realized that Alexander was giving more instructions. The soldiers were saluting, dispersing back into the temple.

Eumenes went with those soldiers. He had much to do.

Being diplomatic with the priests and ensuring that nothing got stolen was part of it—Eumenes also had to issue not-so-gentle reminders that Alexander had laid down a firm mandate that all native Egyptian religions were to be left unmolested. But that task was made more complex by the conqueror's wish to make Ptah's temple the temporary Macedonian HQ. It was the largest building in the city and the most easily defensible. And it was to be the site of the meeting of his top generals that Alexander had ordered take place once his speech to the people of Memphis was concluded.

"Has he told you what he plans to discuss?"

Eumenes turned to find himself looking up at the chief marshal Hephaestion, whose annoyed face was almost as red as his hair. It was plain just how much the question was costing Alexander's lover—particularly given the disdain he bore for Eumenes. They all despised him, of course—a mere Greek amidst the elite of Macedonia. Even though his father had been a guest-friend of Philip, even though he'd been brought up in the royal court—none of that mattered to the Macedonian generals. And they found it all the more galling that Alexander found his secretary's mind so useful. All paperwork, all logistics, all bureaucracy passed through the hands of Eumenes.

But not all confidences.

"He hasn't," said Eumenes. The two men continued to walk down the temple's torchlit corridor, past a series of carved stone crocodiles, guards trailing a respectful distance behind them. "Though I assumed he'd told—"

"Assume nothing," snapped Hephaestion.

Eumenes nodded tactfully. He couldn't even begin to fathom the complexities of Hephaestion's relationship with Alexander, though he had no reason to believe it was immune to the tension that had been gripping the prince lately. But if Alexander was keeping secrets from the man who both shared his bed and headed his network of spies, then that fact boded less than well for the upcoming conference. All this flashed through Eumenes' mind in an instant, and then he instinctively steered the conversation toward safer ground.

"Meleager," he said.

"What about him?"

"Just got word he won't be attending. Craterus has him consolidating our forces south of the city." Hephaestion nodded at this; Eumenes could almost see the wheels turn within his mind as he mulled over what Craterus was up to. Hephaestion's relations with Alexander's other chief marshal were even worse than his relations with his secretary, though Eumenes could practically read Hephaestion's thoughts on this particular matter: that Craterus' power-play wasn't a threat to himself, was instead simply designed to keep out of the room a man who was a particular favorite with the infantry, and with whom Craterus had clashed on more than one occasion. Even better, with Meleager absent, everybody could cast aspersions at him behind his back. Hephaestion nodded to Eumenes; understanding passed between them. They headed through an archway into the records chamber.

The Egyptian scribes who populated that chamber had already been moved elsewhere and replaced with Eumenes' own. They were still setting up shop, though, unfurling scrolls and dispatches, supervised by a man with a copper-toned beard and nervous disposition. He waved a casual greeting.

"Harpalus," said Eumenes.

Alexander's treasurer nodded. "A relief to see you," he said. "I was afraid the conference had already begun."

"He hasn't even left the steps yet," said Eumenes.

Harpalus raised an eyebrow.

"Though he seems to have finished bringing justice to the captured Athenians," added Eumenes.

Harpalus nodded. Had Hephaestion not been present, Eumenes knew that he would have said something cynical. Harpalus was a born accountant—his mind was all logic and numbers, which was probably why he was the only one among Alexander's entourage with whom Eumenes could let his guard down. But right now, with Hephaestion standing there, Harpalus had to content himself with business.

"The priests have cooperated totally," the treasurer said. "Their scribes have been showing me the account ledgers."

Eumenes frowned. "What about the real ones?"

"Ah. Those too."

"Isn't it about time we got started?" said a voice.

People said that Ptolemy's nose was always five steps ahead of him. In truth, it was more aquiline than long, but court wags had never been known for their literal accuracy. Then again, it was an underhanded tribute to his political deftness: his ability to never get tied up in any one faction while somehow remaining on good terms with them all. But right now the expression on that hail-fellow-well-met face was more than a little puzzled.

"He's still out on the steps," said Hephaestion.

"The others are waiting," replied Ptolemy.

"So let them wait."

"We could go join them."

"We could," said Eumenes. He gave some instructions to the scribes, then led the top brass through jackal-painted corridors into a vaulted chamber dominated by a massive marble table. A bearded giant of a man sat at one end while a leaner man paced. They looked up as the group entered.

"So what's it to be?" boomed Craterus. "Are we to march on Carthage?"

"Zeus," said the pacing man, "why are you even *saying* such things?"

"Perdiccas here is so damn *cautious,*" said Craterus, warming to his audience. "All that hesitation, it's a wonder we made it to Egypt."

"Well, we *did* seize it without permission," said Ptolemy, taking his seat.

Craterus laughed sarcastically. "Permission? From the Athenians?"

"From Philip," said Eumenes. "We have yet to receive any word from him."

"What *can* he say?" asked Craterus. "Alexander's presented his father with a fait accompli."

"And war with Athens," muttered Harpalus.

"A war both of them wanted," said Ptolemy.

"But I suspect the old man would have preferred to choose the timing," said Perdiccas.

There was a moment's silence.

"Doesn't matter," said Hephaestion. "If Alexander had failed to take Egypt on the first try, it might be a different story. But Philip's not one to be disappointed with victory."

"Nor am I," said a voice.

They all rose as Alexander stepped into the room. He'd exchanged his armor for a purple cloak. Bodyguards hovered in the archway behind him.

"Leave us," he said.

They did so, closing the doors as they went. Alexander took his seat at the table's head, his voice almost a purr.

"Where's Meleager?" he asked.

"He couldn't make it," said Craterus, seating himself with the rest of them. "Still south of the city, dealing with some Athenian stragglers."

"He should be here," said Alexander softly.

Craterus shrugged. "That's what I told him."

"No matter," said the prince. "You can pass on our decisions to him from now on."

Craterus nodded, faint satisfaction on his face. Alexander looked around the room, meeting each of their gazes in turn. His eyes lingered on Eumenes last. Those eyes were *dikoros*—"of two pupils"; one so brown as to verge on black, the other clear blue. That was supposed to be testament to his divine origins, but Eumenes had seen others with the same condition. Though he had to admit none had been so striking.

"Report," said Alexander.

Eumenes blinked. He was used to Alexander asking him to start meetings with a summary of events, but there was something new and dangerous in the prince's expression. Perhaps the result of so many thousands falling on their knees before him on the temple steps outside. Eumenes held Alexander's stare while he replied.

"The Delta's ours. What's left of Athenian resistance is falling back on Thebes, but we've cut all their communications and they're coming apart even as they retreat. We estimate at least two hundred Athenian ships have been destroyed by the incendiary that Hephaestion's alchemists compounded back East—"

"We should call it Greek fire," said Craterus. "Given it did such a good job turning their asses into cinder."

Everyone laughed, but Eumenes just smiled wanly. Yet another reminder of his own Greekness—though he noted that Alexander wasn't sharing in the mirth either.

"That's enough," said the prince, and the laughter stopped instantly.

"Hephaestion, how much of the incendiary is left?"

"Several vats," said Hephaestion. "But my alchemists are working around the clock to make more."

"What about the black powder?"

"There were several instances where it detonated prematurely. A number of my men were killed. But it brought down their Pharos. A little more refinement, and I'm sure we'll be able to use it more precisely."

Alexander nodded, turned to the man sitting next to Hephaestion. "Harpalus."

"My prince."

"What of the temple treasury?"

"Secure," replied Harpalus. "The Athenians fled too quickly to take it with them. It remains in the custody of the priests—"

"Not for long," said Alexander. "They've agreed to reimburse our expenses."

"Which are considerable," said Harpalus. "And likely to climb higher as the full cost of this new war comes due."

"Don't be so dramatic," said Ptolemy. "Athens has far more to lose than we do. They survive on commerce. The loss of Egypt probably bankrupted half their merchants. I'd give a lot to see the hand-wringing that must be going on in that debate-club they call their Assembly."

"They still have plenty of resources to draw on," said Hephaestion.

"Like what?" asked Ptolemy.

"The rest of the Mediterranean," said Perdiccas dryly.

"Which is why we need to push on Carthage," said Craterus. Eumenes abruptly realized that what had looked like a joke earlier had actually masked serious intent. He said nothing though, waiting on the reaction of others.

"That's a thousand miles west of here." Perdiccas was practically spluttering. "Maintaining our supply lines in the face of the Athenian navy—"

"With the Greek fire, we can annihilate that navy if it ventures too close to the shore." Craterus looked straight at his prince. "Alexander, how *else* are we to finish Athens? We can't strike at her heart directly. Her walls remain impregnable."

"Don't be so defeatist," said Ptolemy.

"I'm being realistic," said Craterus. "We have to chop off the pieces of Athens' empire like so many limbs, and we have to content ourselves with those portions we can get at without ships."

"We'll have ships soon enough," said Hephaestion. "And we already burnt two hundred of theirs in a single night."

"But they have *two thousand* more," said Craterus. "Greek fire or no Greek fire, we can't hope to match them on the ocean."

"Precisely why it would be rash to aim at Carthage," said Alexander. Eumenes exhaled slowly, not realizing till that moment he'd been holding his breath. "Ptolemy's right. Without ships, your supply line would on the knife-edge between ocean and desert."

"But the Greek fire—"

"Doesn't make us invincible. The Athenians could land marines in force at any point they like and long before we reached Libya, our whole army would be guarding its own supply-line. The risk of utter annihilation—"

"So what would you have us do instead?" asked Craterus, and to Eumenes it sounded almost like a challenge. But Alexander, ever unpredictable, didn't seem to take it as such. He simply looked around the room—looked almost like he was puzzled.

"Are there *no* other ideas on the table, then?"

"Keep building up our navy," said Hephaestion. "We'll be ready within a few years."

"Madness," said Ptolemy. "You overestimate the difficulty of building and crewing a fleet that's worth the name. And in a few years—"

"We may not have that long anyway," said Craterus.

"Now *that* may be true, regardless," said Harpalus.

"Exactly," said Alexander. "Say Athens learns how to replicate the fire? Say they have other secret weapons? Their Guilds must be working around the clock to devise them. Besides"—and here he smiled a smile of pure insouciance—"we're still young. Fame and glory are fleeting. Why wait to destroy Athens when we're old? Why not find a way to defeat them now?"

Eumenes mulled this over. It was starting to sound like the move into Egypt wasn't part of some larger plan. Alexander was a born opportunist, but this was taking opportunism to levels that bordered on hubris. Either that, or Alexander really *did* have something in mind. Eumenes hated to think of the expression on Philip's face if his son didn't.

"We're heading west," pronounced Alexander.

Everyone looked at each other. Perdiccas was the first to give voice to the resultant confusion. "Didn't you just say that we weren't—"

"There's more to the west of here than Carthage."

"Such as?" asked Ptolemy.

"Siwah."

"The oasis?" asked Harpalus.

"The Oracle," said Alexander. "Of Zeus-Ammon."

"You're going to ask *Zeus* what to do?" asked Craterus.

"I'm going to *consult* with Him. On a wide range of matters." Alexander's voice was steel. "That's the real reason I came to Egypt, after all."

The group absorbed this. Eumenes suspected he wasn't the only one getting a sinking feeling. Not so much because an oracle couldn't speak truth—indeed, the one at Siwah was particularly famous for combining both the Greek and Egyptian aspects of the All-Father—but because he suspected he knew what was really going on here. He locked eyes with Harpalus across the room, knew they were both thinking the same thing. Olympias. Alexander's deceased bitch-queen of a mother. Who'd despised his father. Who'd filled his head with fantasies about how his father wasn't really Philip—who'd hinted to him that it was Zeus instead. The victories in the East and Egypt had apparently left Alexander on the verge of believing it was true.

Now a trip to Siwah would settle the matter.

Ptolemy made a bid for sanity. "That's a three day journey through trekless desert," he said. "A Persian king lost an entire *army* trying to get there a couple centuries back—"

"I'm not *taking* an entire army," replied Alexander evenly. "Some bodyguards. Some cavalry. Hephaestion, of course." He looked around the table. "And you, Eumenes."

Eumenes tried to dodge it. "Shouldn't I be staying in Memphis to administer the business of empire—"

"The business of empire comes with me."

It took all Eumenes' skill to keep his face expressionless.

CHAPTER THREE

Summer in the Mediterranean made for smooth sailing. But nothing was smooth aboard the fleet. The ships had gotten word of the fall of Egypt while they were still fifty miles out and had turned around immediately. That sat well with neither the crews nor the marines aboard those boats. They wanted to take the fight to the Macedonians. All the more so as the reports out of Alcibidia spoke of utter carnage. Surely at the very least they should be proceeding to the Egyptian coast to pick up survivors? After all, *two hundred ships* had been burnt to the waterline.

Which was precisely why Leosthenes had no intention of doing anything other than heading back to Athens. It wasn't just that he was responsible for the safety of the hundred ships he commanded. He had the bigger picture in mind as well. This was no time to take unnecessary risks; Athens needed every boat now. Besides which, the reports out of Egypt (from all sources... rafts packed with plaintive refugees, fishing-skiffs whose crews were running for their lives, even the occasional river pleasure-barge that had taken to the open ocean in desperation) said that new weapons had been used. Witnesses spoke of gushing fire and detonating powder, facts which made Leosthenes all the more determined to get those witnesses back to Athens where they could be debriefed by the city's sorcerors.

He knew he'd take shit for it, of course. He could sense the mood among his crews—not just of the eight-decker flagship in which he rode but in the other dreadnaughts well. He was an experienced enough commander to know when his men weren't on his side. Had it been a longer campaign, he'd have had time to prove himself. Truth was he was always having to prove himself; it went with the territory of being the youngest of Athens' archons and a direct descendant of the famous Alcibiades. He was popular with the mob, less so with his fellow archons, and every army or fleet he commanded was always skeptical until they'd seen him in battle. So to turn back before combat flew in the face of all his instincts. He knew he wouldn't be winning any popularity contests now. In fact—

"Next session of the archons might be your last," said a voice.

"Thanks for nothing," said Leosthenes, continuing to stare out at the other ships in his fleet. They were sailing in two long columns, fifty ships a column, each ship a symbol of Athenian power, that power emblazoned upon each sail: griffins and dragons and owls and tridents stretching back as far as the eye could see. The men aboard those ships stuck together on and off those boats. They frequented the same dives, the same cathouses. And nine times out of ten, they voted together in the Assembly too. *The rule of the rowers*—that's what Aristotle had once called Athenian government. The man who'd just spoken joined Leosthenes at the rail.

"Just saying."

"That's all you ever do."

Which wasn't quite true. His faithful-if-sarcastic servant Memnon did a lot more than just talk. But it was the talk which Leosthenes found the most valuable. The white-haired Memnon had been born a slave to Leosthenes' father, bequeathed by him to his son, and freed by Leosthenes when he was elected to the position of archon. But really, Memnon's status had never changed—he was Leosthenes' trusted confidant, the one who told him what no one else would, the only one who (even as his master rose through the jungle of Athenian politics) could always be relied upon for candid advice.

Especially when it wasn't welcome.

"You got the sharp end of the stick on this one," he said. "And if you're *extra* lucky, they might even make you a scapegoat for all of Egypt."

"Despite the fact that I never set foot there?"

"All the better."

Leosthenes smiled wryly, brushed a hand through a wave of his hair. It hung in brown locks down to his shoulders; between that and his hazel eyes, the joke in Athens was that it was too bad for him that women couldn't vote, otherwise he'd be guaranteed a lifetime appointment among the archons. But personally, Leosthenes doubted that if women had the vote, they'd use it any different then men. They'd reward success (or what could be made to look like it) and punish fuck-ups. And the real question was who'd fucked this one up.

"The Macks had inside help," he said.

"Of course they did," said Memnon. "One more reason you need to watch your back on the council."

"You really think the rot goes that high?"

"I think it'd be dangerous to assume it doesn't."

Leosthenes nodded slowly. "What about these damn weapons?"

"What about them?"

Leosthenes spat into the ocean. "What else does Alexander have?"

Memnon gazed at the sea as though he'd just been asked a question about the weather. "I daresay we'll be finding out," he said.

Barsine ran a tight ship. She kept Lugorix and Matthias to a rigorous watch schedule: Matthias during the moonlit night, Lugorix during the sun-scorched day. It was while relieving Matthias one morning that Lugorix realized just how frustrated his friend was getting.

"It *was* Athenian," repeated the archer angrily. "Another trireme."

"I didn't say it wasn't," replied Lugorix.

"Then why sound so skeptical?"

"Not skeptical, just obvious. The Mediterranean's their *lake*. You saw a boat out here last night, what else would it be?"

"So why didn't she signal it? Why did she evade it?"

"Because this is a Persian vessel and we lack a good explanation?"

"Then why the hell are we going to *Athens* in the first place?"

Lugorix exhaled slowly, watching the heaving waves. "Been wondering that myself," he admitted.

"Well, there you go then."

"So have you asked her?"

"Asked her? I never even *see* her. She's either asleep or piloting this thing."

"I wonder if that's the real cause of your annoyance," said Lugorix.

"I still think she's playing hard to get," muttered Matthias.

"She must have friends in Athens."

"You trying to make me jealous?"

"I'm trying to make sense of all this," said Lugorix. "We know she's worried about Athenians bought by Mack gold. That's how Egypt fell, right? So she not going to trust *anything* we encounter on the high seas. Maybe least of all an Athenian warship." He looked at Matthias. "You got any contacts in Athens?"

"Never been there."

Lugorix looked surprised. "Really?"

"Really."

"And all along I've been thinking you the worldly Greek."

"And you the uncouth barbarian? Zeus, you've probably seen more of the world than I have."

"Didn't you serve a tour in Athens?" said Lugorix.

"Not *in* Athens. One of the fortresses to the north, before they were all overrun. They don't like to let mercs into the capital. Especially not ones from the Greek cities in Asia Minor who might have a grudge against Athens for selling the whole place out to Persia a few decades back."

"Do you have a grudge against Athens?"

"I take her money, don't I?"

"Answer my question."

"No more than I have a grudge against Persia."

"I'd say that grudge has been paid off. After what Alexander did to the place—"

"Look," said Matthias, "we're just hired hands, is all. And gold talks louder than words. Athens preens herself for her democracy, but all that really means is that a gang of asses in a single place get to decide what happens in a hundred other places."

Lugorix mulled this over. "It's more complicated than that."

"How so?"

"Athens puts democracies in all cities that join their alliance."

"Only the *Greek* ones. And sometimes not even then."

"But when they do, a city's people know that their democracy depends on Athenian power. Without that, local oligarchs take control."

"Oligarchs?" Matthias laughed. "Where the hell does a barbarian learn words like that?

"By listening."

"So Athens plays off the Many against the Few to sustain its empire. So what?"

"So you prove my point," said Lugorix.

"Which is?"

"It's complicated."

"It doesn't have to be. You stay a mercenary long enough, you'll get a little more cynical."

"Fact remains. Dealing with Athens is still a damn sight better than dealing with the Macks. Look at their propaganda. Look at their massacres. You don't hear the Athenians babbling about their right and duty to conquer whole world. If Alexander has his way, we'll all be slaves or dead and that's the truth."

Matthias said nothing.

"And with Egypt in his hands," Lugorix added, "he's on way to making that happen. So the big question now is what Athens will do next."

"If we make it there, we may actually find out."

"And more besides."

"Not if that bitch keeps holding out on us," said Matthias.

But late that afternoon, as the sun was setting, the woman in question joined Lugorix while he was on watch. He didn't hear her emerge from the hatch, though he probably should have, as the ship's *aelio-mekanikos*—wind-motor, as the women called it—was no longer making a racket. It had been turned off and the mast and sails had been extended.

"By Taranis," he muttered. "How long have you been standing there?"

"Not long," said Barsine. The breeze blew her hair about her face. She narrowed her eyes against the glare of the vanishing sun. There was something about the way she did that which stirred at his memory—he wasn't sure why. "But I'm not sure you're doing a very good job at keeping watch."

"I'm watching the *ocean*." He was embarrassed to have been so startled—had almost lunged for his axe which he'd leant against the railing. "If something comes out of the hatch behind me—"

"I'd say something has," she said, her voice bordering on the mischievous. "Who's Taranis anyway?"

"One of my people's gods. What brings you on deck?" In the back of his head, he was thinking that Matthias would be annoyed at missing a chance to speak to her—was thinking he should go wake the man. But of course, that wasn't an option. Besides, Lugorix wasn't averse to having something to hold over his friend. All in good fun, of course....

"We're almost at Athens," she said. "Damitra's piloting. I wanted to get a glimpse of the city."

Lugorix nodded. "So that's why we put the mast up and turned off the engine?"

"No sense in looking too weird," she said.

He drew in his breath. "Who are we meeting at Athens?"

"Friends," she said. "In the government."

"But not *the* government."

Her eyes narrowed at that. "Your friend likes to act like he's the smart one. But you're not all brawn, are you?"

"Never said I was."

"Where are you from?"

"Gaul."

"I realize that. Where in Gaul?"

"Southwest. Village of Sarmax. In the Pyrenees. The Athenian recruiters were in Massilia, so I headed there."

"But why you'd leave in the first place?"

He hesitated. "It's complicated."

To his relief, she didn't press it. "And how'd you hook up with Matthias?"

"Working as marines. Doing raids against the Persian coast."

That drew her up short. "Before or after the Macedonian conquest?"

"Both."

"Ah."

"Your people captured Matthias' city a while back."

"What's his city?"

"Pinara," replied Lugorix. "In Asia Minor."

"That's in Macedonian hands now."

"Yes." And then, curious: "I would have thought your witch would have been able to tell you all this."

"She's no witch. She's a Servant of the Sacred Fire."

His brow furrowed. "What's that?"

"The heart of the Zoroastrian faith. Damitra is one of our magi."

"I thought they were all male."

"You're not the only one who thinks that."

"So she knows a lot of magick?"

"She knows enough. But your question's a crude one."

"Oh, thanks."

Barsine shrugged. "Magick's just another word for something one doesn't understand. The ignorant call it magick. But to the initiated, it's really just a tool. Alchemists, mechanists, sorcerors—they're all just different types of the same thing. The real question is the ends to which they put their power. Damitra and I both serve Ahura Mazda, the One Creator, who set us in motion to play our part in the final battle."

Lugorix had no idea what to make of that. "Final battle?" he asked.

"Between good and evil," she replied.

As she said this, she pointed at the darkening horizon where a speck was growing.

"Athens," she said.

They stared across the minutes as it approached, tower after tower rising from horizon, stacking on and upward toward the twilit heavens, each tower bristling with all manner of war-machines and siege equipment. As they drew near, Lugorix could see ant-like men moving along the battlements, looking down at them.

"It's colossal," he muttered.

"That's just the sea-wall across the outer harbor."

Lugorix shook his head in amazement as they sailed in toward one of the sea-wall's many gates. It opened as though it was expecting them. As they headed in toward it, he turned back to Barsine. And suddenly he realized why he found this woman so familiar—who she reminded him of.

Though he knew better than to tell her.

"War between good and evil," he said.

"What about it?"

"That's what you were saying just now."

"Yes," she replied. "The ultimate struggle. It's a Zoroastrian tenet that—"

"You think that's the war we're fighting now?"

There was a long pause. "Alexander has to be stopped," she said finally. "Sometimes I think he truly believes he'll reign forever. He won't, though he might just leave the world wrecked in his wake."

"But say that's just the least of it?" asked Lugorix.

"How could there be more?"

"If he really *does* discover a way to reign forever."

She stared at the spires of Athens straight ahead of them, made no reply.

Eumenes had no idea it was possible to get this thirsty. Not to mention this blind. The sandstorm had been howling for hours, and only Alexander seemed to think they were anything other than absolutely lost. They were at least a hundred miles west of the Nile, and fifty miles south of the last discernible road. It was all desert now, nothing but sand. Eumenes could see how the Persian king Cambyses had lost his whole army in this mess.

Of course, Cambyses had it coming. He'd burnt down all of Egypt's temples and personally slaughtered the sacred bull Apis. Not the best of ways to prepare for a trip to the sacred site at Siwah, assuming one had any respect whatsoever for the gods. Though Eumenes was starting to wonder if that even mattered—was starting to think that perhaps it was all just divine whimsy anyway. For Alexander and his father to defeat the last of Cambyses' line at Issus—for Alexander to then venture on into the heart of Persia and destroy the oldest empire in existence before turning with utter success on Athens itself—it seemed incredible that it could all come to an end amidst trekless desert. But perhaps it was fitting. Perhaps the gods were angry that Alexander wanted to set himself among them. After all, if that wasn't hubris, then Eumenes had no idea what was.

Though there was always the chance Alexander was right. Eumenes had seen enough of the world to know it could be a very strange place, and that the line between legend and fact often had a way of blurring. No mortal in recent memory had done that like Alexander. So if he really *was* something more than mortal, then the deserts of Egypt would be the place of reckoning. Because at this point it was difficult to imagine any of them surviving under any other circumstances.

The sandstorm ebbed momentarily, allowing Eumenes to spot a horseman trudging just ahead of him. He was relieved to know he hadn't lost contact with the rest. Stragglers kept wandering off in the blizzard, never to be seen again. Each time the storm cleared there were less remaining to follow Alexander. The guides had been among the first to disappear, though Eumenes suspected they'd left of their own volition. Perhaps Athenian agents had paid them off. Perhaps they'd *been* Athenian agents, or Athenian sorcery had called up the sandstorm. Eumenes was too exhausted to care. He raised a flask to his lips, drank just enough to wet his lips and get a little moisture down his parched throat. He edged his horse closer to the man ahead of him, trying to keep him in sight as the sandstorm picked up speed again. Stinging grains of heat smacked against his face. He cursed, drawing his scarf up closer. The other man turned round in his saddle, recognized him anyway.

"Eumenes," he said. Hephaestion's voice was reduced to little more than a croak. There was no trace of haughty disdain now.

"Thought you were up at the front," said Eumenes.

"Not much of the front left," muttered Hephaestion.

"Well, where's Alexander?"

"About fifty meters ahead." Hephaestion gestured through the sand at the faint outlines of more horsemen. "Just past the advance guard. His intuition's the only guide we've got left now."

"Does his intuition say we're getting closer?"

"Sure. Question is closer to *what*."

Eumenes wondered if Hephaestion was trying to lull him into incriminating statements. Then he caught the look in the man's eyes and realized that the chief marshal was way beyond artifice of any kind. Eumenes knew the feeling. So he did something he hadn't done in a long time.

Spoke his mind.

"We might all die out here."

Hephaestion pondered this. "True."

"We're lost in the middle of nowhere, and that's all you can say?"'

"What else would you have me say?" Hephaestion's horse whinnied as sand lashed against it. "If this sandstorm doesn't let up, we're fucked anyway. We could pass within a few yards of the Oasis and never notice."

"There are no roads," said Eumenes, and the words echoed in his head. *"No roads.* And we're down to our last dregs of water."

"Sure. We're in the hands of the gods now."

"Maybe one doesn't have to reach Siwah to hear the oracle's answer."

"We wouldn't be the first to never make it. Cambyses—"

"Don't talk to me about Cambyses," snarled Eumenes. Anger rose in him like the hot wind that swirled around them. "Think about all the *others* who didn't make it. Wayward travelers, lost caravans, seekers of infinity— and all too many found it. A good *half* of those who try to make Siwah never do."

"I realize that," said Hephaestion.

"Then why didn't you say something to Alexander?"

"Why didn't *you*?"

"I think we both know you have a little more influence."

"Zeus, man. No one *influences* him. He follows one voice, and that's his own. Both strength and Achilles' heel, no? Who else would think to cut the Gordian knot? Who else would be so bold as to strike at Egypt without warning?"

"His father may have something to say about that if he ever gets the chance."

Hephaestion laughed harshly. "I think Alexander thinks his real father's somewhere out ahead of us."

"Or above us," said Eumenes, pointing straight up. Through the ceiling of sand overhead, fragments of blue sky were starting to appear. The storm was slackening, dropping as suddenly as it had come on that morning. Eumenes looked around, saw that the desert landscape around them was slowly becoming visible.

"Thank the gods," said Hephaestion.

"That may be premature," said Eumenes.

Hephaestion nodded. Both men looked around as the curtain of sand gradually fell back into the desert all about them. The sun began to beat back down upon them with relentless heat. Its light revealed that there were scarcely a score left of what had once been a hundred-man expedition. Hephaestion and Eumenes spurred their spent horses forward to where the lead figure was riding. He didn't turn around as they came up alongside him.

"Alexander," said Hephaestion.

Alexander didn't answer.

"My prince," said Eumenes.

Still he said nothing. Didn't look at them either. Hephaestion looked alarmed—reached out to take his shoulder.

"The crows," said Alexander suddenly. Hephaestion's hand dropped back to his side. He looked around, confused.

"I don't follow—"

"The crows," hissed Alexander. Eumenes looked at Alexander's sand-covered face—looked out along his field of vision, looked all the way toward sand-smeared horizon. He blinked. Alexander's eyes were better than his.

And then he saw it.

"Birds," he muttered.

"They're crows," said Alexander.

"Crows," said Hephaestion. "Of course."

"The oasis," said Eumenes. "Thanks be to Zeus."

"Now at last I'll hear what He has to say," said Alexander.

He led them in toward Siwah.

"So this is the hub around which it all turns, eh?"

Matthias pulled himself up onto the deck to join Lugorix and Barsine. She shot him an annoyed look, pushed past him, and began climbing back down the ladder. Matthias looked at Lugorix, shrugged.

"What's bugging her?" he asked.

"You," replied Lugorix. "I think she wanted to enjoy the view in peace."

Against the setting sun, it was quite a spectacle. They were still a good half mile off the shoreline itself, beyond which stretched the first layer of Athenian skyline—a sprawl of towers and monuments that put those which had stood at Alcibiadia to shame. Lugorix had never imagined a city could be so large. Each one of the buildings looked like it would dwarf his entire village.

"And that's only the Piraeus," said Matthias.

"Pir-a-what?"

"The harbor-city."

The *Xerxes* was maneuvering among the smaller boats of the harbor now: an armada of fishing skiffs, pleasure yachts and transports. Off in the deeper harbor were vast grain freighters—one of them attended by a huge contraption that reared from the water like some mechanical beast. Crewmembers turned winches to send a long clanking arm swinging out over the docks, then lowered its far end onto the deck of the ship where other workers began to manhandle the containers positioned atop it.

"What the hell is *that?*" said Lugorix.

"They call it a crane," replied Matthias. "It's loading that freighter."

"Why do they need such a device?"

"I guess they don't. But it helps save time."

"But how much time did they spend building that thing?" asked Lugorix. He sensed he was missing the point, but now they were rounding a promontory that blocked the strange machine from sight. Torches hung from many of the ships around them, for it was getting increasingly hard to see amidst the looming dusk. The wind blowing from the shore carried the smell of cooking fires. Lugorix suspected that Barsine had timed their arrival precisely. Had they reached Athens during the daytime, everyone would have been able to see them. Had they shown up in the dead of the night, they might have triggered a false alarm on the part of the Athenian defenses. As it was, they were probably being witnessed by only a few of the ships at anchor, but they'd still been recognized by those who manned the sea-gate. Lugorix had the sense that it wasn't even one of the main entrances—he could see great glowing arches of lights off to the east that perhaps served that function. Those arches grew ever fainter as the boat headed into the far recesses of the harbor.

"Up ahead," said Matthias, pointing.

Lugorix followed the direction of his arm. They were coming in toward one of the docks. It was somewhat ramshackle—it almost looked abandoned, but there were figures standing on it, holding lanterns. Damitra—or maybe it was Barsine—maneuvered the boat alongside, and the men on the dock threw down ropes. Lugorix and Matthias got busy securing them when another man leapt down onto the boat.

"Who's the captain here?" he asked in a nasally voice. His hair was carefully coiffed, his robes were of the finest silk and he was drenched in perfume. The dolphin medallion of an Athenian harbor-master hung about his neck, and he looked at Lugorix and Matthias as though they were the scum of the earth.

"The captain's me," said Barsine as she climbed up onto the deck. "Who are you?"

The man was obviously taken aback. Greeks weren't like Gauls, Lugorix realized. They didn't permit their women much power outside of the house. So to have a mere teenager commanding a boat that could rival the most advanced prototypes the Athenian navy could field—no wonder the man was looking like the whole thing was some kind of strange joke.

"I'm Callias," he said. "Harbor-master for this section of the docks. Your papers, please."

"Papers?"

"Yes, papers. To secure a berth in Athens. You *do* have them, don't you?"

"There must be some misunderstanding," said Barsine. "We were told that we didn't need them." As she said this, a couple more of the men on the dock stepped down onto the boat. Lugorix belatedly realized that they were armed, with swords under their cloaks. They flanked Callias, who stood there with a puzzled-verging-on-annoyed expression on his face.

"If you lack papers, then you lack authorization to be in this harbor."

"And yet here we are," said Barsine. "How do you think we did that?"

"Clearly you've infiltrated our defenses," replied Callias.

"Clearly you're a fool," said Barsine. "No one gets into this city without being permitted. The postern gate let us through because they were expecting us. How is it that you're not?" Lugorix was starting to realize she had a limited sense of tact—one more trait that seemed to be endemic to nobility. Callias' face darkened and a vein on his forehead began to pulse.

"Have it your way," he said. "I'm impounding your vessel. Seize them." One of his guards started forward but—

"Touch her and you'll lose that hand," said Matthias, drawing his *xiphos*.

"Touch me and you'll lose your head," said the guard as he drew his own sword—only to recoil as Lugorix hefted Skullseeker. The other guards eyed the axe nervously.

"Put your weapons away," snapped Barsine. "Why are men always so eager to fight?"

Matthias reluctantly sheathed his *xiphos*—and Lugorix lowered his axe, albeit without any of his friend's reluctance. He knew that if it came to combat, they could slaughter these guards—but once the alarm had been sounded, they'd be meat. Callias looked at Barsine, his eyes narrowing. His guards had kept their weapons out.

"You're Persian, aren't you?" said Callias as though this explained everything.

"Yes," she replied.

"I'd have thought Persian spies could think of better schemes to get themselves into the city."

"I'm not a spy," said Barsine calmly.

"Oh? Then what are you?"

"She's with me," said a voice.

Everybody whirled to see a heavyset man standing on the dock, dressed in the garb of an Athenian sailor. The guards in front of him whipped out their swords and pointed them at his throat, but he didn't seem worried. He just looked down at Callias.

"Harbormaster," he said. "I've orders to take this ship into custody and waive all harbor-fees and duties."

Callias' face was a study in incredulity. "Who the hell are you?"

"Here are the orders."

He handed a scroll down to Callias, who unfurled it and began to read. He'd only got a few lines in before his eyes widened. When he looked up, his expression was contrition mingled with what Lugorix could have sworn was fear.

"Of course," he said. "Of course. She's all yours." He climbed back onto the dock, and his guards went with him. As he passed the newcomer, a thought seemed to occur to him.

"Where do you plan to keep this boat?"

"That's of no concern to you."

"Anything in the harbor is."

The man laughed scornfully. "And here you are talking like you're chief harbormaster! Shall we go wake him up and see what he thinks of your insisting on inventorying this vessel?"

"I'm not insisting on anything. I just wish to know if you're—"

"—planning on keeping her in the harbor? No. Now get lost."

Like any good bureaucrat, Callias knew when he was beaten. He left with his guards, intent on preserving what was left of his dignity. The interloper watched him go, then hopped down onto the boat. Ignoring Matthias and Lugorix, he bowed to Barsine.

"I'm Theramenes," he said. "At your service."

"But you still haven't answered the question," said Barsine.

Theramenes raised one eyebrow. "My lady?"

"Where do we put the boat?"

"In the canals," replied Theramenes.

It was like the sea was made of buildings—like the ship was sailing on roads. Except there was still water beneath them. Lugorix couldn't stop staring at the lantern-bedecked windows passing mere meters from his face. He gazed at his reflection in the water, marveled at the occasional bridge that swept above them. He would have thought they would have been seen by everyone as they made their way through these canals, but they were in the industrial part of town. Most of the workers had gone home for the night. Those that did spot them assumed they were merely one more Athenian warship being towed through the canal, rising through lock after lock: strange segmented areas where doors were closed and pumps forced water up to a new level.

The mules didn't seem to give a shit one way or the other. Theramenes was on the shore with their drivers, leading them as they threaded their way through the maze of freight-canals that led for miles inland, into the heart of central Athens. Matthias and Lugorix stood near Barsine, but she didn't seem to want company right now. A fact that naturally made Matthias all the more importunate.

"So who is this guy?" he asked.

"Someone who's going to help us," replies Barsine.

"A friend?"

"No."

"Then why do you think he's going to help us?"

"He works for a friend. Now please, be quiet."

"Of course. It's just that—"

"*What?*"

"—you told us our job was to keep you safe."

"So?"

"So I'm just trying to make sure we're doing that."

"You might want to think about ducking"—this as she did so herself.

"What?"—but Lugorix was already pushing Matthias down to make sure that the low roof that was sweeping in toward them didn't brain his friend. Barsine looked at them like they were a pair of clowns—then climbed below deck, leaving Matthias more than a little nonplussed.

"That little minx—"

"Never mind that," said Lugorix, "what the hell *is* this place?"

They were in a cavernous cellar, the roof sloping up to a vaulted ceiling. Wooden gates slid into place behind them. Torches slotted into grooves on the wall cast a flickering light on a stone jetty in one corner—and on the iron staircase that rose from it, into the room's ceiling. The boat slowed, nudging up against the jetty. Theramenes unhitched the mules and climbed up onto the deck.

"So you're the hired help," he said.

"Sounds like you are too," said Matthias.

But Theramenes just smiled. "I'll show you to your quarters."

"Where are we?"

"A private residence."

"Not one of Athens' fortresses?"

"Come with me," said the man.

CHAPTER FOUR

Wearily, Eumenes climbed the stairs to the top of the battlements. It was just before morning, and the wind off the Mediterranean seemed to cut right through his cloak. Strange how chilly it could be along the coast, even in the midst of summer. Back on the trek to Siwah, Eumenes had thought he'd never mind being cold again. Now, standing on the battlements of Tyre once more, the wind tearing at him like a living thing, he could scarcely recollect the heat of the desert.

But he'd never forget that oasis.

He looked around. Battlements and towers stretched all around him, encasing acre upon acre of ruins and wrecked buildings. Tyre was a city-fortress that had stood on an island just off the coast of Syria. Though it wasn't much of a city anymore. And now it wasn't an island either. Before striking east into Persia, Alexander's army had built an artificial promontory across the narrow channel that separated it from the mainland—had dumped tons upon tons of rocks and silt into that channel so as to drag their war-machines across and batter down the walls. It had been one of the most epic sieges ever—and the slaughter that followed had been even more thorough than that which had taken place at Alcibiadia. Eumenes remembered well the lines of wooden crosses stretching down the shoreline, a captured defender of Tyre nailed to each one, the stench and screams stretching off to the horizon…

"All because he wanted to sacrifice at that accursed temple," said a voice.

Eumenes turned to see Harpalus stepping from the shadow of a ruined tower. The treasurer looked exhausted, his beard unkempt, dark circles under his eyes. Small wonder, as his work had doubled since the sack of Egypt. And Eumenes knew just how hard Harpalus had already been laboring under the weight of sifting through the Persian finances. When the Macedonian expeditionary force had first crossed into Asia, Harpalus' job was reasonably simple: ensure what little money Philip had alloted his son went as far as possible. But once Alexander had defeated the Great King's army and stormed into the Persian heartland, Harpalus' task became order-of-magnitude more complex. Now he oversaw a vast mobile bureaucracy dedicated to processing the revenue of the richest Athenian province and virtually all the Persian satrapies—not to mention moving the Persian gold reserves out of Babylonia and back to… wherever Philip and Alexander decided. They were arguing about it. They were arguing about everything. Which was why Alexander had been recalled to Pella, the Macedonian capital—summoned to attend upon his father with all the speed he could muster. In response, Alexander had divided his army, leaving part of it in Egypt under Craterus, while the rest of it returned to Macedonia.

Though it would take some weeks to get there. Alexander and his entourage were well out in front of it now—they'd made camp at Tyre last night and were due to move out this morning. To the dismay of some of his advisers, Alexander was following his father's instructions to the letter—he was making utmost speed, and if that meant letting the army play catch up, so be it.

"It's a mistake," said Eumenes.

"Of course," replied Harpalus. "Tyre would have paid tribute without him needing to storm it. When I think of all the men we lost—"

"I'm not talking about Tyre," said Eumenes. "I'm talking about Alexander's… *compulsion* to go and face his father directly. Without the army."

Harpalus nodded. "My sources back in Macedonia tell me that Philip wasn't expecting that. That he was worried he'd be facing civil war. I'm almost surprised he's not getting one. His son's forces outnumber his by almost two to one."

Eumenes shrugged. "Philip controls the crossing to Europe."

"You think that would stop Alexander?" asked Harpalus.

"No. If he had to, he'd just march around the entire Black Sea. But the only winners from a civil war right now would be the Athenians, and Alexander knows it."

"So he's putting his head straight into the lion's den."

"And taking quite a risk." Eumenes' tone was somber. "Can you imagine how angry Philip must be by this point? His son strikes Egypt without sanction—"

"—and succeeds—"

"—and no matter what the sycophants around Alexander say, that'll have made the old man even angrier. Philip's an invalid, trapped in his palace back at Pella, dreaming of his past glory. He was the one who started the war with Persia—and now he's had to watch his son conquer the entire empire—"

"Which no one ever expected—"

"No one except him! Zeus almighty, it's *crazy* to look back on it all. You remember; everyone figured a best case scenario was liberating the Greek towns of Asia Minor, maybe even set up a defensive line in Anatolia. And then next thing, we're sacking Babylon! We've reached Afghanistan! And Alexander's still not satisfied! He wants to continue! Whereupon his father says come back, we need to have a little chat! So he turns around, but does he return? No, he hits Egypt instead and ignites a war with the queen of the seas. And so..."

"Here we are," said Harpalus.

"Here we are," repeated Eumenes, his agitation draining as quickly as it had filled him. He looked out across the battlements at the tide lapping against the beach. Now that dawn was starting to light the ocean, he could see the tops of masts and siege-engines protruding above the water's surface—victims of the withering fire that had poured down from the city's walls during the final assault. Eumenes looked back at Harpalus. "So what did you want to talk about?"

"You know what."

"If Alexander found us meeting like this, he'd say it was a conspiracy."

"He thinks everything is these days. He's convinced that there's a spy among his inner council."

Harpalus' eyes widened. "A spy for Athens?"

"A spy for *Philip*."

"Zeus. Who knows of those suspicions?"

"Besides me—Hephaestion, certainly. Craterus, probably. Beyond that,

I've no idea."

"You and I need to stick together," said Harpalus.

"That's why we're having this conversation."

"If Alexander's getting this paranoid, the others will seek to take advantage of it."

Eumenes nodded. "They already have. Meleager—"

"I heard. He's been imprisoned."

"You mean executed."

Harpalus leaned against the battlements as though he'd been struck. "What? When?"

"Four nights ago. Back in Egypt."

"Does Alexander even plan to announce it?"

"He'll probably tell the army he died in a skirmish with Arab raiders or something—give him a grand funeral, lots of tears, a moving oration, all the usual trappings now he's safely dead."

"Safely?" Harpalus' tone bordered on incredulity. "Meleager was the ultimate loyalist. He would never have—"

"I know. His downfall's thanks to Craterus. Who saw his chance to rid himself of a rival, and used Alexander's mindset to make it happen. So now he can put a more pliable man in command of the part of the phalanx that's been left back in Egypt."

Harpalus seemed to be struggling to absorb all of this. He gazed out at the ocean, slowly shaking his head. Eumenes almost felt sorry for him. Buried in his figures and charts, the treasurer had gradually lost touch with the intensifying pace of court-politics… had lost touch, too, with just how much the character of his boyhood friend Alexander had changed. Eumenes knew there was a time when Alexander and Harpalus had been inseparable. But the fantastic success visited on Macedonian arms had transformed everything. Harpalus looked back at Eumenes, his gaze hollow.

"So what happened out there?" he asked.

"We almost died," said Eumenes.

"I mean, what happened when you reached the oasis."

"The priests hailed him as Son of Zeus."

Harpalus shook his head. "Zeus knows what he'd have done to them if they hadn't."

"And then he went inside the temple. By himself. No bodyguards, no nothing. No witnesses. We waited. And waited. To the point that we wondered whether the priests had been paid by the Athenians to kill him and ride hell for leather out the back door. And then, just as we were about to bust in ourselves, Alexander comes out looking like…." Eumenes trailed off, wondering how to phrase it.

"Like what?" asked Harpalus impatiently.

"Like a man who's just been told his heart's desire." Eumenes thought it over. "But also… like a man who's just had the surprise of his life."

There was a long pause.

"And he was in there for the better part of an *hour*," added Eumenes. "So if it *was* a revelation from Zeus-Ammon, it was rather a long one. Presumably fairly specific too."

"Those damn priests. They could have said anything."

"Assuming it *was* the priests."

Harpalus mulled that one over. "But he didn't tell you what the message was?"

"I'm not sure he's even told Hephaestion. Whatever happened in there is between the prince and the gods. But he's been acting stranger than ever in the weeks since. The paranoia, the moodiness, the drinking—"

"We might be able to piece some of it together," said Harpalus.

"What do you have in mind?"

"Well. Doesn't it strike you as funny that we're here?"

"In Tyre?"

"Yes. In Tyre."

Eumenes pondered this. Try as he might, he couldn't see what Harpalus was driving at. "It's a natural place to stop on the way back north. And Alexander was never a man to resist revisiting the scene of one of his greatest triumphs—"

"Right, but he captured this city so he could sacrifice at the temple of Melkart. That was the whole point, remember?"

There was no way Eumenes could forget. Melkart was the Phoenician incarnation of Hercules, who Alexander had idolized since boyhood. In the wake of Siwah, Eumenes had begun to suspect that identification might have become a literal one, though he hadn't given it a tremendous amount of thought—largely because it seemed to be overshadowed by Alexander's claim to be the son of the father of the universe. But now he found himself wondering if Harpalus knew something he didn't. Still, it didn't add up.

"Melkart was just an excuse," he said. "You know that as well as I do. Tyre was the headquarters of the Persian navy, which Alexander needed to neutralize—"

"Athens had already done a good job with that," said Harpalus. "Back when she took Egypt from Persia, thirty years back. Persia only had a few ships left—"

"Where are you going with this?" asked Eumenes.

"The ambassadors from Carthage," said Harpalus.

Eumenes nodded. He'd personally handled *that* particular problem. The Carthaginian ambassadors had been at Tyre for ceremonies to Melkart when Alexander sacked the place. It had made for a tricky diplomatic situation, since Carthage had been a Phoenician colony—founded by Tyre itself centuries ago. But Carthage had long since passed out of Tyre's political orbit and become a major power in her own right—until Athens had subjugated her and made the city the crown-jewel of her western empire. Eumenes had suspected at the time that Alexander would have killed the ambassadors out of hand had they not technically been under Athenian protection—it would have meant war with Athens before he'd even finished with Persia. So the ambassadors had been permitted to leave Tyre unscathed. But somehow they were still in the picture.

"What about them?" he asked.

"They've been in contact with Alexander," said Harpalus.

That drew Eumenes up short. *"What?"*

"Sending him gold. And African ivory. Which naturally went through the treasury—"

"Bribes?"

"Maybe. But they included correspondence. Which was sealed… but I have my ways."

"Correspondence is supposed to go through my office," said Eumenes, realizing even as he spoke the words just how petulant he was sounding.

"What can I say?" Harpalus spread his arms out. "Our prince likes to keep the left and right hands far apart."

"But—what in Hades' name did the correspondence say? What was the message?"

"They weren't messages—they were *maps*."

"Maps of *what?*"

"The location and layout of other temples of Melkart-Hercules."

"He's got temples all over the place. I could name several right now."

"I'm talking about the westernmost ones in existence."

"Which are where?"

"At the Pillars of Hercules."

There was a long pause. "You're joking."

"I wish I were," said Harpalus.

"The gateway to the outer ocean? Where Hercules is supposed to have bagged the sacred cattle?"

"Don't be so cynical. From what I can make out, the place is real enough. There are two temples, facing each other across the straits. One's called Gadus; the other, Lixus. And Zeus help us all if Alexander wants to worship at either of *them*."

Eumenes' mind was working on overtime. "Did you see any other correspondence from these ambassadors?"

"No."

"I'll bet there was some, though."

"What makes you say that?" asked Harpalus.

"Zeus, there must have been. You just don't send a bunch of ivory and maps without some kind of explanation or context."

"Maybe they went through another channel. Or they were in code."

"Or both. Remember all that talk about Carthage at the council meeting back in Egypt?"

"Unfortunately, yes."

"I'd wager Alexander's working with a fifth column there," said Eumenes. "Trying to get them to rebel."

Harpalus looked thoughtful. "Or they're trying to get him to come liberate *them*"—but as he said this, a blast of trumpets shattered the morning calm. Both men whirled, looking out across the city and promontory, back to the camp. They could see mounted figures riding in — the morning patrols were returning. Soon Alexander would order the day's ride to begin, for the continuation of the journey back toward Macedonia.

"We should leave," said Eumenes, turning back to Harpalus.

But Harpalus was already heading down the stairway.

"I'm sick of this place," muttered Matthias.

Lugorix nodded. He knew the feeling. They'd been cooped up for several days in what they'd quickly come to realize may have as well have been a prison. They'd been allowed to keep their weapons and equipment, but were for all intents and purposes confined to their rooms. *Under house arrest,* was the phrase that Matthias used for it—Lugorix had never heard the term before. In Gallic culture anyone who had a house was a rich man by definition, and anyone who was under arrest was quickly put on trial, either to be executed or released in short order. He'd asked Matthias whether they were here because they'd committed a crime—Matthias said that wasn't the point, that they were in somebody else's hands now, and would just have to wait to see what happened.

Lugorix wasn't sure that was such a great idea. Though he had to admit, their quarters *were* comfortable. In fact, they were more luxurious than anything he'd ever seen. There were real *beds!*—complete with banners that were meant to be pulled over oneself while one slept. Matthias told him they were called *sheets*. Lugorix would have preferred a woman, but he found the sheets to be comfortable enough all the same. The walls were covered with paintings and the floors were bedecked with carpets. There was even something called a *toilet,* which was easily the most remarkable thing Lugorix had ever laid eyes on. One pissed and crapped through a hole and apparently someone at the bottom of that hole was responsible for cleaning the mess up.

One of the slaves, presumably. They were the only people Lugorix and Matthias had seen since being escorted upstairs from the basement where the boat had been moored. Slaves brought their meals, cleaned the rooms, changed the linen, and even furnished wine: amphorae stoppered with wax seals and marked with the symbol of what Matthias assured Lugorix was a very expensive vineyard. Lugorix figured the plan was to keep him and Matthias drunk and happy. He certainly couldn't argue with the success of the first objective.

The house they were in was clearly much larger than the wing to which they were confined. Lugorix had gotten glimpses of it when he and Matthias had been led upstairs from the basement—sprawling landings, spacious hallways, doors left tantalizingly open, but no sign of the elusive owner. Theramenes, the man who had overruled the harbormaster, had escorted them to the quarters they now occupied. Lugorix wondered if in fact *he* was the house's master, but there had been something in the man's bearing that suggested that he was simply what he claimed to be: just a servant. They hadn't seen him since.

Nor had they seen Barsine or Damitra. This seemed to frustrate Matthias above all else, which for Lugorix was clear evidence of a fundamental lack of perspective. Because whatever game Barsine was playing had everything to do with Macedonia and nothing whatsoever to do with Matthias. In the midst of quaffing the contents of a particularly tasty amphora, Lugorix had tried to explain this to Matthias, only to be rudely told he didn't need to be reminded. Tensions between the two men got worse from there. They'd saved each other's lives in the field many times, but confined together in close quarters they were starting to feel like caged animals, able to do nothing but turn on each other.

The view from the window was making matters worse. They were three floors up, looking out over the thicket of trees and vines and ponds that constituted the house's back-garden. Beyond that were more canals and more palatial homes, draped with ivy and vines—and moonlight, now that it was night. The effect was nothing short of haunting; Matthias said it was like the hanging gardens of Babylon, though Lugorix had no idea what that was supposed to mean. They weren't in Babylon, they were in Athens. And he was fed up with it.

"We really need to get out of this dump," he said.

"You said that already," replied Matthias, putting aside yet another empty amphora. He was pretty drunk. "But we're not going to start slaughtering the slaves when they come through the door—"

"We use the bed-linen to make ropes," said Lugorix. "Get down into that garden, find another way into this house. Find out what the hell's going on."

"Best way to do that is to wait here."

"Wait for Barsine to tell you what you should do next?"

"Shut the hell up."

"Place may be gilded, but it's still a cage."

"It's been a nice rest since all the shit we've gone through."

"How's it feel to be a woman's lap-dog?"

"Fuck off."

Lugorix laughed. "Don't like being a kept man?"

"I'll throw you out that window if you keep talking like that."

"What about if we both go out together?"

Matthias was easy enough to wind up. Especially when he was in his cups. In no time at all, he and Lugorix had stripped the beds of all the sheets and created a serviceable rope. They dangled it down to the ground and got ready to climb out.

"Do we take our weapons?" said Matthias.

"What kind of question is that?" asked Lugorix as he picked up Skull-seeker and strapped it onto his back. Matthias did the same with his bow; two minutes later, they were both standing on the patio, looking up at the window three stories above and a fourth story beyond that.

Lugorix stretched his arms langorously. "Wasn't so hard, was it?"

"Keep quiet," hissed Matthias. He swayed unevenly, and then steadied himself against the wall of the house. "Let's check this place out."

They began to circle the house cautiously, treading carefully through the undergrowth nestled alongside the walls. They found several doors; all were locked, and looked even more imposing then the one that led from their quarters. All the windows were barred. There was no sign of movement in any of them. Lugorix was thinking of trying his hand at some lock-picking when—

"Over there," whispered Matthias, pointing. Lugorix followed the direction of his gaze to see a door in the garden wall. They skulked over to it. Lugorix threw back the bars, opened the door and led the way onto the street.

Except it was more of a path—or rather, a towpath along one of the canals that bordered the house. They made their way along it, past the walls of more houses belonging to the Athenian wealthy. The occasional houseboat stood in the canal, festooned with banners. At intervals they passed statues of the god Hermes, each one with an appropriately-oversized phallus.

"These people really let it all hang out," muttered Lugorix.

"It's for luck," replied Matthias. "Every household has one."

"If I had one of those, I wouldn't need luck."

"Well, there was a big scandal involving them once."

"So what?"

"So I'm trying to educate you," said Matthias as he led the way across a bridge that sloped over one of the canals. "The expedition to Sicily was about to depart, led by the man himself, Alcibiades, when—"

"This is ancient history," complained Lugorix.

"A century back. This is how the whole thing got started, man."

"What whole thing?"

"The Athenian Empire. The expedition to Sicily that won them the war against Sparta. The night before it was due to depart, all these cocks"—he gestured at one of the Hermes—"all of them got chopped off. Everyone woke up and went *batshit*. It was blamed on Alcibiades, since he had a bit of a rakish reputation in the first place, but he asked why the hell he'd sabotage an expedition on which he was betting his entire future. His enemies wanted him to sail for Sicily anyway and stand trial in abstentia—"

"No one ever gets found innocent when they aren't at their own trial," said Lugorix.

"Something Alcibiades was keenly aware of. He managed to have it out with his rivals there and then—and then he produced evidence that his fellow commander Nicias—who hated Alcibiades—was behind it all, that he'd had all the Hermes mutilated in order to frame his enemy. So they put Nicias on the rack and did away with the joint command they'd initially been proposing—they sent the entire expedition under the sole leadership of Alcibiades. Six months later Syracuse surrendered. Six months after that so did all of Sicily. Which doubled Athens' revenue and gave them access to all the grain they needed and all the mercenaries in Gaul and Italy and Spain they could hire—"

"Like me," said Lugorix.

"Yeah. Then after Sparta surrendered, Alcibiades led the fleet back west and defeated Carthage. Leaving Athens without any rivals on the sea."

"Thanks for the history lesson," said Lugorix.

"It's not just history," replied Matthias earnestly. Lugorix made a mental note to never ask Matthias about anything when he was drunk. "It's about the way the world works."

"Meaning what?"

Matthias gestured at a Hermes. "Sometimes the fate of an entire nation can turn on the tip of a dick."

"Is that the line you're going to use on Barsine?"

But suddenly Matthias was looking around, entirely distracted. "Where *are we?*" he asked.

"How should I know? You've been leading the way."

"Told you I never been to Athens before. I only know the big tourist attractions—"

"Great," said Lugorix. They were still among the canals, but in a much seedier area now. The houses were shabby and small, and the canals had become dank and slimy—the moon glistened off that slime in unattractive ways. Obviously they'd left the upscale district behind.

"We could go back," said Matthias.

"What's that up ahead?" said Lugorix. It seemed to be a wider street, lit up in a way that the canals weren't. He and Matthias found themselves drawn toward it like moths to a flame. That was the problem with being plastered in a strange city—one just kind of turned off one's brain and went with one's reflexes. Which now brought them out upon a wide avenue, all the more surreal for being so vacant. Lanterns hung from posts up and down its length, each containing the aggregated light of hundreds of fireflies.

"Streetlamps," said Matthias.

"Bugs," said Lugorix.

They could see much more of the city's skyline now—hills all around them, covered with a tangle of buildings. One stood out in particular—a colossal pillared structure atop one of the highest hills of all, a huge bronze statue of Athena right in front of it. Beside the Pharos, it was the largest building Lugorix had ever seen.

"That's the Parthenon," said Matthias. "City's temple."

"Let's go check it out."

"Are you kidding me? It'll be crawling with watchmen just waiting for drunk fools like us. But the Pnyx is nearby—I know where that is, that'll be interesting."

"The what?" But Matthias was already leading the way down a side-street—and through onto another avenue which brought them to a wooded hill. It was a little incongruous to come across it in the middle of the city, but in Lugorix's inebriated state, he was content to roll with it. He was hoping to find nymphs in the middle of the woods but instead—

"What is *this?*"

"What does it look like," replied Matthias.

It looked like a theater. The moon shone down on row after row of seats carved down the side of a slope. But the stage at the bottom was comparatively small—not nearly large enough to put on a play, which made Lugorix wonder just what its purpose was.

"This is where the Assembly meets," said Matthias.

Lugorix looked around. It seemed almost anticlimactic that the entire Mediterranean was ruled from this place. He would have found it more appropriate if that big pillared building—the Parthenon—was where all the action went down; it seemed like the kind of structure that would house a king or emperor or someone really important. But this… he couldn't imagine anything ever getting decided here. It wasn't that he wasn't used to community-decision making—it was how his tribe back home had figured things out. But they were only making decisions for themselves—not for a whole world beyond them.

"Hey Gauls!"

Matthias and Lugorix whirled around. Four men were coming toward them. They didn't look like watchmen. More like—

"Drunk thugs," muttered Matthias. "Just what we need."

"Well if it isn't two Gaulish mercenaries taking in the view," said the largest of them—even taller than Lugorix.

"Mercenaries aren't supposed to be in the city," said another—he had a dirty-looking beard, and eyes that gleamed evilly. "Especially Gaullish ones."

"I'm not a Gaul," said Matthias.

"Well, your friend is," said the man with the dirty beard.

"And you're both mercenaries," said the large one. "So what do you think you're doing here?"

"Not looking for trouble," said Lugorix.

That made them laugh. "Well, you've managed to find it. This city's a clean city, know what I mean? It's not supposed to have any dirty trouser-wearing Gauls in it."

"You certainly hire enough of us," said Lugorix. He knew he was rising to the bait, but all the booze in him made it hard to resist. Besides, these guys were starting to piss him off.

"Of course we hire you," said one of them. "You're useful cannon fodder. Do our bidding for the cash, fight the Macks when we tell you. What else are dirty Gauls good for?"

Lugorix could think of a few things. Like kicking this guy's ass, for starters….

"You're *barbarians,* is what you are." This was the third man, speaking with a pronounced lisp. "Never built a stone building in your life. Probably never seen one either."

"*And* you believe in human sacrifice," said the large man. "We've heard about your druids. About your wickermen. About how you put your prisoners in them and set them on fire and burn them alive."

Lugorix had heard enough. He unslung Skullseeker—whereupon the four men pulled out their swords.

"You don't want to do this," said Matthias. "We're professionals."

"And we're Athenian citizens," said the man with the beard. "You so much as *touch* us and it's the death penalty for you both."

"So let's all walk away," said Matthias calmly.

"First you have to get down on your knees and kiss our blades."

"Screw that," said Lugorix, raising his axe.

"Enough!" cried a voice—and such was the force of that voice that everybody stopped and turned.

An old man was walking toward them. He sported a long grey beard and—despite his age—a thick head of hair. His eyes gleamed with a strange intensity, and the four Athenians seemed to recognize him.

"Your honor," said the largest one, "these men are mercenaries. Carrying weapons in the city!"

"They should be punished!" said the one with a lisp.

"And you should be home in bed," said the newcomer. "Instead of roaming the streets, revelling in how your money's bought you exemption from military service while you look to pick fights. Ironic, no?"

"We weren't looking for—"

"You were," said the man. "And you know damn well the Macedonians are right outside the walls. So if you really want a fight, why don't you try them?"

That seemed to do it. The men turned to go, looking more than a little sheepish. All except for the one with the dirty beard.

"What about these mercenaries?" he asked.

"They work for me," said the man. "Now get out of my sight before I call the watch on you. And don't speak of this to anybody or I'll put my boot so far up your backside your nose will itch."

The four men found the threat credible. They left quickly, their footfalls disappearing into the night. The old man turned to Matthias and Lugorix.

"You gentlemen have caused more than enough problems for one evening," he said. "Shall we return to my house?"

"Not until you tell who the hell you are," said Matthias.

"My name's Demosthenes," said the man. He said it as though he expected it to sound familiar, though Lugorix had never heard of him.

But Matthias had. He looked stunned. "The orator," he said.

"It's nice to be known for something," said Demosthenes. "But these days I don't do much public speaking."

"Why's that?" asked Matthias.

"The Assembly's been closed."

"Closed?" asked Lugorix.

"And I hate to rush you, but we really *do* need to leave. Barsine is back at the house, and we'll explain everything to you."

That was a lie, of course.

But they were about to learn a lot more then they'd bargained for.

CHAPTER FIVE

"Sir," said a voice.

"Leave me alone," muttered Eumenes.

"Sir, you need to wake up."

Eumenes shook his head, spluttered. The smell of brine and salt-air filled his nostrils. Spray smacked into his face in time with the slap of waves. He opened his eyes to see that they were almost there—that they'd traversed most of the Sea of Marmara already. Europe's coast lay ahead; Asia's stretched behind. It was a testament to just how exhausted he was that he'd fallen asleep on such a short crossing.

He stretched, got to his feet. The galley was a standard transport; three rows of slaves hauled on the oars in time with the crack of the lash. Eumenes' aides stood around him as he grasped the rail and looked out at the other ships of the squadron, their black silhouettes framed against the sun. This was the one place on earth where the Macedonians had made themselves supreme upon the water. They'd done so by a simple expedient at the outset of Alexander's attack on Persia: further to the south, they'd stretched vast fortified booms across the Dardenelles, linked up two continents to deny the Athenian navy access to the channel, effectively turning the Black Sea into their lake. Macedonia's ships had crossed with impunity ever since, ferrying troops and supplies back and forth as needed.

The journey here had involved hard riding across Asia Minor—relays of horses carrying Alexander and his men as they rode back over territory which they had wrested from the Persians more than half a decade previously. Once they made landfall in Europe, they'd proceed directly to Pella, the Macedonian capital, where King Philip awaited his son—a prospect that filled Eumenes with more than a little foreboding. The Fates alone knew how that conversation would turn out.

Eumenes' reveries were interrupted by a shudder that ran beneath his feet as the ship hit the shallows and its prow ground up the beach. The smoke of Byzantium's chimneys was dimly visible to the north. Crossing there would have made more logistical sense—the Bosphorus was only a couple miles wide—but Byzantium undoubtedly contained Athenian spies, and Alexander wanted to keep a low profile. Sailors threw ropes over the side and the passengers climbed down and waded through the surf. Eumenes resisted the urge to kneel in that surf, silently thanked the gods he'd been allowed to see Europe again. For many years he had thought he never would—all those endless Persian armies, all those deserts and mountains of the East until finally he thought that Alexander meant to continue on to the very edge of the world and beyond.

But then had come the order from Philip: for the army to turn back, leaving the hellhole called Afghanistan behind, along with the refugee Persian nobles and pretenders who infested it. The Macedonian soldiers had been as jubilant as Alexander was furious: he regarded returning west as nothing short of a ignominious retreat. Yet he had obeyed his father. Oraxthes, the brother of the deposed Darius III had been placed on the Persian throne as a puppet; the job of the Macedonian garrisons deployed across Babylonia was to keep him there while the main bulk of Alexander's army returned to the Mediterranean coast. Though it was all too clear that the subsequent plunge into Egypt would be the primary order of business in the upcoming confrontation between father and son.

A loud shouting reached Eumenes' ears. There was some kind of commotion aboard Alexander's ship, which had almost reached the shore. Eumenes ran along the beach toward the boat, one hand on the hilt of his sword, while others ran alongside him. An assassination attempt on Alexander? An Athenian attempt to kill him? As he approached the ship, a man was hurled from it, into the water. The man rolled in the surf, his face bloody. Eumenes was the first to reach him.

It was Harpalus.

Alexander's bodyguards leapt down into the ocean, and picked him up, shoving past Eumenes as they dragged him onto the beach. Alexander himself was next to follow, Hephaestion at his side.

"What in the name of all that's holy is going on?" asked Eumenes.

"It's very simple," said Alexander, his voice dangerously calm. "He's a spy."

"That's not true," yelled Harpalus. He started to pull himself to his feet, but Alexander pushed him back into the surf, declaring that he had the proof. Which was when Ptolemy reached them—he'd run further than anyone else, as his ship had beached a short distance from the others.

"What's the proof?" he asked.

Everyone fell silent. Alexander grasped Harpalus by the hair, who stopped resisting. He looked at all those gathered around him.

"Documents from Carthage," he said. "Not only has Harpalus been embezzling Persian gold, but he's been corresponding with the same Carthaginians we freed when we took Tyre."

Harpalus began to loudly protest his innocence. Alexander seized a spear from one of his bodyguards, stepped back from Harpalus, and in one smooth motion impaled his treasurer through the chest like he was spitting a boar. Harpalus fell back into the water, his legs kicking and thrashing, blood everywhere. Even now he seemed to be trying to deny his guilt—but all that spouted from his mouth was blood. Then he convulsed once more, and lay still.

Alexander pulled out the spear, handed it back to the bodyguard.

"Bury him," he said.

They rode inland, and there wasn't much talking. Alexander and Hephaestion were up in front, Eumenes and Ptolemy closer to the back. Eumenes urged his horse down the narrow road, watching peasants stare as they charged by. His mind was racing even faster than his horse. Had Alexander killed his boyhood friend because he wanted his own correspondence with Carthage to remain a secret? Or had he just been enraged that Harpalus had intercepted that correspondence? None of which made a great deal of sense—if Alexander was conducting surreptitious negotiations with Carthage, there wasn't any compelling reason why he would hide that from his inner circle.

Unless those conversations went beyond a mere attempt to subvert Carthage from Athenian rule. Eumenes thought of what Harpalus had been saying about the temples just beyond the Pillars of Hercules. Perhaps

Harpalus knew more than he had told Eumenes? Then again, *what* Harpalus knew may have mattered less then what Alexander *thought* he might know. Eumenes thanked the gods above that Alexander hadn't realized that Harpalus had said anything to him.

Though…. maybe he *had*. Being around the prince was starting to feel like walking on very thin ice. Eumenes could only imagine how much worse it was going to get when they reached Philip. Which—now that Eumenes reflected on it—may have been the issue, after all. Alexander had been worried that there was a spy *for his father* among his advisers. Why he believed this, Eumenes didn't know. Maybe he had evidence, maybe it was paranoia. Though such paranoia ran in the family: Philip would certainly have been doing his utmost to corrupt or turn one of his son's men. But if Alexander had become convinced that Harpalus was his father's man, then no wonder he had acted as he did. A spy for a foreign government—that could be punished. A spy for the King of all Macedonia—well, technically such a spy couldn't be touched. There was nothing illegal about that. Which might explain why Alexander had used the Carthage excuse to execute Harpalus there and then. And if whatever Harpalus knew about Alexander's intentions vis-à-vis the Pillars had been passed back to Philip, who knows what might happen when the two met face to face.

Or maybe it was all just more paranoia. There was nothing to prove that—even if Philip *did* have a spy—it had been Harpalus anyway. Eumenes let the wind rush against his face, tried to empty his mind as he looked out at the hilly countryside. Clouds bedecked the horizon toward which they were riding. It was hard to believe that scarcely an hour ago he'd been looking forward to returning. He felt like turning around and swimming back to Asia. But he was—despite everything—a loyal servant of his prince. He never thought to question that. There was no reason he would. He'd followed him to the end of the earth and back, followed him for years. He drew himself up in his saddle: he was a Macedonian nobleman, and if he wasn't Macedonian, he'd just have to be even more of one. There was a code. They all knew it. And Eumenes was prepared to die by it if necessary.

He just hoped it wouldn't be in the manner that he'd just witnessed.

It was almost dawn by the time they got back. Demosthenes led them through the gate into a house that was already well into its morning routines. Slaves were cooking and cleaning; gardeners were showering the plants with water. Other slaves had breakfast ready.

"We'll bring it upstairs," said Demosthenes, taking a piece of proffered barley bread and dipping it in wine. A slave handed him some figs. Lugorix and Matthias helped themselves, followed Demosthenes up the stairs, up to the rooms they'd been sequestered in—

"Not this again," said Lugorix, still chewing on his bread.

"No," said Demosthenes, leading them up more stairs, up to the top floor of the house and into a cluttered study filled with furniture and strange devices. Shutters were thrown back on a wide balcony that looked out upon Athens—a far more expansive view then that which had been possible on the lower floor. The Parthenon gleamed in the morning sun in all its radiant colors; far beyond that, Lugorix could see the massive city-walls and battlement-laden towers visible between some of the buildings. The smoke of cooking fires hung everywhere.

"Here," said Demosthenes, gesturing to what Lugorix had assumed was a large abstract mosaic that filled most of one wall of the study. Demosthenes started tapping one particular area of it.

"That's Athens," he said.

"What?" asked Lugorix, totally confused. He pointed out the window. "I thought *that's* Athens out the—"

"It's called a map," said Barsine as she entered the room. She was dressed in a light blue gown, Greek-style rather than Persian. Somehow that made her look even more familiar to Lugorix—made him want to look away. Her hair was done up behind her head, and she appeared to be far more rested than Lugorix felt. Matthias bowed, though the effect was rather spoiled by his dropping crumbs as he did so.

"My lady," he said, through a mouth half full of bread.

"What's a map?" asked Lugorix.

"A representation of geography, from a bird's eye view," said Demosthenes. Lugorix was about to ask what *representation* and *geography* meant, but the old man explained what really mattered: "This depicts the empire of Athens."

Lugorix stared, beginning to see. The blue represented water—the Mediterranean Sea, hemmed in by the brown and green and yellow land of Europe, Asia and Africa. Demosthenes drew his hand from Athens up into the mountains of northern Greece, and from there to—

"Pella," he said. "The Macedonian capital. Which now controls all this"—he swept his hand to the right—"past the Tigris and Euphrates rivers, and on toward Bactria and Sogdiana and a myriad other provinces."

"And then closer to home," said Matthias, "there's Egypt."

"Egypt. Yes." Demosthenes gestured at chairs, sofas and cushions around the room. "Please, make yourself comfortable."

"We've been a little *too* comfortable these past few days," said Matthias edgily. As he said this, Lugorix settled himself into a couch—but the couch slid backward and knocked into an elaborate contraption of levers and pulleys nestled in a corner. It hit the wall, making a strange whirring noise. A wooden bird emerged and began whistling—then fell off its perch altogether and struck the floor. The whistling ceased.

"Nice one," said Matthias.

Lugorix turned an abashed face toward Demosthenes. "Your pardon," he said.

"Not to worry," said Demosthenes. "It's just a clock. But do please sit down before you break anything else."

They did. Barsine sat cross-legged on Demosthenes' desk—which struck Lugorix as somewhat unladylike. But Demosthenes remained standing. The born orator, thought Lugorix as the old man cleared his throat.

"Where's Damitra?" said Matthias suddenly.

Demosthenes looked annoyed. Barsine just shrugged. "She's meditating."

"About what?"

"The future."

"Naturally."

"Can we get back to the matter at hand?" asked Demosthenes.

"Sure," said Matthias. "You were telling us why you'd locked us up."

Demosthenes shrugged. "We needed to keep you here while we awaited more information and resources."

"Horseshit," said Matthias. "You were still deciding what to do with us."

"Were we now?" Demosthenes didn't seem offended. "Maybe that's so. It's like that clock your friend just broke: there's a lot of moving parts. And the situation outside is very volatile."

"You said they shut down the Assembly," said Lugorix.

"They did," said Demosthenes. "The archons closed it."

"Who are the archons?"

"The generals of Athens. They made the announcement in the wake of

Alexander's taking of Egypt."

"I'm not sure I follow," said Matthias.

"Think about it," said Barsine, her tone implying that was the last thing Matthias was capable of doing. "It's the worst disaster to ever befall Athenian arms. Particularly since a tenth of the navy got destroyed too, and the navy's thought to be invincible. When the news reached Athens, there was panic in the streets. The lending markets collapsed and the banks shut. Merchants went bankrupt. Several of the archons in charge were thrown out. And those that took over shut down the Assembly for fear of what the people would do next."

"Like listen to Mack peace overtures?" asked Matthias.

"Like open the gates of the city and bend over," said Barsine, which Lugorix thought was very unladylike indeed. "This is the problem with democracies. The mob is fickle. They want one thing one day, and something else the next. Works only as long as they're not being threatened by a dire menace. How Athens ever won their war against Sparta is beyond me."

"Well, we did," said Demosthenes, a certain edge to his voice. Lugorix wondered just how much arguing he and Barsine had been doing these last few days.

"They threw you out," she said. "The best man, and they threw you out of power."

"Oh," said Matthias, "*you* were one of the archons—"

"They needed a scapegoat," said Demosthenes mildly. "I fit the bill."

"You were lucky not to be ostracized," she said. "Exiled altogether. Now you have to fight for your people behind the scenes."

"My obligations didn't end with my being drummed out of power," said Demosthenes. "I'm still an Athenian citizen. Now if we could get back to the business at hand—"

"Your enemies closed the Assembly to stop you from speaking," said Lugorix.

There was a moment's pause.

"It's true, isn't it? You're the greatest talker in city, so the only way to stop you talking is to let *no one* talk."

"That might be part of it," admitted Demosthenes. "But it's all part of the larger problem: at this point, anything could happen if you let the people debate."

"But what about if the *archons* decide?" Matthias asked.

Demosthenes grinned wryly. "That's an issue too."

"There are appeasers among them," said Barsine. "That may be why they've shut down the Assembly. So *they* can do a deal with Macedonia. They certainly have no idea how to wage a war against Alexander and Philip."

"And you do?" asked Matthias. "Didn't your whole empire just get its ass kicked?"

"*I'm* still fighting," Barsine snarled.

"And so am I," said Demosthenes. He looked at the mercenaries. "And for all your cynicism, I suspect you know that there's room for neither of you in the world that Alexander is bent on creating. Lugorix—Athens barters with you. Pays you gold for honest labor. They've never tried to conquer you. Matthias—the only way your city will ever be liberated is if Macedonia collapses. As for me, I've fought Philip since long before he even *had* a son to afflict the world with. Back when he was just the leader of a small kingdom on the outskirts of Greece. I tried to warn Athens as his power grew. I tried to warn everyone. But by the time they listened, it was too late. Philip had already conquered the northern part of Greece—had seized the Bosphorus in a surprise coup, and secured the Black Sea and Pontus. Then when he turned on Persia, I begged the Assembly to ally with her against Macedonia."

"But your people's hatred of the Persians ran too deep," said Barsine.

Demosthenes sighed. "They were too myopic to see the real enemy—too fixated on ancient names like Thermopolae and Salamis, where they'd defeated your ancestors and covered themselves with honor. Past glory is so much easier to dwell in then present danger. Yet even so, I thought the problem was over when Philip was gravely injured fighting the Persian satraps at the battle of Granicus. The man lived, but only as a hollow shell of what he'd once been. I and so many others thought his son was a callow youth—too young to be a real threat, too impulsive to last long. Who would have thought he'd have all his father's talent and then some? And now we're talking about what I always feared we would. The very survival of Athens."

"Why do you care about Athens?" said Lugorix suddenly.

Demosthenes' smile held a trace of sadness. "Her rule isn't perfect," he said. "But since she defeated Sparta and conquered Carthage, the Mediterranean has been at peace for the first time in history. Surely that counts for something?"

Lugorix gestured at Barsine. "I was asking *her*," he said.

Another pause. Then: "Told you he was the clever one," said Barsine to Demosthenes.

"Wait a second," said Matthias, "what the hell is that supposed to—"

"She *doesn't* care," continued Lugorix. "Not in the slightest. Persians and Athenians fought wars for almost all of last century. She's simply interested in defeating Alexander."

"I've made no secret of that," said Barsine.

"You think all Asia should be ruled by your people," said Lugorix. "By a single Persian king."

"He'd dead now," snapped Barsine. "His traitor brother sits on a false throne."

"Sure," said Lugorix. "But even if Athens stops Alexander, how does that free Persia?"

"Alexander is going to throw the bulk of his and his father's power against Athens," said Barsine. "Break that power, and you break Macedonia. And as soon as Macedonia loses its ability to control my homeland, tens of thousands of Bactrian cavalry will sweep into Persepolis and Babylon."

"And put you on the throne?" asked Lugorix.

She smiled, but her eyes held Lugorix in a way that made him feel like a mouse gazing at a bird of prey.

"Females cannot rule in Persia," she said.

"And magi can't be female either," said Lugorix.

That made her laugh. "Look at me," she said. "I'm just nineteen." Laughing now, she looked younger than that, but Lugorix wasn't fooled: this was a girl who'd had to grow up fast. "I can't rule Persia and I can't lead my people. But I can do my best to save them."

"And where do we fit in and how much are we getting paid for it?" asked Matthias.

She stared at him in disgust. "Money is all mercenaries ever think of, no?"

"It's easy for rich girls to say money doesn't matter," replied Matthias.

"You'll get paid," said Demosthenes. "In silver."

Matthias's face was the picture of indignation. "We were told in gold!"

"But you weren't told how much."

"Oh?"

"We'll give you and your friend two talents apiece."

Lugorix and Matthias looked at him open-mouthed. A silver talent was a decade's wages. Demosthenes was offering them enough to retire on. Which led to the natural question—

"In exchange for what?" asked Lugorix.

"Accompanying me and Damitra to Syracuse."

That took Matthias aback a little. "That's all? We escort you to Sicily, and get two talents each?"

"It'll be dangerous," said Demosthenes.

"Any sea voyage is," said Lugorix, thinking of the journey from Syracuse to Egypt he'd made less than a year before. The Athenian recruiters who'd hired him at Massilia in the south of Gaul had herded him and the other newly hired tribal mercenaries into the holds of great grain transports that had reached the coast of Sicily after four days of choppy sailing down the boot of Italy. Half a day after that, they pulled into Syracuse's aptly named Grand Harbor. At that point in his life, Lugorix had never seen a city so big—even now it remained the third largest he'd laid eyes on, after Alcibidia and (of course) Athens. From there, the haul to Egypt was about another week. He guessed it would be a little less time trying to reach Syracuse from Athens—

"I'm not referring to the voyage," said Demosthenes. "That should be simple enough." He pointd to the map. "From here around the Pelop-ponese, and then a straight run to Megale Hellas. Probably make landfall in Tarentum, on the boot of Italy. And then from there to Syracuse."

Lugorix's brow furrowed. There was something about all this that wasn't quite adding up for him. "If you want to fight Alexander, shouldn't we be remaining in Athens?" he asked. "If Alexander overruns the city, it's all over anyway."

"He might try," said Matthias. "But I think he knows he won't succeed."

Lugorix shook his head. *Won't succeed* and *Alexander* are words that don't go well together. Didn't they say Tyre couldn't be taken?"

"Athens isn't Tyre," said Matthias.

Demosthenes cut in. "In terms of physical defenses, that's certainly true. The moats of Athens are half a mile wide, and patrolled by the latest ironclad dreadnaughts. The walls are lined with rapid-fire bolt-throwers and sulphur-fueled flamethrowers. Each tower contains lenses that concentrate the sun-light into rays capable of frying flesh at a distance of more than two miles."

"Doesn't mean Alexander can't find way his through," said Lugorix.

"I'm not disputing that—"

But Lugorix was still talking: "Particularly how good he is at locating the weakest point in any defenses."

"Which in this case is the defenders themselves," said Barsine.

"Now *that* is the primary danger," admitted Demosthenes. "It was Alexander's own father who once said that he could take any fortress as long as he could get a donkey carrying enough gold up to the gates. And much as I'd like to say that donkey will be flash-broiled long before it gets near the city-gates, you're right: Macedonian deployment of Persian money carries as great a risk here as it did in Athens. But that's all the more reason for speed in your mission."

"Especially because you're all missing the point," said Barsine, gesturing at the map. "The fortress isn't *Athens*. The fortress is the *Athenian Empire itself*. I know how Alexander thinks. Like the Gaul says, he's adept at finding weak points. His attack will develop on the periphery of the empire and move inward from there."

"But why would he strike at Syracuse?" asked Lugorix. "It's on an *island*."

"If I had to guess, I'd say he's targeting Carthage," said Barsine. "It's brewing with unrest these days, particularly now that the Baal cults are active again."

"So why don't we go there instead?"

"Because we need to go meet somebody in Syracuse."

Matthias and Lugorix looked at each other. "Are you kidding me?" asked Matthias.

"What's wrong?" asked Demosthenes.

"Off to meet *another* mysterious stranger?" said Lugorix.

"Who we get kept in the dark about for as long as possible?" muttered Matthias.

"No need to be so bitter," said Demosthenes. "Barsine didn't know if she'd be able to contact me. She didn't even know if I was still alive. Nor did she know if she could trust you."

"So who do we need to meet in Syracuse?"

"Someone who is the key to defeating Alexander," replied Demosthenes.

Matthias scoffed openly. "Who is this superman? Zeus himself?"

"Not quite," said Barsine. "His name is Aristotle."

CHAPTER SIX

P ella had changed.

Its numbers had swelled considerably in the time Eumenes had been away. It was still far from the equal of an Athens or a Babylon, to be sure, but more of the swamp around the town's core had been filled in to make room for the sprawl of city-blocks, all of them laid out in those sterile grids that the kings of Macedonia favored. Eumenes had always seen such rigor as over-compensation—an attempt on their part to prove they weren't barbarians, that they were proud members of greater Greece. Of course, no sane Greek would have built a city in these marshes, but that was the Macedonians for you. And there were far more defenses in evidence now—a bona fide city-wall, punctuated by the occasional tower. Not really enough to withstand a truly serious siege—but then again, Pella wasn't a city which expected to ever have to undergo a serious siege. Its invincible armies would see to that.

Yet it was what *hadn't* changed that Eumenes found most disconcerting. The city still didn't feel like an imperial capital. It didn't even have the vibe of a provincial town. It still felt like an artificial creation—as though the word of a king had established it by fiat, and forced the dwellers in the countryside around it to move within. All around him, Eumenes saw people who looked like they'd be a lot happier on a farm or behind a plow. They glanced up as Alexander's cavalcade thundered past, but it wasn't clear they realized who they were staring at. There was certainly no cheering.

Which worried Eumenes. These people did what they were told—they thought what they were supposed to think, and their lack of reaction meant that Philip hadn't given them any cues—hadn't arranged for any kind of welcoming committee. Certainly nothing worthy of a conquering general, let alone his son.

Ahead, the road narrowed. They rode onto the bridge that connected the city to the palace—a bridge that was essentially a promontory that stretched out into the lake that pressed up against Pella on the south. An inlet led from that lake to the Thermaic Gulf, but it had been filled up long ago, given Macedonia's lack of anything resembling a navy. The last thing Philip needed was a bunch of warships sailing right into his own backyard and beaching under the walls of his palace.

And it *was* one hell of a palace.

In a sense, it was the imperial city that Pella wasn't. The bridge ended in giant gates set into a huge wall—but now those gates rolled aside with a creaking shudder to reveal a vaulted archway, the walls of which were covered with so many torches that made the interior almost as bright as the day outside. Guards stood on balconies lining the archway, looking down at Alexander as he and his entourage rode beneath them. No one saluted him. No one even acknowledged him. It didn't seem to bother Alexander in the slightest. He led the procession into a courtyard, where rows of retainers awaited them. The court chamberlain stepped forward, bowing, his words stiff with studied formality.

"Sire," he said. "Your king is expecting you."

Eumenes's eyes narrowed. *Your king.* Not *your father.* Again, it didn't seem to ruffle Alexander. He just gave the chamberlain an easy smile.

"So take us to him," he said.

Having said this, he dismounted, his retinue following suit. The chamberlain led the way; Alexander walking just a step behind him, with Hephaestion, Ptolemy and Eumenes trailing in his wake. Eumenes doubted that any more than that would have been acceptable to Philip. More guards awaited them at the throne room's antechamber—their uniforms those of Philip's personal bodyguard. The chamberlain turned.

"Sire," he said. "We need you to surrender your weapons."

That got Alexander's attention. But his voice remained calm: "Since when was that a Macedonian custom?"

"You've been away a long time, sire." The chamberlain looked more than a little uncomfortable. Eumenes almost felt sorry for him. But he recognized the predicament they were all in now. He had his own sword at his side, but he didn't surrender it. None of them did. They were all waiting for a sign from Alexander—who was in a delicate position. It was unthinkable that a Macedonian should be asked to surrender his weapons. To go before his father without a sword under those circumstances was tempting fate to its very edge. But the alternative was even worse. Civil war was one thing. But right now Alexander was hundreds of miles from any soldiers loyal to him save the few men back in that courtyard—who were probably being disarmed right now. All this must have flashed through Alexander's mind in an instant, because that was all the time he needed to decide what to do.

"Keep these safe for us," he said, unstrapping the blade with which he had carved his way across Persia. He doffed his ram's-head helmet too, took off his breastplate. Eumenes, Hephaestion, and Ptolemy followed suit. And then the doors opened, and they were led into the throne room.

Which was even larger than Eumenes remembered it. Apparently more walls had been knocked down in order to expand the room still further. It was as though the invalid master of Macedonia could only keep pace with his son's conquests by expanding the domain of his private chambers. Granite pillars held up the mosaic-encrusted ceiling. Banners on which were emblazoned the royal lion of Macedonia hung from mammoth cantilevered arches that loomed overhead. Alexander and his three companions walked silently toward a massive throne set on a dais against the far wall. Guards stood to either side of that chair. The figure who sat on it was lost in shadow.

Though his voice was not.

"I understand you have a new father now," he said.

Alexander said nothing. Just kept approaching that throne—which was another new addition. It looked like it was carved from a single giant tree, its arms spreading out like gnarled branches. Alexander walked toward it, trailed by his ever-more-nervous comrades. The guards around the throne were on edge too. They stepped forward to bar his way.

"That won't be necessary," said the voice. Its owner shifted in his chair, his face catching the light of the nearest torch. Eumenes drew in his breath even as Alexander halted on the very edge of the dais. He knew Philip had changed, he just hadn't realized how much. The man who sat in that throne was a mountain of muscle gone to fat, his body mute testimony to a lifetime of battle-wounds. Ten years ago, the arrow of a Thracian archer had taken out one eye, shattering the cheekbone and giving the king the look of a demented cyclops. Five years after that, two fingers had been lost to a Theban cavalryman whose head was severed from his body in the very next moment. But the crowning injury was that which Philip had sustained beside the river Granicus, in Asia Minor—only six months into his Persian foray, fighting the combined forces of the western satraps. The blow of one of those satraps had knocked him to the ground; the blow of another had cut through his spinal column and left him paralyzed from the waist down. But the Macedonian phalanx had swept all before them anyway. Two hours later, Philip was carried off the field of his greatest victory—in no small part thanks to the heroics of his son, who personally killed one of the satraps and stood over his father's prostrate body while the battle raged on about them. That had been the pinnacle of their partnership. After that, Alexander had been tasked with continuing the war against Persia while his crippled father returned to Macedonia. In retrospect, it was a no-win situation. If Alexander lost, so did Macedonia. But if he won, then he would surpass his father, even while his father still sat on his throne.

Yet now the prince went down on one knee before the king.

"Rise," said Philip tonelessly. "Come closer." Wordlessly, Alexander did so. Eumenes and the others remained kneeling, watching as Philip reached out for his son, who leaned down and embraced him. Was this all for show? Eumenes had no idea whether one of them was about to try to strangle or stab the other.

But then Alexander stood up and took a few steps backward. Philip looked over his son's shoulder at the three men he'd brought with him. He greeted each of them by name. Each of them knelt, addressed him as lord and king. For a moment, the years swept away—for just a moment, Eumenes was a child again, being introduced by his long-dead father to Philip at a banquet filled with Macedonian nobles. Philip had been in his twenties then—a bull of a man more impressive than anyone Eumenes had ever met. He remembered that almost palpable sense that this was a being for whom anything was possible.

But then he rose and beheld the ruined king before him.

Philip turned toward his son. "I understand Harpalus is no longer in our service," he said.

"He was a traitor," said Alexander. "In league with Carthage."

"In league with me, you mean."

Alexander said nothing.

"That's what you thought, isn't it? That's why you killed him."

"He was in league with Carthage," repeated Alexander.

"I hope *somebody* is," said Philip. "Because unless we reach a deal with them, it's going to be very difficult to finish what you started down in Egypt."

"I've given you a great victory," said Alexander.

"You've given *yourself* a great victory."

"All I've conquered is in your name."

"I summoned you so we could talk frankly and this is the prattle you spout?"

"What would you have me say?" asked Alexander.

Philip's hands shook. Spittle dribbled down his beard, and he wiped it away. His eyes gleamed. "I'd have you admit that there's such a thing as winning a battle but losing a war."

"I don't intend to lose a war with Athens."

"Executing your competent subordinates is an excellent way to ensure you do. First Meleager, then Harpalus—who's next?"

"I was thinking you had in mind me."

Philip smiled grimly. "In truth, it *had* crossed my mind."

"Although then you'd have no general able to command your armies."

The two men stared at each other for a long moment. Eumenes knew what both were thinking. Parmenio: Philip's best friend and most trusted general. Eumenes recalled the king's words—"the Athenians elect ten generals every year, but in all my life, I only ever found one." Parmenio had been the king's right-hand man across his consolidation of greater Macedonia—but he'd died in a skirmish mere days before Granicus. Had he lived, the rest of the Persian expedition would almost certainly have been entrusted to him, and Philip wouldn't have had to rely so exclusively on his son. Then again, the secret to Parmenio's success had been his caution—something that Alexander had thrown to the winds in his conquest of Persia. Parmenio might never have achieved so much. Certainly Parmenio would never have struck at Egypt and triggered a war with Athens without Philip's leave.

Which was, of course, the whole point.

"Harpalus wasn't my spy," said Philip.

"Then who was?"

"You're assuming I had one."

"Of course you did."

Philip nodded. "Look at the man standing next to you," he said.

"What?" Alexander looked at Eumenes for a brief moment—Eumenes frantically shook his head, but Alexander was already looking past him at—

"Ptolemy," said Philip.

What happened next was almost too fast for Eumenes's eyes to follow: Alexander whirled toward Ptolemy and felled him with a punch to the jaw that sent him sprawling. He was about to leap on the fallen man when—

"Enough," said Philip. And such was the force of his voice that Alexander stopped, looked at his father with an expression of smoldering rage. The guards on either side of the king gripped their spears, but Philip seemed to find the whole thing amusing. "It's almost refreshing to see that you've still got weaknesses," he said. "And yet: how many times have I told you that your emotions are akin to the reins of a chariot? You either hold them tight or else you'll be undone. Perhaps by being blind to truths beneath your very nose."

Ptolemy hauled himself to his feet, keeping a wide berth of the furious prince. "Alexander," he said, "I can explain—"

"I don't want to hear it," said Alexander.

"You already know it," said Philip. "He's been reporting back to me. Good information, too—"

"You bastard," said Alexander.

"Well, that's exactly what your lifelong friend is. My bastard son."

Now Alexander looked like *he* was the one who had been punched. "What?"

"Do I have to spell it out for you? My son via someone other than your dead and rotting mother. You remember her, don't you? The one who had a dream the night before I married her that a lightning-bolt penetrated her and then flame shot out from between her legs to engulf the world? And who then became convinced that it wasn't me who had conceived you, it was Zeus? An interesting theory, one guaranteed to attract the attention of fools and peasants the world over."

Now Alexander was angrier than Eumenes had ever seen him—and also more confused. "But Ptolemy's father—I thought Lagos—"

"—was given Arsinoe by me when I'd finished with her. She was a peach, I tell you—excuse me, Ptolemy. So she received her reward—I raised her from concubine to the wife of one of my barons—not such a bad deal, really. But raising the seed I'd left within her was part of the bargain."

Which wasn't an atypical arrangement for Macedonian nobility, Eumenes reflected. But usually the bastard in question was identified as such, rather than being left under the legitimate son's nose. It was no wonder that Alexander was still breathing hard, still struggling to control his temper—no wonder that Philip was enjoying himself so much.

"So if you don't wish to be my son," he said languidly, "I can hardly regard myself wholly deprived."

"That leaves you with a bastard *and* an idiot," snarled Alexander—this last a reference to Arrhidaeus, Philip's other legitimate son, who was mentally retarded and incapable of any kind of command. "Such impressive progeny."

"Well, we can't *all* be gods," said Philip. "I suppose I'll have to content myself with being just a king."

"You put your statue amidst the Olympians," said Alexander. "If that's not the seeking of divine honors, then what else would you call it?"

"I call it propaganda," said Philip. "In preparation for the march into Persia. I figured that if you're going to go to war with a king that half the world thinks is blessed by heaven, then it might help to have a little sacred mystique up your sleeve. Whereas you... you seem to actually *believe* this shit. You heard exactly what you wanted to at Siwah—"

"What I saw at Siwah would be blasphemy to repeat," said Alexander.

"*Everyone* heard you addressed outside the temple as son of Zeus," said Philip. "I'm sure it only got more interesting once you got inside. Did the priests suck you off? Or did they get the temple whore to do it?"

He's goading him, thought Eumenes—wondered if Philip wanted Alexander to spring at him like he'd done at Ptolemy. In which case he'd promptly be cut down by the guards. Perhaps Philip really *had* decided Alexander was too unreliable. Perhaps he wanted to make Ptolemy his heir and general. Perhaps there was no reason behind it other than blind rage. Or maybe (it abruptly occurred to Eumenes) Philip intended to make peace with Athens. In which case the sacrifice of Alexander would be an excellent way to kick off the negotiations.

But suddenly—as though Eumenes was reading his mind—Alexander's face became as calm as a statue.

"It would be blasphemy," he repeated softly. "Which may come easy to you, but not to me. Regardless: you are the father that gave me life and I'm still your heir."

"So nice to hear," said Philip. "Though I suspect the latter means far more to you than the former. And I can't help but notice you're still evading my question."

"I won't talk about what was broached to me in trust at Siwah—"

"So don't. Just tell me straight up: beside myself, do you or do you not believe yourself to have any *other* fathers?"

The ghost of a smile fluttered across Alexander's face. "Zeus is the father of us all," he said.

Philip laughed outright. "I forgot how well Aristotle instructed you in sophistry."

"Are the rumors about him true?" asked Alexander.

Philip stared at his son as though deciding whether to let him get away with changing the subject. "They are," he said at last.

"So he really left."

"He really did."

"Did he give you a reason?"

"Only a letter he left behind."

"Which said?"

"That you had betrayed the Greeks by going to war with Athens."

"You should have stopped him from leaving."

"He's a resourceful man," said Philip. "Escaped from the palace by a boat of his own devising. And he must have had accomplices waiting for him on the shore with horses. My agents tell me he reached Athens within the week."

"And where he is now?" asked Alexander.

"We have reason to believe he went to Syracuse."

"Why didn't he stay in Athens?"

"Presumably because he knows the place is crawling with agents on my payroll."

"And Syracuse isn't?"

"I'd ask you to give me time." Philip picked up a goblet at his side, drank from it. Wine dribbled onto his tunic. "Which, of course, you didn't."

"I did what you always taught me," said Alexander. "I saw an opportunity and took it."

There was a long pause. The two men stared each other down to the point where Eumenes became convinced neither would blink. It felt like the next words could prove explosive—like anything could happen.

And then suddenly Eumenes heard his own voice filling in the silence.

"War with Athens was inevitable," he said.

Both men looked at him—as did Ptolemy and Hephaestion, the latter of whom raised his eyebrows at such daring. Philip put down his goblet. "Ah, Eumenes. I've missed your candid counsel these last several years."

"I serve Macedonia, sire."

"No doubt." But the tone said that Eumenes was as expendable as anyone else. "Tell us what's on your mind."

"Athens is a democracy—"

"Such insight," said Hephaestion.

Eumenes ignored him. "That means they are fickle and inconstant. Their Assembly is a glorified mob. It decides one thing one day, and something else the next. No peace with them can last. We can never trust them."

Philip nodded slowly, absorbing this.

"Besides," added Eumenes, "to them, *you're* the one that can't be trusted."

"Because?"

"To them, you're a tyrant. As Demosthenes never tires of pointing out."

"He's been removed from power," said Philip.

"But he'll be back, sire. That's the point. Political office in democracies is like a wheel. What's down one moment is up the next. And Athens has been filling up with Persian refugees during the Prince Alexander's conquests. Persian refugees—and their gold. In a democracy, influence is measured in money. So the more successful our war against Persia has gone, the more anti-Macedonian influence in Athens has risen."

"Persian refugees," repeated Philip. He seemed to be mulling this over. "Many of whom are noble."

"They're the ones with the money," said Eumenes.

"And some of them might be royal." As Philip said this, he glanced at his son. Eumenes realized there was something here to which he wasn't privy. He cleared his throat.

"It's a bit of a fine distinction, sire."

Philip looked impatient. "Meaning what?"

"Legitimacy in the Achaemenid dynasty runs—*ran*—through the paternal line. The son of a concubine was technically eligible to succeed to the throne, unlike, say in"—Eumenes was about to say Macedonia, but suddenly saw the trap he'd set for himself—"most other places. Several generations of Achaemenid kings have resulted in hundreds—possibly even thousands—of would-be royal heirs. At this point, most of the noble houses in Persia have at least some royal affinity. So, yes, there is almost certainly Persian royalty in Athens."

"Well," said Philip, looking back at his son, "we'll just have to keep an eye on them, won't we?" Then, turning back to Eumenes—"so how would *you* proceed against Athens?"

This is what I get for opening my mouth, thought Eumenes. "There are many options, sire," he said carefully.

"I'm sure there are," said Philip, brushing off the all-too-transparent attempt to buy time. "Which one would you stake Macedonia on?"

But Eumenes had his answer. It wasn't the most original one, but it would get the discussion moving again. "Treachery," he said.

"Indeed."

"We bring the entire army up to Athens and put on a show. Let the elephants trumpet while the men bang their *sarissae* against the shields. Indicate we're willing to assault the city unless it surrenders unconditionally. Meanwhile we make contact with those inside who would spare Athens that fate."

Philip drained the last of his wine. "Those people being?"

"I'd start with the archons who threw Demosthenes out of power."

"I thought you said you weren't in favor of peace negotiations."

"I'm not looking for those who would negotiate," said Eumenes. "I'm looking for traitors. Those who despise democracy. Those who want oligarchy. Our foremost priority should be to find such individuals."

"The problem isn't finding such individuals," said Hephaestion. "It's those individuals finding the means to act. Athens has built countless safeguards into its defenses. No tower is ever left under a single commander. No gate is ever entrusted to a single unit. The ships in the moats are from multiple commands. And they have two walls, the inner of even greater strength than the outer, each one just as hard to enter from the inside as the outside."

"Nothing's impregnable," said Ptolemy.

"Sneak into Athens and convince me," replied Hephaestion.

"Ptolemy's right," said Alexander. "Any wall can be scaled."

"So you'd assault Athens?" asked Philip.

"I'd assault their empire."

"Easier said than done," said Ptolemy. "The Athenians have done what any sensible naval power would do. They base themselves on islands."

"Athens isn't an island," said Hephaestion.

"It may as well be," said Alexander. His delivery was crisp, self-assured. Eumenes realized that he'd been holding back, letting others commit before he stated his own views. "You couldn't make Athens any more difficult to reach if you put it in the middle of the Mediterranean. Same with the rest of their empire. Our problem is defeating a naval power from the land. We face the added problem that even if Athens falls, it doesn't mean their empire will go with it. Whereas the converse *does* apply—if we peel their empire away from them, Athens no longer matters. She will wither, like unplucked grapes upon the vine." As he spoke, Philip nodded in agreement, and Eumenes wondered if father and son had been on the same page all along—if the real issue in this discussion had been whether the two could put aside their rivalry in order to cooperate on the defeat of Athens, and now that was settled, the rest was simply the ratification of the plan.

"So you want to march West," said Philip.

"It's the only way," said Alexander. "We had to march to defeat Persia, and it's by marching that we'll defeat Athens. Father, what happened to your wall-maps?"

"I found something better," said Philip. He gestured to a guard, who pulled a lever on the wall. There was a rumbling and part of the floor in front of the throne-dais begin sliding aside. The men moved to get out of its way—and stared at the map of the Mediterranean that was thus revealed. It was as beautiful as it was expensive, made mostly of precious jewels. Azure was the ocean; gold the land. Cities were marked with rubies, while Athens and Pella were both denoted by diamonds, scarcely a fraction of a yard apart on a map that was more than ten across. So very close… and not for the first time, Eumenes pondered how much easier this all would have been if Athens had lost the war against Sparta a century ago. The world would have been a very different place, most of it for the better as far as Macedonia was concerned. Sparta's world-view was fundamentally negative: it had neither the vision nor the manpower to impose itself on all of Greece, let alone the Mediterranean. Had Athens' expedition to Syracuse not succeeded, the subsequent runaway chain of conquests would never have occurred, and the rise of Macedonia would have found a Greek world factionalized and bickering: easy meat.

But the gods never made things easy.

"I'll marshal the army on the Black Sea," said Alexander. "We'll use the captured merchant vessels from Phoenicia and Egypt to get the troops back from the East quicker than if they marched—keep them within bolt-thrower range of the coast so the Athenian fleet can't get at them. Once we've got them mobilized, we move north up the Danube and then turn southwest to reach the coast of Gaul. If we can catch Massilia by surprise and raze it, so much the better, but regardless: we keep going, through the Pyrenees, south into Iberia, to Gibraltar."

He paused momentarily. Everyone except Philip was looking at him in stunned amazement. Alexander turned to one of the guards and—almost absently—plucked the spear from the surprised guard's hands, before turning back to the map and using the weapon to illustrate the overall route. "So across Europa and then down into—"

"Put down the spear," said Philip.

Alexander looked genuinely surprised. "I thought we were past that."

"We're never past that."

"You don't trust me?"

"When you won't even acknowledge me as father?"

"I called you that earlier—"

"A man doesn't have two fathers. A prince even less so. *Now put down the spear.*"

It would have taken Alexander less than a second to hurl that spear and the range was so short he couldn't miss. Then again, Philip's throne was clearly no ordinary chair. And Eumenes doubted that the lever that revealed the map was the only lever in this room. Was Alexander weighing all this even as he weighed the weapon? With a flourish, he stuck the spear into the floor. The guard came to retrieve it.

"No," said Philip to the guard. "Don't touch it."

"Sire?" asked the guard, but Philip was already turning to the guards on either side of his throne.

"Take him away," he said.

For a moment, Eumenes thought Philip meant Alexander. But then he understood: the guards came forward and seized the other soldier by either arm, led him out of the throne room. As the door closed behind them, another guard came over and took the spear.

"Execute him with it," said Philip.

"Sire," said the guard, and went out that same door. Philip turned back to the others, shrugged. "Just so we're clear," he said. "If a bodyguard loses his weapon, he loses his life. They're the only ones entrusted with carrying arms within my palace. No one else is. And that includes my son, my bastard son, and it *certainly* includes any man who wants to renounce the idea of *being* my son."

Alexander shook his head. "I haven't renounced—"

"Tell me more about your plan," said Philip.

"I'd be happy to," said Alexander. His eyes were as fiery as his voice was cold. "We bridge the straits of Gibraltar the same way we bridged the Bosphorus, and cross into Africa, setting fire to its granaries as we close on Carthage. Which we will catch in a pincer movement: because while I'm moving through Europa, Craterus will lead the cream of the forces that assaulted Egypt across North Africa. He and I link up at Carthage, after which the Carthaginian navy goes over to us. At that point, Athens will sue for peace on our terms."

Eumenes couldn't believe what he was hearing. Nor could he believe that everyone seemed to be going along with it. Even Philip was nodding. Eumenes tactfully cleared his throat.

"Yes?" asked Alexander. There seemed to be a look of warning in his eyes, but Eumenes didn't care. "You're talking about marching for thousands of miles," he said.

"As we did in Persia," replied Alexander.

"That was mostly desert. Here you're looking at tractless forests filled with wild barbarian tribes. Each one of whom will want to be known as the people that stopped Alexander."

"Each one deserves the chance," said Alexander.

"And we'll able to rely on ships for much of the Danube," said Hephaestion.

"But the Danube's upper parts are unexplored," protested Eumenes. "We don't know if it emanates from Ocean itself, or if it disappears amidst the worst portions of the Alps."

"We'll find out," said Alexander.

"And Craterus?"

Alexander's brow furrowed. "What about him?"

"Back in Egypt, you said it was madness to send an army across North Africa—"

"I fear you misheard me."

That was the moment when Eumenes realized he had better shut up if he wanted to keep his head. He suddenly understood the true nature of the terrible confluence of wills which he was witnessing. Philip wanted Alexander to go forth where he would conquer or die—wanted his son to either provide him with an empire that stretched from the rising to the setting sun, or else rid him of the greatest menace to his own throne. Alexander wanted the chance to defeat the only power worth more than Persia and prove himself as the greatest soldier who ever was. And as for the drive across North Africa, perhaps it might have been pure folly its own right. But as a diversion, it made just the right kind of sense. A march out of Egypt would attract Athenian attention—would focus all Athenian resources—perhaps even to the point where they missed the army moving beyond the northern edge of the known world. Eumenes didn't doubt that Alexander intended to capture Carthage—that his contacts with subversive elements in that city were real, and in deadly earnest. But he also suspected that Gibraltar was more than just a stop on the way. Particularly as bridging it would be a far greater task than spanning the Bosphorus. No doubt about it, something about Gibraltar had definitely gotten Alexander's attention. Eumenes thought about those temples that Harpalus had mentioned—wondered about their connection with the one at Tyre… with the one at Siwah…

"Eumenes?" said Philip.

Eumenes looked up. Everyone was staring at him. For a horrible moment he thought he'd been thinking out loud. But then Philip repeated the question.

"The weapons from the East," the king said. "We were wondering if you could give us your report on them."

"Of course," said Eumenes. He pulled from his belt the parchment containing the report he'd prepared on the way back from Asia—the compilation of the work of Hephaestion's alchemists and his own engineers. He cleared his throat.

"There are three major categories of devices," he began.

Or maybe it was two. Or four. Or more. In truth, there were as many ways to classify the new weapons as there were weapons. But in the end, Eumenes had settled on the organizing principles of earth, fire and gears. Some of the devices fell uneasily between those boundaries; some were combinations thereof. But it seemed the most expeditious way to analyze their effectiveness—to decide how to allocate the labors of the sorcerors and mechanists of Macedonia… a group which now included the priests of Egypt and the seers of Babylonia. Eumenes spent perhaps twenty minutes bringing Philip up to date. And all the while the man on the throne kept smiling like he had a secret.

When Eumenes had finished, the king stretched and poured himself more wine. "Well done, Eumenes," he said. "The faithful servant, as ever. Now I have one more task for you."

"Name it sire," said Eumenes.

"Take Hephaestion and Ptolemy and follow Antipater."

A man stepped into the room. He was so thin it didn't seem there was much man to him. He wore the uniform of Philip's bodyguard, but was older—probably almost fifty. He bowed to Philip, and then to Alexander.

"Sires," he said.

"I need to talk to the crown prince in private," said Philip. "The rest of you have a vital task that requires your immediate attention."

Eumenes didn't like the sound of that, but he was heartened by Ptolemy and Hephaestion's involvement. And frankly he was only too happy to get out of that throne room. Antipater led them through the labyrinthine corridors of Philip's palace—up and down stairs, through carpeted rooms, through rooms of dank stone. Eumenes saw no servants—only more body-guards. Finally, Antipater reached a set of double doors, and threw them back. Eumenes, Hephaestion and Ptolemy entered.

And stopped in amazement.

There were so many scrolls, at first Eumenes thought this chamber was a library. But as he looked around, he could see it was much more than that. Sketches and diagrams were heaped everywhere. Beakers and jars shared shelf-space with a variety of stuffed animals, each one frozen in a lifelike pose. Much of one wall was taken up with the most complex set of astro-logical charts Eumenes had ever seen. A long glass tank on the opposite wall was heaped full of earth; insects scurried within. And in a corner was a boney pair of massive jaws—Eumenes had no idea what kind of animal it was, but its bite was easily twice the length of a man. He hoped never to meet the owner of those teeth. He wandered if he ever would meet the owner of this room. He heard Ptolemy asking who that man was.

"It's the laboratory of Aristotle," said Antipater.

CHAPTER SEVEN

"Who's Aristotle?" asked Lugorix.

The looks he got said he really should have known better, but he was used to that. It seemed to be a hallmark of civilized people that they confused knowledge with intelligence—mixed up the marshalling of facts with the sharpness of the mind. Demosthenes and Matthias started talking over each other—saying that Aristotle was the foremost thinker in the Greek world, that he ran the school that had once belonged to Socrates and Plato, that he had taught in Athens for years…

"Until he received an offer he couldn't refuse," said Demosthenes.

Matthias fell silent as Demosthenes went on to explain how King Philip had offered Aristotle the opportunity to tutor the young Alexander. Aristotle had been promised his own weight in gold, but was already a wealthy man by that point. He was believed to have accepted because of the opportunity to shape the education and character of a crown prince from whom much was expected. Though no one at that point was aware of just how hostile that prince would ultimately be to Athens.

"The wisest man on Earth succumbed to the oldest dream of all," said Demosthenes. "Plato called it the idea of the philosopher-king: the perfect, incorruptible monarch who rules his subjects in the name of virtue."

Barsine was practically spluttering. "You could not be more wrong," she said.

"That's how he conceived of the role of royalty," said Demosthenes. "I'm not saying for a moment Alexander lived up to that ideal—"

"I'm not talking about *Alexander*," snarled Barsine. "I'm talking about *Aristotle*. We may need him, but that doesn't mean I have to bow down and celebrate his ideas. This is the man who once told Alexander that the barbarians—by which he meant *my people*—should be ruled as *animals*." She threw back her head and snorted. Lugorix glanced over, saw that Matthias was quite transfixed by the outburst. "He doesn't even think we're *human*. No wonder Alexander treated us the way he did—with a teacher like that to guide him—"

"My point isn't to dissect the man's thinking," said Demosthenes. "Neither he nor Socrates nor Plato had much love for the democracy. None of them like the masses very much—they're too dirty, too messy. They don't do what they're *told*. But there's been a widening gulf between Aristotle and his pupil in recent years. He stayed behind in Macedonia when Alexander set off for the East and founded a new school in Pella—endowed by Philip of course. My agents tell me that Aristotle maintained a robust correspondence with Alexander until the prince struck at Egypt. Whereupon he abruptly fled Macedonia; headed south and passed through Athens like a thief in the night before taking ship for Syracuse. No one even knew he was here."

"So how did you?" asked Lugorix.

"I have my ways," said Demosthenes.

"His legal ways," said Barsine.

"Very funny," said Demosthenes.

"Can someone tell me what the hell we're talking about?" asked Matthias.

Demosthenes sighed. "Oratory in the Assembly pays no bills. I'm a lawyer by trade, and I specialize in harbor-law. I've represented practically every ship's captain, shipowner, shipbuilder and moneylender who does business in this harbor, and not all of them could afford my rates."

"So he gets paid in secrets," said Barsine. "Like those involving Aristotle's whereabouts."

"But why didn't the man stop here?" asked Matthais. He gestured out the window at the sprawling city. "Given that he lived in Athens for so long."

"He's not exactly popular in these parts," replied Demosthenes. "Like I said, he's known to have a low opinion of the democracy—"

"But apparently he's loyal to Athens nonetheless," said Matthias.

"Or just loyal to himself. At any rate, the mob has the same disdain for him he does for them. There's a lot of talk in the streets about how he 'nursed the serpent in his bosum,' that kind of thing. The archons know he'd be useful for the city's defenses, but the mob doesn't care. He'd probably have been lynched if he'd stayed Athens. Or put on trial."

"He still might be," said Barsine. "Syracuse is Athenian territory. They might take him into custody before we can reach him."

"First they have to find him," said Demosthenes. "Syracuse is a big place and none of my contacts there know where he is. Which is all the more reason why you need to leave quickly." He sat down as though he were exhausted. He probably was; he was an old man and he'd been up half the night chasing after them, reflected Lugorix. Matthias got to his feet.

"When do we sail?" he asked.

"This evening," said Demosthenes. "In the meantime, I suggest we all get some sleep."

Eumenes slept fitfully in the bedchamber he'd been alloted in Philip's palace. He dreamt of vast interlocking sets of gears; of metal mouths belching fire. Huge wheels rolled across his consciousness, crushing all before them. He felt himself a tiny speck in their wake, dragged by them to the ends of the earth and beyond while flames raged about him, burning endless pieces of papyrus containing endless diagrams of devices, all of them consumed by the fire which swept through Eumenes' head.

Only to be snuffed out in an instant.

Eumenes opened his eyes, suddenly wide awake. He sat up in bed. It was dark, but he could still tell there was someone in the room with him. Someone sitting right on the edge of his bed. He fumbled for the dagger he kept under the pillow.

"Put that away," said Alexander.

As he said that, he turned his head into the moon's light that shone through the window. Eumenes could see that the prince's eyes were bloodshot. He smelled strongly of wine. But there was no slur to his voice.

"Contradict me again in front of the king and I'll send you to join Harpalus," he said.

Eumenes wondered if he was still dreaming. At first he couldn't remember how he might have offended Alexander. Still groggy with sleep, he could barely recollect the details of the meeting in Philip's throne room. The only reality for him was the dream he'd just been in and the long hours in Aristotle's work room before that. But then it all came rushing back—the maneuvering between father and son, the discussion over grand strategy; his own rash questions as Alexander outlined his mad plan to march across half of Europe and cross over to Africa.

"Alexander," he said. "Your pardon. I merely acted as I would have were we in your own council chamber."

"But we weren't," said Alexander. "We were in front of Philip. Where I look to you for support rather than challenge. Is that understood?"

Eumenes nodded.

"In front of me alone—in private—you can say anything you want to. That hasn't changed."

"Then I would beg that you reconsider the march you're planning."

There was a long pause. Eumenes wondered if once again he'd gone too far, Alexander's invitation notwithstanding. But finally Alexander just exhaled deeply. "Why?" he asked.

"I don't believe your father thinks you'll return from it. If he can't beat Athens, he'll at least be rid of you."

"Do you think I don't know that?"

"I don't know *what* you think, Alexander."

Alexander got up. Walked to the window, looked out at the flickering lights of Pella. Turned back to Eumenes.

"This march will be easier than Persia. We'll be fighting tribes instead of civilized nations."

"Nations know when they're beaten. Tribes don't."

"They will when I get through with them." Alexander laughed softly. "Don't lose your candor, Eumenes. I have need of it now, more than ever. But keep it just for me. No one else."

Not even Hephaestion? Eumenes wanted to ask, but he didn't. There was something troubling the prince—probably all too many things, and Eumenes had no idea which one was foremost. The fact that there was still one human being in the world to whom he had to bow? The fact that one of his confidantes had proven to be a treacherous half-brother? The fact that even his military genius might not be able to reach Gibraltar? Or was it what lay at Gibraltar itself? And what did all this have to do with what he'd seen at Siwah? Eumenes heard himself murmuring assent, saw Alexander nod in satisfaction—saw the prince sit back down on the bed.

"What did you find among Aristotle's papers?" he asked.

Eumenes sighed. He'd wondered why Philip had sent Alexander's own men to look over Aristotle's recently vacated laboratory. Why didn't he send in his own sorcerors? But of course he must have already done so. At first, Eumenes decided that the king simply wanted a fresh perspective. Hephaestion, Eumenes and Ptolemy were used to working together—and yet since Ptolemy was Philip's man, he would ensure that any insights made it back to the king. But insights regarding what? What was it that made it so imperative to have extra sets of eyes inspect the room? Eventually Eumenes had realized that there was only one question that mattered.

"It's what we *didn't* find," he said.

Alexander nodded. "Exactly," he said.

"Aristotle didn't leave just because he disagreed with you," said Eumenes. "He stumbled upon something."

"Of course. But what?"

That was the problem. Too much had been removed from the lab. Too much that was easy to carry off. Pages had been torn from bestiaries. Maps were missing. Explorers' journals had been stripped. Papers had been rifled of their contents. And though specifics were lacking, the overall pattern was difficult to mistake....

"It relates to the West," said Eumenes slowly. "He's looking for something there." Alexander's multi-hued eyes bored into him in a way that made it seem like he already knew all of Eumenes' secrets. Did he suspect the conversation with Harpalus? What was it that Harpalus had taken to his grave?

"The king blames me," said Alexander. That wasn't quite what Eumenes had been expecting him to say, so he held his tongue and waited for more. "The king blames me," repeated Alexander as though it was the height of injustice.

"Why should he do that?"

"Those scrolls we discovered in the East."

Now Eumenes understood. They'd found rather a lot that didn't make sense in all those years of trekking through the eastern reaches beyond Persia. All those lost caves and temples—all those devices that admitted of no clear purpose, all those scrolls that couldn't be translated—they'd all been sent to Pella for Aristotle's perusal.

And all the notes on them had gone.

"He took those papers with him," said Eumenes.

"Of course he did."

"We need to find him."

"And so we shall. What about what was left?"

"Left?"

"In his lab."

"I'm not sure where to begin," said Eumenes carefully.

"With the most interesting thing in there."

Eumenes hesitated. "He has something called a steam engine."

"What does it do?"

"It seems you boil water in order to turn levers that can do work. That could hurl boulders or power ships, in theory."

"In theory," said Alexander.

"You're skeptical?"

"I'm skeptical of anything that old man left behind in that chamber. Anything he wanted us to believe might be of value."

"Or that he forgot to burn," said Eumenes.

"He could have torched that whole chamber."

"Not if he wanted to get out of Pella without being noticed."

Alexander scratched his head absently. "What about Ptolemy?"

"Um... what about him?"

"Did he say anything about what I did to him in the throne room?"

Why don't you ask Hephaestion? thought Eumenes. Was Alexander no longer trusting his lover? Or was he simply checking up on Eumenes? He and Ptolemy had always been friendly, and even now he really had nothing against the man. He chose his words carefully: "Ptolemy seemed to share our opinion that it was pointless to bring that up."

"Pointless because?"

"Tempers were short as it was. If we all ended up putting daggers through each other, that would serve neither you nor your father."

"He's not my father," said Alexander.

Shit. "I know that," said Eumenes. It seemed dangerous to say anything else.

"He used to whip my mother."

"I didn't know."

"Yes. When he was drunk. He was drunk a lot. She told me how Zeus came to her in the form of a dove and impregnated her with me. He can deny that, but it's still true. I'll visit her tomb tomorrow. I'll swear on her grave that I'll avenge her. He's going to pay." Alexander was rambling now.

"Perhaps he really *does* want to put Ptolemy on the throne. Could Ptolemy lead our armies? Could Ptolemy really be a king? I don't see how. I always thought of the man as a brother. It's beyond me how he could betray me. If I ever get the chance I'll strangle him until his eyes pop out."

At least now we know who the spy is, thought Eumenes. But Alexander's paranoia had clearly only gotten more intense in the wake of the revelation that he'd been right to suspect something. He rose, stretched. "In any event, I just came from drinking with the king. We were discussing the real plans. Not the ones we talk about in front of people we don't trust."

This was all news to Eumenes. He'd have loved to have been a fly on the wall for *that* conversation. He ignored the insinuation that he wasn't trustworthy, instead went for the more immediate issue: "So we're *not* going to the headwaters of the Danube?"

"We will. But first, we're going south."

And suddenly Eumenes understood all too well. "When do we march?" he asked.

A smile crossed Alexander's face—a smile that scared Eumenes more than anything else so far.

"We already have," he said.

Waking to the sound of screaming is never a pleasant experience. And the noise now dragging Lugorix from sleep was particularly shrill. He stumbled out of bed, pulled on his trousers, buckled his belt. Turning to the wall, he grabbed Skullseeker—if they were in for a fight, he'd need it. Matthias was right behind him as they headed out into the hallway and looked down into the atrium.

"Shit," said Lugorix.

Damitra lay down there, convulsing on the floor, white foam pouring from her mouth while slaves struggled to help her. Theramenes stood down there as well. The heavyset man who seemed to be Demosthenes' chief of staff had some medical knowledge, as he'd had one of the slaves force a leather strap between Damitra's teeth, while another placed a cushion under her head to stop it from banging on the floor. Lugorix and Matthias raced down the stairs just in time to run into Demosthenes, who was emerging from his own quarters.

"What's wrong with her?" he asked.

"Just got here," said Lugorix.

"Where's Barsine?" asked Matthias.

"Here," said Barsine. She strode over to Damitra, knelt, cradled her head, whispered to her in Persian as Damitra grasped her hands. Demosthenes turned to one of the slaves. "Fetch herbs," he said. The slave nodded, ran off. Barsine continued to try to comfort Damitra.

"What happened?" said Demosthenes.

"I didn't see it," said Theramenes.

Barsine looked up. "She'd been in the trance all day. I checked in on her about half an hour ago. And then when I heard the noise, I looked in her room, and she was gone."

A slave muttered something about how the old woman had walked as though transfixed into the center of the hall and then began screaming. Another slave entered the room with herbs and a vial.

"Valerian root," said Demosthenes. He handed the vial to Barsine, who helped Damitra to drink some of it. It seemed to calm the old woman; she fell back against the cushion, and started muttering in Persian. Demosthenes cocked his head as though listening.

"Do you speak Persian?" asked Matthias softly.

"Shhh," said Demosthenes, brushing him aside. But his face was growing pale. Whatever Damitra was saying was getting to him. Abruptly there was a loud hammering on the front door.

"Go see who that is," he said.

Accompanied by a slave, Lugorix and Theramenes went through several lavishly-appointed rooms to the front-entrance. The pounding on the door was getting louder. "Who's there?" yelled Theramenes.

The hammering stopped. "Isocrates," said a voice.

Lugorix peered through the peep-hole. A weasely looking man stood there.

"What do you want?" asked Theramenes.

"I don't have time for this," said Isocrates. "Get me Demosthenes."

Theramenes nodded to Lugorix. "He works for the boss. We should let him in—but carefully."

Lugorix understood perfectly. He raised Skullseeker while Theramenes threw back the bolt and opened the door onto the late afternoon sun. Isocrates entered—and blinked at the sight of Lugorix's axe. "You want to put that down, friend?" he asked.

"Don't know you," said Lugorix.

"I aim to keep it that way," said Isocrates. "Take me to him. And for Zeus' sake, close that door."

Lugorix swung the door shut while Theramenes walked Isocrates back to where Demosthenes stood. As soon as Isocrates saw him, he broke free of Theramenes' grip and ran to Demosthenes' side, his hands stretched out imploringly.

"Demosthenes! Thank the gods you're here! All hell's broken loose! You've got to go *now*—"

"Calm down," snapped Demosthenes. "Tell me what's happening."

"The mob's coming for you."

"Are they now," replied Demosthenes calmly. "Why would that be?"

"The city's in a panic," said Isocrates. "Someone said it was time to root out the traitors and then—"

"My name came up?"

"They're saying you're harboring Gauls"—as he said this, Isocrates glanced uneasily at Lugorix—"and that you've got a Persian witch." He looked at the prone Damitra. "That you're practicing magick against the people. For all I know the archons themselves set them in motion to get rid of you once and for all, and if you don't move now, they're going to succeed—"

There was more hammering at the door. Much louder this time. Along with the sound of way too many voices...

"Too late," said Demosthenes. Theramenes began yelling at the slaves: "Get the furniture against the doors and windows! Get the arms out of the weapons-locker!" Demosthenes turned to Lugorix and Matthias. "You two need to take Barsine and Damitra to the ship and get out of here. The rest of us will stay and buy you time and try to talk some sense into that mob out there."

That sounded like a tall order, Lugorix thought. He helped Barsine get Damitra to her feet. The old woman seemed to be conscious now; she staggered with some difficulty, still mumbling to herself.

"What's she saying?" he asked Barsine.

"That we need to go," she replied.

Lugorix took the hint and shut up. He helped Barsine get Damitra down to the basement, to the trapdoor that led to the sub-basement and the waiting ship. But as Matthias pulled that trapdoor open, Barsine turned to Lugorix.

"I need to retrieve something from my quarters," she said. Before they could protest, she was gone, sprinting back up the corridor, leaving them holding Damitra. They stared at each other for a moment.

"We should go after her," said Lugorix.

"I will," said Matthias. "You stay here."

"First we get the crone into the boat," said Lugorix. He and Matthias helped Damitra down the stairs and onto the dock. The ship lay in the water as though they'd only just left it—rising and falling slowly with the swell of water. It seemed doubly strange to see it here, for it forced Lugorix to admit to himself that being in that contraption had been no dream. Matthias leapt onto the deck; Lugorix handed Damitra down to him as though she were a rag-doll. Matthias pulled back the hatch; Lugorix leapt down and Matthias lowered her into his arms. She was demanding to be placed in front of the controls, so he set her in the seat there.

"You well enough to pilot?" he asked.

"Yes," replied Damitra weakly. She fumbled in her robes. "But I need my amulet," she added.

"Amulet?" asked Lugorix—but suddenly it all flashed back into his head—that bizarre device that Damitra had used to control this boat....

"*Shit,*" said Matthias, scrambling back onto the deck.

"That's what Barsine went after," said Lugorix. He climbed up the ladder, but Matthias was already running up the stairs. Lugorix took off after him, bellowing at his friend to wait. Matthias hollered back at him that he should stay where he was. Lugorix pointed out that splitting up probably wasn't the best idea ever, whereupon Matthias let the slower man catch up with him.

Which was just as well. Because when they got back up into the house, everything was pandemonium—a bedlam of shouts and screams. Fire had broken out in several places. Lugorix couldn't believe the place had gone to hell so quickly. Though he didn't have time to speculate on this, because wild-eyed assailants were already hurling themselves at him. They looked like the same kind of thugs he'd met back in the Assembly—and this time Lugorix didn't care if they were Athenian citizens or not. He swept Skull-seeker before him with the zeal of a barbarian who hasn't killed anyone in more than a week. Surprised-looking heads flew through the air in the wake of his axe; their owners hadn't been expecting to run into any serious resistance. Matthias had his short-sword out—the two of them fought their way through a throng of crazed Athenians into Barsine's quarters only to find them—

"Ransacked," breathed Matthias.

There was no sign of Barsine either. "Back the other way," said Lugorix.

There was a rumbling as part of the roof above them gave way—the two men ducked aside as they were showered with a rain of wood debris. The smoke was starting to get pretty bad now, billowing up in the two mens' faces in great choking clouds. Lugorix could hear the noise of the mob falling back, retreating outside to avoid death in the flames. He led the way out into the atrium.

Demosthenes lay against one of the walls, blood dripping from his mouth, a couple of bodies nearby. He looked up as Lugorix knelt down next to him, his head lolling to one side from the gash in his neck.

"Macedonians," he muttered.

"He's delirious," said Matthias.

"Macedonians, damn you," muttered Demosthenes. "In the house. Just now."

"That was the mob," said Matthas.

"Instigated by Macedonian agents," said Demosthenes. "They took Barsine. Heading for the city-wall."

"By Taranis," said Lugorix. "Where on the wall?"

"Don't... know. Go to stables. Theramenes was heading there."

"You're coming with us," said Matthias. "We can't leave you."

"You can," said Demosthenes, "and you will. My time is done." Lugorix started to help him up, but Demosthenes shook off the larger man's grip with surprising strength—and collapsed back against the wall as though the effort had cost him what reserves he had left.

"Find Barsine," he said. "Save Barsine. Everything depends on her."

"What about Damitra?" asked Matthias.

"She's not going anywhere," said Lugorix.

"I'm not talking to you," snapped Matthias. And then, to Demosthenes: "I meant, what was she saying earlier?"

Demosthenes looked at him blankly, as though trying to remember. Then: "She had a vision," he said weakly.

"And what did she see?" asked Matthias. But Demosthenes was fading quickly. His head sagged forward. Lugorix put his hands under the old man's chin and lifted it so that his eyes were looking directly into those of Demosthenes.

"What she say?" he hissed.

"That Alexander is on his way," whispered Demosthenes.

After that, it was a blur. Demosthenes was dead even as he spoke his last words, and Lugorix and Matthias were on their way to the stable, which was already wreathed in flames. They found Theramenes just as he was riding out the door to try to rescue Barsine by himself. Lugorix stripped the saddle off one of the horses—in his tribe, it was considered the height of decadence to ride with a saddle. In short order, the three men were on horses galloping into the canals of Athens—straight into what was left of the mob which had surrounded the house. Lugorix had never realized just how much fun it was to trample someone beneath a good set of hooves. Especially since these were the guys who had just killed Athens' greatest orator. Among his people, the men of wisdom were treated with honor. He couldn't understand why things should be different in cities. His horse charged straight ahead; people hurled themselves left and right to get out of his way. And over the din he heard Matthias yelling.

"We need one of them alive! Take one of them alive!"

Lugorix responded instinctively, reaching out from the saddle and grabbing a fleeing man by the tunic—lifting him into the saddle and then punching him in the jaw. Not very hard; just enough to quieten him up a bit. Then he followed Matthias and Theramenes as they turned their horses down some of the narrower canals and towpaths, putting Demosthenes' house behind them.

Finally they stopped and took their bearings. Smoke rose from Demosthenes' house in the distance. Lugorix had been expecting all of Athens to look like the burning buildings of Alcibidia, back in Egypt, but the city seemed quiet.

"Too quiet," said Theramenes.

Matthias nodded, dismounted—pulled Lugorix's captive down and dropped him sprawling onto the ground.

"Which way did they go?" he asked.

The man tried to look puzzled. "Which way did who"—but Matthias kicked the man in the balls. Then drew a knife. He didn't even have to threaten to use it—

"They threw the bitch in a covered wagon and rode for the northwest tower!" squeaked the man.

"Who were they?"

"They said they worked for the archons! We each got half a drachma in return for helping to give the traitor what he deserved—"

"Bastard," said Matthias, kicking the man again. He then leaned in with the knife—"this is for what you've done"—whereupon Lugorix grabbed his knife-hand.

"No time," he hissed in Matthias' ear.

Matthias nodded—climbed back on his horse. "I presume you know where the northwest tower is," he said to Theramenes.

Theramenes nodded. His own sword flashed. The man's severed head bounced into the canal.

"Follow me," he said.

It was when they got out of the canal district that they began to realize what was going on. The city was in a state of alert. The side-streets were empty, but the central ones were alive with armed men, all of them heading to the walls. What was a mob around the house of Demosthenes was a citizen-militia everywhere else—organized by those who directed Athens' defenses rather than those who would disrupt them. Which, really, was the best possible cover three armed men moving at speed to the west gate could ask for.

Problem was, those they pursued were enjoying the same advantage. Theramenes stopped quickly to ask an infantryman for information about what was going on.

"Word is that the Macks are moving up to attack in force," the man replied.

"Could be another false alarm," said Theramenes.

"It's not," said the man.

"Let's go," said Matthias. They rode hard through the streets, Theramenes leading the way through alleys and roads as they raced northwest as fast as their steeds could carry them. Straight toward the setting sun...

Which all at once was blotted out.

"Holy shit," said Lugorix.

The sky was almost black with projectiles arcing in toward them. Some of them were burning. Some weren't. They streaked down, began to disappear amidst the buildings up ahead. The earth began to shake.

"Looks like that guy wasn't kidding," said Theramenes.

The Macedonian bombardment seemed to be concentrating on the very portion of the city toward which they were heading. But all they could do was keep riding in toward it—in toward all the shaking and the screaming and the clouds of dust starting to rise up like a wall in front of them. Theramenes had them keeping largely to the secondary roads and side-streets, avoiding most of the troop-traffic on the avenues. Lugorix urged his horse onward, not sure how much more the beast would be able to stand.

But then he caught a glimpse of motion in an adjacent street.

"Chariot," said Lugorix.

It might not have anything to do with what they seeking, but they'd seen nothing else going so fast. They spurred their horses forward, Theramenes steering them down more short-cuts—through a cul-de-sac to a narrow passage forcing them to ride in single file, then down what seemed like a series of blind alleys. All the while they were heading toward that bombardment. They could hear the noise of the impacts as rocks tore through buildings.

They came out into the same street as the chariot, saw that they'd managed to get ahead of it. Lugorix glanced back, sizing up the situation. The chariot was pulled by two horses. Three men rode within—one at the reins, one holding a sling, the other with several javelins. Further back was a covered wagon, pulled by three more horses, two men riding atop it. A second chariot was bringing up the rear. The procession was moving at full-tilt, racing past the marching militias heading for the wall. And the chariots were being driven with a skill that said those who rode them were no amateurs.

"That's them," said Matthias.

"How can you be sure?" said Theramenes.

"They're Macks," insisted Matthias. "Barsine is in that damn wagon."

And if she wasn't, then they weren't going to catch her. Lugorix knew that Matthias was fishing in the dark, but what other choice did they have? But then Theramenes narrowed his eyes, looking more closely at one of the men atop the wagon.

"That's one of them," he said. "I saw him back at the house."

Lugorix nodded at Matthias, who immediately started galloping forward, putting more distance between himself and the oncoming procession. Lugorix waited a moment, then spurred his horse in the opposite direction, straight at the chariot, Theramenes trailing in his wake. The chariot's driver had now noticed the oncoming threat—pointing at them with one hand, holding onto the reins with the other—and his two comrades responded. A javelin just missed Theramenes; a stone streaked past Lugorix's head: way too close given that they were still more than thirty meters out. The slinger drew back for another chance—and then toppled out of the chariot, an arrow in his head. Matthias' bow had found his mark. The javeliner lowered his head to gain more cover, waited while Lugorix charged in, raised himself to hurl the javelin at point-blank range. But even as he did so, a second arrow hit him, straight through the chest. He fell down in the vehicle; Lugorix swerved his horse past the chariot, turned in behind it.

And leapt in.

To jump into a chariot from horseback is a maneuver with no middle ground—you have to climb onto your horse and hurl yourself from it in a single fluid motion, which usually leaves you looking either very impressive or very dead. Lugorix's tribe called it the salmon-leap—and the driver of the chariot barely saw it coming before Lugorix was right beside him, hurling him from the chariot with a barbarian shout of exaltation. Matthias took up the cry, unleashing another arrow at the wagon, hitting one of the men on top of it. The other turned the wagon toward the road's edge—sending it hurtling down another street that slanted off at an angle. The second chariot accelerated in order to cover its departure. Lugorix hauled tighter on the reins, forcing his newly acquired chariot to slow; restraining his own instinct as much as the horses, since it meant allowing the chariot behind him to draw nearer to his exposed back.

A slingstone streaked past and smashed Theramenes in the skull; the man went down and his riderless horse raced away. Matthias was now riding straight at Lugorix—straight past him and at the chariot behind him, firing an arrow that went wide of the driver. But as the driver focused on Matthias, Lugorix pulled in the reins, suddenly braking his own chariot. As the opposing chariot shot past him, he tossed a javelin at the driver, hitting him in the neck while Matthias simultaneously put an arrow into one of the horses. The chariot went out of control, cartwheeling behind the remaining terrified horse, disintegrating even as it tossed its hapless riders through the air.

"Let's get after that wagon," snarled Matthias. Lugorix nodded.

"What in the name of all the gods are you guys doing?" yelled someone from a window.

"Killing Macks," said Lugorix—next moment, he and Matthias were riding down the road the wagon had taken. The chariots had bought that wagon time—maybe enough to matter. Through the buildings the walls were becoming visible. They rounded a corner, and had to ride through people racing past them, doing their utmost to escape the Macedonian bombardment which was crashing down like rain all around them. Ahead of them was the end of the road—shots of fire streaking in and around the northwest barbican-fortress, a mass of towers and battlements that stretched across both inner and outer walls. But its interior gates lay open. The wagon charged inside.

"Come on," said Matthias, as they galloped across the open ground toward the barbican. A huge stone smashed into the ground only a short distance away. Another impacted on the inner wall, sending pieces of the battlements tumbling into the city below. Still another projectile crashed onto the far side of the open ground, near some fleeing soldiers. It seemed to be some kind of vial—and where it had just shattered, a murky yellow gas arose. Lugorix didn't feel like getting anywhere near it. And now those soldiers who had been caught within the growing cloud were suddenly writhing, clawing at their eyes, rolling over and over upon the ground as though they were possessed.

"Demons," muttered Lugorix.

"Worse," said Matthias. "Poison."

They rode through the gate and into the fortress. Which was a madhouse. It was as though civil war had been unleashed within. They were in one of the courtyards; Lugorix found himself looking up at balconies, ramps and stairs. Men were fighting with each other everywhere. All wore the uniform of the Athenian army.

"Complicated," said Matthias.

"*There,*" said Lugorix.

He gestured to the wagon, which had come to rest against the far wall. A door lay open nearby. Matthias and Lugorix rode over to the wagon. A quick look within ascertained that its drivers had fled with the contents. The two men headed through the door, found themselves in a corridor.

"They'll be making for the outer wall," said Matthias.

"Or helping let the rest of the Macks inside," said Lugorix.

"Or both," shot back Matthias. The corridor ended in a metal ladder. They started to clamber up it, Lugorix becoming increasingly unsure that they were on the right track. But all they could do was keep going. They could hear the noise of combat all around, but this route took them directly into the fortress' rafters. They went up for what seemed to be at least a hundred feet—rather a long way when one didn't know what was at the top of it. Finally they emerged onto a platform.

And their jaws dropped at the view.

CHAPTER EIGHT

Eumenes walked through the dirt-walled trenches. Macedonian soldiers raced past; those who noticed him saluted. All around were the noises of siege machinery: the clanking of levers, the whir of gears, the crackle of flame as missiles were set alight, the telltale whine as they were released, all of it multiplied by hundreds of times… the sound of impending death, a sound that all too often wouldn't even be heard on the receiving end. Eumenes could only imagine what it would be like within Athens right now. All the more so as the city hadn't been expecting this so soon.

For that matter, neither had he. Thanks to Philip, none of them had. The master-manipulator had once again shown why he was the ruler of them all. He'd talked a good game about the schemes to take down the Athenian Empire, the whole time brewing his own plan. Eumenes kicked himself for not anticipating it. The one thing that Philip was particularly proud of was his siege-train—something that was notoriously immobile, save for the few elite engineers who had accompanied Alexander east against Persia. Athens was Philip's big chance to show the world what he'd been building. Egypt or not, Philip would have eventually struck at Athens. Everything they'd discussed in that meeting had been mere contingency planning.

Except, of course, it wasn't.

Wheels within wheels, a convoluted chain of logic: for even if they captured the center of everything—even if they took Athens and raped its women, killed its men, sold its children into slavery… even if they won it all, there would still be the West to deal with. There were some empires where the capture of the capital spelled doom for the rest of the imperium. Athens wasn't like that. After all, Persia herself had taken Athens only to have the entire population flee to the island of Salamis, from where they annihilated Persia's navy. This time, the people could flee much further, on the backs of hundreds upon hundreds of ships. Without a navy to do the pursuing, the Macedonians were going to have to use the land. So one way or another, Alexander's expedition would set forth.

But first Philip wanted to gain the greatest prize of all.

The trench through which Eumenes was walking gave way to a tunnel, which in turn led to a chamber carved out of the earth. Windows on the far side of that chamber served as viewing-slits to look out upon the ground between the siege-works and Athens. Several Macedonian officers were in the room, most of them standing around a table poring over charts showing firing angles and trajectory vectors. Alexander and Hephaestion stood in a corner, deep in conversation.

"My prince," said Eumenes as he joined them.

As always, Hephaestion looked less than thrilled to have a third party enter a conversation between him and Alexander. Alexander, on the other hand, just looked tired. Dark circles were set under his eyes. The nightly drinking sessions had been picking up. That was one thing Eumenes was glad he didn't get invited to—such parties could be dangerous, as Cleitus and Philotas had both discovered. Alexander had personally killed both men in the midst of arguments while everybody was deep in their cups. Eumenes found it hard enough to deal with his prince sober.

"We were wondering where you'd got to," said Alexander.

"Your father detained me," replied Eumenes.

Alexander smiled wanly. "Let's hope that's not literal," he said.

"If it was, would he be here?" muttered Hephaestion.

"He wanted to talk with me about logistics for the march up the Danube," said Eumenes.

Alexander glanced over his shoulder as though he was speaking too loud. "What about it?"

Eumenes handed Alexander a scrollcase. "All details in there, Alexander. Men, horses, equipment, machinery, food, supplies, everything."

"What about intelligence on the local tribes?"

"We already have the data on that," said Hephaestion, breaking in.

"You have the older figures," said Eumenes. "That data has now been revised."

"Revised?" asked Hephaestion. He looked incredulous; after all, it was his network of spies. "You mean the scouts and traders got it wrong?"

"No," said Eumenes. "They got it right. It's just that the tribal populations have changed."

"Why the hell would they have changed?" said Hephaestion—and then broke off, as he realized that Alexander was laughing. Eumenes couldn't help but smile; apparently Alexander had never bothered to mention this part of Philip's plan to Hephaestion. Hephaestion managed a grin that fooled no one.

"What am I missing?" he asked.

"What do you know about the walls of Athens?" asked Alexander.

Hephaestion stared, not enjoying this Socratic exchange in the slightest. "They're going to be a tough nut to crack," he replied.

"How many Macedonian soldiers do you think will be killed storming them?"

"Too many," said Hephaestion.

"Exactly," said Alexander. "By definition, too many."

There was a pause.

"And such soldiers are our scarcest resource," added Alexander.

"Sure," said Hephaestion, "so that's why we use mercenaries—*oh.*" He broke off as he finally saw the point—managed a broader grin this time. "Did you see them on the road, Eumenes?" he asked.

"In untold numbers," replied the Greek.

The platform was roofed and made of stone, protruding out from the inner wall, allowing one to look over the lower, outer wall and at the plain surrounding Athens. Fire and smoke cut across the sky as more and more projectiles streaked in toward the city. The Macedonian siege-lines were dimly visible through the haze. The moat that surrounded the outer walls looked like a sea on which a storm was raging; as Lugorix watched, slabs of rock impacted around one of the Athenian warships in the middle of the moat—and then there was a crash as another landed directly on top the warship, sending pieces of meat and wood flying through the air, leaving nothing remaining of the ship.

"*There,*" said Matthias, pointing along the platform. Lugorix nodded—

they ran to the end of the platform, started down some stairs that led along
the underside of one of the arches that connected the outer wall with the
inner wall. The steps were steep—and as the two men clambered in toward
the inner wall, they could see that it had been swept of defenders, that
now soldiers were raising the ramps and barring the grilled doors that gave
way to the battlements on either side, effectively blocking off access from
the top of the north and west walls to this corner barbican-fortress. Those
soldiers wore Athenian uniforms, but so did the men who they were firing
darts and arrows at through slits in the grilles.

"More Macks," said Lugorix. "Trying to seal off this corner of the city's
defenses."

"Let's take 'em," said Matthias.

"Thought we were here to find Barsine."

"We need to let the Athenians in here or we'll never reach her alive."

Lugorix nodded. They reached the wall and turned toward the closest of
the doors. Lugorix charged forward while Matthias halted and began firing
arrows. They whizzed past Lugorix and buried themselves in backs.

The men holding the wall-gate turned, just as Lugorix reached them and
swung Skullseeker, taking off two heads with the first blow. The Athenians
on the inner wall just outside the barbican-fortress began cheering. The
remaining Macedonians had their swords out and began swiping at the
Lugorix, who used his axe to stave off their blows while Matthias kept on
firing.

It wasn't the first time the Gaul had trusted himself so totally to Matthias'
razor-sharp precision—an arrow passed so close to his head he could feel
its breeze; blood sprayed against his face as that arrow found its target in
a man's throat. He used the space that bought him to step back and swing
the axe again, curving it low, slicing through a leg, then pulling the blade
back to block another flurry of blows aimed at his chest. He shouldered
into the man opposite him, knocking him to the ground—kicking in his
head as he brought the axe down on the rope that held the ramp to the rest
of the inner wall up.

That ramp came down with a crash; the Athenians outside clustered
forward, pressing up against the iron-wrought door, shoving their spears
through the bars at the Macedonians battling Lugorix. That did it: the
Macedonians fled, two of them leaping down to a platform just below the
summit of the inner wall, a third racing to another staircase that led along

the nearest arch, back up to the outer wall.

That last man was the only one to make it—Lugorix's axe caught one of the men as he leapt to the platform; Matthias' arrow hit the other in the leg, causing him to trip as he landed—stumble, fall screaming off into space. Even before he hit the ground, Lugorix was already opening the gate, letting in the Athenians, who charged past him and Matthais. An officer bringing up the rear stopped to acknowledge the two.

"What's the situation elsewhere?" asked Matthias.

"The Macks are concentrating on this corner of the wall," said the officer. "Just bombardment so far, but they obviously planned to open the barbican's gates from within."

"Still might," said Lugorix. As he spoke, he was scanning along the structures around them, looking at all the gates and ramps and arrow-slits set into the walls. He realized that Matthias was doing the same—

"Zeus," said Matthias, pointing. Lugorix followed his gaze, down to where a group of men had emerged from a small door at the very bottom of the inner wall, right against the moat. They looked like ants down there. But two of them carried a carpet-sized bundle.

"Must be them," said Lugorix. Which was when a chorus of trumpets sounded from the Macedonian lines—followed by an almighty yell that echoed, intensifed, was taken up by far too many voices. The shouting carried in across the plain, but already the source of it was becoming visible.

"By Taranis," muttered Lugorix.

"Here they come," said the officer.

"I don't believe this," said Hephaestion.

"Believe it," said Alexander. "It's how the king thinks. Always in search of a bargain."

That was putting it mildly, thought Eumenes. It was a truism that in war one used mercenaries for the dirty work, but this was taking that maxim to new heights. Philip's recruiters had hired more than fifty thousand barbarians from the tribes of northern Thrace—had promised those barbarians first crack at ransacking Athens once they'd breached the walls, along with a hefty bonus for doing so, and all the loot they could haul out of there. Undoubtedly it was an offer that sounded great in the huts along the Danube—but in practice it meant that they were cannon fodder, intended to give the Athenian defenses something to shoot at besides the Macedonian machinery that would comprise the main thrust of the assault. And even if not a single one of them made it to the walls, that was still all to the good.

"The king has depopulated the entirety of the eastern Danube," said Eumenes. "The figures are all in those scrolls, but it's all the tribes. Triballians, Getae, Serdae, the lot: when we march through the region, we'll face almost no resistance. Even if the barbarians manage to break down the walls of Athens, their numbers will be so thinned down as to be laughable."

"Not a very sporting way to win war," said Hephaestion.

"You don't win wars by being sporting," replied Alexander.

The room shook as though the place was being hit by an earthquake—a rumbling that became steadily louder. Alexander led Eumenes and Hephaestion over to the window-slit, the officers standing there stepping aside to let the three men through. The rumbling kept on building in intensity. It seemed to Eumenes like the sky was falling in—like the earth was about to swallow them all up. A vast shadow fell across the window.

The ground was black with men moving toward the walls—many of them pushing mantlets ahead of them for added security as they closed on the Athenian defenses. There were thousands of them, and they kept pouring out from behind the Macedonian lines, boiling up like ants whose nest had been disturbed. Battle-cries echoed across the plain, drifting among the listeners who stood atop the walls.

"Let's move," said Matthias.

They raced along the battlements and down the first staircase they came to. That led to a passage, which ended in a trapdoor—they hauled it open and clambered down a ladder as fast as they could, reached another passage that led along the very edge of the inner wall, past a series of arrow slits. Lugorix didn't bother to look out those slits.

Matthias did.

"Fuck," was all he could manage. Lugorix skidded to a halt, glanced out. At first he couldn't believe what he was seeing. It was like the horizon itself had come alive, raised itself up toward the skies. Then his eyes focused.

Much as he wished they hadn't.

"What the hell are *those?*" he muttered.

They looked like the titans themselves had returned to earth: gigantic man-shaped figures stalking across the landscape toward the city. There were three of them, the carpet of men around each parting as massive feet lifted into the air and shook the earth with their impact. Lugorix looked up at Matthias, his eyes wide with astonishment.

"They're some kind of siege machinery," said Matthias. "Probably a few hundred mules in each one, with levers and gears to amplify everything. Look, their feet are hardly rising. What counts is forward momentum—"

"Don't care *how* they're doing it, said Lugorix. "I care about beating them to the bottom of the wall."

There was a noise all around them like a thousand birds alighting. The Athenian defenses were swinging into action. They'd endured the bombardment in silence until now, waiting for the actual assault to start. As Lugorix dashed past more arrow-slits, the view blurred as the walls unleashed thousands upon thousands of projectiles of every shape and size. Moments later, the missiles began striking home, scything great swathes into the Macedonian onslaught. Lugorix caught a glimpse of a rock bouncing through the first wave of men, smashing them each time it made contact with the earth; he saw another projectile impact and detonate with a force that sent soldiers flying in every direction. The defenders were causing frightful damage to the oncoming infantry; the mantlets behind which that infantry was cowering didn't seem to be having much effect on the stones heaping up such slaughter. But the gigantic machines were a different story. Lugorix saw huge bolts smash into the side of the foremost one—but it just kept coming.

Matthias stuck his head out an arrow slit. "Those Macedonians are at the edge of the moat," he said. "Wait a minute—*oh shit*."

"What?" asked Lugorix.

"They just got picked up by a ship."

"Athenian?"

"It flies that flag. But I'm sure that's about it."

Lugorix nodded. He and Matthias raced along the corridor and practically threw themselves down the stairs at the end of it. Now they were on another of those platforms; this one was enclosed, and contained several large bolt-throwers, each one positioned in front of a large aperture to allow for a wide field of fire. The quarter-mile wide moat glimmered beneath them. Flotsam scattered across the water testified to the relentless efficiency of the Macedonian fire. The ship was moving steadily away from the shore.

"They're getting away," said Lugorix.

Eumenes stared out at the plain. The Athenian defenses had timed it well—had waited till the oncoming assault had closed to a mere several hundred yards before they let them have it. The slaughter going on out there was frightful. But the Leviathans were continuing implacably toward the walls, shaking the ground with every stride, surrounded by a sea of barbarians that kept rippling outward to avoid those feet. For those mercenaries, the dilemma was palpable—cluster around the Leviathans for shelter, but not so close that you got stomped. The bolt-throwers atop the shoulders of the Leviathans fired back, but there was so much smoke hanging over the walls it was hard to see what was going on.

"This'll help," said an officer, passing Eumenes a thin metal cylinder. And then, off his quizzical look—"they're farseekers, my lord. Put it to your eye. You focus it by turning this dial."

Eumenes nodded. He understood now—he'd actually seen the plans for these earlier, back in Aristotle's lab, though he hadn't realized they'd already been constructed. It made him wonder just how much else had. Were the Leviathans a design of Aristotle as well? He lifted the farseeker to his eye, and suddenly his vision was transformed. Suddenly it was like he was at one with the object of his attention: as he scanned the plain, he could make out the fur worn by the barbarians—could make out their individual weapons, could see the blood that flew in all directions as a stone crashed down amidst them. Yet still those barbarians kept coming—more of them pouring in from the siege-lines with every minute. But this second wave simply looked more scared than savage—as though they were just as afraid of what lay behind them as the walls that sprawled ahead.

"The Persians had whips at Thermopylae," said Alexander, another farseeker in his hands. "To drive their masses into battle. We've got something even better."

Eumenes nodded. He'd seen the devices on the road into camp—gigantic bellows pumping toxic fumes at those who were about to charge, ensuring that they charged all the faster. The chemicals involved dissipated quickly into harmless smoke, though it was still taking one hell of a chance with the wind. But the barbarians thought they were dealing with the breath of dragons, and preferred a clean death on the walls of Athens to a last few minutes writhing on the ground and puking so hard one's bones broke. Eumenes turned his attention back to the walls and focused the farseeker on the corner-barbican that the commandos inside the city were supposed to be capturing. Getting them in there had been no easy task; it had involved a great deal of captured weapons and armor from Egypt, not to mention plenty of bribery of various harbor-masters.

Yet it didn't look like they'd been successful. He could see Athenians clustered atop the battlements of both inner and outer walls, manning the siege engines that kept on firing out at the waves of mercenaries. He could see every detail of those siege-engines; as he watched, a steam-powered chain spun around a rotating drum, dropping bolt after bolt into that drum and flinging them out at high speeds. Just next to that was another device—just a piece of glass, it seemed, until Eumenes followed the direction it was pointing and saw barbarians literally catching fire as the sun's concentrated rays hit them. He swung his farseeker back toward the wall, lowered it just enough to take in the moat.

And stopped.

"Alexander," he said. "That ship—"

"I know," said the prince.

"You should take another look," said Eumenes.

Matthias stared out at the ship that was making a beeline for the far side of the moat. He turned to one of the bolt-throwers, began loading it—slotted in an arrow-projectile easily half his own length, then pulled back some latches and—

"Start winching," he yelled to Lugorix. The Gaul stared for a moment, then bent to the task, letting his muscles pour tension into the super-attenuated strip of leather he was winding back. He kept on winding, till it seemed like the cord must snap—like any moment it would break and take his nose off in the process. Meanwhile, Matthias was busy slotting a rope onto the end of the bolt now encased within the machine. Lugorix suddenly realized what he was planning.

"You are *not* serious," he said.

"If you've got a better plan," said Matthias, "now would be a good time to name it."

Lugorix didn't. So he just kept on winching—the resistance against him increasing until he could barely turn the screws any further. Matthias finished attaching the rope—looked up at him.

"That's enough," he said, locking in the springs. "Now let's aim this thing." He moved behind the device and proceeded to rattle off a series of directions to a bemused Lugorix, who turned the contraption leftward on its hinges and shoved its nose downward in accordance with Matthias' instructions.

"Further left," said Matthias. "No, a little bit more to the right. Okay, let's pull up the nose. No, back a bit more the other way—"

"Will you make up your mind?" said Lugorix.

"I'm trying to allow for the speed of the ship," replied Matthias, looking through the sites. "So shut up and move it downward. No, that's too much. There—that's it—now to the right… a little further. A little more… okay, here we go."

He pulled on a lever; there was a clanging noise and Lugorix cursed as the back of the machine slammed against him—the bolt hurtled away, trailing rope behind it, arcing down toward the lone trireme, finally burying itself in ship's rigging. The rope sagged toward the ground, but the ship's forward motion was drawing it ever more taut.

"Let's do this," said Matthias—and before Lugorix could protest he leapt out the window and onto the rope, holding fast with his gloves and boots while he slid down it, rapidly rocketing away from Lugorix, dwindling as he closed in on the boat. For the first time in his life, Lugorix found himself hesitating. Facing down men and monsters didn't worry him, but a few things did, and he suddenly realized that jumping from the wall of a besieged city onto an enemy ship was one of them. For a moment, he envisioned other members of his tribe beside him, mocking him; spurred by that impetus, he leapt out onto the rope.

And hurtled downward. The wall shot away above him; he thought he was plunging directly toward the water and then he felt the rope above him, kicking like a living thing as it grew taut and he zipped in toward the boat. All around him was missile-fire: stones arcing down toward the fortress, bolts leaping up from the fortress… he caught a glimpse of that vast army steadily closing the distance between its ranks and the moat—those infernal machines towering above it, leading the way—and then in front of him was a sail and a mast and the stern of the ship, the latter filling his vision as he stretched out his legs and slowed, the rope burning against his gloves until he smelt smoke and leapt off, sprawling onto the deck.

Matthias stood there, blade out, already hard-pressed by half a dozen men. But those men were too busy with Matthias to have spotted the approach of the second interloper—and even less prepared for the giant axe that started shearing through them as Lugorix waded in. They were taken completely by surprise—and before Lugorix knew it, those who were left were fleeing toward the front of the ship.

Lugorix and Matthias headed to the stern to find the helmsman. Lugorix led the way as they hacked their way to the man's side, Macedonians scrambling out of his path and leaping into the water.

"What gives," said the helmsman, who was clearly Athenian. The ship slowed momentarily as the rope went completely taut—and then the boat jolted forward again as that tether snapped altogether.

"Who are you working for?" asked Matthias.

"That'd be you," replied the helmsman, eyeing Lugorix's axe.

"So turn this ship around."

The helmsman started to do just that—and ducked as a spear flew past his head, thrown by one of the Macedonians now regrouping further down the deck. Matthias and Lugorix ducked behind some barrels; Matthias unslung his bow, nocked an arrow and fired, catching a Macedonian in the chest. The rest of the Macedonians took cover behind the port forecastle.

"It's a stand-off," muttered Matthias. "There's more of them but they have to come to us."

"You sure about that?" asked Lugorix—gestured at the far bank of the moat. The foremost of the Leviathans had almost reached that bank. One of its arms hung limp at its side, and the rest of it was battered and dented, but as a fighting machine it was still very much intact. Ballistae and bolt-throwers were mounted atop it; a massive and unholy clanking emanated from within.

"Zeus save us," muttered Matthias as it crashed into the water and began striding toward them.

Eumenes didn't know which was more interesting: what was going on in the moat, or Alexander's reaction to it. The prince's attention was totally fixed on the struggle for the ship. Matters weren't going according to plan—the Athenians had managed to get men back into the barbican, and now they'd done the same for the ship, which was turning around in the water even as a Leviathan bore down on it.

The question was why the boat was so important in the first place. Eumenes didn't know. What he *did* know was that he was looking at a plan known only to Alexander, Philip and Hephaestion. And maybe not even the latter... but as Eumenes studied the marshal's body language, he realized the man was in on the secret for sure. Hephaestion wasn't just responding to Alexander's obvious tension. He knew something. Something specific, and it involved that boat which was rapidly becoming the center of everyone's focus. For a brief, crazy moment Eumenes wondered if whatever was aboard was the whole point of the entire assault. But then he dismissed the notion as ridiculous.

After all, nothing could be worth so much.

The colossus strode through the water. The moat was deep, but nowhere near deep enough—the water came up to the machine's waist, which kept on moving forward. A lone Athenian warship was nearby; crowded with archers and siege-engines, it unleashed a withering stream of fire—but the shots bounced harmlessly off the armor of the Leviathan. Next moment, the machine lowered one of its arms and unleashed a titanic jet of flame from nozzles set into its wrist. Fire enveloped the warship—men turned into screaming human torches leapt into the water. The burning ship drifted aside as the Leviathan bore down on its quarry.

"Shit," said Lugorix.

Now that it was getting close, he could see the way in which its head had been built to look like a real one—eyes that looked down upon him, giant jagged teeth which decorated a mouth set into an awful leering grin. He could make out Macedonians manning bolt-throwers mounted on the monstrosity's shoulder—they were firing at the battlements on the barbican. The ship kept on turning away from the oncoming Leviathan but it wasn't turning fast enough.

That was when the Macedonians aboard the boat rushed the stern. Matthias' hands were a blur as he fired arrow after arrow. Lugorix waited till they were almost upon him before he emerged from cover and began laying about with Skullseeker, arcing the axe through the air in great strokes. The blade smashed through a man's chest while the hilt splintered another's teeth. But the Macedonians were veterans and pressed in regardless. Matthias stood off to the right, still firing arrows—now at the very rearmost point of the stern, and if anyone came any closer he'd have to drop the bow and draw his blade and make do as well as he could with it. Above them all towered the Leviathan, kicking up waves of such force that the boat was bobbing like a wooden cork. Hatches in the machine's belly opened; through the Macedonians pressing in against him, Lugorix caught a glimpse of a rope dangling from the Leviathan, its end disappearing into the hold. Next moment, two Macedonians were being hauled up along it.

Along with Barsine.

She was kicking and screaming and all to no avail as she was hauled into the belly of the beast. Lugorix stepped forward, lopping the head off another Macedonian—continuing to hack about him with his axe, pressing his advantage until the Macedonians retreated back down the deck. There were only a few of them left now and they knew the game was up—they were leaping up to grab more ropes sidling down from the Leviathan. But whoever was driving the Leviathan had more pressing priorities. There was a clanking noise as the colossus lurched to the side, began turning around. Those Macedonians who had grabbed onto ropes found themselves swinging helplessly—two smashed against one of the machine's legs and lost their grip, tumbling into the water. Another fell back onto the ship's deck, his head splitting open like overripe fruit. But Lugorix was already sprinting past him and onto the ship's prow. And as the Leviathan strode past them he did the one thing he could.

Jump.

He hurled himself against the monstrosity's legs, managed to grab onto the edge of one of its armor-plates. He hung there for a moment, then began clambering up from plate to plate. The fact that the leg was in constant motion made that all the tougher. The Leviathan was now striding back the way it had come, and Lugorix could only wonder what the onlookers on the Athenian walls were thinking as it retreated toward Macedonian lines.

Not that it was any less a target for the Athenian defenses. Projectiles and bolts streaked past Lugorix as he kept scrambling ever higher up the Leviathan's leg. One hit the area where he'd just been with such force that he almost lost his grip. But then he was at the level of the machine's waist. That was when he was spotted by some of one of the bowmen perched besides the siege-machines on the shoulder. The archer drew back his bow—only to be suddenly hit through the chest by an arrow fired by Matthias, standing on the ship's deck and watching for just such a moment. The Macedonian fell back screaming and Lugorix breathed a sigh of relief.

Only to suddenly find a hatch right beside him. An archer leaned out, drew a bead on Lugorix—who hurled himself forward, ducking under the arrow and grabbing onto the man's arm, pulling himself into the hatch in one fluid motion even as he yanked the man out. Lugorix glanced back at the now-dwindling Matthias, gave him the thumbs-up sign and then continued deeper into the huge machine. He ducked low through some doorways—a soldier whirled to face him and Lugorix cut him down. Moving past the still-twitching corpse, Lugorix could hear plenty of activity coming from the next room. He peered on through.

It took a moment to take it all in. He was looking at what was clearly the Leviathan's central hub—a cavernous chamber that occupied what had to be almost the entirety of the machine's chest cavity. Several wooden platforms were stacked on top of one another, and on on each of them was a massive horizontal wheel, each wheel being turned by slaves, each slave chained to his position on the wheel. Ropes and pulleys and cables were everywhere, all of them cranking and groaning as the wheels turned and the machine lurched onward. Slavemasters with whips and Macedonian soldiers with drawn swords ensured that the pace never slackened.

Until Lugorix stormed forward.

So stunned were the Macedonians that they barely even recognized they were under attack until several of their number had already been butchered. Lugorix was a barbarian possessed as he hacked at both cables and flesh; limbs and rope flew across the room as he fought his way forward. A slavemaster slashed at him with a whip—only to be suddenly pulled off his feet by the slaves nearby and gutted with his own dagger. Next moment, the slaves were using that dagger to cut themselves free. As slaves swarmed away from the object of their servitude, the Leviathan shuddered, stumbled—then leaned to one side, shuddered and stopped.

But Lugorix didn't. He strode forward, grabbed a wounded Macedonian, shoved him up against the tilting wall.

"Where's the woman?" he growled.

"Upstairs," said the man—and those were his last words as Lugorix tightened his grip, crushed his windpipe before he whirled and began clambering up the stacked platforms. Slaves helped him up, cheering. Others were engaged in an orgy of destruction—smashing the wheels wholesale, seizing the weapons of their Macedonian overseers and using them to break open vats set along one of the walls. Black tarry pitch leaked out. A slave hurled a torch—just as Lugorix noticed tubes leading from one of those vats through the wall, in the direction of one of the arms. He remembered how the Leviathan had torched that Athenian ship to the waterline. But he made the connection a little too late.

"Don't do it," he yelled.

There was an explosion. Sheets of fire tore through the room. Flame began roaring up the platforms as slaves scattered through every exit they could find. Smoke billowed around Lugorix as he climbed through a hatch in the room's ceiling and ran along a walkway. Two Macedonian guards tried to block his way—he ducked past their blades, and then sliced through them both with a single massive stroke. Blood went everywhere as he pushed past the still-twiching bodies and up some stairs.

Straight into the control-chamber. A tilted view of the Macedonian siege-lines was dimly visible through two huge porthole-eyes; much closer was the edge of the moat. Levers and tubes filled the room, but whoever had been manning the controls had fled.

Except for one man. The Leviathan's captain stood in the center of the room, his eyes trained on Lugorix. He held a dagger in one hand, Barsine in the other.

"Turn around," said the captain.

"And miss all the fun?" Lugorix's tone was light but his mind was racing. This is where having Matthias around would have been useful. All he had was the axe. It could possibly be used as a throwing weapon in an emergency, but not as a precision one. Which meant he had absolutely no idea how to get Barsine out of this alive. As if realizing this, the captain laughed.

"I'm serious, barbarian."

"So am I," said Barsine as she suddenly dropped a dagger from her robe into her hand and stuck it through the captain's stomach. He gasped, tottered backward—Barsine ducked away as Lugorix strode forward and swung Skullseeker, sending the captain's blood spraying all over the port-holes. He turned back to Barsine.

"We need to get off this thing," he said.

"You think?" she muttered. She dashed past him, going back the way he'd come, along the walkway—only this time right past the hatch and out onto the weaponry platform on the Leviathan's right shoulder. Smoke was everywhere now and the tilt of the Leviathan was becoming more pronounced. Slaves were swimming away from the doomed colossus in all directions. There was a crash as one of the arms fell off, flame licking from it as it hurtled into the water. Lugorix looked around.

"Only one way to do this," he said. Barsine grabbed his hand. He stared ahead. It was a long way down. "On the count of three," he said. "One… two…."

"Screw that," said Barsine. As one, they leapt forward, away from the Leviathan. The moat rushed up toward them and they hit, crashing through the surface and plunging down until blue turned to black and Lugorix could barely tell which way was up. He still had hold of Barsine's hand, but she wasn't reciprocating—she was going limp. He grabbed her, hauled her back up toward the surface. They broke back out into the air—Lugorix realized the shock of hitting the water had momentarily winded Barsine, for she was gasping for breath and seemed stunned. He wrapped an arm around her, trying to keep her above the surface while he swam back toward the walls of Athens.

That was when he heard a terrible creaking noise above him. A shadow fell across him as the Leviathan toppled into the water with an almighty splash, crashing through where he and Barsine had just been. Everywhere people were struggling to stay afloat—Macedonians swam back toward their own side, slaves swam toward Athens. Lugorix was with the latter group—and despite his burden, he quickly forged out ahead of them. But it was a long way to go. And two more Leviathans were striding into the water. Along with thousands upon thousands of barbarians, who began using their mantlets as boats as they paddled toward Athens, heedless of the blizzard of fire and shots that poured down upon them.

"Over here," yelled a voice.

It was Matthias. He was in the prow of the ship that had originally taken Barsine—and which was now heading straight toward the swimming Lugorix. At the last moment, the ship turned aside—Matthias reached down and grabbed Lugorix's arm. Together, they helped a spluttering Barsine into the boat, which then began to slide at speed across the water, back toward Athens. Lugorix realized that while he had been in the bowels of the Leviathan, the Athenians had fired more ropes out across the water, attaching crampons to the ship with Matthias' help. Now the ship was being pulled back the way it had come with as much speed as the men hauling at those ropes could muster. Out in the moat, a battle royale began to develop between several Athenian ships and scores of barbarian boats—though it was a one-sided battle, as the two Leviathans kicked and smashed their way through the Athenian vessels, moving in toward the walls—

"Heads up," said Matthias.

Lugorix turned as the ship they were in ground onto the shore of the moat. Athenians reached out to help Barsine, but he and Matthias shook them off, helped her off the boat and onto the shore, the wall towering above them. Even as they ran toward it they could see stone sliding aside and nozzles protruding from the wall. Liquid began spraying from those nozzles, coating part of the surface of the moat.

"Oh fuck," said Matthias. Lugorix said nothing. There was nothing to say—faced with the assault about to hit them, the Athenians had decided to cut their losses. Everyone out in that moat, friend and foe alike, was now forfeit. Just as the three got back inside the doorway through which the Macedonians had carried Barsine scant minutes earlier, there was a sudden whooshing noise. They felt a burst of intense heat on their backs as the moat suddenly burst into flame. For a moment none of them could breathe—the air was too hot, the pressure too much. With his fast-dimin-ishing strength, Lugorix and another Athenian manhandled the door shut. Everyone stumbled on into darkness.

Face expressionless, Alexander turned away from the window. The sky was black with smoke and flame; the cries of those caught out in that inferno was deafening. The Leviathans were pillars of flame now. And yet even now a third wave of barbarians was pouring from the Macedonian siege-works out into the plain. Eumenes had learned enough from Alexander about generalship to know that throwing more bodies into a slaughterhouse only added to the scale of the slaughter. Common sense dictated that the ad-ditional troops be held back for another attack, at another time. But if the assault had failed, the cannon-fodder still had to be spent. Had this been the critical moment in the battle, Alexander's actions would have been precisely calibrated to achieve the decisive breakthrough.

But as Eumenes gazed out at the smoke and fire, he knew in his heart that no such moment was at hand. He wondered what those dying for Macedonia under the walls of Athens would say if they knew that Alex-ander was even now leaving his command post—if they knew that they were just pieces that had to be cleared from the board of a larger game. They had been hired not to conquer but to die; they were being snuffed out so that they'd never return to their homelands—perishing so that the commander who'd bought them could lead an army up the Danube with as little resistance as possible. Eumenes suspected that Alexander had never intended to capture Athens—that he wanted his western expedition to be the straw that broke the camel's back, rather than a glorified mop-up expedition. Perhaps the defenses of Athens were so strong that nothing could have shattered them. But if Philip had been there, he'd have made sure those defenses were truly put to the test, with diversionary attacks to cover the main assault, rather than simply throwing everything against a single section of the walls.

Though clearly Alexander had possessed some other reason for aiming at that section of the walls. Whatever had been in that boat before it had been sunk or incinerated (for it was impossible to see any sign of it amidst the flames and wreckage that covered the moat) had presumably been lost for good. Could it have been some kind of information? A stolen document? Or perhaps it was an artifact of Aristotle's. Or maybe something of symbolic value to the people of Athens... Alexander certainly understood the value of symbols, as he'd demonstrated with the Gordian knot. But usually his symbols were displayed for all the world to see—flaunted to advertise his triumphs. Which today certainly wasn't. Alexander had concentrated on a single section of the walls of Athens, as part of some plot that remained obscure. Except that it involved treason within the walls of Athens.

And perhaps within Pella too.

For that was at least part of the key, thought Eumenes. Philip *couldn't* have commanded the siege in person. He couldn't leave his palace. To do otherwise would render him vulnerable to the plotting of his own son. Whether or not Alexander wanted to be a god, he certainly wanted to be king. To achieve that all he had to do was eliminate his father.

Whereas Philip had no such options. Perhaps he hoped to build up Ptolemy as a potential successor, but the truth of the matter was that until the war with Athens was won, Alexander was irreplaceable. So the old king was going to sit in his palace in Pella, surrounded by his bodyguards and army. Only a civil war would get him off the throne. And with the capital of an enemy superpower scarcely two hundred miles to the south a civil war would be fatal to Macedonia. Meaning the final reckoning between father and son would have to wait until victory over Athens. Unless the king died of natural causes. But not many Macedonian rulers had died of those.

More rumbling shook the room. Eumenes looked up with a start—

found the eyes of Hephaestion staring into his own with an intensity that suggested the man knew exactly what he'd been thinking. He gazed back at Hephaestion, willed himself not to look away.

"Something on your mind?" he asked.

"Trying to figure out what's on yours," replied Hephaestion.

There were three of them who rode away from the smoking wreck of the Macedonian siege-lines that night. They were king's messengers, and the fact that today they bore the prince's messages was all the same to them: they served the royal house of Macedonia. One made for Pella—he had the shortest journey but the hardest task, for he had to break the news of the failure of the siege and face the wrath of Philip. The second bypassed the capital, rode north, into the mountains of Thrace, heading eastward, toward the mouth of the Danube where officers of the Macedonian navy were busy assembling a vast supply of grain and weapons. They would have to accelerate such preparations if they wanted to keep their posts, let alone their heads. This was the kind of message that the king's couriers relished delivering—all the trouble went to the recipient, and none to the messenger himself. There was no feeling quite like the one of standing there stone-faced, awaiting orders while the recipient read the message with sinking comprehension.

But it was the third man who had the longest journey. He would have to cross the Bosphorus, heading through Asia Minor before turning south into Lebanon. He would use the royal roads of Persia that ran across mountains and desert, linking all the territories that the Great Kings had once ruled. Their empire had lasted for centuries, in no small part because of their first-class system of roadways. So now the messenger made haste along them, making all the speed he could, acutely aware that he could never go as fast as the more conventional system of using relays of messengers—but speed had been sacrificed for security, as the message he was carrying was deemed too sensitive to entrust to more than a single man.

Not that the courier knew what it said. All he knew was that he had to hand the sealed orders personally to Craterus, chief marshal of the Macedonian forces in Egypt. After which it would be Craterus' problem. The messenger knew that whatever he carried involved the titanic struggle now underway between the ruler of the land and the mistress of the sea. But he didn't really concern himself with that. He was just the bearer of tidings.

That was all. He was a worshipper of Hermes, the messenger god, whose spirit he prayed would guide him on these roads above, keep him off those roads below.

It was a good day for the birds.

Dust drifted over the Attican plain, mingled with the groans of the dying. Smoke rose from the wreckage of mantlets and siege engines. The melted wreckage of the Leviathans was strewn through the now-dry moat. Bodies were everywhere. Some had died by heat. Some had been trampled by their own comrades piling up behind them. But the bulk of them had succumbed to the time-honored way to die in a siege-assault, struck by one of the myriad projectiles flung from the walls which they were charging. Nor had there been any retreat. The toxic gas being pumped in behind them had ensured that the barbarians had been forced to keep charging forward until they were all dead. Those who had reached the moat had been greeted by inferno. Most had never got that far.

The birds were eating their fill. Vultures, kites, hawks, ospreys—they must have come from all over Greece, for the sky was black with them. To the archon Leosthenes, inspecting the walls with guards in tow, it seemed less like the aftermath of victory than a portent of the gods, the sun over the Parthenon blotted out by creatures that fed on anything lifeless.

"Quite a sight," said Memnon.

Leosthenes nodded. He wasn't in the mood for conversation right now, particularly not Memnon's. The last few days had pushed them all to the brink. Had the Macedonians launched an assault against all sides of Athens—well, the war would have been decided there one way or another. Perhaps that was why Macedonia hadn't. Philip would ultimately have had to commit the bulk of his shock troops, and those troops would have had to either conquer or die. It may have been in Alexander's nature to gamble everything on one throw of the die. But not in Philip's.

And now the reports indicated that Macedonian forces were deploying west, to probe for weakness on the periphery of the Athenian imperium. On the one hand that was good news—at the very least, a reprieve. But there had been disquieting reports from the spies... that Alexander's real objective in the west involved something that would not only bring down the Athenian Empire, but would establish a new order that would last (according to one spy) 'until the Sun burnt out and the Earth withered.'

Heavy stuff... probably bullshit... and yet Leosthenes had gone so far as to show (via an agent reporting to Memnon, who was a master of deniability) the disgraced Demosthenes the latest intelligence estimates. He didn't leave a copy with him, of course—but Demosthenes had been his mentor and supporter in his early days on the council, and unlike everyone else on that council, he still trusted the man. *Had* trusted the man—for now Demosthenes was dead, the victim of Macedonian agents or Athenian treason or both. Apparently he'd been engaged in his own private games even after leaving the council—well, Leosthenes would have expected nothing less. In fact, that was precisely why he'd shown Demosthenes the compilation of what Athenian spies based in Pella were saying—what Aristotle was rumored to have discovered prior to his fleeing the Macedonian capitol. If the Persian witch who had passed through Athens didn't trust anyone still holding office in Athens enough to contact them—well, Leosthenes couldn't say he blamed her. Hopefully Demosthenes had helped her with whatever schemes she was concocting against Alexander.

It wasn't like Leosthenes was in a position to do shit. Memnon's fears that he'd be scapegoated for Egypt had almost been borne out. Only the rivalry on the council between Phocion and Hypereides had allowed Leosthenes to keep his post: his belonging to neither faction meant that both still hoped to win his support—and he gave each faction just enough hope to keep them interested. Yet while survival under those circumstances could be considered quite an accomplishment, right now his political triumph seemed as hollow as that of Athens' military one. Because this war was just beginning.

It was going to be a long one.

CHAPTER NINE

The messenger travelled by night now whenever possible, turning off the road to skirt past towns and cities. It seemed only prudent to do so. It was true that all those settlements were technically under Macedonian overlordship now. But what did that mean? Who really ran them? Who reported to who? Like any good courier, he had an acute sense of politics—not in the manner of a player of those games, but in the way a sailor knows the direction of the tide and where the more treacherous shoals might lay. That there was tension between father and son was obvious. Same with the the tension that simmered among the the son's generals. There was word that at least one of them had been declared to be a son of Philip in his own right—a rival for Alexander, or just a cat's paw, the gods above only knew. The messenger certainly didn't.

So he rode on, ever further south, through the forests of the Levant, the smell of pine all around him, the blue of Mediterranean occasionally visible through those trees. As a Macedonian, that sea made him uneasy. It was forbidden territory. And yet somehow they would have to conquer it. Which was a disquieting thought. If Athens really *was* impregnable, then how much more so was her empire? The messenger wondered how Alexander intended to come to grips with it. He had no doubt his prince was up to something.

Lugorix would never have believed it would have taken several more weeks before they could get out of Athens. But the city was on too high a military alert to do it sooner. They'd been lucky to get away from the walls in the first place—had been stopped by Athenian soldiers while trying to leave the barbican, and placed under guard. But the officer whose men Lugorix and Matthias had assisted recognized them and ordered their release.

Of course, his decision might have been influenced by the gold that Barsine was carrying. She'd given him a month's wages. Two more bribes were necessary to get back to the wreckage of Demosthenes' house, and even those probably wouldn't have sufficed had it still been day. But they used the cover of night to slip past the sentries posted around the still-smoldering debris—and then shoved some of that debris aside to gain access to one of the trapdoors and make their way down to the hidden dock. Damitra was right where they left her, still aboard the *Xerxes,* meditating calmly, her countenance totally at odds with her hysteria of a few hours ago. She professed not to remember any of it, and simply said they needed to leave the city as soon as possible.

Not that they needed a seer to tell them that. One of the reasons why bribery was so effective in getting back to the house of Demosthenes was that no one seemed to be in charge anymore. There were rumors that the archons were fighting among themselves, that a search for traitors was underway at every level. How else could a Macedonian commando force get into one of the critical strong points on the wall? The sense of hysteria was mounting. It wouldn't be long before all foreigners were arrested on sight, no matter how much gold they had to offer. They stole down the canal that very evening and into the harbor, where some of Demosthenes' men hid the *Xerxes* in one of the warehouses and bid them wait for the right moment to slip out of the city. Lugorix was certain they'd be betrayed, and had relaxed only slightly when Demosthenes' henchman Isocrates showed up. The man who had warned his master of impending mob action said there had been mass arrests, but that he was working on getting one of his men installed as commander as one of the harbor-gates. It turned out that was only one part of the equation. The others were the shifting schedules for the harbor patrols and the location of the barricades that had just been scattered throughout the harbor. Getting those took some time. Lugorix and Matthias passed it by a throwing a lot of dice, day after day, until finally they thought they'd be throwing dice forever in that warehouse by the sea. Spring slowly gave way to summer—and then one day, Isocrates reappeared and said he had what he needed to get them out of there.

The harbor was still on the alert the night they left, but all the defenses were focused on keeping ships out, rather than on making sure they stayed in. Barsine gave the orders while Damitra piloted—Lugorix and Matthias kept watch on top, but their presence seemed almost superfluous as the *Xerxes* followed the route that Isocrates had given them, sneaking past a long line of triremes at anchor, and in between some sea-walls, then through a maze of those barely-submerged barricades and out the gate that was operated by Isocrates' henchman.

By the time dawn broke, Matthias had gone below to get some rest. They were well out away from Athens now, but the summit of the Acropolis was still visible in the distance, as Barsine had given her lookouts a strange cylinder that magnified views. Lugorix had heard that commanders presiding over battles sometimes used magick snakes to inform them of all that transpired beyond their eye. Hadn't Herodotus said Xerxes used such a creature at Salamis? Perhaps this cylinder was one of those snakes. With the right incantations, maybe it even reverted to snake like form in order to bite the enemies of whoever wielded it. Lugorix felt more than a little nervous putting it up to his eye.

"It won't bite you," said Barsine, climbing up onto the deck.

"Because I'm on your side?"

"Because it can't." She joined him at the rail, looking out at the fading city. "We're leaving quite a mess back there."

"But Alexander lost."

"*Macedonia* lost. I doubt Alexander feels defeated."

Lugorix said nothing. Such distinctions meant little to him. Besides, it felt like Barsine was standing beside him for a reason. Like she had something she wanted to say. Something she was only able to say now they were free of Athens. She cleared her throat.

"Thank you for saving me," she said in the tone of a someone not used to thanking anybody for anything.

"That's what you hired us for," he said gravely.

"Nevertheless. You put your life on the line for me."

"Why does Alexander want you so badly?" asked Lugorix.

For a moment her face did that thing that faces do when the mind behind them is trying to decide what to say. "He's afraid of me," she said at last.

"Why?"

"He knows that I could rule in Persia some day."

"Despite what you said earlier?"

"What did I say earlier?"

"You're a woman. So you can't rule."

"That makes it more complicated," she admitted. "But you don't have to be on the throne to rule."

That felt closer to the truth. "In whose name would you?"

"Any suitable male member of the Achaemenid house."

"But why *you?* What makes you so dangerous to Alexander?"

"Because I'll stop at nothing to defeat him."

It wasn't an answer, and both of them knew it. Lugorix shifted gears. "So that assault on Athens—was it all aimed at you?"

"Nothing Alexander does is ever aimed at one thing. He always has multiple objectives. He's nothing if not devious."

"Just like you?"

To his surprise, she laughed. "Are all barbarians this impudent?"

"No," he said.

"Is that why you left your village?"

"No."

"So you still won't tell me."

Not for the first time, Lugorix felt baffled by this woman. "Why is it you want to know?"

"I owe you a blood-debt."

"So?"

"So that's not something a Persian noble takes lightly."

"It really isn't that big a deal."

"I beg to differ."

Uncomfortable as this woman made him, Lugorix was beginning to get annoyed. "Why should I tell you anything if you won't tell me why Alexander wants you?"

She hesitated. "He wants me because…" She trailed off, looked uneasy. "I'm the only one who understands how to beat him. All the other members of my house are fighting for the scraps in the east. They're all in Afghanistan, pinned down by Macedonian garrisons and skirmishers. I'm the only one who came west, to seek the weapons that will stop him. Weapons that Aristotle is the key to."

"Did you persuade him to leave Macedonia's service?"

"No. Macedonia's own actions did that."

"And you believe he knows how to build these weapons?"

"Yes," she said. Lugorix mulled this over. He knew Barsine was still hiding something. It wasn't even that she was telling lies—Persians were supposed to abhor lies. Barsine was telling the truth. She just wasn't telling the *whole* truth.

Though two could play at that game.

"I was exiled from my tribe," he said.

"Because?"

"They found me guilty of killing my parents."

If that surprised her, she didn't show it. "Did you?"

"No."

"Who did?"

"My brother."

"He framed you?" Lugorix nodded, but now Barsine was looking skeptical. "You're telling me the penalty for patricide and matricide is *exile?*"

"It's his tribe's ultimate punishment," said Matthias.

They turned to look at him as he climbed onto the deck. He was swaying as he walked toward them, and it wasn't just because of the pitching of the deck. As the smell on his breath amply confirmed.

"You've been drinking," said Barsine.

"Some wine I took from Demosthenes' place. Good stuff."

"So drink below. I'm talking to Lugorix."

"Who happens to be my friend."

"Which is why you need to back off," said Lugorix. "We're talking about my parents."

Matthias' expression was that of a hurt dog. "You and I have talked about that before."

"Not while only one of us was sober."

"Don't do this to me," said Matthias.

"Do what?" Lugorix was aware the situation was getting volatile, but he wasn't sure precisely why. Matthais knew all about his family—should have known better than to barge in on a conversation about them. But then he saw the way the inebriated Greek was looking at Barsine, and he understood all too well.

As did Barsine.

"It's time I cleared up any misconceptions," she snapped. "This isn't like in the stories. I'm not a fairytale princess. I'm a *real* one. I'm a daughter of the royal house of Persia. I've hired both of you for your services, in return for which I will deliver you two talents apiece in silver when I get my hands on Aristotle. Is that clear?"

From the expression on Matthias' face, it was all too clear. He turned and stalked off, climbed back down the hatch. Lugorix sighed. Then met Barsine's gaze.

"So are we *kidnapping* Aristotle?" he asked.

"That won't be necessary. He and I will see eye to eye."

"Just because he ran from Macedonia doesn't mean he'll work to defeat her. He may just want to keep a low profile."

"I had in mind an offer he can't refuse."

Lugorix looked scornful. "You really think he needs money?"

"Who said anything about money? The only currency that means anything to a mind like that is information. That's how you bait his kind of hook. And we don't have much time: as soon as Alexander finds a chink in the armor of Athens' empire, the whole edifice will come apart at the seams. By the way, what is it about your friend that makes him such an asshole?"

It took Lugorix a moment to register the switch of subjects. "I prefer the term *troublemaker*."

"Tell me something I don't know."

"His father was a builder by trade and a wrecker by nature. Matthias ran away to sea when he was fifteen but he tried to seduce the captain's wife. So he enrolled in the Athenian marines, but they threw him out for insubordination. So he joined the mercenaries. That's where I met him."

"And you've been inseparable ever since," said Barsine sardonically.

Lugorix shrugged. "He's my friend."

"Even though he lacks all social graces?"

That made Lugorix laugh. "You think *I* have them?"

"That's different. What makes you so close?"

The question annoyed Lugorix. How was he supposed to explain it? *We're soldiers. We've saved each others' lives. We've fucked whores side by side.* "We're both exiles," he said.

She stared at him for a long moment. "I know the feeling."

From his perch atop the bluff overlooking the Danube, Eumenes could see at least half the army, a carpet of men and beasts extending along both sides of the sloped banks, with barges and warships moving in stately procession between them. The occasional elephant was visible—there were eighty in all. Cavalry outriders patrolled along the hills, keeping a watchful eye on the endless treeline beyond. For the last several days they had been moving ever further into terra incognita. The army was watchful in a way it hadn't been during the initial, downstream portions of the river. All the tribes in that area had been decimated beneath the walls of Athens—and now what was left of them had either offered submission or fled into the vast northern forests. There was of course no pursuit; Alexander knew better than to chase stragglers into those tractless woods, beyond the edge of the known world.

Which didn't mean that one couldn't make some deductions about what was out there. Scouts were well out ahead of the columns, in some cases many miles up. Eumenes had spoken with a trader last night who had talked with other merchants who dealt in amber; that trader claimed to have conversed with a man who had walked along a coast far to the north and looked out upon an ocean littered with giant chunks of *hardened sea*. Those were his exact words. To Eumenes, such claims seemed a sure sign that the man was lying through his teeth—one more tall tale to throw in there with all the ones about dragons and monsters. But the notion of a coast on the other side of all these forests made sense—or at least, it accorded with the theories of the geographers that the world that encompassed the Mediterranean was in turn surrounded by the *Okeanos*—the world-ocean. So Eumenes had scrupulously recorded the babblings of that trader, the same way he kept detailed notes of all such conversations; not just from an intelligence-gathering perspective, but also with a more long-term goal in mind, for once Athens was defeated, what else would be left save exploration and the pushing back of the frontiers of the unknown?

But at least for now they were on the move. Out of benighted Pella and godforsaken Macedonia. Eumenes had hated every day he'd spent there in the aftermath of the attack on Athens. For the sake of appearances, he'd even had to stay with his *wife*. Artonis: it had been years since he'd seen her, and he hadn't missed her for a day. She hadn't either, from the looks of it. She was the daughter of one of the Macedonian barons; their marriage was purely political, and all her servants were spies for one faction or another. Being with her was like being an actor in a play; one wore a mask and performed one's role. Eumenes' was to tell her *all about his adventures* while god knows how many other ears hung on every word and she asked ever more probing questions about Alexander. He knew better than to give her honest answers.

The fact that he didn't know those answers himself made it easier. When one was with someone every day, one could lose track of how they were changing. They could become a different person under your eyes, and if they did it gradually enough you'd never even notice. Eumenes had followed Alexander into Asia because he'd believed him to be a man of destiny. But now the prince didn't even seem to think he was a man. And yet Eumenes owed him everything—for Alexander had been the first to see his ability, and had promoted him above the heads of jealous Macedonians until Eumenes administered the nerve-center of a mobile empire larger than any the world had ever known. And if he knew a growing disquiet about his master, well, surely he wasn't the first servant to have known *that*...

A shout plucked Eumenes from his reverie. He whirled in his saddle to catch a glimpse of Macedonian soldiers riding through a gully about a quarter mile away, closing on a pocket of woods, moving like hunters who had just picked up a scent. Automatically, Eumenes gripped the reins and rode down after them—conscious in so doing that he was now out of sight of the rest of the army, entirely within the purview of the perimeter-patrols that were now converging on a particular area of the forest. He heard more shouts, and then the unmistakable clang of steel on steel.

Combat.

Eumenes knew he ought to turn around and ride back to the river. But it was a long while since he'd gotten close to the action—in fact, he hadn't seen combat since the pitched battles in Persia. Almost without thinking, he spurred his horse among the trees, saw mounted tribesmen closing from both directions. And then all at once they were on him—he twisted in his saddle to avoid a descending blade, then sheared off the man's face with a sudden backhanded swipe of his sword. The tribesman fell to the ground screaming and Eumenes' horse trampled him, before careening straight into the steed of yet another tribesman. This time the distance was too close for Eumenes' sword—but not the tribesman's dagger which sliced into Eumenes' armor and stuck there. Even as the tribesman tried to pull it free, Eumenes was dragging that man from the saddle, hurling him onto the ground, where another Macedonian ran him through with a spear.

More Macedonians rode past.

But now Eumenes reined his steed in, drew it up short. If this skir-mish was the first part of a larger attack, then his responsibility was to be back with Alexander, not out beyond the edge of the perimeter. Catching his breath, he stared down at one of the dead barbarians. The blood that obscured the man's features couldn't mask the fact that this didn't look like any tribesman Eumenes had seen. He wore thick furs of some animal Eumenes didn't recognize; his legs were practically bowed from spending so much time in the saddle. There were strange tattoos up and down the man's arms. The shouts and screams up ahead were receding: the tribesmen were drawing off, galloping back into the forest. And Eumenes could see why, for their quarry had eluded them: another rider bolted in amidst the Macedonian cavalry—a Macedonian courier, the one who the tribesmen had been chasing.

"Thank the gods," he muttered. "They almost had me."

"Forest must be full of the buggers," said someone else. A chorus of ques-tions followed, but then—before Eumenes could intervene—the voice of an officer barked above the clamor: "In Zeus' name, let's get him to the river. Those bastards could be back at any moment."

Soldiers saluted as the officer designated one patrol to keep covering this section of the forest while the other escorted the courier back to the Dan-ube. Eumenes cantered in among that second patrol—there were more than a few eyebrows at suddenly finding one of Alexander's top lieutenants right in their midst. In short order, Eumenes was riding alongside the courier.

"My lord," said the man as he spotted the general's stripes on Eumenes' shoulder.

"You have correspondence?"

"From Pella. The king. A satchel of papers."

"Then why in Hades did you ride through the forest? Why not just fol-low the army up the river?"

The messenger looked sheepish. "I was taking a short-cut. Between bends in the river." He caught sight of the look that Eumenes was giving him. "We were told the eastern part of the forest was clear!"

Eumenes kept his voice level. "By who?"

"The fleet captains back on the Black Sea."

"Who are safe back on their boats at the coast. And can thus indulge in such fantasies. Next time, stay within sight of the river."

"My lord." They rode out onto that river bank, the columns of marching infantry parting to let them through. The messenger's eyes went wide as he saw the fleet arrayed out on the river—his eyes focused in particular on the massive octere that was Alexander's eight-leveled flagship, although it wouldn't retain that status for much longer. Soon the deeper-keeled warships would have to turn back, and the fleet would rely ever more heavily on the barges, some of which were bigger than the warships, and crammed with men and horses and supplies.

Most of the boats were far smaller, of course. Eumenes glanced at the skiff that was now reaching the shore; barely larger than a typical fishing vessel, and manned by three Macedonian sailors. They helped the courier in; Eumenes climbed aboard as well and they rowed out to Alexander's flagship.

So far Alexander had spent all his time there. He hadn't even bothered to go ashore; indeed, neither had any of his high command, which was why Eumenes had felt compelled to check out conditions shoreside for himself. Now he was returning to the flagship with a messenger from Philip, which struck him as more than a little ironic. Eumenes wondered what that messenger carried. Hopefully not orders. That might be awkward. Alexander had made it all too clear that he regarded himself as his own law out here. But the messenger was evidently carrying *something* of importance—his sealed satchel testified to that. Eumenes led the weary courier up a lowered ramp and onto the deck of the flagship, past bodyguards, beneath folded sails and between rows of ballista—and then into the pavilion-tent that occupied the entirety of the rear portion of the deck. This was Alexander's command center.

Which also meant it was a lounge and drinking-parlor. Alexander had been holed up in here with Hephaestion for the last few days, his mood darkening the further up the Danube they got. Eumenes had been trying to stay clear of him, which wasn't easy. But that was one of the reasons why he'd gone to the shore earlier—obstensibly to conduct a personal inspection of the vast moving city that was the Macedonian army, but also to stay out of Alexander's hair. Eumenes entered the pavilion to find the prince and Hephaestion and two officers playing dice on a table littered with charts and maps.

"So what's this about a skirmish on the shore?" asked Alexander.

"Scythians," said Eumenes.

The reaction to that made him want to laugh. It was as though he'd tossed a burning brand into the center of the pavilion. No one wanted to hear that one of the fiercest tribes in existence—right up there with the Amazons themselves—was on this part of the Danube. Scythians were supposed to be way out in the steppes. Everyone stared at Eumenes—everyone except Alexander, who just looked like he'd been expecting this.

"Are you sure?" said Hephaestion.

"No," replied Eumenes. "I'm not."

"Then why—"

"The bodies don't look like any tribesmen I've ever seen. They're not Dardanians or Cicones—not like anybody we were expecting to find along this section of the river. They're altogether exotic."

"Really?" said Hephaestion. He sounded altogether skeptical.

"Philip himself fought them, didn't he? And Herodotus discusses them in detail—"

"Fuck Herodotus," said Hephaestion. "I'm sick of you quoting that *Greek* to paper over the fact that you don't know what the hell's going on out there."

"That's enough," snapped Alexander. "The Scythians are real. Let's not pretend they're not."

"Doesn't mean that they're *right on top of us*," said Hephaestion. "We've got scouts out in force, Alexander. Eumenes is acting like the woods are full of bogeymen."

"I said nothing of the kind," snapped Eumenes. "All I'm saying is that we have Scythians in the vicinity and we should be prepared for further incursions."

"We should *assume* further incursions," said Alexander, waving his hand languidly. "Power abhors a vacuum, no? We emptied the whole eastern portion of the Danube, so no surprise that some of the more fearsome tribes from the north might have been moving down to take advantage of the disruption."

"But surely they'd be moving in *behind* our path of march," said one of the officers. "Into that vacuum—rather than directly against us. Who would try that?"

"The Scythians would," said Eumenes.

"And that's why we're on the alert and ready for anything," said Alexander.

He looked at the messenger, who had been standing there awkwardly this whole time. "Who's this?"

The messenger drew himself up straight and saluted. "I bring word from your father, sire."

Your father: the wrong thing to say, but the courier was too tired and too low-ranking to be sensitive to such nuance. Alexander stood up, face darkening—gestured at the courier's satchel.

"Open it."

The messenger hesitated. "He was most insistent that only you do that, sire."

Alexander looked at Hephaestion, who was shaking his head. Eumenes knew what they were thinking—some kind of trap. But if that was the case, there were better ways to spring it. Subtler ways, and Alexander knew it. Still, why take chances...

"I said open it," repeated Alexander.

The messenger nodded, broke the seal, slowly removed the lid....

And jumped backward as though he'd been bitten by a snake.

For a moment, Eumenes thought that's exactly what had happened—that the messenger would collapse and start frothing at the mouth and Alexander would turn the entire army around and march back to Pella for a final reckoning with his father. But the messenger was still standing there, breathing a little heavily—then stepping forward again to pull out the contents of the satchel.

A human head.

Withered by whatever preservative agent it had been steeped in prior to being placed into the satchel, its features almost unrecognizable. But Alexander recognized them anyway: his eyes went wide. Then he looked at the messenger.

"At least your return trip will be easier," he said quietly.

The messenger gazed at him, confused. Alexander signalled to two of his bodyguards, who grabbed the man and forced him to his knees. He began begging for mercy.

"Spare you?" said Alexander. "Spare *us*"—gestured with one hand. Another bodyguard stepped forward, grabbed the messenger's hair and swung his sword, hacking off the head in a single stroke. Blood sprayed across the floorboards. The bodyguard placed the freshly hacked head in the satchel.

"Throw that box and body overboard and let them drift down the river," said Alexander. "That's my answer to the king. And you"—this to the junior officers and remaining bodyguards—"all of you, *get out*."

The bodyguards saluted and dragged the corpse out of there, the white-faced officers following, pulling the tent-flaps down behind them. Now it was just Alexander, Hephaestion and Eumenes—and the shrivelled head sitting on the table. Alexander regarded it calmly.

"It was worth a try," he said.

Eumenes finally remembered where he'd seen the sightless face staring up at them. It was one of Philip's own bodyguards. He realized that Alexander and Hephaestion were both staring at him, as though awaiting his reaction. He looked back at them evenly, decided that boldness was the best course.

"So what was the plan?" he asked.

"There were two of them," said Hephaestion.

"Two plans or two men?"

"Men."

"Both bodyguards?"

"The other was a page."

"With access to Philip's bedchamber?" said Eumenes.

"Yes. It's not clear what went wrong."

You were in charge of it, thought Eumenes. He could see it loud and clear on Alexander's face: Hephaestion had failed his prince. Which was why Eumenes had been ordered to stay behind, to help clean up the mess. Eumenes recognized it as a subtle increase in his own standing, but now Hephaestion was going to hate him more than ever. And being dragged into a plot when it had already failed was never the most salubrious of propositions. Eumenes looked from the anxious face of Hephaestion to the far-too-calm face of Alexander. He chose his next words carefully.

"Philip has that palace locked up tight," he said. "He's set everyone to watch each other. Maybe the page betrayed you, maybe another of the bodyguards suspected something."

"Not like it matters," said Alexander. "We'll never know."

"No," said Eumenes. "You won't. But if you were going to try this again, I'd recommend it be done outside the palace."

"Philip never leaves it," said Hephaestion.

"He would if you burned it down."

Alexander stared at Eumenes. A slow smile crept across his face.

"We're not in a position to do that," said Hephaestion.

"Not yet," said Eumenes. "Wait till this expedition's done. What's the hurry?"

"The hurry is I'd like to be king," said Alexander.

"You can proclaim yourself that anytime," said Eumenes.

"Macedonia can't have two kings," said Hephaestion.

"Not when it was a tiny kingdom. But now it's a world-spanning empire. Perhaps it *needs* two kings. I could certainly draw up a reasoned treatise proposing that. Release it in the name of some anonymous philosopher, get them all arguing." Alexander looked thoughtful. "Wait till your next great victory," added Eumenes. "Preferrably one that has allowed the army plenty of looting."

"That could be some time," said Hephaestion. Alexander shot him a look but Hephaestion wasn't backing down—he was still the one man who could talk back like this to Alexander: "Why not? It's true. It's hard to rack up historic victories in the middle of nowhere. And in any event, the problem isn't whether or not you're king. The problem is what to do about Philip. Not to mention what he's going to do about you."

"Nothing," said Eumenes.

"Nothing?" asked Hephaestion with more than a tinge of disbelief.

"What *can* he do?" Eumenes was smiling now. If there was one thing he knew, it was how the mind of the King of Macedon worked. "More than half the army is under arms on this river, under the crown prince. Even if someone arrived with orders to arrest or kill Alexander, how precisely would they do it?"

Hephaestion didn't reply. Alexander looked as though he'd expected Eumenes to say exactly this. Eumenes had the odd feeling he'd been asked to stay in order to settle an argument. He warmed to the task, gesticulating for emphasis. "The fact of the matter is that professional assassins wouldn't be professional if they didn't want to *survive the deed*. There's not a one out there who would try his luck in the middle of this army. And—more importantly—why would Philip even *want* to kill his son? Who else offers a chance of leading this army to victory? Any move the king makes either leaves this army without its best commander or else results in that army going back to Pella to tear down everything the king has ever built."

Hephaestion nodded slowly. Alexander stood up as though the matter was settled.

That was when they heard it.

Distant shouts—a far-off din, followed by a nearer uproar, a maelstrom of shouting and screams—and then the clanging noise of all the bells atop the masts of fleet, all of them sounding the alarm. An almighty yell went up from all directions—all too much of it the product of voices echoing in from outside the Macedonian perimeter.

The tent-doors to the pavilion flew open. A bodyguard stood there, a grim expression on his face. Before he could open his mouth—

"Bring me my armor," said Alexander.

CHAPTER TEN

Charging through the flaps of the tent, Eumenes found himself looking out upon a sight that made him wonder if his eyes had rebelled against his mind. The fleet had just rounded a bend in the river to behold a barrier that stretched from shore to shore less than half a mile ahead. It was as though the Danube was a harbor with a boom stretched across it—and as Eumenes looked more closely he saw that it was a tangle of boats and wood and metal and all manner of debris, all of it chained together to form a barricade propped in place against the river's current. Tribesmen armed with bows and slings crouched behind a makeshift wall of spikes and wood that stretched across that barricade; as Eumenes watched they began firing at the foremost ships in the fleet.

But Alexander never stopped moving. His bodyguards were strapping on his armor while he bellowed orders. Signal flags ran up the masts of the flagship even as the oarmasters beat a faster time on the drums—Alexander's ship sped up toward the barricade, the rest of the fleet following suit. The soldiers on the shore began running, keeping pace with the fleet.

Alexander stared at them for a moment, frowned—then reeled off another string of orders with an impatience that made it seem he would shove the signal officer aside and run those flags up himself. As he strapped on his rams-head helmet, more flags were going up along each shore, relaying his directives down the chain of command. The squares of infantry and cavalry stopped and began forming up, facing outward, away from the river. Adopting a defensive formation, Eumenes thought... against what?

And then he saw it.

Flames had appeared all along the tops of the hills bordering the river on both sides: a line of fire that blossomed into full-on incandescence and began rolling downhill. They were wagons that the tribesmen had set alight; as hordes of screaming warriors charged in behind the careening wagons, the full extent of the Macedonian predicament became terribly apparent. Trumpets sounded along the river; the infantry squares along the river clustered into an integrated phalanx and then began advancing up the hills toward the oncoming wagons. Alexander had given his orders, deciding in the instant that the situation called for eschewing defense and going straight into an attack formation. Eumenes could only guess as to why. Perhaps so the soldiers could put as much distance between themselves and the river-bank behind them as possible. Perhaps because that was always Alexander's instinct, regardless of the circumstances. The burning wagons would be hitting the phalanxes on both sides of the river within the next thirty seconds.

But the men on the flagship had more pressing concerns. The ships and barges and skiffs now formed the two sides of a V behind Alexander's ship, stretching out toward either bank. The scene on the deck of the flagship was one of controlled chaos. Marines pushed the pavilion overboard, setting up mantlets in its place. Eumenes and Hephaestion crouched behind one such barricade. The latter was ashen-faced. He seemed to be in a state of near-shock.

"You were right about the Scythians," he muttered.

"I'd rather not be," replied Eumenes as a dart shot past him.

"But how—in Zeus' name, *how* did they achieve such surprise?"

Eumenes shrugged. "They must have taken out all our scouts and outriders. Then moved in from all sides."

"We were careless."

Eumenes wasn't about to disagree. Nor was he going to say anything out loud. Particularly when the man most responsible was within earshot: Alexander stood on the main-deck, totally exposed to the fusillade of Scythian darts and arrows streaking past. He was yelling at one of the siege-engineers, who in turn was gesturing frantically at some of his subordinates as they struggled with something below deck. Then Alexander turned to some marines crewing one of the ballistae, began pointing out the field of fire he wanted. Hephaestion looked aghast.

"Can't he keep his fucking head down?"

"I think we both know that's not his style," said Eumenes.

"He could save the fleet right now." Hephaestion was practically sputtering. "Just turn around and go back down the river to regroup."

"But then he'd lose the army."

"The army's already *lost*," spat Hephaestion—and as he said this, the wagons reached the phalanx. With practiced precision, segments of that infantry formation were already sliding aside like beads on an abacus: a last-moment series of orders opening up gaps in the phalanx through which many of the wagons passed, their fires hissing out as they plunged into the Danube.

But there were too many Macedonians and too many wagons for them all to miss. Men flew into the air while others were simply crushed. Wrapped in flames, others ran screaming for the river shore, leaping in as the smoldering wagons crashed after them. The phalanx was reeling; before its gaps could close, the mass of howling barbarians charged into it with a gigantic crash. A pitched battle raged up and down both sides of the Danube. As one, the latter ranks of the phalanx moved in to shore up the gaps torn in the front lines.

"They're holding," said Eumenes. But the phalanx was already in considerable disorder, fighting in conditions about as suboptimal as could be imagined—on ground that was far from level, with enemies already in amidst its ranks. In places, the forest of massed *sarissae* pikes was still intact, a hedgehog on which barbarians impaled themselves as though it were a gigantic pincushion. But in all too many areas, the *sarissae* were down, the swords were out, and hand-to-hand combat was underway. As more barbarians poured down the hills and into the fray, the Macedonians on both banks were gradually being forced backward, remorselessly, toward the river.

But Alexander had never lost a battle—and he clearly had no intention of starting now. Even if this particular fight had begun in the worst way possible, he continued to yell orders. More darts whipped past Eumenes' head; the flagship had almost reached the barbarians' barricade. Eumenes caught a glimpse of a jagged projectile streaking along the deck, just missing Alexander and skewering several marines behind him. More marines moved in to take their place, surging up from below-deck, getting ready to leap onto the barricade as soon as they reached it. Eumenes and Hephaestion led more squads forward from the mantlets to join Alexander. The air was filled with missiles as every barbarian within bowshot concentrated fire on that ship. Those aboard the boat screamed a war-cry—one that was taken up by the rest of the fleet. The barricade filled Eumenes' vision—rows of barbarians along it, waving fists and brandishing weapons. The flagship put on one final burst of speed.

And then they hit.

A terrible, grinding crash: and Eumenes was knocked to the deck. Struggling to his feet, he saw a scene of total shock and confusion. The flagship had embedded itself in the barricade, but failed to break through. Alexander had already leapt over the railing and onto one of the barricade's platforms, where he personally was battling it out with at least six Scythians. Alexander's purple cloak and ram's-head helmet left those tribsemen with no doubt who they were facing, leaving them mad for glory and the chance to end both battle and war right there. Even as Eumenes raced forward to help his prince, a thrown axe sailed past Alexander's head. Alexander whirled aside and struck the man who'd hurled it a gigantic blow, cleaving through helmet, skull and neck in a single stroke just as Eumenes and Hephaestion and several marines reached him—Eumenes thrust his sword through the guts of a Scythian, withdrew it in a spray of shit and blood just in time to parry the blow of another tribesman that almost knocked him from his feet. The tribesman advanced for a second swing, only to be cut down by Alexander himself—who nodded quick acknowledgement at Eumenes before whirling aside, slicing off the arm of a Scythian about to unleash a vicious swipe at Hephaestion. Recovering from the collision, marines were pouring off the flagship, while barbarians simultaneously tried to fight their way onto the boat, sending up a howling cry that was echoed by their fellows along the riverbanks, pressing forward as they sought to drive the Macedonian phalanx to destruction in the Danube.

Then both deck and platforms shuddered anew as the ships to the immediate left and right of the flagship impacted. Men spilled off boats and barricade. The air was almost thick with stones, darts, and arrows. Eumenes took all of this in a moment—and then all the screaming and howling were drowned out by his prince's voice:

"Get away from the flagship!" screamed Alexander. "Get distance! Get some fucking distance!" Still shouting, he led the way along the barricade, putting the flagship behind him even as barbarians continued to leap on board. Eumenes was starting to realize just how heavily outnumbered the Macedonians who had made it onto the barricade were. It was scarcely clear who was attacking who—whether the Macedonians were battling their way along the barricade or whether they were being chased away from their own boats.

But amidst it all Alexander was like a man possessed, wreaking deadly slaughter with his blade while not forsaking the other weapons at his disposal—a swift kick in the crotch to leave a barbarian howling before being run through, a shoulder-charge to knock another into the river. It seemed incredible that so much steel could be thrust at him and still miss, but Alexander was dodging with almost superhuman agility, his body contorting as he danced through the maze of swords and axes thrusting at him. The cost of keeping up with him was considerable—a barbarian's blade grazed Eumenes' shoulder, while a club crashed into his leg; but he kept on fighting, covering his prince's left while Hephaestion covered the right, the three men operating as a brutally effective combat unit that fought their way ever further from the stricken flagship. Only a few marines from that ship were left now—all of them utterly surrounded by screaming Scythians who pushed in from all directions. Somewhere up ahead, Eumenes could see the other ships that had reached the barricade, in similar states of being overwhelmed—to the point where they were now backing their oars, Scythians clinging to them as they tore free of the barricade and reversed into the Danube. Now Alexander and his two lieutenants were the only ones who still fought on. Scythians swarmed in toward them from all sides. As the sparks of clashing steel burnt against Eumenes' face, he found his life reeling past him—sunny days from a childhood in Cardia, teenage years in Macedonia where it seemed like anything was possible, the conquest of Persia where the impossible became everyday occurrence, and finally the growing shadow of Alexander's meglomania—a quest for divinity which had led the prince to push past mortal limits once too often and that would now leave him to die on this godforsaken river, torn apart like a dog. For just a moment, Eumenes caught sight of Alexander's face—still utterly determined, still totally confident. The prince caught his eyes.

"Get down," he said, hurling himself at the feet of the barbarians.

Eumenes and Hephaestion followed suit without hesitation.

Behind them, the Macedonian flagship detonated.

Pieces of wreckage were still raining down as Eumenes hauled himself to his feet to find most of the barbarians had been knocked from theirs. Alexander was already off and running, his boots slamming against backs and heads as he raced pell-mell toward the gaping hole in the barricade where the flagship had been. Flaming wreckage dotted the water. The blackpowder charges that his engineers had rigged in that boat's bowels had done their work well, though Eumenes hated to think what would have happened if they'd gone off prematurely. It seemed like half the barbarians in this section of the barricade had been tossed clean into the water. He and Hephaestion and Alexander charged through those who remained, practically bowling them over as they raced back the way they came. But their momentum was rapidly slowed as more and more barbarians got back into the fray—once more, numbers began to take their toll as the Scythians pressed in upon the prince and his companions. Eumenes found himself face to face with a huge tribesman, who waded in, lashing out with surprising speed, preventing Eumenes from even getting near enough to launch his own blows. But Eumenes couldn't retreat—to do so would be to give up Alexander's flank. The barbarian smashed away with the club, battering in Eumenes' shield, systematically breaking down his guard—until suddenly Alexander lunged leftward with the speed of a striking snake, impaling the barbarian through the throat with a blow so quick it left Eumenes wondering if it had really happened until a jet of warm blood hit him square in the face and the barbarian toppled as though poleaxed.

Another Scythian stepped in behind his dying comrade—only to abruptly stumble and fall, an arrow in his back. All around, it was the same—barbarians dropping as darts and arrows struck them, a rain of missiles flung in from the ships and barges of the Macedonian fleet now sailing through the opening in the barricade. One of the warships swerved hard as soon as it had done so, turning along the barrier's unprotected rear, coming alongside the tangle of metal and wood, close enough for Alexander and his two lieutenants to spring across. A cheer went up as the prince leapt onto the deck—a cry that was taken up by the rest of the vessels in the fleet as the warship shoved off, plowed back out into the Danube. Alexander gestured at the barricade.

"Burn it," he said.

Flaming arrows and projectiles poured like a carpet from the Macedonian ships. Alexander hadn't wanted to set the barricade on fire earlier lest he temporarily render that obstacle even more formidable—but now it no longer mattered. As each ship cleared the barricade, it turned sharply toward one of the two shores, archers and siege-engines discharging fiery bolts into the sea-wall that had seemed so unbeatable mere moments ago. The barricade was alive with fire and screaming—the barbarians dimly visible through wreaths of smoke as they leapt into the water or desperately tried to run back toward the shore. Meanwhile Alexander was conferring with the ship's captain as Eumenes reached him.

"How many horses?" he was asking.

"We've got twenty, sire," replied the captain.

"I'll require three."

The captain nodded—turned his attention back to the helm as the rowers' drumbeat increased in time and the ship surged in toward the shore. Eumenes followed Alexander and Hephaestion as they headed below decks. The horses were there, stamping impatiently, whinnying as they smelt the smoke wafting past them from the nearby barricade. Cavalrymen were already climbing aboard the horses—and Eumenes felt the almost tangible wave of excitement that swept through them as they realized that they were about to fight alongside their prince. Cheers went up; Alexander called out for silence.

"We couldn't turn the ships aside before that barricade," he said, his voice soft, beguiling, utterly convincing. It seemed strange to Eumenes that he would eschew a traditional pep talk for a discussion of tactics—but suddenly it was as though he was simply a regular officer explaining the most basic of operations to his platoon. The men listened raptly, a silence broken only by the rowers calling out time and the screams and war-cries of those outside.

"If we had turned immediately and landed on the shore to support our army there, we'd have just been feeding more men into the slaughter. Deploying cavalry behind infantry would have been pure catastrophe. But now we've broken through. So we can turn their flank. So when the doors go down, follow me and ride like the hounds of Hades are baying at your heels"—he kept talking, his voice growing ever louder, as what had been a tactical analysis swelled into the exhortation that everybody had been expecting all along. A raucous cheer filled the hold—only to be drowned out by the yell of the beat-timers screaming reverse. The deck shook as the ship ground into the shallows—Eumenes was blinded momentarily by a burst of sunlight as the ramp at the front of the ship dropped; even before he'd reattained full vision, he was spurring his horse forward along with all the others—charging down the ramp, splashing through the water and onto the river bank. Alexander galloped out ahead, turning sharply, the stallion he'd chosen the spitting image of his first steed Bucephalus, now long dead in the Afghan hills. Other ships kept hitting the shore; their own ramps dropping as more cavalry poured out into the mass of horses already charging back toward the barricade and the pitched battle still raging further downstream. And now the first of the barges reached the shore—unlike the warships, it didn't need to beach in the shallows. It plowed onto the beach, the entire front side dropping open to reveal men.

Except they weren't men.

Their bodies were as metal as the swords they carried. A clanking noise came from their innards—the noise of the gears inside them. They were one of Aristotle's inventions, and now they were being put to the test. Eumenes knew their inner workings better than any man who wasn't a mechanist, but he still felt a chill ran along his spine as the golems broke into a run that was fast enough to allow them to keep up with the cavalry. Those horses had been acclimated to their presence: trained in long sessions in the fields at the mouth of the Danube not to panic under such circumstances. Now they regarded the golems as they would men. Indeed, those automata had been coated with human sweat to make that adjustment easier. Somehow Eumenes found that fact more disturbing than any other. The golems and cavalry raced along the shore, past the burning barricade. For a moment, Eumenes was entirely surrounded by smoke—and then he emerged from the haze to see the pitched battle raging almost immediately in front of him. The phalanx had been forced back into the water; the men were standing in the shallows, battling ferociously, contesting with the onrushing Scythians for every step—but they had no more room to fall back into. They had lost the asset most precious to battling infantry: maneuverability, and were being hacked down where they stood in the water.

But then the first wave of Macedonian cavalry hit, plowing into the flank of the barbarians like a spear through exposed flesh. Many of the barbarians were packed too tightly against the phalanx to even turn—the Macedonians trampled them underfoot, spearing them like fish as they went. A shout of triumph went up from the phalanx, which surged forward again, finally forcing their way out of the river and back onto the shore. The same scene was being repeated on the far bank of the Danube. The barbarians were turning, breaking into full flight now.

Only to find the golems moving in behind them. While the cavalry had struck the flank, those metal automata had slanted inland. Now they were cutting off the Scythians' retreat—and those barbarians were doing everything they could to get away from creatures that seemed like nothing short of abominations. Eumenes saw more than one barbarian turn back to die under a Macedonian sword, rather than be sent to the underworld by creatures that weren't human. It was like the Scythians' own gods had turned against them. The only way out was further downstream, along the shore. Some of the barbarians headed that way.

Except now the elephants appeared.

Alexander had been too impatient to wait for their full marshalling, so they'd been left behind at the Danube. Eumenes had known that they'd set out, were catching up with the army—but he hadn't realized how close they'd come to doing so. Presumably when the elephant-masters had seen the smoke billowing up ahead, they'd charged forward. Now they'd reached the battle just in time to cut off the Scythians' last route of escape. A despairing cry went up from the barbarians as they watched the grey monstrosities charging toward them, trumpeting furiously. What had started as an almost perfect ambush was quickly becoming an encirclement. What had been a fight became pure slaughter as the elephants began trampling Scythians beneath their feet. Eumenes remembered very little of what followed. For long minutes he was transported back again to the plains of Asia, when the Macedonians had wreaked such havoc amidst the Persian hosts. It was the same way now—the rise and fall of steel, the scream of men, the wash of blood. Glory days had come again. And glory meant the blood of enemies. The Macedonians set about their task with relish.

Hot, pitiless wind blew along a barren shore that had no beginning and no end. The army had left Cyrene more than two weeks earlier. The journey to that city had been bad enough. The last Greek outpost on the African desert, four hundred miles west of the now-renamed city of Alexandria at the head of the Nile delta: it wasn't even in Egypt. It was in a place called Libya. Men were starting to die of thirst even before they got there.

None of which had boded well for venturing west of Cyrene. There was absolutely nothing out here. Not even a road, unless you could dignify the hardened strip of sand between desert and beach with that title. Which the messenger certainly wasn't about to do. Not for the first time, he cursed the gods that he'd gotten swept up into this crazy march. Though it wasn't like he'd had a choice—he was a soldier, he did what he was ordered. And as a courier, that meant you either carried messages to their intended destination or you waited to be given such messages.

He fell into the latter category now, thanks to the events of the last several weeks. He had made all haste down the Levant and across the Sinai, had arrived at the Nile bedraggled and exhausted, whereupon he'd immediately been ushered into the presence of Craterus, commander of the Macedonian forces in Egypt. That bear of a man had broken the seal, unfurled the scroll, read the message with a growing smile that afforded the messenger no little relief, since this was the part where those who bore bad tidings sometimes got carved into pieces or fed to crocodiles. The latter type of death was quite fashionable in this part of the world. The priests of Egypt had resorted to it often, and all of Macedonia had heard how Alexander had employed it himself to such dramatic effect only a few months before.

But for the messenger there were no such punishments—only the wine and refreshments that were the reward of one who had brought good news. That suited him just fine. Cavorting in the whorehouses of Alexandria suited him even better. One never had time for such distractions while en route. Especially because such diversions might be the artifice of those seeking to intercept the message. No courier could afford to take to strange beds while on the job. Once the destination was reached, of course, it was a different story. Pleasure was something to wallow in; one never knew when one would be able to do so next.

The messenger's relief lasted only as long as he was in the dark about the contents of the correspondence he'd been carrying. Within hours it was all over the city: they were marching west. They were going to cross the African desert and capture Carthage. At first the messenger figured that the rumor-mill had gotten it wrong. Or that he'd gotten so drunk in the bars and brothels he was starting to hear things. But everyone had the same news, and by dawn the messenger had a splitting hangover and the sickening knowledge that he'd been the one who brought the tidings that set all this madness in motion.

Because madness was what it was, of course. There was no way an army could reach Carthage without the navy the Macedonians didn't have. Nor did the common soldiers have any knowledge of geography, because if they did they wouldn't have been so happy about marching again. Egypt had given them a chance to rest, and now they were hungry for more booty. Too bad they had no idea how far away it was. Though they were starting to get it now.

Of course, the messenger had known all along. Distances weren't something his profession was ignorant of. Even if he didn't know precisely how long it was to Carthage—even if he'd never be called upon to deliver a message to it—he knew just how impossible it would be to ever reach it. Not that it really mattered. It was too bad that Macedonia felt the need to throw a whole army away in the same harebrained way that Cambyses of Persia had once done, but ultimately it wasn't the messenger's concern. Taking word of the expedition's departure back to Pella was.

Except it wasn't.

Two days later, with all of Memphis buzzing with the marshalling of the army for the march into the western desert, there was a loud knocking on the whorehouse door. The messenger paid no attention until bodyguards of Craterus himself entered his own room and ordered that he report for duty. The messenger extricated himself from the arms of the less-than-conscious woman he'd hired earlier that day, splashed cold water on his face and went with the bodyguards. He figured that he'd be heading back to Pella within the hour.

No such luck. Instead he was ordered to join the headquarters of Craterus. That's when his worst fears were confirmed. He wasn't going back to Macedonia at all. He was going with the army to certain death. His only hope now was that he was one of the first messengers to be dispatched back to Egypt to say how terrible everything was going and beg for reinforcements. After he'd delivered *that* message, if he was sent back to the expedition again, he figured he'd salute, say yes sir, and then promptly desert. That was the one advantage of being a messenger—no one kept tabs on you between stops. And he'd seen plenty of places he could hide during his various travels—various out-of-the-way towns, seaports, hillside forts, forgotten temples. It didn't matter, as long as he could go incognito. Something he was good at, since messengers didn't exactly advertise themselves while on the road. He spoke several languages, and could pass for a native in more than one place. Blending in with the local inhabitants was a specialty of his.

But the the only inhabitants of the desert were crazed savages who stalked the army by day and picked off stragglers by night. *Berbers,* they were called. There'd be no blending in with them. The messenger wondered where they were coming from—how they survived out in those tractless wastes. Presumably there were oases out there. Everyone had heard of the one at Siwah—the one that contained the god that had spoken with Alexander and told him he was one too—but that place was fortified and civilized. These barbarians must be coming from oases that no one knew of, from places deep within the desert. Places that would remain unseen to civilized eyes. It wasn't like anyone was about to ride off and look.

"Why the fuck not?" said Perdiccas.

"What good would it do us?" said Craterus.

The two men stared at each other across the table. A flagon of wine sat between them. The torches that lit the tent were burning low. Craterus sighed—picked up the flagon, refilled his goblet. He downed half of it, set it heavily back on the table. Gazed at the still-silent Perdiccas.

"I'll answer that for you," he continued. "None at all. We'd lose every man who rode off into the desert. And that's exactly what these savages *want* us to do."

"But how else do we stop them?" Deep circles underlay Perdiccas' eyes. He wasn't getting much sleep. The march was taking its toll on him. Much as he hated to admit it, so was the lack of Alexander, who would have known how to get this army to do the impossible. Sure, he'd himself said that a march on Carthage would be pure folly. But that was back in that conference chamber in Memphis. Now things had changed. They had a specific plan of operations. But having a plan was one thing, executing upon it was another. And neither man was Alexander.

Much though Craterus was trying to be.

"We *don't* stop them," he said. "They're going to keep raiding, they're going to keep picking off our men here and there. That's how attrition works. Besides, you've got to keep your eye on the big picture. We're losing a lot more to thirst than we are to raiders."

Now it was Perdiccas' turn to reach for the wine. "That's supposed to make me feel better?" he asked.

"It's not supposed to make you *feel* anything," replied Craterus. "You're the commander out here. Second only to me. So rise above these petty emotions. Armies lose men every day even while they're just on garrison duty. Put an army in the desert, the rate increases. The only question is whether the rate's acceptable."

"I'm starting to think it's not."

"Again, that's your feeling." Craterus shoved figure-laden papers across the table. "These say differently."

Perdiccas scanned the casualty rates. His eyes widened. "Are you nuts? These show a loss of—"

"That's among the mercenaries. The auxiliaries. The foreign hirelings. Not among the Macedonian core. We've scarcely dropped below the ten thousand we started out with. Meaning we still have a phalanx that can roll through anything. So the Persian conscripts are dying like flies. So what? That's what they were meant to do."

"No one explained that to them."

"You'd make a shit recruiting sergeant." Craterus' laugh rattled around the tent like some disembodied and perverse extension of himself. Perdicas smiled wanly, but all he could think of was what lay beyond the tent. The largest desert known to man....

"Cheer up," said Craterus. "We'd never have conquered Persia with that attitude."

"Persia had cities. Not like this—"

"What do you think Carthage is?"

"It's not taking the city that I'm worried about," said Perdiccas. "It's getting there—"

"You *should* worry about taking the city. It's almost as bad as Athens. Three massive walls, each one higher than the previous one so the defenders can rain shit down on whoever's managed to storm the wall beneath them. And the harbor isn't even on the sea."

Perdiccas threw back some more wine, tried to clear his head. "What do you mean, the harbor isn't—how can a harbor not be on the sea? How else could it be a harbor?"

"Because it's a *lake*. They dug a channel through the city and walled it off and dug a huge basin and put the harbor there."

"So their navy is utterly secure."

"It is."

"Alright, genius. So how *do* we take Carthage?"

Craterus laughed another of those booming laughs. "You see? Suddenly you believe it too—we'll make it there after all. You're such a born pessimist that you can't believe we won't live to face the most unsolvable problem of them all."

"Cut the shit. How do we solve it?"

Craterus drained his goblet with a flourish. "There's no fortress strong enough to defend against the enemy within," he said.

"That didn't exactly work at Athens, did it?"

Craterus shrugged. "Carthage is on the the western edge of Athens' empire. Which was always a ramshackle structure to begin with, and is now falling apart. The latest messenger brought reports that Syracuse is on the brink of revolution."

Perdiccas looked skeptical. "That could mean a lot of things."

"Of course it could. But if Syracuse is precarious, Carthage is even more so. The Phoenicians have no love for Athens."

"And even less for Alexander. After what he did to Tyre—"

"It's not like the Phoenicians are a united front. Carthage is the daughter city. So sure, she mourns the destruction of her founding city. But now she's pre-eminent among the Phoenician cities, and you'd better believe there's more than a few Carthaginian merchants who are grateful for that fact. And there's even more of them who are chafing for liberation from Athenian rule. They know full well they should be the dominant power in the western Mediterranean, not Athens."

"Nor us?"

"No need to disabuse them of their dreams so quickly. Liberation before conquest. Romance before rape. You know how it goes."

Perdiccas nodded. He was used to Craterus' crude analogies. "And Alexander? You said you'd had word from him?"

"Indeed. He went up the Danube. Just like he said he would."

"I didn't think he really was crazy enough to do that."

"Said the man who's three weeks into Libya."

"Very funny."

"So halfway up the river, the Scythians sprung an ambush."

"And?"

"Oh, he won of course. Annihilated them. Our garrisons along the lower Danube reported thousands upon thousands of barbarian bodies drifting down the river. Soldiers went *thirsty* waiting for the river to clear. Those primitives won't fuck with him now. After that he took the title of king—"

"King of the barbarians?"

"King of Macedonia."

"What?"

"Well, co-king, anyway."

"What did Philip do?"

"What could he do? I gather Alexander already tried to kill him, and it failed."

Perdiccas looked incredulous. "This was all in the latest message?"

"No, that bit was scrawled in code in the margin."

"By who?"

"Who else could make an unofficial annotation to an official record?"

"You don't mean—Eumenes?"

Craterus nodded. Grinned. Poured more wine.

Perdiccas shook his head. "Why should that Greek impart such information to you? It could be his hide—"

"Let's just say I've done him one or two favors. And vice versa. Just because we despise each other doesn't mean we can't cooperate."

Perdiccas looked thoughtful. "Do you think he's mad?"

"Eumenes? He's the sanest man I've ever—"

"I'm talking about Alexander."

Craterus gave him a long stare. "Now *that* is a dangerous question."

"The answer might be even more so."

"How much wine have we had?" Craterus peered blearily at the flagon. "We'll feel this in the morning."

"I will." Perdiccas eyed Craterus' bulk. "You'll be just fine."

"Save for saying what was on my mind. Look, the man thinks he's a god."

"Precisely why I'm asking."

"Well—maybe he's right."

"You really think so?"

"Not being a god myself, I can't say for sure."

Perdiccas rolled his eyes. "If the priests at Siwah hadn't told him what he wanted to hear, he'd probably have torched the whole place."

"Probably. But isn't this conversation academic?"

"No more academic than him saying he's now king. This stuff matters."

"Not out here it doesn't. We're in the middle of the desert and we have to get through to the other side. After that we can worry about—"

"We'll have to start slaughtering the camels soon," said Perdiccas.

"Despite the diggers?"

"We've only got three left."

Craterus nodded. The expedition had been outfitted with machinery sent down from Pella and supposedly developed by Aristotle himself: contraptions that belched smoke and dug through sand, boring shafts through the desert, down to where the water was. Such equipment was part of the edge that Alexander believed would carry the expedition through to victory. But either Aristotle's conception had been faulty, or the engineers had botched it, because they weren't very reliable. The army had started with twenty of them, and the ones that remained wouldn't last much longer. Worst, they needed water to run, and were starting to use more than they were providing. Craterus gulped more wine down, belched.

"How many camels *do* we have?" he asked.

"Two thousand," replied Perdiccas.

"Walking water tanks, glutted on the Nile. Just slice one open and drink and eat your fill."

"I'm not going to be the one to make the first cut."

"You won't need to. Leave that to a common soldier."

Perdiccas smiled ruefully. "A common *Macedonian* soldier."

Craterus nodded. "Like I said, keeping our boys moving is the main goal. If they have to, they'll drink the blood of everybody else to stay alive."

"Speaking of blood, I heard a rumor."

Craterus shook his head—he looked as bleary-eyed as Perdiccas felt. "I'm either too drunk to follow you or you're too drunk to make any sense."

"I mean I've heard there's a bloodline at issue here."

"Ah." Craterus raised an eyebrow. "I've heard the same thing."

"From Eumenes?"

"Or from your sources."

"*My* sources? What are you talking about?—back in Pella?"

"I know about your correspondence with Ptolemy, if that's what you mean."

Perdiccas tried to mask his surprise, but to no avail. He decided that there was no point in denial. "How in Hades' name do you know about that?"

"Because I've *read* it. Because like I said earlier: you're only second-in-command. I'm Alexander's marshal, and this is my army. And I know everything that goes on here and don't you forget it—"

"Fine," said Perdiccas. "You're the boss. Relax."

But Craterus had drunk more than his fill—had crossed that point where alcohol stopped loosening tongues and started riding roughshod on them instead. "Relax? You're telling *me* to relax? You bring up treasonous questions and then you raise the question of *bloodlines*—which is even worse than treason. It's pure stupidity. It's fucking madness."

Perdiccas wasn't backing down. He knew how to handle Craterus when he was in one of these moods. That's why he'd been the man's deputy for five years. They were friends and yet they weren't. It was what being a member of Macedonian high command was all about. "Treason's treason," he said mildly. "Nothing's worse than that. But nothing I'm saying is—"

"Zeus, what *are* you saying? Why don't you just come out and say it? The last Persian princess is on the run, and Alexander has to find her because she's a way bigger problem than she should be."

"And he can thank himself for that."

Craterus stared at him. "So you know all of it," he muttered.

Perdiccas nodded slowly.

CHAPTER ELEVEN

They reached Syracuse at night.

It wasn't just a matter of minimizing the number of eyes that might be watching. It was also because they had no clue as to what was going on within the city. So they snuck past Syracuse after sundown—the lights of the town a distant glow on the horizon, framed by the mountains of Sicily set against the rising Moon. Besides Lugorix, none of them had ever been this far west. They were in terra incognita now, relying on the dark and their low profile on the waterline to keep them from being spotted, the lights of the Great Harbor fading as they made their way down the coast. The indirect approach didn't surprise Lugorix. There were more discreet ways into the city that to just sail right in. Apparently Barsine had one in mind.

It had been a long strange trip. They'd stuck to the coast, sailing around the southern portion of Greece—the Peloponnese, once the center of Spartan power—before crossing the Adriatic to Megale Hellas, the Athenian enclave that encompassed the Greek cities of southern of Italy. They'd made landfall on a forested coast adjacent to Tarentum, the foremost of those southern cities, on the heel of the Italian boot, where they'd filled the ship's holds with the wood the engines burnt. Matthias had even shot some deer to supplement their endless diet of fish and beans. But they'd never entered Tarentum itself—it contained a considerable Athenian garrison, and Barsine was of the opinion that showing up in the harbor in a ship like the *Xerxes* was a great way to get the boat impounded and themselves arrested.

Presumably that meant she had no contacts in Tarentum. Maybe she didn't have any in Syracuse either, because now the the lights of the city had disappeared entirely as they continued to move south. But staying too close to the shore was never without risk—Lugorix kept his eyes peeled while Matthias took depth soundings. It was a task made somewhat more difficult by the fact that he and Lugorix weren't talking. They hadn't been talking since the argument on the deck during the departure from Athens. Lugorix knew his friend was seething with jealousy that Barsine was fond of him... he'd tried to explain to Matthias that part of the reason for that fondness was that he had no aspirations to bed the Persian, but that just made Matthias all the madder.

Besides, Matthias knew damn well what Lugorix thought of his crush on Barsine—and he'd finally realized who Barsine reminded Lugorix of, knew the real reason Lugorix didn't want Matthias anywhere near her. The situation was way too complicated. They were both captivated by Barsine for very different reasons. So now Matthias shoved past Lugorix, dropped a weighted rope into the water, called out readings down to Damitra and Barsine as they steered the ship along the coast, navigating past a series of peninsulas, and down a long stretch of rocky shore that gradually rose up into cliffs. Spray dashed itself against those cliffs.

But all at once the ship turned straight in toward them.

"What the hell?" said Lugorix. Matthias began yelling at the women below to turn aside.

But then he stopped as he saw what they were steering toward.

To say the cove was hidden would be a bit of an overstatement. But it was certainly tough to spot, a gap in the cliffs that you really had to be looking for to see. Nestled in that cove was a harbor all its own. Torchlight illuminated shacks; more lights gleamed in caves higher up those hills.

"We made it," said Barsine as she climbed onto the deck.

"What is this place?" asked Matthias.

"Smugglers' cove," she said. "It's filled with traders—"

"Criminals," said Matthias.

"—men of commerce trying to avoid the Athenian tribute. Which, as you might have heard, is considerable. And which has to be paid by any ship entering an Athenian port."

"But this looks like a more-or-less permanent settlement," said Matthias.

"So?"

"So you're telling me the authorities in Syracuse don't know about it?"

"Of course they know about it," said Barsine.

"And they're bribed *not* to know about it," called up Damitra.

"Oh," said Matthias.

"*Oh,*" mimicked Barsine. "Paying the bribes is often cheaper than paying the tribute. And for the officials doing the collecting, it's often a damn sight more profitable. Every port in the Athenian Empire's got at least a few of these places. And no one at any of these places breaks the code: no one asks any questions. That should give us at least a few days."

"So who do we bribe?"

"We don't," said Barsine. "I left that to my friends."

A roof slid over the ship as it pulled inside a watershed set alongside one of the docks. Men were in that shed working over a trireme. One of them looked—and turned, did a double take. He leapt from the trireme to the dockside, came over to the *Xerxes*. His skin was dark, his black beard was sharpened to a fine point, and though he wore the dirty tunic of a worker, he carried himself like a man wearing much finery. He addressed Barsine in Persian.

And then fell to his knees in front of her.

"Hey," said Lugorix, "relax."

But the man did not. He babbled on and on and it got a little embarrassing. Finally Barsine stepped forward, and raised the man to his feet before kissing him lightly on each cheek. He looked like he was going to die of happiness. Matthias looked like he was going to expire from rage.

"This is Mardonius," said Barsine. "A Persian merchant."

"It's an honor," said Mardonius in Greek that (Lugorix had to admit) was far better than his own.

"You're not a merchant," said Matthias. "You're a spy."

If Mardonius took umbrage, he didn't show it. "I'm a businessman," said Mardonius. "And you must be the mercenaries."

"Riiiight," said Matthias, sounding a tad offended.

Mardonius seemed genuinely puzzled. "Are your services not those of the sword? Are you not getting paid for them?"

"We are," said Lugorix.

"So then you're mercenaries."

"And *you're* the one with information about Aristotle," said Lugorix.

Mardonius glanced at Barsine. "Direct," he said. "I like it."

"I don't," snapped Barsine. "We should have this conversation in—"

"—Persian?" asked Matthias. "I don't think so."

Damitra climbed onto the deck. "Are the men making trouble?" she asked.

"No more than usual," said Barsine. Turning back to Mardonius. "Where is he?"

"I don't know," said Mardonius. And then, as her face darkened: "But I know who does."

Syracuse was a blaze of color and smells and noise, the sprawling rock of the Epipolae plateau towering along its western side. Skirting along the very summit of those heights were the main defensive walls and the houses of some of the wealthiest men in the city—but fortunately the rendezvous with the man who knew the whereabouts of the man in question didn't require venturing up onto over-policed high ground. Instead they rode among the throngs in the packed eastern district of Tyche, Barsine wearing a loose hooded cloak that concealed everything about her, including her gender. There were a lot of Athenian soldiers in the crowd. And the harbor was packed with Athenian ships, far more than when Lugorix was here last. It was a full-scale armada—hundreds upon hundreds of ships riding at anchor in front of the Ortygia: the vast citadel Athens had built on the promontory that stretched across the harbor.

"Why is it called the Ortygia?" asked Lugorix.

"How bad *is* your Greek?" Mathias scoffed. "Ortygia means 'little island'."

"But it's a promontory."

"There's a channel dug through the far side of that strip of land, with some fortified bridges across it. So actually it *is* an island, jackass."

"It's also the key to Syracuse," said Barsine. "Nothing gets in or out of that harbor without the blessing of those who command in the Ortygia. Which is why it's full of Athenians."

"So is this whole city," muttered Matthias.

"They seem to have sent a good chunk of their fleet here. Trying to keep pace with Alexander's move westward, no doubt." Then, spotting the place she'd been looking for: "There it is."

The Gorgon's Locks was one of many dockside bars. A stylized picture of Medusa and her snakes hung over the door. Lugorix shoved on through and into a crowded drinking hole filled with sailors and whores. He made his way to a corner table while Matthias ordered three cups of wine. That done, they sat down to wait.

"Are you sure this is the right place?" said Lugorix.

"This is where Mardonius said to go," said Barsine, sipping her wine.

From the look on Matthias' face, that fact didn't fill him with confidence. Nor did the fact that five minutes after they'd arrived, the door opened and a squad of Athenian marines entered the room. They ignored the dirty looks from the locals, and settled down to drinking. Before long they were in the midst of an uproarious party, cavorting with the bar's women and calling for more rounds. Lugorix eyed those girls, wishing he could get involved. There was one with red hair and a freckled nose who reminded him of a beauty whose favors he'd enjoyed in Alcibidia. She was almost certainly dead now. As was that city: he'd heard that the fraction of it that hadn't been destroyed had been renamed *Alexandria*.

"May I join you?" said a voice.

Lugorix looked up to see a young man standing over the table. His blond hair bordered on the golden, and was done up in a ponytail that mirrored his longish nose. The overall effect was unflattering, yet somehow magnetic, almost in the manner of a court jester. Or a trickster... he sat down next to them—looked straight at Barsine.

"My lady," he said.

"Is it that obvious?"

"To me, deceptions usually are."

"Who are you, friend?" asked Lugorix—with maybe a little bit too much emphasis on the latter word. The man smiled.

"Fortunately for you, I am. Mardonius and I have done much business with each other. Always through intermediaries, of course. I doubt he even knows who he's been dealing with."

"Neither do we," said Matthias dryly.

"Easily remedied," said the man. "My name's Agathocles."

Barsine' eyes widened in recognition. "The outlaw," she said.

"I prefer to think of myself as a patriot."

"Would someone care to fill me in," said Matthias.

"This man's a key figure in the resistance against Athens," said Barsine. She glanced at the Athenian soldiers yukking it up nearby, leaned forward. "Aren't you taking a risk in meeting us out in the open?"

"This is my city," said Agathocles. "I move where I like, and I don't always look like this. Besides, the Athenians have more to worry about right now then trying to round up the insurgents in Syracuse. That fleet out there isn't here on my account, I can assure you."

Barsine nodded. "What are Alexander's latest whereabouts?"

"No one knows for sure." And then, as Barsine frowned: "But word is that there was a great battle on the Danube, and his phalanxes and ships wreaked a bloody slaughter among the Scythians. And there's a second Macedonian army as well, moving across Africa."

"I hadn't heard anything about that," said Barsine.

"Well, you're hearing it now. It's not looking good for Athens. All the more so as there continue to be reports of division among the archons back at Athens."

"You see this as the moment to throw off Athens' yoke," said Barsine.

"The Pax Athenica made my city's people very prosperous—almost enough to make them forget about the glories that were Syracuse. But the war has reminded my countrymen of the perils of entrusting their destiny to that of another power. Our cause has been bolstered every day—all the more so now that the harbor is filling up with an Athenian fleet."

"And where are those ships going?"

"Reinforcing Carthage? Bolstering Massilia? Landing troops behind the Macedonian lines of advance? Staying here and making my life miserable? I don't know. Why don't you ask the viceroy, Cleon? He's up in the Orgytia citadel and I'm sure he'd be only too happy to discuss Athenian strategy with you."

"Very funny," said Lugorix.

"Well, you're going there anyway, so why not?"

"Excuse me?" said Matthias.

"I said you're going into the Ortygia. Though truth to tell, you should probably stay away from Cleon. He's a bit of an asshole, from what I hear."

From the look on Matthias' face, that was precisely what he was starting to think of Agathocles. "And we're going into the Ortygia because…?"

Barsine nodded her head, understanding. "Because that's where Aristotle is."

Agathocles nodded. "He reached Syracuse about a month ago—snuck into the city incognito—and hid out with some wealthy friends of his at one of the well-heeled villas up on the Epipolae. Nice neighborhood, you know the sort—the best private tutors for the kids and the latest sex-toys for the wives. But all of a sudden, Athenian marines swept in and busted everyone in the villa. Textbook special forces raid. They rounded up everyone in the place—there were at least a couple of families in there—and took them all into the Ortygia. Aristotle among them. He's been locked up ever since."

"Wonderful," said Mathias.

Agathocles chuckled. "It *is*—from the Athenian perspective. They need him, but this way they don't have to advertise their need to the mob back in Athens—don't have to broadcast the fact that he's assisting them against the Macedonians."

"How do we know he's assisting them?" asked Barsine.

"I doubt they're giving him much of a choice. Besides, doesn't he hate Alexander now?"

"Doesn't mean he's supporting Athens," said Barsine. "He may just want Hades to take hindmost. Why else was he hiding out from everybody?"

Agathocles shook his head. "If he was hiding out from *everybody*, he would have left the Athenian domains altogether."

"Maybe that was his next step."

"Enough," said Lugorix. Everyone looked at him. "All that matters at the moment is getting into the Ortygia."

"Which is supposed to be impregnable," said Matthias.

"Let those who dwell there think that," grinned Agathocles. He pulled a piece of paper out of his pocket and slid it across the table to Barsine. "That's a map of the citadel," he said. "Including the section where Aristotle is being held." His voice veered into the sardonic. "All you need are two brave strong men to infiltrate the place tonight and get him."

Matthias looked at Barsine. "I never agreed to raise my hand against Athenians."

"Try living under their rule for decades," said Agathocles.

"My people once did. It wasn't that bad, actually. Don't they allow you to have an Assembly?"

"This city's Assembly's a joke," said Agathocles. "It's not allowed to take any decisions worth the name."

"Never mind the politics," said Barsine. "Athens is divided against itself. They can't be trusted to resist the Macedonian onslaught. Look at what happened in Egypt. For all we know this viceroy—Cleon—is in the pay of

Macedonia." She turned to Lugorix and Matthias. "This is the part where you earn your silver."

"Fine," said Lugorix.

Agathocles took a swig of his drink. "Good luck," he said.

"Fuck you very much," muttered Matthias.

Unless one planned to turn invisible and sneak across one of the fortified bridges, the only way to get into the Ortygia was by water. And the only way to go by water that wasn't total suicide was to approach via the seaward side. There was simply too much traffic in the harbor, too much of it clustered near the citadel itself. But out in the Mediterranean the waves were high and the currents were strong, and Lugorix could think of a million places he'd rather be—pretty much anywhere that didn't involve paddling right next to Matthias in the middle of the night, holding onto what amounted to a piece of driftwood. But that was how they were staying afloat, and staying together, gradually closing in on the towering hulk of the Ortygia. Its walls came right down to the water itself. There was no beach, nowhere to land. But there were water-gates through which boats could enter. None of them were large. All of them were shut.

Except for the one that was underwater.

Agathocles had pointed it out on his map—Matthias had memorized the exact spot while Lugorix looked on, marvelling at the way in which civilized people used paper to communicate. The real question was where Agathocles had got the map, but the Syracusan demurred when asked, simply saying he had his sources. Those sources were obviously inside the Ortygia; not only did have the layout of this section of the wall, but they knew the position of the tides along it. This particular gate was visible during low tide and covered at the high.

That was why Matthias and Lugorix were now floating in toward it, their driftwood in danger of being crushed against the wall by the waves that slapped against it. The tension simmering between them had subsided as the promise of combat grew closer. Above all else, they were professionals, and capable of acting like a team even when they felt like nothing of the kind. Through the noise of those waves they could hear sentries talking on the lower sections of the battlement. But those sentries were looking for ships, not men harebrained enough to be swimming out in the Mediterranean. Only meters from the wall now, Matthias let go of the driftwood and dove, Lugorix following him through the inky blackness, his eyes stinging with the salt—but ahead of him he could see the shadowy form of Matthias, lit up now by torchlight filtering through the water. They had swum straight through the water-gate—and were now emerging, sputtering, into an interior harbor. A stone jetty loomed before them. An Athenian guard stood on the edge of that jetty, staring at them as though they were mermaids.

Then he drew his sword, and opened his mouth to scream the alarm.

He never gave it voice. Lugorix seized the legs of the guard and dragged him into the water. The guard tried to drive his sword at Lugorix, but the Gaul had already grabbed that sword-arm, twisted it sharply—the sword sunk into the water. The guard was sinking too, dragged down by the weight of his armor, trying to fend off Lugorix's hands around his neck—but he was out of air. Lugorix grabbed his head and twisted. The guard hit the bottom and stayed there. Lugorix kicked off the stone floor, propelled himself back to the surface. Matthias was now standing on that jetty, looking down at him.

"Good work," he said.

Lugorix said nothing, just pulled himself onto the jetty, breathing heavily while he caught his wind. He had his axe strapped onto his back but that was it: both he and Matthias were entirely bereft of clothes—the less encumbrance, the better for the swim. And it had been quite a swim: one of Mardonius' men had taken them out in a fishing skiff, before depositing them about quarter of a mile off the Mediterranean-side of the Ortygia. Now they needed to find Aristotle.

But first they had to find something to wear. Or more precisely, guards' uniforms that weren't soaking wet. Meaning they had to find more guards. Again, Agathocles had shown them which direction to take. From the jetty, they went down stairs, walking through a series of torchlit tunnels. Some of those tunnels adjoined on storage chambers, but everything stored within was useless to the two intruders—just supplies to enable the fortress to withstand a long siege. That was when they heard voices coming from down the corridor—emanating from a lit room just ahead.

"Shit," muttered Matthias.

"Let's go a different way," whispered Lugorix.

"We can't. There's a storehouse of armor and weaponry just beyond this room."

"Then let's go through 'em," said Lugorix—and strode into the room.

The three Athenian soldiers throwing dice within looked up from the table around which they sat. The last thing they were expecting to see striding into the room was a naked Gaul carrying a huge axe—and then bringing that axe down on the first man's head, splitting him almost in half. Matthias was already lunging forward, pulling that dead guard's sword from its scabbard, kicking over the table as he did so, sending the other two guards sprawling—and then leaping at them, stabbing one repeatedly with his comrade's sword. The third man turned to flee—but Matthias hurled the sword into his back. He fell onto the floor, badly wounded.

"Now we got uniforms," said Lugorix.

"We need clean ones," replied Matthias as he bent down beside the wounded soldier. "Where's Aristotle?" he asked.

"I don't know… what you're talking about," replied the man.

"The scientist," said Matthias.

"The what?"

"The *sorcerer*," said Lugorix.

"In the northwest tower," muttered the soldier. "At least that's where I think he is. No one's seen him in days. Only the bodyguards of the viceroy are allowed in."

"Looks like they'll have to make an exception," said Matthias as Lugorix ran the man through. He didn't want to, but he couldn't see that they had much of a choice. Dressed in uniforms, they proceeded through the rest of that particular section of the basement and up some stairs into the main part of the fortress. Lugorix grimaced in his armor—the breastplate was a tight fit, since Greeks rarely came in his size. But their helmets were classic hoplite fare, their faces only partially visible beneath the cheek-plates and nose-guard. That suited the two men just fine as they walked down corridors and up more stairs. The fortress was quite a place—almost a city in its own right. And there was enough diversity of weapons so that no one paid attention to his axe. Making it all the easier for two interlopers to proceed with anonymity up stairs and ramps, climbing ever higher. Occasionally they encountered other guards. But no one challenged them.

Until they reached the northwest tower. The two men who stood in front of the barred entrance wore the purple sashes of the viceroy's bodyguards.

"Move along," said one impatiently.

"By all means," said Matthias, whipping the edge of his sword across the guard's throat. Lugorix was already hacking down the second man. Then Matthias lifted the bars of the door and opened it.

"We need to hurry," he said. Lugorix pulled both bodies through the doorway. Matthias closed the door behind him, and then the two men raced up the spiral stairs within. This tower was several stories high; at the top was a ladder that led to the roof, as well as another barred door. Matthias pointed at the ladder—Lugorix nodded. He climbed up that ladder and peered through the opening.

The single soldier on the rooftop had his back to him, was leaning against the battlements. That made it easy: Lugorix put down the axe, drew a dagger, uncoiled himself onto the roof like a snake—and then lunged forward, stabbing the man from behind while grabbing his mouth to ensure he made no sound. Lugorix then released the body, let it drop to the roof. Peering over the edge of the battlements, he could much of the fortress sprawling out beneath him—the city itself beyond that, a vast grid of torchlight and lanterns.

"What the hell are you doing up there?" asked Matthias.

"Telling you to shut up," said Lugorix. He pulled himself away from the view, climbed back down the ladder. Matthias stood there impatiently—then turned to the door, pulled back the bar and swung it open.

The room within was filled with parchments and scrolls. A young woman sat on the floor, intent on a collection of gears and shafts spread out all around her. Her lips had been painted as black as her hair and clothes, and her skin was a pale white at odds with the redness of her irises. She wore a silver ring in her nose, and her arms were covered with tattoos. She was, beyond doubt, the strangest woman Lugorix had ever seen.

And she was just getting started.

"Who are you?" she asked.

Matthias recovered quickly enough. "We're looking for Aristotle," he said.

"He's dead."

"You're joking."

"He was my father, asshole. Think I'd joke about that?"

"He was—your, um…"

"That's right. Which, since you seem to be kind of slow, makes me his daughter." She stood up. "The name's Eurydice. How about you?"

Lugorix figured he'd better step in before Matthias fucked this up any further. "I'm Lugorix. This is Matthias. We were sent to rescue your father."

Her eyes narrowed. "Sent by who?"

"Her name's Barsine. She's a Persian noblewoman with a lot of money who—"

Eurydice cut him off impatiently. "I know that bitch."

"You what?" Matthias again.

"My father corresponded with her. Might have known she was behind this. Well, you can go back and tell her she can find another plan to stop Alexander. My father died of fever two weeks ago."

"I'm sorry," said Lugorix. He didn't know what else to say. Eurydice just looked scornful.

"*You're* sorry? Not only is my father dead, but this prick of a viceroy—Cleon—is convinced that I can be useful to him anyway. His scientists keep asking me annoying questions, and they keep getting pissed when they don't understand my answers. Which is frustrating as all hell. Not to mention that Cleon himself is a fucking pervert. Won't stop staring at my—"

"Come with us," said Lugorix.

"What?"

"Come with us," he repeated. "If you stay here, you'll be a prisoner of Athens for the rest of your life. Come with us, and you can listen to what Barsine has to say and then do whatever you want."

"Besides, Barsine isn't really a bitch," said Matthias.

"Maybe she isn't on her good days." Eurydice shrugged. "She comes across a little snotty on paper though. Whatever. I suppose it's better than cooling my heels here." She started picking out some of the scrolls, tossing them into a satchel. Then she scooped up the gears and threw them in as well. After which she turned to the desk and began rummaging through it.

"We don't have all night," said Matthias.

"I don't *need* all night," snarled Eurydice. "Just another few minutes."

"You won't even get that," said a voice. They all whirled as part of the wall slid away to reveal a hidden corridor. Several Athenian archers stood in that doorway, their bows trained on the three who stood within. A weaselly looking captain stood beside them, laughing.

"And here I was thinking it was going to be a slow night," he said.

"Demetrius," said Eurydice. "You bastard."

"I won't deny that," said the captain.

"You've been spying on me the whole time I've been here."

Demetrius smiled. "One peephole and one false door: I'm surprised it took a clever girl like you so long to figure that out."

"Fuck *me*," snarled Eurydice.

"You know how much I'd love to. Now are your would-be liberators going to drop their weapons or am I going to have my men use theirs?"

Lugorix had already calculated the distances and vectors. They'd been caught on the far side of the room. He knew he could down at least one of them by hurling Skullseeker but the rest would then take him and Matthias out with a burst of bolts. He bent down and put the axe on the floor. Letting go of it felt like cutting off his own limb. Matthas had already done the same with his sword.

"A wise choice," said Demetrius. "Now let's wake up Cleon. I love it when he's in a bad mood."

Cleon had the look of a man who was irritable even under the best of circumstances. And being woken up in the middle of the night clearly didn't qualify. The Viceroy of Syracuse, the Exalted Ambassador of the People of Athens, and the Guardian of the Western Ocean had a host of other impressive titles, all of it in mockery of his actual appearance: he was short and old and fat, with rheumy eyes that nonetheless gleamed with animal cunning. He stood in his audience chamber, still clad in his sleeping gown, his bodyguards flanking him while he inspected the results of the abortive raid on the Ortygia. The weapons of the intruders had been stacked at his feet, and Lugorix and Matthias had been corralled off to one side, bows pointed at their backs while Demetrius the guard captain looked on, a self-satisfied smile plastered on his face. Eurydice stood in front of Cleon, her arms crossed.

"What the hell were you thinking?" he asked her.

"I wasn't," she replied, her voice dripping with contempt. "These two showed up on my door and said let's go—what was I supposed to do?"

"Not try to escape."

"Well, that's an interesting choice of words, Cleon. 'Escape.' And all this while you've been calling me a guest."

"Save your word games for someone with the time to tolerate them." Cleon stalked over to Matthis and Lugorix. "So… the Greek traitor and the Gaulish barbarian have come to Syracuse."

That wasn't quite what they'd been expecting him to say. "You know who we are?" asked Matthias.

"Scum," said Cleon. "That's what you are. But yes, I know what your game is. Working for a certain Persian witch. How much did she pay you to break into my palace?"

"Two talents," said Matthias. Lugorix's jaw dropped; it was all he could do not to punch his friend right there and then. Matthias caught his look and tried to backtrack. "Um…though it's not like she actually *paid* us. She just promised us that once we'd—"

Cleon laughed. "It's a scant fraction of what Aristotle's work is worth." He thought for a moment. "Does she know that the great man is dead?"

"*No one* knows," hissed Eurydice. "You've kept it secret rather than admit to the world that you no longer have—"

"Be quiet," said Cleon. Then, to Matthias: "Does she know?"

Matthias shrugged. "She told us nothing about that," he said.

"So you thought you'd leave here with his daughter instead?"

"Better than doing it empty-handed."

"You should never have come at all."

"How do you know who hired us anyway?" asked Lugorix.

Cleon looked up at the taller man, laughed scornfully. "So the barbarian knows how to speak Greek. Wonder of wonders—"

"You had spies in the house of Demosthenes," said Lugorix. "Didn't you?"

"What makes you say that?" asked Cleon.

"Most likely way for you to know so much about us," said Lugorix. "Or you interrogated his surviving servants."

"We took what steps we needed to. Demosthenes was a man who craved power. He couldn't stand to be without it. So he conducted his very own foreign relations. And fell prey to the coils of this Persian witch. All of which is playing into Alexander's hands." Cleon gestured at one of the open windows. "He's out there even now, you know. Coming west with an army so large it beggars description. And you two are his unwitting dupes."

"Barsine *hates* Alexander," said Matthias. She's working day and night to bring him down."

"She's working *for* him, you moron."

"Alexander conquered Persia! So why would Barsine—"

"Zeus almighty! Do you realize how many Persians are now working for

Alexander? Do you realize who sits on the throne of Persia? Who serves in Persia's armies? Troops who accept the new order, that's who! Troops in the pay of Macedonia!"

"Barsine is different," said Matthias.

"Barsine is the worst of all," said Cleon.

"How can you say that?"

"Because she was fucking Alexander!"

Matthias lunged forward at Cleon, only to be restrained by the viceroy's bodyguards. Cleon laughed. "My poor little lovestruck soldier. Alexander has so many ways of conquering his foe. And Barsine fell for the oldest one of all. He met her in Persepolis and seduced her in Babylon and she was loving every moment of it. And then he sent her out into the world to do his bidding and now you're doing hers. Is this really coming as a surprise?"

"May you rot in Hades," snarled Matthias.

"You're the one who's going to do that," said Cleon. "For slaying the soldiers of Athens. For lifting your hand against her viceroy. For stealing her property—"

"Oh, so now I'm *property*?" said Eurydice.

"Now you're going to *shut the fuck up,*" said Cleon. He turned to his bodyguards. "Take Eurydice back to her room and take this man"—he nodded toward Matthias—"to the cells until I can think of a punishment fit for the likes of him."

"What about the Gaul?" asked one of the archers.

"A quick death," said Cleon. "Execute him."

The archer drew back his bow; Lugorix tensed himself to lunge one way or another. He knew he was done for, but he was damned if he was going to make this easy. If he could beat the first round of bolts, he might be able to get in among the archers and then people beside himself would die.

But all of a sudden people were dying all around him.

Afterward, Lugorix and Matthias would try to piece together what had happened—would argue over the precise sequence of events. They both agreed that something burning had shot through the window and detonated behind the bodyguards, knocking some onto the floor and setting some of them on fire. After that it got hard to see; Lugorix thought that was because everybody was still partially blinded by the light of the explosions, but Matthias swore that a strange mist was getting into everybody's eyes—something that was really more like gas than smoke and that added to the confusion by dint of its peculiar smell. But Lugorix said that was really the stench of burning bodies—and there were certainly enough of those, as absolute pandemonium gripped the room.

Lugorix was intent on taking advantage of it. He stormed forward, grabbed an archer just as that man fired—the arrow sailed into the back of one of the man's comrades even as Lugorix grabbed his victim's neck and twisted. There was a snapping noise and Lugorix threw aside the grotesquely flopping body, ducked down onto the floor himself. Getting low seemed like the best way to live longer. He couldn't see a thing, but arrows were flying everywhere—he could hear them whirring past him, could hear the thwack! noise as they smacked into flesh. Lugorix crawled forward over a couple of bodies—his hands grasped along the floor.

And closed around that oh-so-familiar axe.

"Skullseeker," he muttered like he was talking to a lover. No longer would he skulk like a dog. He got to his feet and strode forward—straight into an Athenian. This close Lugorix had no problem seeing him—and cleaving him in two with a single sweep of the axe as he stormed past him and reached the wall. Turning alongside it, he made his way toward what he hoped was the door.

It wasn't. It was the window. From it he could see the battlements and lower towers of the Ortygia. Guards were already running along those battlements, sounding the alarm. Beyond them was the sprawl of Syracuse. Fires had broken out in several places in the city. Lugorix drew in a deep breath of air—it was getting hard to breath in that room—and then drew his head back in and continued fumbling his way along the wall. In short order he reached the door. A man was dimly visible in that doorway, though Lugorix was too blinded to see his face. But he wearing an Athenian uniform. The Gaul drew his axe back.

And stopped as the man turned around.

It was Matthias. He had an Athenian's sword in one hand, Eurydice's hand in the other.

"You moved fast," said Lugorix. Matthias grinned like the cat that ate the canary.

"How'd you get in here in the first place?" asked Eurydice.

"Through the water gate."

"That'll be totally blocked off by now." She thought a moment. "Act like you two are escorting me." Then she let go of Matthias' hand, led both him and Lugorix down the corridor with a purposefulness that made Lugorix wonder who was rescuing who. She clearly knew the palace's layout. She took them through a series of side-corridors, back-passages and storage rooms that were clearly off the main avenues of traffic. Occasionally they hung back at intersections while squads of guards rushed past them. Shouts and orders echoed all around. The fortress was in a state of considerable upheaval. And the situation back at Cleon's chamber seemed to be the least of it. There seemed to be a major incident going on at the gates to the fortress. Lugorix reckoned that Agathocles was the man behind that. Perhaps it was a diversion. Or perhaps *they* were the diversion. They were passing through a weapons-storage room when—

"There," said Eurydice.

"What?" asked Lugorix.

"That's how I'm leaving," she said, pointing at an *oxybeles*—a large crossbow, mounted on a wheeled platform.

"You want us to fire you into the city?" asked Matthias.

Eurydice didn't bother to answer. She bent down, squeezed herself under the platform, clung onto it. She was all but invisible—only her foot stuck out.

"Now let's hit the front door," she said.

Lugorix and Mathias looked at each other, shrugged—began pushing the oxybeles out of the room, heading in the direction where the noise of soldiers shouting was loudest. The oxybeles attracted much more attention than Eurydice had. But it was far more likely to be allowed out of the fortress than she was. One more ramp took them into a courtyard that bordered the main gatehouse. The gate itself was open. Lugorix and Matthias pushed the oxybeles through it—

"Yikes," said Matthias.

Lugorix knew the feeling. It was only now that he could see just how narrow the peninsula connecting the fortress to the city was. It was more of a bridge, really—a winding ramp that sloped steeply downhill, battlements on either side, another gatehouse at the bottom, at the entrance to the city. Soldiers were moving at speed down the ramp.

"Let's do this," said Matthias. He started pushing the oxybeles onto the ramp. The apparatus immediately began rolling away from him. Lugorix dashed past it, stepped in front of it before it could gain much speed. His eyes met those of Matthias.

"Idiot," he said.

"How was I to know it was going to start rolling so quick?" protested the Greek.

"By thinking," said a voice from under the oxybeles.

Lugorix started walking down the ramp, letting the oxybeles press against his back to keep it from sliding past him. Matthias grasped its rear—tugged on the platform to lessen the load. But Lugorix was doing most of the work. As he walked the oxybeles carefully forward, he was scanning the city toward which they were descending. Many of the buildings along the dockside had now caught fire; it looked like whatever civil disturbance was going on was largely concentrated in the districts nearest the harbor. Which would make sense if the goal was to funnel troops out of the Ortygia and into the city and in so doing allow the three within to escape. But what Lugorix hadn't expected was the scale of what was taking place.

"You there," said a voice—stentorian, commanding. It was coming from the gatehouse they'd just left. A sergeant-at-arms stood there. Lugorix half-turned—continued to walk the oxybeles down the ramp as he responded.

"Yes?"

"Where do you think you're going with that?"

"Our lord Cleon wants more firepower to deal with the rabble."

"Does he really?" said another voice. Its owner stepped out of the shadows behind the sergeant-at-arms. It was Demetrius, the guard captain. Beside him was Cleon, looking seriously pissed.

"Shit," said Matthias. He leapt onto the oxybeles-platform, swiveled the oxybeles itself around so that it pointed directly at Cleon—pulled a trigger that sliced through a rope, unleashing the compressed energy of the weapon. There was an enormous twanging noise as a giant bolt shot from the oxybeles. Cleon was already hurling himself aside with a speed that belied his girth, but Demetrius wasn't so quick. The bolt lifted him off his feet, hurled him backward. He never made a sound. But the soldiers who were rushing up behind him did. They swarmed down toward the oxybeles screaming bloodlust.

"Time to go," said Lugorix. He scrambled around behind the oxybeles and gave it a hard shove as it began rolling down the ramp unchecked. Then he gripped the back of it, running behind it, giving it some more momentum before leaping on. He steadied himself on the rear, grasped the edge of the platform, looked back up at Cleon. The Exalted Ambassador of the People of Athens was on his feet again, entirely beside himself with rage. He screamed curses and insults as his soldiers ran after the accelerating oxybeles-platform. But they were quickly left behind as the contraption careened down the ramp. Lugorix grinned.

And then a hand appeared right in front of him. He grasped it, helped its owner onto the platform.

"I figure the time to keep a low profile's over," said Eurydice.

Lugorix nodded. The wind tugged at his hair. They were going faster than any horse could carry them, and they were still gaining velocity. Eurydice took in the steepness of the ramp, ran her eyes along its sinuous length.

"You know," she said, "this was a really stupid move."

"You're the one who wanted to use this thing," said Matthias.

"Not in this fashion."

"Small comfort now," shot back Matthias.

"How about both of you shut up," said Lugorix.

The planks holding the accelerating platform together were starting to creak alarmingly. Soldiers leapt out of the way to avoid getting run over. Ahead of them the ramp sloped to the right, curving down toward the lower gatehouse.

"We need to throw our weight to the right," snarled Eurydice. *"Now."*

The three of them did just that. Lugorix swung himself as far off the right-hand side as he could, holding onto the oxybeles itself, feeling the platform tilt to the point where it seemed it was about to tip altogether. The platform scraped against the left-hand wall, ripped along it, careened down what remained of the ramp and shot through the lower gatehouse. Stunned soldiers stared as it whipped past, into the streets of Syracuse. Which were far too narrow and winding to allow them to slow down. Ahead of them was a nasty-looking wall.

"Hang on," said Eurydice.

"Oh *shit,*" said Matthias.

The crash that followed was as loud as it was spectacular.

CHAPTER TWELVE

Back from black: Lugorix swam slowly upward through the layers of awareness. He was dimly aware of pain in his head, of some kind of overwhelming heat that waxed and waned at odd intervals. Shadows hovered over him. Someone was mopping his brow, telling him to rest. But the resting had gone on for eons. Then at last light flickered above him, shimmering through all that dark. Gradually more sounds began to suffuse his brain. Chief among those noises was a hammering. It got louder. And louder. And then—

"He's awake," said a voice.

Lugorix wasn't so sure about that. He opened his eyes, but all he could see was a blurry haze.

"Can you hear me?" said the voice.

"Yes," said Lugorix.

"Turn your head."

Lugorix did.

"Move your left foot."

Lugorix did. Several more instructions followed. A hand grasped his wrist, checked his pulse. A light weight fell on each of his knees, checking his reflexes.

"He possesses full mobility," said the voice.

"Of course I do," said Lugorix.

"Then I shall leave you, my lady."

"I'm not a lady," replied Lugorix.

"That'd be me," said Barsine.

Lugorix focused on the shadowy form that was sitting on the edge of the bed. He squinted as that form resolved itself into the features of the Persian noblewoman. He realized he'd been dreaming about her. He wondered if this was a dream too.

"That was the doctor," she added.

"How am I doing?" asked Lugorix.

"I think he's surprised you woke up."

"How long have I been here?"

"Some weeks."

"Some *weeks*?"

"The blow on the head was followed by a fever. One that nearly consumed you in your weakened state. How do you feel?"

He thought about that. "My head hurts."

"That's to be expected. But Damitra's been a damn sight more useful than that doctor. She's been dosing you with herbs every day."

"Where am I?"

"At the house of Mardonius. Back at Thieves' Cove."

"Ah," said Lugorix. He thought about this for a few moments. It seemed a more fundamental question was in order. A few more moments, and he realized what that question was.

"So what the *fuck* is going on?" he asked.

"You put your life on the line and earned your two talents," she said. "But I need you to come further west with me."

There was a pause. Lugorix said nothing. She looked up, met his eyes.

"It's your choice, of course. But regardless, I owe you an explanation."

"You owe Matthias one as well."

"He's already heard it."

"Was he injured in the—"

"No. And I'm pleased to say that he's forgotten all about his silly crush on me. Thanks to that slut of a sorceror's daughter."

"Eurydice?"

"She's a creature of considerable appetites. And she's taken a fancy to your friend."

"Oh. That's, um,"—Lugorix searched for the right phrase—"great news."

"It certainly made the news that I'd been in Alexander's bed easier for him to deal with."

Suddenly it all came rushing back. "Taranis," muttered Lugorix. "That was *true?*"

"It *was.*"

"You were working with Alexander?"

"If I had been—if I still was—do you think we'd be having this conversation?"

Lugorix mulled this over. His head really hurt. "What's that hammering noise?"

"That? Eurydice is supervising some adjustments to the *Xerxes*. Enhancements of her own design that are going to be make the next phase of this journey much easier. One more reason we've been holed up here for so long. She may be a sex maniac but I can't deny she's got talent. Fortunately Agathocles didn't realize that."

Lugorix nodded. "He was planning to take Aristotle for himself, eh?"

She smiled wryly. "I wasn't going to trust Agathocles further than I had to. Those plans for the Ortgyia and that diversionary attack of his... he was helping us out so that he could get his hands on a sorceror who might help him overthrow Athenian power *and* keep the Macedonians at bay as well. Needless to say he wasn't too pleased to hear of Aristotle's death. Matthias and Eurydice gave him some of the scrolls and told him that was all they'd managed to get out."

"And Aristotle didn't really die of sickness, did he." It was a statement not a question.

She shrugged. "Probably not. All the more suspicious given how quickly they seem to have gotten rid of the body. Eurydice tells me she was left alone with his corpse for less than ten minutes."

"The Macks got to him."

"Presumably. If you could get into the Ortygia, so could others."

"Or they were inside the Ortygia already."

She sighed. "I know Cleon was about to ship the old man back to Athens. Which isn't to say he would have been safer there. As we've had ample cause to learn, the whole Athenian command-structure is plagued with those who've succumbed to Macedonian gold. I've asked Eurydice what she thinks happened to her father, but she refuses to even discuss the issue. My guess, she was in considerable danger by the time you reached her. The Athenians have been waking up to the fact that she has a good chunk of her father's abilities, and that means the Macedonians were going to be after her as well. She's lucky you got her out when you did."

"All the more so as you're not working for Macedonia." Same inflection as before, but now it had the hint of a question. Barsine sighed.

"Alexander's forces captured me after the battle of Gaugemela," she said. "Darius ordered all members of his household to fall back on Ectabana, but the Macedonian cavalry moved too fast. We were brought before him at Babylon. That was when I saw him first."

She stopped talking, seemed to be searching for words. Or maybe she was just lost in memories. When she looked up at him, her eyes were glistening.

"I'd like to tell you he forced me. That would make it easier, wouldn't it? But the truth of the matter is that I loved him from the moment I laid eyes on him. I thought he felt the same. It took me a long while to realize the only thing he's capable of loving is his own reflection. It took me even longer to realize what he thinks that reflection really is."

"That of a god."

"And he truly does possess the means to become one."

"Is that why we're going west?" asked Lugorix.

Barsine stood up. Walked over to a window and looked out it. Then turned back to Lugorix. Her voice sounded far away.

"Alexander thinks himself to be the incarnation of Hercules. That much the world knows. But what the world doesn't is how literally he takes it. The legends say that Hercules had twelve labors. Two of those were in the far west, at the Gardens of Hesperides, near the gateway to the Ocean… the Pillars of Hercules that he gave his name to. One of those two western labors was to steal the golden apples from the nymphs who dwelt there. Supposedly, tasting one of the apples confers immortality."

The word hung in the room. Outside the window, the hammering had finally stopped.

"Perhaps that's what godhood means," said Barsine quietly. "I don't know. As for the other labor, it involved stealing the cattle of the monster Geryon."

"Which probably weren't cattle at all," said Lugorix.

"Exactly. That's how you need to think about this. Just because a myth is a metaphor doesn't make it any less real. The edge of the world contains artifacts of tremendous power. From sharing Alexander's bed, I learnt that he thinks of those artifacts night and day. And now he's coming west to get them."

"And to conquer the western reaches of Athens' empire."

"Like I said, he never does anything that's aimed at a single purpose."

"So we're going to this Garden?"

"First we need to find out where it is."

"I thought you just told me—didn't you say the legends say it's near the Pillars?"

Barsine laughed. "The myths also say it's 'beyond the sunset,' but that description could use a little precision, don't you think? So we've been working on it. As was Aristotle. Unfortunately, Eurydice wasn't privy to all of his secrets. She and I have been trying to piece together what we can, and we think the answer lies at Carthage."

That brought Lugorix up short. "Why there?" he asked.

"The Carthaginians have explored more of the west than any other people. They've been out beyond the Pillars into the Ocean. They've journeyed to the Islands of Thule, and down the coast of Africa. They've discovered so much they've forgotten half of it. Maybe more. Some of their map-rooms suffered damage when Athens took over. Other parts of their library were buried during the Athenian bombardment. So Carthage is where we need to go. But getting there won't be easy."

"We can't just sail there?"

"There's no 'just' about it. West of here is where things get dicey. No one's quite sure what's going on out there. There are reports that monsters are prowling the sea-lanes."

Lugorix sighed. Now he'd heard it all. "What kind of monsters?" he asked.

"Probably the usual kind—something real dressed up in bullshit. But whatever's going on, ships are disappearing. Individual ships are no longer safe. Only well-armed convoys seem to be getting through to ports west of here. And with a Macedonian army closing in from the land, Carthage seems to be on the brink of rebellion. Agathocles told me that a week ago, Cleon dispatched a fleet of a hundred ships to reinforce the Athenian position there. So we're going to have to tread carefully. Speaking of which, can you get out of bed?"

"I can try." He pulled himself to his feet, clutched at a bedpost for balance, steadied himself.

That was when he saw what lay out the window. He was looking through an interior wall, down into the watershed in which they'd moored the

Xerxes. But that vessel was practically a different ship now. It lay in a large drydock—and not only did it sport new armor plating, but large containers had been positioned along the sides and under the ship itself.

"What do those containers carry?" asked Lugorix.

"Right now they're empty," said Barsine. "But when the time's right, they'll fill with water."

Lugorix mulled this over. For a ship travelling out of sight of land to carry water was nothing new, but it seemed crazy that they'd need to drink so much of it. He sensed that there was something about this that he wasn't quite getting. He was about to ask Barsine. But the words faded in his mouth as he spotted Matthias and Eurydice. His friend had his hand on the ass of Aristotle's daughter as the two of them kissed on the aft-deck of the *Xerxes*. Lugorix was surprised to hear Barsine chuckling beside him.

"An excellent development on two fronts," she said. "Not only does it stop your friend from importuning me every time I get near him, but it also means he's coming with us."

This was news to Lugorix. "Why's that?" he asked.

"Because that way he gets to be with Eurydice."

"So she's agreed to go with you?"

"Indeed."

Lugorix mulled this over. "Maybe she *does* believe Macks killed her father."

"Maybe. Though in truth, she doesn't seem to be that interested in politics. I think for her it's more about uncovering the secrets her father might have been keeping from her."

"That sounds healthy."

"I prefer to think of it as useful."

"And it'd be even more so if I agreed to come along as well?"

She looked up at him. "You could put it that way."

"Not until after I've returned to my village."

"To deal with your brother?"

"With the silver you owe me, yes."

That brought her up short. "How will that silver help?"

"Do you mean you don't have it?"

She looked offended. "My word is my bond. Mardonius has the silver, so it's yours whenever you want it. I'm just trying to figure out how it will help in fighting your brother."

"My brother won't fight fair," said Lugorix. "Nor will his retainers. So I need to buy some of my own."

"Can't you appeal to your village's chief?"

"My brother *is* the chief."

"Ah," she said. "But can't your brother wait?"

"*I* can't wait."

"Neither can I," she replied. "I need you, Lugorix. You're smarter than your friend, and you're the better fighter."

He said nothing. She cleared her throat as though hesitating. Then—

"Besides, Matthias told me."

"Told you what?"

"About your sister."

Lugorix felt the color drain from his face. "Why did he do that?"

"Probably to make you mad."

"He's succeeded."

"Look. I'm sorry if I remind you of her. I wouldn't have wished that on you."

Lugorix blinked rapidly. There was something in his eyes.

"What happened?" she asked softly.

It was a few moments before he could answer. "My brother wanted her," he said, though it wasn't the *want* he should have had to mean and it didn't even sound like his own voice talking. He felt like he was staring down at his own body while it spoke with this woman who—when all was said and done—was nothing more than stranger. "He tried to force himself on her. She screamed and my father came to her aid, and then my brother slew him. And then he slew my mother and… everybody else. I was hunting all night, but when I got back I knew the truth. It was written on his face, but he'd already blamed me. He'd done the killing with my own blade and bribed the elders, so it was easy."

"How did he become chief?"

"My father was chief before him. He'd become chief for nineteen years, from when my sister was—when she was born…"

To his horror, Lugorix realized tears were running down his face. Men weren't supposed to do that, but Barsine didn't seem to mind. "It's okay," she said. She reached forward and cradled him in her arms. He pulled her to him and kissed her cheek, ran his fingers through her hair. Sexually, he'd never wanted a woman less. Emotionally, he'd never wanted one more.

"I won't let harm come to you," he said.

"You should go back to your village."

"It can wait." A moment's pause, then: "Your baby can't."

Her eyes went wide. But she didn't deny it. There was no point.

"Does Alexander know you carry his child?" he asked softly.

"Why do you think he pursues me so remorselessly?"

Lugorix stroked her hair. His sister was dead. Barsine wasn't. Nor was Alexander. As if in a dream, he heard Barsine telling him they'd received word his army had emerged from Europe's interior and made landfall on the Mediterranean. He heard himself asking where. He heard her whispering the answer.

By the time Eumenes rode through the city gates, there wasn't much left of the city to ride through. Bodies were everywhere. Most of the buildings that hadn't been destroyed during the Macedonian bombardment had been set on fire subsequently. And those that were still standing were mostly filled with soldiers raping and killing whoever was in them. The screaming made Eumenes' skin crawl. He hadn't heard anything so bad since Egypt.

It didn't have to have been this way, of course. But the commanders of the defenses of Massilia had made the mistake that so many had made these last few years: underestimating Alexander. Secure in their command of the Rhone delta, high walls around them and the ocean at their backs, they'd defied the king and declined surrender. And in so doing, they'd doomed the population. This was partially because the best way to get Alexander motivated was by refusing him. But it was also a function of the soldiers he'd augmented his army with since that battle against the Scythians. The headwaters of the Danube had given way to endless dark forests, reputed to be the dwelling place of all manner of goblins and spirits—not to mention a myriad barbarian tribes which Eumenes had expected would set upon the expedition from all sides. Given how many men the Macedonians had lost against the Scythians, it had seemed to Eumenes that the writing was on the wall—that the attrition of constant barbarian attacks would gradually whittle the army down till Alexander was forced to turn back.

Yet the exact opposite had occurred. The victory over the Scythians had spread word of Alexander's renown as no threats or proclamations could ever have done. Tribes practically trampled each other to join the man they believed to be the conquering sun-god from the east. From all sides, the best warriors of each tribe flocked to join him. Alexander was only too happy to oblige. In short order, he had a barbarian auxiliary that was almost ten thousand strong. And those numbers were just the beginning. By the time they'd emerged from the forest into the Rhone river valley, most of those who joined the expedition were Gauls: tall blonde barbarians covered with tattoos who were only too happy to sign up with the Macedonians when they heard what Alexander's next objective was. All too many of those Gauls saw the merchants of Massilia as bloodsuckers. The merchants of Massilia saw the Gauls as being in their economic orbit. Perhaps both were right. But now it no longer mattered.

The siege had been over quickly. Massilia was well-protected, but the army that had taken Tyre had made short work of defenses intended to protect against scattershot tribal activity. Alexander might not have been able to bring with him high-end siege technology like the Leviathans, but he had his engineers, and they had all the wood they needed to construct a whole range of ballistae and catapults. So energetically did the Gauls set to work felling the requisite trees that the bombardment began mere days after the city had been invested. The defenders were swept from the walls even as those walls crumbled. Elephants and horsemen charged in through the breaches. At the height of the assault, Alexander unleashed a series of fire-ships: rafts packed with the black powder that drifted down the Rhone to destroy river-gates and bridges alike, thereby paving the way for more rafts packed with Macedonian shock-troops. There was never even a need to commit the golems—they remained to defend the Macedonian camp in case the Athenians happened to have had the foresight or resources to have hidden reinforcements outside the city.

But they didn't. According to the figures Eumenes had assembled subsequently, the garrison of Massilia had numbered less than five thousand. And only a thousand of those had been Athenians; the rest had been Gaulish mercenaries, most of whom deserted en masse when they saw so many of their brethren amidst the attacking forces. The result was as inevitable as it was bloody: in the space of a day, a city that had been Greek for almost three hundred years was laid to waste, along with any illusion that Alexander was incapable of reaching the western regions of the Athenian Empire.

Yet Alexander was in a furious mood all the same. He was always in a mood these days. He'd been acting ever stranger as they moved into the headwaters of the Danube. The drinking parties had stopped and he'd taken to leaving the camp for hours at a time every few nights. Where he went, Eumenes had no idea. Even worse, he took no bodyguards. Sometimes while he was out there, storms ripped through the woods; the weather in the forests was terrible and getting worse. Eumenes feared that the king would get struck by lightning or killed by wandering barbarians. But he returned just before dawn each morning to stumble past the stunned sentries, a hollow look on his face and the burning need for a goblet or two of wine before he was up to giving orders. Of course, by the time reveille was sounded, he was looking his normal self again—every inch the warrior-king, ready to lead his troops on to victory.

But now that victory had been achieved at Massilia, he was pissed. And Eumenes could guess the reason why—a guess that was confirmed when he finally reached Alexander at the burnt remnants of the city's dockside. The king was yelling at Hephaestion in front of several bodyguards—an almost unthinkable public show of temper at the one man who he'd always made a point to never criticize in public. As Eumenes rode up, Hephaestion was turning away and stalking off, having been dismissed. Eumenes dismounted and saluted.

"My king," he said.

"Look at that," snarled Alexander, gesticulating at the burning boats sinking into the harbor. There were a lot of them.

But nowhere near enough.

"Their fleet escaped," said Alexander.

Of course it did, thought Eumenes. *It was a fleet.* But he kept silent. More than three hundred ships had been in that harbor, and from the looks of the wreckage out there only fifty had been sunk. Another fifty had been burnt in drydock. But that still left about two hundred that had made it out into the Mediterranean.

Hephaestion had been the man responsible for stopping them. It was the same plan that had worked so well at Alcibiadia—deploy Greek fire from rafts and small boats close to shore. Only this time the Athenian ships hadn't waited obligingly; as soon as the assault on Massilia had begun, they'd put to sea, forging out of the harbor in an enormous V-formation that made it difficult for the smaller attackers to get to grips with them. The death toll among the Macedonian commandos was considerable. None of which was necessarily Hephaestion's fault—he was playing from a weak hand. But if there was one thing Alexander hated, it was excuses.

"This is a new kind of war we're fighting," said the king.

Eumenes nodded, said nothing. He knew better than to reply. Not till he knew where this was going. Alexander stared out at the harbor, wiping sweat and ash from his face.

"It's a new type of war," he repeated. "And it requires a new kind of soldier. We're used to pitched battles, and this is something else. So far we've had success with it, but we need to take the organization to the next level. Special operations: I need you to take command of it."

Are you fucking nuts? thought Eumenes. But all he said was, "It would be an honor."

"You'll partner with Hephaestion, of course. He is my rock. But I've come to realize his strengths aren't in the conduct of covert warfare. He excels at working behind the scenes to develop the new machines that will guarantee our victory. But the deployment of those machines doesn't necessarily translate into their use—the bold gambits that take our enemies by surprise when they least expect it."

Eumenes' mind was racing furiously. All of this meant he'd have to work even closer with Hephaestion. Thereby increasing the danger to Eumenes in more ways than one. Particularly if the task that Alexander was asking him to do really was as impossible as it seemed. Deploying innovative weaponry was one thing. Taking on the Athenian fleet was quite another. But managing expectations was a delicate art. Eumenes calculated the variables rapidly, decided on the risk of candor.

"I worry that you're being too harsh on Hephaestion," he said.

Alexander's eyes flashed. "What do you mean?" he demanded.

"We have wondrous armaments, but we lack a navy. All the artifice and ingenuity can't keep pace with the Athenian fleet when it puts to sea."

"I won't accept that," snapped Alexander. That was the signal for Eumenes to shut up, but he kept going, mustering what tact he could:

"All I'm saying is that I can't promise to bring destruction to their fleet when they're out of sight of shore."

"Nor should you," said Alexander. "That's my job." He seemed to hesitate, then—"Just because they're out of sight of shore doesn't mean I can't get at them."

"I don't understand," said Eumenes.

"You don't have to." Alexander's tone was that of a man who had said more than he intended. It wasn't a tone Eumenes had ever heard his king use before. He wondered just what the hell Alexander meant. He knew that if he ever found out, it wasn't going to be in this conversation. He'd come too close to bringing Alexander's inchoate anger down upon himself as it was. So he did the most prudent thing he could.

Change the subject.

"I brought the staffing plans you requested," he said. "The next phase of the march. Down the coast of Iberia to Gibraltar for the link-up with Craterus' forces."

"Forget them," said Alexander.

"You want a different approach? We need to stick close to the coast if we're to—"

"We're not going to Gibraltar."

For a moment, Eumenes thought Alexander was joking. But Alexander never joked.

"Where then?" asked Eumenes.

But he knew the answer even before Alexander said it.

It was late at night, but Lugorix didn't care. He could finally walk without getting dizzy, and he had someone he needed to have a word with. He stormed through the halls of the house of Mardonius and pounded loudly on Matthias' door. There was the sound of movement within and then the door opened.

It was Eurydice. She was clad in a gown and not much else. Nor did she look surprised to see Lugorix.

"He's all yours," she said to him—and stepped past him and down the corridor. Lugorix smiled appreciatively as he watched her go—whether at her nerve or her ass, he couldn't tell—and then stepped into the room, which smelt of sex and booze. Matthias was sitting up in bed, a wine jug in his hand, an awkward smile plastered on his face.

"I heard you were up and about, but I've been a little busy...."

He broke off as Lugorix grabbed the jug and smashed it onto the floor.

"Why did you tell Barsine?" he demanded.

"Because she deserved to hear it," said Matthias.

"Explain."

"You've been mooning after her when the truth is that she's—"

"I've been mooning after her?" Lugorix couldn't help himself from laughing. "What about *you?"*

"Not anymore, sport. Case you haven't noticed."

Lugorix sat down on the bed. He wondered if he looked as exasperated as he felt. "You jump from woman to woman seeking love you will never find."

"Don't be so sure of that. Eurydice is quite a peach."

"Only thing that girl's in love with is her own brain."

"At least I like 'em talented," said Matthias.

"So I like whores?" snarled Lugorix. "So what? At least I'm honest about it."

"At least none of them will remind you of"—Matthias broke off as Lugorix drew his fist back to hit him. "Zeus man, *wake the fuck up*. You've always blamed yourself for her death because you weren't there. Now you're here and this woman needs your help and if I hadn't spoken up you would have *just walked away*."

Lugorix took a deep breath. "So let me get this straight," he said. "You're besotted with your new girl and want to follow her to the ends of the earth and you need me to come with you before she manages to get both of you killed."

Matthias stared at him. "Maybe," he said.

Suddenly the whole building shook. They heard screams outside, followed by the unmistakable noise of battle-cries.

"Shit," said Matthias and lunged out of bed. Lugorix was already racing down the corridor to get Skullseeker. Through the windows he could see that several of the buildings in the smugglers' cove were on fire and armed horsemen were riding through the streets, trampling anyone who got in their way. He grabbed his axe, whirled—

Only to find Damitra standing there.

"Mistress says it's time to go," she said. Lugorix took the old woman's hand and led her down the corridor. As they went down the steps, they were joined by Matthias.

"It's the Athenians," he snarled. "They're killing everybody. Except the women."

"But why should they do"—Lugorix stopped. He knew damn well why. The only people that mattered at this point were Eurydice and Barsine. Everyone else was expendable, and given that the ratio of men to women in this place was about ten to one, rounding up all the women and then sorting them out later made a nasty kind of sense. He and Matthias half-dragged Damitra around the corner and into the doorway.

Mardonius was lying in that doorway, two arrows protruding from his back, blood pooling from his mouth.

"Save her," he said. "Save her…"

But that was as far as he got before he died. Damitra leaned forward, placed her hands on his temple and muttered something in Persian.

"We don't have time for this," said Matthias. She ignored him, kept on muttering for about ten seconds. Then she stopped and shut Mardonius' eyes.

"He was a good man," she said softly.

"I'm sure he was, but we need to go," said Matthias. He and Lugorix led the old lady through the doorway, out into the streets.

Which were a total shambles. Most of the surviving smugglers and ne'er-do-wells had retreated to the rooftops, from where they hurled a whole array of rocks and debris and furniture down onto the Athenian horsemen. But the Athenians had responded by hurling flaming torchbrands into the buildings, and the fire was in the process of spreading to the roofs. Smoke was everywhere. But that smoke gave the three trying to make their exit enough cover to move along the side of Mardonius' house, around the corner and out onto the docks—where the full extent of their predicament become apparent. The entrance to the cove was entirely blocked by Athenian ships; they'd obviously blockaded the harbor before the soldiers moved in, to ensure that the trap would be complete. Lugorix led the way inside the warehouse.

The *Xerxes* was at the end of the pier. A squad of Athenian soldiers had just dragged Barsine off the ship and onto the dock. But even as they did so, a figure leapt off the boat after them, limbs flying in every direction, hurling Athenians into the water and along the dock. The remainder rallied, slicing away at the figure, who leaped backward like an Olympic gymnast. But there was only so much room on the pier to maneuver. Lugorix and Matthias were already running forward, Damitra not too far behind them. As they reached the combatants, Lugorix's eyes went wide as he realized who the figure in black was.

"Well don't just stand there," snarled Eurydice.

He didn't intend to—he brought Skullseeker up in a scything motion, chopped an Athenian in two. Matthias was right beside him, his blade flashing, while Eurydice redoubled her strange yet highly effective hand-to-hand combat. The Athenians were now caught between two threats, and the fight in them broke. They tried to run, but had nowhere to go, except into the water, which was where most of them started jumping. But now more Athenians were appearing at the entrance to the shed. Eurydice leaped back onto the *Xerxes*.

"Cast off," she yelled. Lugorix and Matthias used their weapons to slice through the ropes while Damitra helped a shaken Barsine onto the ship and the Athenians raced along the dock toward them. One drew back a bow, took at aim at Lugorix. Matthias yelled a warning; Lugorix stepped aside as the arrow flew past him and straight at Barsine. She didn't even see it coming. But Damitra did.

So she stepped in front of it.

The arrow hit her in the chest, knocking her onto the deck. Barsine shrieked and dropped to her knees beside her. But Eurydice was already starting the ship up—there was a clanking as the gears shifted and the motors ignited and steam poured out as the *Xerxes* began moving out into the water. Lugorix and Barsine carried Damitra below while Matthias unleashed his bow and returned fire, shooting the Athenian archer through the face and bringing down an officer for good measure. The rest of the Athenians drew back as the ship accelerated out into the harbor, buildings burning all around it as it made speed for the open ocean—straight toward an Athenian ship blocking the way. Lugorix stuck his head out of the hatch to see it turning, bearing down on them, a massive galley with *opthalmoi*-eyes painted on either side of the menacing looking ram. Its oars flew through the water as it picked up speed. Barsine looked up from the stricken Damitra and yelled instructions to Eurydice, who began pulling on some levers. All of a sudden there was a hiss—Lugorix felt the ship shake; he saw what looked like a very fast fish streak away from the *Xerxes* and into the darkness.

Next moment the Athenian warship exploded.

One moment it was there; the next moment it was enveloped in sheets of fire as it basically just folded up and sank, the *Xerxes* surging past it. Lugorix couldn't believe how things had come to this; just a few weeks before this, they'd been tempted to pick up Athenian stragglers off the coast of Egypt. Now somehow the Athenians had become the villains. Or maybe these Athenians were in the pay of the Macedonians, or they were acting on the orders of those who were, like so many of them seemed to be.

The other ships were trying to give chase, but the *Xerxes* was without lights, moving steadily out into the ocean. The Athenians lost the scent rapidly. The *Xerxes* had made it.

Damitra didn't.

The sea felt different to Lugorix.

It looked the same, though. It was the same Mediterranean that they'd traversed to get from Egypt to Athens, and from Athens to Syracuse. Same blue-green stretching off to the horizon. But something had changed across the last twenty-four hours and Lugorix didn't know what it was. When he finally got a chance to discuss it with Matthias—and to try to clear the air—it turned out there wasn't much to discuss.

"Forget it," said Matthias.

"Never mind then," said Lugorix.

It was well past midnight, their second night out of Syracuse. The two of them were standing on the aft-deck of the *Xerxes*. This was Lugorix's watch period, but Matthias had come on deck anyway. He looked haggard and tired.

"That wench is draining me dry," he muttered.

"You're tagging the daughter of Aristotle and you're asking for sympathy?"

"No," said Matthias. "Just a break. Meaning I'm not in the mood to listen to your ramblings about how the *sea feels weird*."

"Well, it does."

"Said the Gallic landlubber. Don't tell me you believe all this talk about monsters?"

Lugorix scowled. This was what annoyed him about Greeks. They had this thing called *skepticism*, and skepticism was supposed to mean they didn't believe in anything they'd never seen. Which was all very well. But not when it led them to disbelieve in anything that didn't fit their definition of the word *rational*. These days that was a very shaky concept.

"I don't know *what* to believe," said Lugorix. "That's the point. We're in uncharted waters now."

"Actually we're not," said Eurydice.

She'd come up behind them with all the stealth of a wraith. Matthias practically jumped out of his skin. She was dressed in a green robe that it looked like she'd just thrown it on. Her hair was unkempt and she was no longer wearing that nose-ring. She was holding a strange device—a bronze disc covered with markings and notches that Lugorix immediately knew was some kind of sorcery. She held it up to her eye, made adjustments as she sighted along it at one of the stars.

"What on Earth is that?" asked Matthias.

"It's not on Earth," she said. "That's Polaris. The North Star." She lowered the instrument: "And *this* is an astrolabe."

"What's that in Greek?" asked Lugorix.

"That *is* Greek," she replied. "It means *taker-of-stars*." She busied herself making adjustments to the astrolabe. Since Damitra's death, she'd assumed co-piloting duties with Barsine, who—unsurprisingly—was still in something approaching a state of shock. Lugorix was the only one whom the Persian would confide in about her. She'd told him that Damitra had raised her from a baby—that she'd been a servant of her father Artabazus, who had attached her to his court with the specific purpose of raising Barsine in the ways of the prophet Zoroaster. But Artabazus had got a lot more than he bargained for, since Damitra's knowledge extended into some fairly arcane areas. She hinted that had something to do with what she'd seen at the side of Alexander. Now she and Eurydice were spending increasing amounts of time in conversation. The strange part was that the two women made no secret of their dislike for each other—they had very different styles and attitudes, so maybe that wasn't a surprise. Eurydice regarded Barsine as a stuck-up aristocrat; Barsine thought of Eurydice as a crude-talking guttersnipe. But when it came to science and magick, they apparently had a lot to talk about. And they talked out of earshot of the men whenever possible, but Lugorix kept hearing the same words over and over... *maps.... ancients.... secrets....*

Secrets.

Eurydice held up the astrolabe for them to admire.

"It's a device that my father invented and I perfected," she said.

"You're very modest," said Lugorix.

"I'm very smart," she replied. "And I'd be stupid to deny it."

"That's my girl," said Matthias as he put his arm around her. She yanked that arm off her with a force that nearly broke it—proceeded to flip Matthias onto the deck where he lay there, a dazed expression on his face.

"Why did you do that?" he said.

"I'm not in the mood."

"You were ten minutes ago."

"What kind of move was that?" asked Lugorix. She glared at him; for a moment he thought she was going to be rash enough to try the same thing to him—but then she seemed to realize that he wasn't talking about bedroom acrobatics. Her voice took on a *glad-you're-impressed* tone—he remembered how she'd laid into the Athenians earlier with nothing more than her hands. "My father said that ladies shouldn't carry weapons, so he had a Spartan teach me hand-to-hand combat."

"Must have been an interesting childhood," said Matthias, grimacing as he pulled himself to his feet.

"Growing up at the court of Macedonia was a little *too* interesting for my taste."

"See much of Alexander?" asked Lugorix.

"See him? He wouldn't leave me alone."

"He made advances on you?"

"No, I don't think he likes girls much. But he idolized my father, so he was constantly bugging me to figure out my father's 'secrets.' He always thought my father was holding stuff back from him."

"Well, wasn't he?" asked Matthias.

"Fuck I hope so." She frowned. "What's that on the horizon?"

They followed the direction of her gaze, saw what she'd just noticed. Faint flashes sparkling along the horizon. Which could only be—

"Lightning," said Lugorix.

"I've never seen lightning like that."

It *was* a little peculiar, Lugorix had to admit. Purple flared, illuminated huge clouds strung along the horizon—turned to green and then to yellow before fading to dark. It was too far away to hear any thunder.

"Must be a big storm," said Matthias.

"At least we're heading south of it," said Lugorix. "Far away."

"*Very* far away," said Eurydice. She seemed to be lost in thought. "If we can't hear the thunder, that's being reflected over the horizon. Must be some kind of atmospherics. Hard to tell how far."

"What's north of here?" said Matthias.

"Not much. Just ocean, all the way to Gaul."

Matthias mulled that over. "Didn't Barsine say Alexander had captured Massilia?"

"I don't know if *captured* was the precise word," said Eurydice. Her face was grave. "It was a massacre. Ordered by Alexander himself." She stared off at those flickering lights. "My father… he thought he could shape the boy's character. Guide his actions. But the prince fell prey to the dreams of his own glory. He has a way of captivating all who listen—himself most of all. And now he's king in defiance of his father."

"Barsine said the same," said Lugorix. "But how is it that a kingdom can have two kings?"

"It can't," said Eurydice. "One of them must make way for the other, or else there'll be two kingdoms." She paused. "Which may yet happen, of course. If Alexander's campaigns in the west are successful, Macedonia will stretch from the Pillars of Hercules all the way to the plateaus of Iran. And perhaps no one man could rule so vast a domain."

"But a god could."

Eurydice gave Lugorix a strange look. "That's precisely his problem. He thinks he possesses superhuman abilities, and the world has yet to show him otherwise." As she spoke, she took the astrolabe out again, began taking more measurements of the stars around Polaris. It seemed as much a nervous gesture as anything. But Lugorix was still fascinated by it.

"So what are they anyway?" said Lugorix.

"What are what?"

"Stars."

"Oh," said Eurydice. "Most likely other suns."

"Just like ours?"

"Maybe smaller. Definitely further away, but like the Sun, revolving around the center."

"That center…you mean us?"

"You have to start from first principles," said Eurydice. "Trace the movements of those stars, and you'll see that the stars wheel through the heavens around us. *They* move and *we* do not. Meaning the position of the stars is so predictable we can steer ships by them. So we use the celestial globe overhead to navigate our way across the globe on which we sail."

"Globe?" Another term Lugorix had never heard of.

"The sphere of the world."

"Damitra told me the world is flat."

Laughter: "She's wrong." Then, correcting herself even as the laughter stopped: "*Was* wrong."

"What does Barsine think?"

"She thinks it's flat too. But my father said it's round."

"Why?"

"He developed several proofs. The first of those was elephants."

"Elephants," said Lugorix, wondering if he was being made fun of again.

"If you travel to the west, to Africa, you find elephants. If you travel to the east, to India, you find elephants too. But there aren't any elephants in between. So these creatures must come from the same land, on the other side of the world."

Lugorix thought that one over.

"But he didn't stop there," said Eurydice. "Look at the shadow of the Earth on the Moon during an eclipse. It's circular. Naturally, his detractors said that that didn't mean shit, that the Earth could still be a flat disc. They persist in the error of their ways, though at least it shut up the disciples of Anaximander, who maintained that Earth was a rectangle." Her voice took on a scornful tone. "His ideas were among the most absurd ever proposed. Do you know, he thought the stars are just pinpricks in the sheet of night, with a great fire beyond them! At any rate, the final proof of the Earth's spherical nature will have to be left to me." She gazed at the sky overhead. "My father left a lot of unfinished business."

"Fathers often do," said Lugorix. When she didn't reply: "What does Barsine say to all this?"

"She said if the the Earth was round, then ships sailing away from us would eventually disappear over the horizon."

"They *do* disappear," said a confused Lugorix.

"She says that's just because they fade away because of distance—that if the Earth were round, they'd be fading quicker." A pause, then: "The ultimate proof will be showing how the stars change positions in the sky depending on where one is on the Earth. But there isn't enough data on that. Travellers lie, instruments are unreliable—at least until now. But I hope to make the proof during our journey. Given how much ground we'll be covering."

"Travelling to Carthage will show you that?"

"Um. Yes, exactly. Carthage." But there was something weird about her tone—and Lugorix wasn't reassured when she changed the subject. "Mathematics and astronomy can be very tricky things. Did you know that there is a number that *isn't a number?*"

Lugorix wasn't in the mood to argue with such obvious absurdity. "No."

"There is. It's nothing. Which is its own number. We call it the *zero*."

"Crazy," said Lugorix.

"Numbers are!" she said with the enthuasiasm of one who had successfully ditched a line of conversation that she didn't like. "Same with words. That's why my father's teacher's teacher—Socrates—never wrote anything down. He thought his work was purer that way. There's a reason the Egyptian god Thoth was not only the god of writing, he was the god of trickery." She had yet to notice that Lugorix had stopped paying attention. "Perhaps it's because there's such power in words and equations." She gestured at the stars: "Just because you're far away from something doesn't mean you can't make it a basis for logical questions."

Lugorix cleared his throat. "Like that of who killed your father?"

Afterwards, he wondered why he said that. Perhaps he was getting tired of this young woman who was so smart and yet so troubled. Or maybe it was because he was sick of her avoiding the one subject that mattered most to her. But for a moment he really *did* think that she was about to try to hit him. She raised her hand—but he just stood there, not even moving to defend himself. He could afford to be complacent: he stood a full two feet taller than Matthias, and his prowess at close-quarters combat was something that the Greek could only dream of. The truth was that he was perfectly prepared to let her strike him for what he'd just said. Perhaps recognizing this, she restrained herself.

"You shouldn't have said that," was all she said.

"You're probably right."

"Why are you trying to make me revisit this?"

"His death was a little too convenient."

"Zeus almighty," she said. "Do you think I'm blind?"

"Who do you think did it?"

Her lips quivered. Her face was white. "Someone who's going to pay," she muttered.

CHAPTER THIRTEEN

Cleon woke with a start. He'd been dreaming of that woman again. Wondering how in the name of all the gods she'd slipped from his grasp. He was master of all Syracuse—he could have done whatever he wanted with that wayward daughter of a dead sorceror, and she'd slipped through his fingers. That fact galled at him more than a little. It would have been sweet to have her join him in this bed he lay in now, at the top of his personal tower in the Ortygia. Sweet—but stupid. There was no use dwelling in dreams. He opened his eyes.

And froze.

Someone was in the room with him. He couldn't see them in the dark, but somehow he knew it all the same. Someone was standing there, right at the foot of his bed. Someone who was convinced he was helpless, who only needed another moment to kill him—or who was waiting for him to wake in order to gloat or make some pointless demand. Cleon didn't care which; his response was the same regardless. The paranoid slept with knives under their pillows, but Cleon had something better. Very slowly he reached out along the edge of the bed and grasped the miniature crossbow-pistol that hung concealed there. He slid it toward him, raised it up to point at where he thought the intruder was.

Only then did he speak.

"I'm awake," he said. For a long moment there was silence. But then—

"I realize that," said a voice.

"Have you come to kill me?"

"I came to bring you a message."

"You could have just sent it."

"I'm not sure you would have listened."

"I'm listening now."

"Good," said the figure. There was the sound of iron striking flint; a lantern flared into view. The man who held it had a sword in his other hand. He was of medium height, with a thick black beard, an aquiline nose, and a wolfish grin. He put the lantern on the floor and drew a second sword.

"Don't you think one will be enough?" said Cleon.

"Is this the part where you try to assure me you're unarmed?"

"I wouldn't dream of it." *He probably thinks I have a blade.* "Who are you?"

"I'm Ptolemy," said the man. "Son of Philip."

"You mean the *bastard* son of Philip," said Cleon. Ptolemy looked surprised—Cleon laughed, enjoying the man's discomfiture. "You Macedonians have your spies in Syracuse. We Athenians have ours in Pella."

"Then they must have told you how unhappy Philip is with you."

"Why should he be unhappy?"

"Because you took our gold."

"In return for which I killed the old man."

"But not his daughter."

"She knew nothing."

"You must think *I* know nothing if you expect me to believe that."

Cleon forced his voice to sound casual. "She escaped."

"How could you be so careless?"

"I was distracted by her tits," said Cleon sarcastically.

"Precisely why I thought I might find them right here beside you."

"One of my many mistakes."

"Not killing her was the worst of them." He paused. "You really didn't even *fuck* her?"

"Only with my eyes."

Ptolemy spat on the floor. "But why did you try to fuck *us?*"

"I'll admit I was hoping you were less informed." His mind was racing furiously. "How many of my guards did you kill?"

"Just the ones outside your door. The rest I simply avoided. But let's talk about the girl. She has at least half the knowledge of her father. She's smart enough to figure out the rest. *So why the hell didn't you kill her?*"

Cleon took a deep breath. The only way out of this was to get Ptolemy off balance. The Macedonian would be seeing him merely as a fat old man in bed. But the angrier Cleon could make him, the better. The truth was the best vehicle for that. "I was trying to sell her to Alexander," he said.

There was a moment's pause. "You're shitting me," said Ptolemy.

"Nice to see you can be surprised."

"He was bidding against his own father?"

"Doesn't the one serve the other?" asked Cleon disingenuously.

"If you really do have decent spies in Pella, they'll have disabused you of that notion."

"So the old man isn't too happy about his son proclaiming himself king?" Cleon grinned at the look that flashed across Ptolemy's face. "I mean his real son, of course." For a moment he thought Ptolemy was going to attack him there and then. But instead the Macedonian noble took a deep breath.

"Let Alexander adorn himself with titles," he said. "Let him heap his head with crowns. What does it matter? He may stand at the head of the largest army in the Mediteranean, but it's his father that really pulls the strings."

"You sure about that?"

"All the more so since Alexander doesn't even realize it."

"I guess when you're the commander of eighty thousand hardened veterans that might be hard to spot," said Cleon.

"Your sarcasm is duly noted."

"And here I was thinking that Macedonians were too thick to register it."

"But not too bereft of clue to follow your schemes. So: you thought to play the father and the son against each other, and in so doing maybe draw out the schemes of both. But irony of ironies—the one who stole your prize out from under you turns out to be a prize all her own. Especially to Alexander."

"The Persian? I never saw her."

"No," said Ptolemy. "You didn't. She just struck a deal with outlaw scum and organized a little fishing expedition. Which makes me merely the latest person to underscore just how pathetic your defenses are. What happened to the contents of the old man's laboratories?"

"I heard he left most of those in Pella," said Cleon.

"I can assure you he brought the best ones here. And it's a safe bet she took them west with her when she split."

Cleon tightened his finger on the crossbow's trigger. "Perhaps she'll even find what she's looking for out there."

"You'd like that, wouldn't you?" snarled Ptolemy. "Do you even *realize* what's at stake?"

"Does *anyone* know exactly?"

"We have our suspicions."

"You mean your fantasies," said Cleon.

Ptolemy's face darkened. "I mean our knowledge. You who had Aristotle at your beck and call should know better than to indulge in such mockery. The superstitious think the gods used to walk the earth. The skeptics think it's all just horseshit. The elect know they're both wrong. These were *people,* same as us—"

"No," said Cleon. He'd seen the reports prepared by Athenian intelligence, the reports that had been suppressed by the archons upon pain of death. "Not the same. Not the same at *all.*"

But Ptolemy was just talking right over him. "—who unravelled the secrets of the universe. A mere *fraction* of those secrets would conquer all the armies that ever existed. All of Alexander's strategic genius—all the armies of the warring powers—all of it would be as nothing compared to the magick of the ancients."

"And if that magick falls into your hands, you'll build a Macedonian Empire that will last forever."

"No one builds an empire intending it should last for less."

"I'm sure the ancients said the same thing. And look where they are now."

"Yes," said Ptolemy. "Where. Exactly. *That's the fucking question."*

Cleon laughed. "And how does Philip plan to answer it? Your half-brother already has two armies in the western Mediterranean. Your father has none." Ptolemy's hands tightened on his swords. "No one loyal to him for a thousand miles save you." Cleon smiled, met Ptolemy's smoldering eyes. "I knew Philip was past his prime, but I never dreamt for a moment that the *cripple* would be so foolish as to send the *bastard* to run his errands—"

The combination of those two words did it. Ptolemy was already leaping forward at Cleon, charging over the bed, both swords out.

Which made him a sitting duck.

Cleon raised his crossbow. Ptolemy started to hurl himself aside, but not fast enough. The bolt flew straight at him—

And glanced off one of Ptolemy's blades, shooting up and burying itself in the ceiling.

For a moment all was still.

Then Ptolemy picked himself off the floor.

"Would that I could make this slower," he said, walking toward Cleon.

"Wait," said the viceroy. "I have gold."

"That which we gave you," snarled Ptolemy.

The last thing Cleon saw was that blade coming at him.

"Dying was the best thing that asshole ever did."

It wasn't the most tactful of eulogies, but it might just be the most accurate, Leosthenes reflected. Though to be sure, not everyone in the room shared the opinion. In particular Phocion, whose patron Cleon had been, was looking less than pleased with Hypereides' judgment. The death—and by all accounts, the abject failure—of Cleon would mean that the advantage passed to Hypereides on the council. And that man was going to try to make the most of it. Hypereides met Phocion's eyes, smiled broadly.

"You don't look too happy," he added.

"How can I be happy?" said Phocion in that rumbling voice of his. It sounded like Zeus himself; the fact that the man who possessed it was so much less impressive was merely one of life's little ironies. "A servant of Athens is dead. His faults notwithstanding—"

"His faults are precisely the issue here," shot back Hypereides.

"We don't know the details," said Phocion mildly.

"We know enough of them," said Leosthenes. All the other archons looked at him, and there were more than a few eyebrows raised. Was Leosthenes at last committing himself in the ongoing struggle between Hypereides and Phocion? Or was this just his perpetual tacking back and forth, throwing support to first one, then the other? "The situation in Syracuse is a *disaster*," Leosthenes added. "For all we know, Agathocles and his rebels are—"

"Perhaps you'd like to go out there and take charge of the city yourself?" asked Phocion.

"Maybe I should," said Leosthenes, and he could see how that remark set more wheels to turning, as the other archons wondered if he was serious and how his absence would affect the council.

"*Someone* is going to have to," said Hypereides. "Someone we trust."

"We don't even trust each other," muttered somebody, and there was general laughter at the understatement. That Macedonian intelligence had been in touch with members of the council wasn't open to dispute. Leosthenes was reasonably sure that everyone had been approached—he certainly had been, on multiple occasions, though it was hard to tell which inquiries were serious and which were jokes and which were attempts by Athenian intelligence to entrap him. But there was no denying Athens was a hotbed of espionage these days.

It was also a hotbed of sedition. The situation in the wake of Alexander's assault on the city had only grown more volatile. That was why the archons were meeting in secret, in the northern wing of the Propylaea, the gateway to the Acropolis. Through the windows, the moonlit city was visible below; pictures of the city's famous battles lined the walls. The meeting had started late and was probably going to run much later.

"And Aristotle? Have we heard whether he's still in Syracuse?" said Thrasybulus impatiently. He had extensive business interests in the West, and those who knew him knew that business was all he really cared about. Which was all very well—Athens' economic power constituted the sinews of its strength, but viewing everything through the lens of money could lend itself to a certain myopia. And if the smart money started to think that Macedonian rule might actually be more profitable....

"We haven't heard shit," said someone.

"I don't know about that," drawled Hypereides lazily. "I heard that Phocion here has heard something." All eyes turned to Phocion, who looked uncomfortable.

"That may have been what Cleon got himself killed over," he said softly.

"Do tell," said Hypereides.

"Cleon may have taken Aristotle into custody," said Phocion, and his voice was almost a whisper.

"I didn't hear you," said Hypereides. "Can you say that louder?"

"I think you heard me just fine," said Phocion, and for a moment the two men exchanged a look of pure hatred.

"But we could use some help on the implications," said Erasinides. A retired veteran, he spoke little but when he did speak, his voice carried more weight accordingly. "If Cleon was killed not by Syracusan rebels but by Macedonians—then Aristotle may be back in Macedonian hands."

"He's not," said Phocion, "he's dead." Hypereides' face remained expressionless, but Leosthenes knew in that moment that this was the admission he'd been intending to force from his rival. Consternation broke out amidst the council-chamber; it seemed like every archon in the room was talking. But then Hypereides' voice rose above the din.

"Aristotle is alive," he said. Everyone stared at him.

"So where is he?" asked Thrysabulus.

Hypereides sighed. "That's the part I'm still trying to figure out," he said.

Moonlight lit the desert as the man staggered through the sands. His horse had long since died, and he knew that he was halfway there himself. He was only capable of moving at night now, and he realized with what little cognition he had left that the coming day would almost certainly finish him off. His tongue had swelled to the point where it felt like someone had shoved their foot down his throat. He could no longer swallow, and he had forgotten what water tasted like. But he kept on moving forward, up one dune and then down the next until he wondered if he had already died and gone to a hell of sand that stretched out in all directions forever.

But he was still alive. Still lost in the middle of the desert known to man.

The worst of it was that he'd been going home. He'd finally been given the task of returning to Egypt as the bearer of a message from the expedition that had been charged with taking Carthage. The expedition that would almost certainly never reach that city. He'd been so busy thanking the gods for his deliverance it was a long while before he realized that they'd abandoned him. They'd done it in their time-honored fashion: by cursing him with hubris. He'd been trying to take a short-cut west of Cyrene where the land bulged out into the sea. Naturally he'd gotten lost. Now he was well and truly fucked. It was hard to see how this could any worse.

That was when he heard the howling. It sounded like wolves. But there were no wolves in this desert.

Other than the human ones.

Adrenaline surged through him, fueling him with sufficient strength to somehow pick up the pace. The Berbers had found his trail. Or they'd smelt him out. Flesh-eating marauders who had harassed the army ever since it had left Egypt, picking off stragglers—and now he'd become one himself. He could hear them calling to each other in their barbaric tongue, incomprehensible to him yet filled with the dire warning of all the things they would do if they took him alive. He resolved not to let that happen.

Ahead of him the desert was so flat it looked like water.

He blinked. It *was* water, moonlight shimmering off its rippled surface. He'd reached the sea once more. As he raced down the sand dunes and onto the beach, he realized that it offered him one final chance at survival. Waves lapped at his feet as he charged toward the water. Behind him he heard the cries of the Berbers intensify as they closed in on him. As he waded out into the surf, he chanced a glance backward, saw shadowy figures coming over the crest of the dune. They were sprinting toward him—but now he was neck deep in the water that they believed it was death to enter. As they reached the edge of the ocean, he was already swimming, paddling out to sea, their furious cries dimming in his ears as the waves crashed over him. There was so much salt in the water that he had no trouble keeping his head above the surface. He kept on swimming, praying for a miracle from heaven. Athenian ships had been stalking the expedition since they left the Nile, keeping pace and keeping watch. Maybe one of them lay off the shore tonight. Maybe they would spare him in exchange for the secrets he carried.

But only if he knew them.

His hands clutched frantically at the scrollcase at his belt. He lifted it above the water, slid away its lid, drew out the scroll enclosed within and broke the seal of Craterus, the man to whom he'd delivered the message from Alexander and Philip all those weeks ago. He continued to thresh his way further from the voices on the shore as he read the words by the light of the moon overhead. Had Craterus and Perdiccas discovered a way forward? What would they do if they reached Carthage? Did they have a plan for getting out of the mess they'd gotten into?

Incredibly, they did.

The scale of the lie he'd been fed—the lie the whole army had swallowed—was so colossal that he started laughing in spite of himself. The truth was on the paper in front of him and yet he still couldn't believe it. Nothing was what it seemed. Everything was a subterfuge. He laughed and laughed, and couldn't wait to tell somebody—anybody—the truth.

He barely noticed the tug on his foot.

At least, it felt like a tug. And the nudge against his leg felt like just a nudge. But as the blood pooled on the surface of the water around him he realized otherwise. He didn't even have time to scream—next moment he was pulled under as the sharks that had found him fought one another for his flesh. He broke the surface once more—thought he heard the jeering voices of the Berbers back on the beach. Then he was hauled under for good, leaving behind that single piece of paper floating on the surface, the water making the ink run until it was just another piece of flotsam floating beneath the starry field above.

Perdiccas tore his gaze away from the lights in the sky, returned his attention to the lights around him. It was cold in the desert at night, and there were nowhere near enough fires to keep the army warm, for the simple reason that there were no trees out here. The dung of the pack-animals was the only fuel the army had available, but those animals had been dying off in alarming quantities.

As had everyone else. Even the Macedonians were suffering. Nearly all of the camels had been slaughtered, their water and blood guzzled, their meat eaten to keep the army moving, staggering forward, westward along the Mediterranean coast toward Carthage. The maps said they weren't that far from the green plains of Tunisia, but the terrain they were in remained as barren and inhospitable as it had been since they left the Nile delta, trudging along the tractless coast. The endless expanse upon which the coast bordered had given way to the heaped rocks of mountains—no longer flat, but still unrelenting desert.

At least the Berbers were no longer a factor. They'd been left behind; the problem was they'd been replaced by a new threat that was all the more menacing for going largely unseen: the mountains were infested by small creatures called troglodytes who lived in caves and rolled down stones upon any Macedonian so foolish as to venture into the heights that overlooked the coast. But the blocking of the mountain heights made it almost impossible to get any perspective on the army's position. Was greenery in sight? Was there ever going to be an end to this? Or would the trogolodytes venture down into the coastal lowlands and attack the Macedonian army directly? During the day, that wouldn't be a problem. Even an enervated army could deal with them handily.

But night might be a different story. That was why Perdiccas was now standing on the edge of the army's encampment, inspecting the sentry positions personally, staring out into the black. The army had fallen a long way that it should be scared of midgets, but Perdiccas knew that one more disaster might just drive them all into the sea. He paced along the trench that marked the edge of the camp line, before slowly retracing his footsteps back toward the command tent, past the pockets of men gambling what remained of their water rations. No one was getting enough water, so the temptation to chance what one had in the hope of getting more was considerable. Of course in the morning some wouldn't have water to make it through the day, and their bodies would contribute to the trail now littering the wake of the Macedonian army. Turning a blind eye to the gambling was a small price to pay to minimize the butchery that had already started to occur. Every day when the army rose and dismantled its tents, a few of them were left standing—and those who entered found only lifeless husks inside, drained of much of their blood. Such tents were nearly always those of the auxiliaries and allies. The conclusion as to what was happening was as obvious as what to do about it: nothing. Appalled as he was by what was taking place, Perdiccas realized that in truth he should be grateful that his Macedonians had discovered a simple expedient that would allow them to march further. His army was adopting the habits of nocturnal demons in its quest to stay above the ground. He lifted the flap of the command tent and entered, ignoring the smell of sickness that assailed his nostrils.

He walked through into the main room where Craterus lay on piles of pillows. Every time he saw him he couldn't believe how much weight the man had lost. The man who had once been a giant was rapidly becoming a wizened husk. It was as though Craterus had aged years in the space of days. Perdiccas thanked the gods above that the illness that had laid his commander low hadn't turned out to be a plague capable of spreading like wildfire among the ranks. Not yet anyway. The fever had settled on Craterus' lungs, gradually tightening its grip. The end couldn't be that far away now. Perdiccas was the acting commander, and very soon he would be the actual one. But until that happened, he continued to observe the formalities, consulting with his senior officer every evening. Craterus raised his head, opened a pair of bloodshot eyes.

"I told you to come back tomorrow," he muttered.

Perdiccas felt uncomfortable. "It *is* tomorrow," he said.

Craterus closed his eyes. "So what happened today?"

"We marched."

"How many died?"

"Close to a hundred."

"How many were Macedonians?"

"Eleven. But that number is going to increase if we don't find water soon."

Saliva dribbled down Craterus' chin. "There's water in the mountains."

"Undoubtedly."

"So find it," ordered Craterus.

"We will," said Perdiccas. Though he knew they wouldn't. Because they weren't even going to look. The troglodytes had ensured that. It wasn't until three scouting parties searching for water had been lost that Perdiccas had realized they were dealing with a new menace—and when survivors from the fourth party told the story of how miniature demons had sprung an ambush and dropped stones upon their heads, he had ordered no further incursions into the rocks. The bastards had probably poisoned the wells anyway. Perdiccas had tried to explain all this to Craterus, but Craterus kept asking the same questions over and over again—kept ordering a move into the mountains to find water. Now Perdiccas just nodded until Craterus got tired of the subject. And he certainly had no intention of telling him about that his beloved Macedonians were turning into a pack of blood-drinkers. There were some things that were better left unsaid. Easier to just let Craterus' mind run in its accustomed circles. Easier—and more merciful.

"How close are we to Carthage?" asked Craterus.

"I wish we knew."

Craterus looked anxious. Mustering what must have been considerable effort, he raised his head. "But you know what to do when we get there," he said.

"Yes."

Craterus relaxed, leaned back on his pillows. "I was telling him I could rely on you."

"Telling who?"

"The physician."

Perdiccas drew a deep breath. A nasty feeling was creeping up his spine. "What did you tell him?"

"That you could be relied on to carry out the plan."

"Oh."

"When we get to Carthage."

Perdiccas kept all emotion out of his voice. "And did you tell him what the plan was?"

"I don't remember."

Perdiccas stepped backward, his mind racing. Only he and Craterus knew the ultimate objective of the army. Two people in all—and Perdiccas had assumed that Craterus' illness meant that number was about to drop to one. That assumption had been a rash one. He straightened up, looked into Craterus' eyes.

"It's all right," he said. "It doesn't matter." And then he leaned forward and put his arms around Craterus' neck, began strangling him. Once that bear of a man would have had responded by ripping off Perdiccas' arms and then beating him to death with them. That man had taught Perdiccas nearly everything he knew about soldiering. They'd crossed the world together and it seemed unfair that their partnership should come to an end in this squalid little tent on the edge of nothing. When Craterus stopped thrashing, Perdiccas let go. Then he called for the captain of the guard outside the tent. The man entered and saluted.

"Our noble commander has breathed his last," said Perdiccas.

"Sir." The captain cast a quick sidelong glance at Craterus' form, but that was all. If he knew either suspicion or regret, he displayed neither.

"Find the physician who attended him and have him executed for incompetence," ordered Perdiccas.

"Sir." The captain saluted, turned and left, leaving the new commander of the army of Africa with the body of the man he'd just killed. For long moments Perdiccas stood there, looking down at Craterus' face. Somehow it seemed that it was he who lay there and that Craterus was the one staring down at him. Perdiccas knew that had their situations been reversed, his commander wouldn't have hesitated to do what he'd just done. Craterus had been a hard man to deal with, but he'd been fair, and consistent. And foolish—he would have attacked Carthage even without the twist to the plan that Alexander had devised. But now he would never see the walls of that city. Perhaps none of them would. He reached out and closed Craterus' eyes.

Abruptly, there was a commotion outside the tent. Perdiccas put one hand on his sword. Had Craterus' death triggered a long-overdue mutiny? Were the Macedonian soldiers going to slay their new commander even before he'd had a chance to give more than one order? His mind flashed down the list of junior officers who would be most likely to try to replace him. He braced himself to do some fast talking and even faster swordwork.

The flaps of the tent burst open and two soldiers stepped into the room.

"Sir," said one, "the sentries have detained a horseman."

That wasn't what Perdiccas had been expecting. "Leaving the camp?" he asked. Deserters had nowhere to run, but that didn't mean they hadn't been trying.

"No sir," said the soldier. "Entering the camp."

"Not a messenger either," said the other. "Not one of ours. He wants to speak to Craterus."

Perdiccas exhaled slowly. "Bring him to me," he said. "Now."

It was the first day in a long while that explosions hadn't rung through the mountains. The detonations had become such a regular occurrence that Eumenes had gotten used to it—could scarcely believe they had stopped. In theory that meant the journey had gotten easier. But the snow was still continuing, falling downward in ever-thickening white chunks, coating the roof of heaven. They'd been winding their way across jagged peaks and twisted contours of that roof for some time now.

The Alps, they were called. Beyond them lay Italy.

The elephants were suffering particularly badly. Several had died already, and many more were ailing. Eumenes still found it difficult to believe that Alexander had elected not to strike toward Gibraltar. Not because such a move would have made military sense... but so many of the trails seemed to point in that direction, regardless of how difficult a journey along more than a thousand miles of coast might have been. Though Eumenes had to admit that the numbers of Gaulish mercenaries had swelled still further when Alexander had announced his intent to invade Italy. It turned out there were other Gaulish tribes on the far side of the Alps whose forefathers had achieved considerable success raiding central Italy. In particular, they'd sacked and burnt a city called Rome, though failed to take its citadel—and as a result Rome had risen from the ashes of defeat like a phoenix. From the intelligence Eumenes could piece together, a resurgent Rome had proceeded to conquer the Samnite peoples, thereby establishing hegemony over much of central Italy. None of it sounded like it would pose much of a challenge to Alexander though.

But the Alps had given him more than enough trouble anyway. Avalanches and falls were a daily occurrence. Sometimes the trails became so narrow that the men had to march in single file. When night fell, those who stood on those trails had no choice but to sleep leaning against the rocky wall. When morning came, many were gone. They'd shifted during sleep, woken up screaming as they dropped toward valley floors far below. There was no doubt about it, the mountains were worse then any human enemy.

Though, to be sure, there were plenty of human enemies in these peaks. The tribes that inhabited the Alps had dwelt up here for eons, and they didn't take kindly to intruders. They rained arrows and rocks down on the heads of the Macedonians, and ultimately were only thwarted when Alexander offered a talent apiece to each man that could get above them. It was a group of mercenaries from the rugged peaks of Anatolia that claimed the prize, climbing up ice-covered cliff-faces at night to get above the positions of the tribesmen, then catching them in the rear as the Macedonians launched diversionary feints from below.

But no such solution was available for the parts of each trail that were blocked by landslides and rocks. The Macedonian high command rapidly came to understand the real value of guides in these mountains—not because they *knew* the way, but because they could *find* the way. The landscape was mutable, shifting constantly as moving rocks and snowfall blocked some paths and opened others. But all too often there was no path available. Rocks had blocked the way entirely.

So they used explosives.

Specifically, the black powder that Hephaestion's alchemists had devised: powder that (now he was in on the secret) Eumenes knew to be a combination of saltpeter, sulphur and charcoal. It was effective, blasting the way forward again and again. It was also dangerous as hell, going off prematurely more than once, each time utterly consuming the hapless engineers in charge of it. But across the last few weeks the army had gotten used to stopping for hours at a time, only to start moving again following the boom of explosions. Eumenes had taken to spending much of that time engaged in discussion with one of the sorcerors Alexander had brought back from the east, a wizened sage by the name of Kalyana. He hailed from the lands that lay to the east of Afghanistan and had agreed to accompany Alexander back to the West in order to spread the word of *Nirvana*.

Not that Eumenes understood what that meant. Truth to tell, he wasn't sure Kalyana understood it either. Hours and hours of conversation, amphora after amphora of wine, and it seemed to mean less and less the more they talked. Maybe that was the point. But conversations with Kalyana were never boring, and they weren't confined to philosophy either. The man was interested in everything, from ways to improve the black powder to devising remedies against swamp fevers to measuring the true dimensions of the world.

But today there had been no conversation: no stopping and no explosives; just constant marching through the falling snow, which had Eumenes wondering what else was about to go wrong. It didn't surprise him in the least when he heard rumbling from the front of the line—rumbling that sounded like a continual landslide of considerable proportions.

Yet landslides were supposed to subside. This didn't. It kept going, building and building. And the fact that Alexander was up near the vanguard today made it particularly alarming. He forced his way forward, over the slippery rocks, almost losing his footing more than once, moving past Macedonians, then Persians, then more Macedonians, then hordes of Gauls, then some barbarians from a tribe whose name he couldn't pronounce. All the while the rumbling grew louder. Finally he rounded a corner.

And saw Italy.

The vanguard was spread out along a lower part of the trail, cheering lustily at the Italian plains far below. The echoes of their cheers had reverberated back along the trail until its original source was indiscernible. Eumenes looked down through the clouds at the slopes and peaks falling away beneath them. The descent would be almost as hazardous as the crossing. There would be more casualties. But in a few more days they would be in northern Italy, with a few more months of campaigning season left in the year. Eumenes allowed himself a small smile. Then walked over to where Alexander and Hephaestion stood together in silence, gazing at the green fields far below.

Lugorix was sick of rowing. But he was even more sick of Matthias bitching about it. Especially because the Greek was only doing a fraction of the work. They'd been at it for some hours now. Which in itself was nothing new. Lugorix had rowed ships before—given his size and bulk, the Athenians had often had him on rowing duty on the trip east, in the weeks after they'd hired him. So he was used to hauling on oars.

But never underwater.

They'd submerged shortly after sighting Carthage—battened down the hatches, filled the tanks with sea-water, and slipped beneath the ocean surface. Lugorix had never been so scared in his life. He could understand why Eurydice and Barsine had been so coy as to the actual purpose of the modifications made to the *Xerxes*. If he'd known, he would never have gotten into this boat that so totally defied the natural order of things. But now it was too late. Before they went under, he'd had the chance to fortify himself with a skin of wine, which took some of the edge off the fear. But only some.

And now they'd done what no ship had a right to do—sink without sinking.

Lugorix sat behind Matthias on a metal bench that had unfolded from the walls. Mardonius' artisans had been busier than he'd realized. They'd installed oars that were stranger than any oars Lugorix had ever seen— these swung out from the walls and tugged on an elaborate series of pulleys and gears that in turn pulled at what Eurydice were a number of "fins" rigged along the outside of the ship. Matthias had asked her to repeat that, and Eurydice had merely smiled that smug smile of her and spelt it out—F-I-N-S—fins, like a fish. Which was pretty much what they were this point. They'd turned off the main engine and were relying entirely on muscle-power now. It wasn't like that main engine couldn't function underwater. But it still made noise. And they were trying not to make any.

Since they were in the middle of a squadron of Phoenician warships.

Or maybe those ships were merely an elaborate conjuring trick on Eurydice's part. Immediately after they'd submerged, she'd sat down beside Barsine, begun peering into a strange-looking instrument that seemed to be yet another addition installed at Syracuse. Eurydice had gazed through those eyepieces for some time, calling out course adjustments to Barsine. No one paid any attention to the two rowers until Lugorix demanded they be let in on the secret. He'd expected the women would tell them to keep quiet, but instead Eurydice had simply unfolded a series of ever-smaller glass discs, and then pointed the last of those on the wall in front of them. The whole thing had been altogether weird, and it got even weirder when a ship appeared on that wall.

It was a standard Phoenician quadrireme, of which there were maybe a hundred in the Athenian fleet: four banks of oars and two masts, with catapults rigged both aft and rear. It was a bit fuzzy, but it looked quite realistic. Lugorix congratulated Eurydice on conjuring such an excellent painting, whereupon she had rolled her eyes and told him that what he was looking at was the real thing, thanks to her *periscope*. Lugorix had no idea what the hell that was, but it certainly seemed to work: Eurydice toggled the discs back and forth—made some kind of adjustment, and all of a sudden the view was quite clear. The ship was one of many. And those ships were all *moving*—the ocean lapped against the bottom part of the picture, and the ships rose and fell in the sway of the waves. Beyond them was Carthage, getting ever closer—a series of white-walled battlements and towers stretching along the horizon.

"We're right in the middle of their squadron," said Eurydice, using the same low tone of voice she'd been using this whole time. "So try not to shout."

Lugorix was too out of breath to think about doing that. He was amazed that he and Matthias alone were somehow generating enough oarpower to keep pace with ships that had hundreds of rowers—but Eurydice said the pulleys and gears served to *amplify force,* whatever that meant. As far as Lugorix was concerned, it was all witchcraft—same way they were able to see the ships even though they were underwater. But he had to admit that Eurydice knew what she was doing. Transporting them via spells beneath the waves was nothing to sneeze at. Maybe she'd even manage to keep them alive. A task that was getting ever more tricky as they drew ever nearer to Carthage and the ships clustered ever closer together and the number of eyes watching them from the walls grew. Those walls were almost as tall as those of Athens, and Lugorix pitied anyone who had to try to storm them.

"Faster," said Eurydice.

It was the first time she'd asked them to adjust their speed, but it wasn't the last. Across the next few minutes, she called on them to redouble their pace three times more—and then had them slow down. Once they had to back water. The Phoenician ship in front of them was so close it looked like they were about to crash into it. Lugorix felt like he could practically reach out and touch it. He kept pulling on the oars, conscious that more and more of the work was falling on him as Matthias tired. Sweat dripped down the faces of both men. It was hot work. And even though Eurydice had rigged an air-supply to the surface, Lugorix felt like they were running low on air. He took deep breaths, fought down his fears, kept rowing as they passed through the opened sea-gate and into the harbor.

It was gigantic. Not quite as big as the one at Athens, to be sure, but still crowded with ships at anchor, lined up along the docks. But all those ships were merchant-vessels, and the squadron they had infiltrated wasn't stopping. It was continuing on through, straight into—

"Shit," said Lugorix.

The outer harbor gave way to an inner harbor: a gigantic circular construction, the outer wall of which was lined by pillars that stretched down into the water. Warships were nestled between each of those pillars, their eye-painted beaks like monstrous birds looking out upon the harbor. At the core of that interior harbor was an artificial island—a domed building of colossal proportions. Warships were lined up within it, only unlike those around the exterior, these ones had been hauled entirely out of the water, up into drydocks while swarms of laborers worked them over.

The squadron dispersed: two of the ships rowed in toward that drydock while each of the remaining boats headed toward a different slot around the pillared outer wall. For a moment Lugorix wondered how the ship-captains knew their assigned berths—but then he saw signalmen on the inner island's roof, waving flags and pointing at each boat.

"That way," said Eurydice—she pulled on levers while Barsine worked the helm and suddenly the view was covered by waves as the *Xerxes* sunk beneath the surface. Lugorix could feel the ship drifting toward the bottom. He breathed deep, kept waiting for the crunch as they smashed into the bottom.

But there was no crunch—just a gentle shudder that passed through the craft, which finally ground into motionlessness. For a moment all was still. Then Eurydice stood up.

"Let's get out of here," she said.

Lugorix threw open the hatch, found himself peering through a sluice-gate at the harbor outside. The *Xerxes* had managed to sneak through the space beneath, into one of the drainage channels that served the harbor. Now the *sub-marine* (for that was what Eurydice had declared their vessel now was) was attached like a limpet to the wall, waiting for those within to make their next move.

Nor did it take long to get that underway. Barsine and Eurydice had planned this out beforehand—there was neither argument nor discussion. Eurydice clambered past Matthias—who followed her, Lugorix bringing up the rear. Barsine was apparently going to stay behind.

"Keep yourself safe," she whispered to Lugorix. He nodded, grasped a ladder and clambered up to a crawlspace cut into the ceiling, wriggled past coils of rope and vats of what looked like oil. Gaps cut into the floor looked down upon the ships resting at anchor: murder-holes intended to provide a last-ditch means to destroy any hostile ships that happened to make it into the harbor. At the far end of the platform were some stairs. They headed down those stairs until they came to a large door. Eurydice looked up at Lugorix.

"All you," she said.

Lugorix's axe made short work of the door. On the other side was a long stone corridor. It looked like a great deal of fighting had gone down here. Blood stains were all over the walls, along with the scars of axe and blade. Matthias scanned them as they passed.

"All fresh," he said.

"And everything we've seen so far is Phoenician," said Eurydice.

"What?"

"All the ships. All the soldiers. All of it native to Carthage. All of it Phoenician."

"So what?" asked Matthias.

"So where are all the Athenians?"

Lugorix mulled this over. He'd been thinking along the same lines himself. Things were going bad enough for Athens further east; why should they be any better further into the empire's hinterlands? Carthage lay at the edge of the Athenian Empire. Her people weren't even Greek. And there had already been much evidence to suggest that the unrelenting pressure of the encroaching Macedonians was shaking that empire's foundations.

Now there was still more.

"But what about the fleet that Cleon sent from Syracuse?" asked Matthias.

"For all we know it never reached Carthage," said Eurydice.

"Looks like whoever was losing made a stand here," said Matthias, examining the blood. "Fell back down those corridors there."

"Where they were probably butchered to a man," muttered Lugorix.

"Let's not jump to conclusions," said Matthias.

Lugorix laughed. "All I have to do is step."

"Both of you shut up," whispered Eurydice. She led them down more corridors until they reached a ladder that led up to a storage attic that looked to have fallen into disuse. Piles of rope and rolled up sails were everywhere, along with casks of pitch and oil. The three intruders treaded cautiously across the floor, all too conscious of how their footfalls were echoing. At the far side of the attic they found another set of stairs; these wound down, then up again, twisting sinuously until it seemed impossible to Lugorix that anyone could possibly know what direction was which.

But Eurydice didn't seem phased. She stopped at a stairway landing covered with carvings of serpentine gods, grasped one of those snakes—then pulled. A stone slid away to reveal a hidden passage with a roof so low it looked almost like a chute. Everyone had to stoop, except Lugorix, who was forced to crawl.

"How do you know where we're going?" he asked Eurydice.

"Philip's agents stole the plans," she said. "In anticipation of one day attacking Carthage. And my father made copies."

Lugorix nodded—drew in his breath as far as he could, collapsing his ribcage, willing himself to be smaller. But altering the pattern of his breathing only made him feel more claustrophobic. He'd already had to unstrap Skullseeker from his back, was reduced to holding it out in front of him. He began to feel like he was already trapped—would never get out of this place in the middle of this alien city. He wondered if the Athenian garrison had ended up down here—if this was where the Carthagnians had put the bodies. He wondered if they were still down here.

And then he emerged from the passage.

"Zeus almighty," said Matthias.

It was another storage attic. But this one was filled with weapons: shields, swords, spears, helmets. All of them Athenian. Lugorix hefted his axe.

"So much for the garrison," said Eurydice.

"Show some respect," said Matthias.

"Why's that?"

"Isn't Athens your homeland? Shouldn't you be showing some loyalty?"

"Loyalty?" Eurydice scoffed. "Athens threw my father out. *Exiled* him."

"But then he fled Macedonia. Which had harbored him and given him—"

"Exactly. Loyalty to nations is a fool's proposition. Only thing I'm loyal to now is *knowledge*. That's the one thing that can't betray you."

"You sure about that?" asked Lugorix. Eurydice didn't reply, just walked around a corner to another wing of the attic. There were even more weapons heaped here than by the door. But there was also a slitted window. The three men peered out it—found themselve gazing at the skyline of Carthage: temple-bedecked hills, villas everywhere, aqueducts twisting amidst them, smoke rising from a thousand fires.

"Gorgeous," whispered Matthias.

"Especially because you can't see the slums," said Eurydice. "The rich live in the hills, the poor struggle at the bottom."

"So where's this library?"

"On the other side of the palace."

"And where's the palace?" asked Matthias.

"We're in it," said Eurydice. They stared at her. She laughed—"That passage took us in from the docks. Everything's interconnected. Come on, this way."

She led them into another crawlspace. This one wasn't quite as narrow as the one before, but it was still low enough to make Lugorix nervous. Evidently it ran alongside one of the palace walls, because those slits continued along the left wall, the view changing from city to courtyards and finally to gardens. By the time they reached that greenery, the stone had transitioned to wood—they were skulking over an enclosed catwalk through which were slotted metal pipes that rained down water on the plants below.

Those plants were of a kind that Lugorix had never seen. Huge fronded trees, tangled thickets, a wealth of flowers, all of it packed incredibly closely together. The air in here was hotter, too, and Lugorix could see a wooden roof stretching overhead. Steam drifted against that roof. Brightly-colored birds flitted here and there.

"What the hell is this?" whispered Lugorix.

"It's called *jungle*," said Eurydice. "Plants from regions south of the desert."

"Oh," said Matthias in a voice that made it clear he didn't give a shit. Lugorix couldn't believe how many insects were buzzing around the catwalk. If that's what a jungle contained, he didn't want any part of it. The catwalk continued through another stone wall, into a different garden. The plants here reminded Lugorix of those back home, the trees of Europe reaching up toward him. The smell of oak made him so homesick he wanted to jump down amidst them. But he restrained himself.

Which was just as well, given the men who were standing in the clearing below.

One looked to be a Carthaginian noble—he was fat, and wore robes almost as purple as his face. He was doing most of the talking, while a translator rendered his words into passable Greek. A barrel-chested Carthaginian officer stood at his side; he wore leopard skin over his armor, and carried a vicious-looking barbed spear in one hand. Several Carthaginian soldiers stood sentry duty at respectful distances so to give the Carthaginian leaders and the man they were talking to some semblance of privacy. And as for that man—

"You have *got* to be shitting me," muttered Eurydice.

He wore the uniform of a Macedonian general and carried his helmet under his arm. He looked pale and exhausted, though his eyes burnt with a strange intensity. He nodded brusquely as the Carthaginian noble spoke, but his mind seemed to be elsewhere. Finally he gestured at the translator.

"I've heard enough," he said in Greek. "Tell the Sufete Hasdrubal that we don't have time for these speeches. I've got thirty thousand men encamped outside the city, and they're getting tired of waiting." The Sufete Hasdrubal and the officer who stood next to him listened as the translator turned this into Phoenician. Then the Sufete began talking in turn, the translator a few words behind.

"With all due respect, the Sufete Hasdrubal says you must be patient. We've only just succeeded in throwing off the yoke of the tyrants. Nor have we fully exorcised their baleful influence. Moloch must be placated before we can take any action."

"Moloch shall be beyond placating if your delays cost him his victories," snapped the Macedonian general. The translator began to speak, then stopped and glanced nervously back at the general, who merely looked impatient. "They're my words, not yours," he said. "So go ahead and tell your master what I just said." The translator nodded, resumed—only to be slapped across the face by Hasdrubal, who began ranting angrily, the translator struggling to keep up.

"General Perdiccas, you may be favored in the eyes of the one they call Iskander, but do not presume to instruct us in the ways of pleasing Moloch. The Baal is a jealous god, and a hungry one. We must feed him flesh to give thanks to him for giving us our city back, and we must feed him in the way that he demands. If you crave a boon from our city, then you will wait until we have sought his counsel and then you will do as Moloch demands—"

But the general called Perdiccas was interrupting once more. "I'm already doing it," he said. "Because Moloch and I are *on the same team.* Neither of us wants to see Carthage burnt to the ground and all your works put to the torch."

Yet now the Carthaginian officer broke in angrily, his hand clenched around his barbed spear. The translator relayed his words: "That *already happened*," he said. "We were already burnt. When Athens conquered us." And then, his voice calmer: "Have you heard of the Garamantes?" Perdiccas shook his head. "You have surely encountered them, though. They dwell in the Atlas mountains and along the edge of the great desert. They are only three feet high and—"

"*Those* assholes," muttered Perdiccas.

The officer kept talking. "Perhaps you have heard about the sleeping draught they brew. It makes a man seem as if he is in the grave. He breathes so faintly his chest no longer rises; his pulse beats so faintly you cannot hear it. They use it for sacred initiations, and it is as though the living die and then come back to life. Thus it was with the resurrection of our city. The world thought Carthage was dead, but she was only sleeping. As our ally, I would beg you not to make the same mistake."

"I have no intention of doing so," said Perdiccas diplomatically. "I'm just saying that I'd hate to see your city suffer still further as the result of indecision. I'd much rather see your enemies suffer instead."

The officer stared at him. "Let me show you how we deal with our enemies," he said.

CHAPTER FOURTEEN

The Carthaginians led Perdiccas from the room through a pair of double doors, the guards trailing in their wake. The three hidden in the rafters watched them go. No sooner had the doors closed then—

"That was Perdiccas," said Eurydice.

"Who's Perdiccas?"

"One of the top Macedonian generals. Alexander left him behind in Egypt. He reports to one of the marshals, Craterus."

"So they must have gotten across the Sahara," said Matthias.

"Isn't that supposed to be impassable?" asked Lugorix.

"Well, they certainly didn't swim," said Eurydice. "They've got no navy to speak of. They must have marched."

"But to have done all that and *not* attack Carthage—it doesn't make any sense." Eurydice looked puzzled. "Why would they come all this way to *negotiate?*"

Lugorix had an answer for that. "It's a trick. The Macks will launch a surprise assault."

"Maybe," said Eurydice. "But not while one of their generals is inside the city. And why send that general in the first place? Why not just send heralds? It's as though Perdiccas doesn't want his men to know he's negotiating. That suggests that he really *is* serious about talking."

"Sure," said Matthias, "but what's he talking *about?*"

"Let's keep moving," said Lugorix. "Maybe we'll find out."

They skulked down the catwalk and left the garden-room—only to find themselves looking down at a similarly-sized room that had clearly once contained plants but that now contained something else altogether. All the shrubbery had been uprooted and ripped away. To make room for…

"Zeus almighty," whispered Matthais.

"Now we know where the garrison went," said Lugorix.

What was left of it, anyway. The room below them was filled with Athenian soldiers, wearing only tunics and packed together like cattle. Most of them were sitting on the floor, though a few were standing along the walls. All of them looked totally miserable. All the more so as they were being scrutinized through a barred door by the men who had just walked out of the garden-room. Perdiccas and Hasdrubal could be seen deep in conversation, but now they were too far away to hear.

But the result of their discussion was clear enough. Suddenly another door flew open and Carthaginian soldiers shoved their way into the room. Their shields were locked together and their spears were out, but none of the prisoners attempted anything. Instead the Athenians were doing their best to stay away: reeling backward with an alacrity that bordered on panic as they practically trampled each other to get away from the Carthaginians. But there was nowhere to run. The soldiers grabbed several of the prisoners and hauled them struggling from the room. The door slammed shut.

"That doesn't look good," said Mathias.

"This way," said Eurydice.

She led them away from the room and into a honeycomb of torchlit passages—turning left, then right then right again. Then down a long flight of stairs—so far down that Lugorix knew they must be going deep into the bowels of the earth. The carvings on the walls became more and more disturbing. Gods and demons and monsters leered at each other and at them.

Finally Eurydice stopped at a bend in the passage. She gestured to Lugorix and Matthias, who peered round the corner to see two spear-wielding guards standing in front of a pair of heavy stone doors. A gong stood beside them.

Matthias drew his bow—was about to step around the corner when Eurydice shoved in front of him. "I'll handle this," she muttered as she turned the corner and walked toward the guards. They tensed as they saw her coming—then relaxed as they realized she was just an unarmed woman.

She began started speaking to them in Phoenician. Whatever she was saying must have been funny because they were laughing now.

But the smiles were wiped from their faces when Eurydice suddenly whirled and spun in the air—her foot connecting with the head of one of the soldiers with a resounding crack that was followed by another as he hit the wall and slid onto the floor. As the second soldier drew his blade, Eurydice grabbed his wrist in a maneuver that Lugorix recognized as being a repeat of the one she'd discomfited Matthias with—only she went a step further this time, snapping the soldier's wrist. His scream of pain was cut off when she shoved an elbow through his face—a blow calculated to drive his nose back into his brain. He dropped.

Lugorix and Matthias rounded the corner to join her, a little taken aback at what they'd just witnessed. Lugorix noticed that Matthias seemed particularly ill at ease—his face was a little green. There was nothing like the realization that the woman with whom you'd been cavorting in bed could snap your neck like a twig. Eurydice was standing over the bodies of the men she'd just killed, her face flushed, breathing heavily. She was enjoying this a little too much, Lugorix decided.

"Get this door open," she said.

Lugorix was happy to oblige. While Matthias pulled a burning torch from the wall, he lifted away a series of heavy bars, then set Skullseeker to work. In short order the ornate door was a mass of broken wood. He tore it away to reveal—

"Welcome to the Library of Carthage," said Eurydice.

Light flickered on a square room whose shelves were filled from top to bottom with scrolls. Each of the walls contained an arched doorway. Eurydice showed no interest in any of the scrolls—instead she simply pointed at the leftmost of the archways, whereupon they proceeded into an identical room: four more walls packed with scrolls, four more doorways. This time Eurydice pointed at the one to the right. The process went on for some time while they wended their way through rooms that were essentially indistinguishable from one another. Eventually Lugorix realized that was the point.

"It's a maze," he said.

"Very perceptive of you," said Eurydice.

"It's also a deathtrap," said Matthias.

"Now what would make you go and say a thing like that?" asked the daughter of Aristotle.

"This library contains much of value," said Matthias. "Right?"

"Indeed," said Eurydice.

"Yet the locks to this library were from the *outside,*" said Matthias.

"Good point," said Eurydice.

"And there aren't even doors within this place."

"From which you deduce?"

"That we're not alone in here."

"Astute reasoning," said Eurydice, beaming as though she was a teacher pleased at a student's insight. "Drawing on several different points to build up a broader theory—that's what my father would have called *induction.*"

"I call it obvious," said Lugorix, pointing at the center of the room they'd just entered. In the middle of the floor was a large chunk of animal dung.

And it was still steaming.

"Not human," he added.

"Could be a big human," said Matthias, looking nervously around. "Someone who was reading late and decided to take a—"

"Not human," repeated Lugorix. He'd known something was strange about this place. Anything that contained items as valuable as Eurydice and Barsine seemed to think would have its guardians. And they were bound to be a damn sight more impressive than those sentries at the front door.

"There's a reason why nobody's allowed in the library late," said Eurydice.

"You're talking like you know what's in here," said Matthias.

"In point of fact I don't," she replied. "But I daresay we're about to find out."

"Did you hear that?" said Matthias.

"Hear what?" asked Lugorix.

"Shut up," hissed Eurydice. Lugorix stepped in front of her torch, blocking off the light, for there was too much of it. As his eyes adjusted, he found himself staring straight ahead, through doorway after doorway, out into the middle distance. With a start, he realized that two eyes were looking back at him. He couldn't tell what kind of animal they belonged to, but they were watching him with a predator's intensity.

And then they were gone. Whatever it was had moved off to the side. And from the looks of the labyrinth they were in, it could be moving in toward them from one of several directions. Without taking his eyes from the darkness ahead of him, Lugorix relayed to the others what he had just seen. Matthias nocked an arrow, while Eurydice stepped into a corner. Matthias looked at her curiously.

"That's the plan? Wait for it to come to us?"

"A damn sight more sensible then going after it," said Eurydice. "It's an animal, and it's probably hungry. It'll be here soon enough."

Lugorix nodded. That was the kind of thinking he understood. He hefted his axe and braced himself for whatever was out there. He knew what the feeling of being stalked was like. Everywhere you looked was nothing. Just a feeling. But he'd seen those eyes. He knew whatever owned them was coming closer. Closer…

Then it was on them. A shadow rushed from out of the darkness, straight at Lugorix, who stepped aside at the last moment as what looked to be a gigantic cat hurtled into the room. It had stripes and extremely sharp teeth and that was all Lugorix really saw before Matthias dropped his bow and pulled an entire shelf of scrolls down onto the creature. Papyri flew everywhere as the animal bellowed and hissed and began to wriggle out from under the shelf.

But that was when Lugorix stepped in, wielding Skullseeker like a cleaver, hacking and chopping away. He felt his blade bite deep into flesh; he ground it in further, jumping into the air to avoid a clawed paw that swiped suddenly at his hamstrings. Then he leapt backward and let the axe fall like an executioner's blade, trying to stay out of range of those claws. There was an anguished howl and the creature began convulsing, its blood spurting everywhere. Yet it was still struggling out from under the shelf. Until Lugorix stepped forward and chopped its head off. The animal shuddered and went still while the head rolled over to stop at Eurydice's feet. She hadn't moved the whole time.

"Interesting," she said, looking down at the face glaring up at her. "A tiger."

"A what?" said Lugorix, looking around in case there was another one on its way.

"Tiger. A large cat from the jungles of India, which is the furthest east that Alexander's scouts got—"

"Stow the geography lesson," said Matthias. "Are there any more of these damned things?"

"Only one way to find out," said Eurydice.

So they waited, in that room with the scattered scrolls and the dead beast. They waited and waited… until finally Lugorix couldn't take it anymore.

"This is not the warrior's way," he said. "We need to go."

"We should stay," said Matthias.

"Until what?" asked Lugorix. "Morning? We need to go. Now."

And with that, he hefted his axe and set off into the darkness. His two companions hesitated a moment, and then followed him. They had no choice: splitting up was crazy, and—Eurydice's skills notwithstanding—Lugorix was the only one of the three that a large cat was going to have to reckon with.

But there were no more cats. Just more rooms, which Eurydice continued to navigate through. All those glyphs and runes and markings were making Lugorix more nervous than any tiger. Finally they stopped in one of the rooms. Eurydice looked around.

"This is the one," she said.

It looked like a normal room, but Eurydice wasn't buying it. She began sweeping scrolls off one of the shelves until the outlines of another door became visible—though really it was more of a hatch. She knocked on it in a curious staccato pattern, and it swung open of its own volition. Which Lugorix found more than a little weird.

It got weirder when they ripped aside the shelves and went through—and then down a passage and into a room that was much larger than the others: a circular rotunda of a chamber with a ceiling that vaulted overhead. Lugorix thought there was something familiar about the markings on that ceiling but he couldn't place it. Tables lined the tapestry-covered walls, and scrolls were scattered on those tables, along with strange artifacts and instruments.

A man sat at one of the tables. He wore a grey robe and had a white beard. He looked up in surprise as they entered—asked them a question in Phoenician. Eurydice replied, whereupon he switched to Greek.

"Your accent is horrible," he said.

"Thanks for nothing, greybeard," said Eurydice.

"Who are you?"

"We've come for the map."

"Help yourself," said the man. He gestured at the room around him. "There are many here."

"We're looking for the only one that matters," said Eurydice.

The man shrugged. "You'll have to be more specific than that."

"The one that Adherbal the Navigator compiled of his journey to the West," said Eurydice. "In which he sailed beyond the Pillars of Hercules and discovered the route to the fabled domain of Atlantis. I'm sure you know what I'm talking about."

There was a long pause. Finally, the man rose. "I have that," he said. He walked to one of the tables, shuffled through papers—held up a weather-beaten scroll.

"Here you go," he said.

Eurydice glanced at it. "I had in mind the real one," she said.

"Precisely what this is. See, those are the Pillars, these are the Fortunate Islands, and then west of that is—"

"Bullshit," snapped Eurydice. "I said I want the real one."

"I'm the Librarian," snarled the man. "Think that I don't know what the real one is?"

"Of course you do," said Eurydice. "And we know you're sworn to protect it. And we both know that what we're looking for is only *half a map*, so how about you cough it up?"

The man's face had gone pale as his beard. "I'm not sure I understand," he said.

"But you do," said Eurydice. "You only have half the map. I've got the other half."

"You lie, whore."

"I'm not a woman for hire and I'm not lying," said Eurydice. "A Persian noblewoman named Barsine recovered the lost half of your map in the labyrinth beneath the ziggurat of Babylon, to whose priests the thief who stole it from you had bequeathed it when he was dying of plague."

"An interesting story," said the Librarian. "But I'm not sure I can—"

"Sure you can," said Eurydice.

And with that, she knocked the old man onto the floor and proceeded to start beating the truth out of him. It was painful to watch. Lugorix felt he should stop her, but it wasn't like he had an alternative way to get the information. Several more choice blows, and the beating was over—and the old man was dragging himself over to one of the tables, where he reached up and pulled a hidden catch—pulled out the contents of the hidden space within.

"Thanks," said Eurydice, taking the proffered piece of parchment. As she did so, Lugorix heard shouting, echoing through the door they'd just come through. Someone had found the dead tiger. His eyes met those of Matthias, who nocked an arrow.

"How do we leave this place?" Eurydice asked the Librarian. He said nothing—but glanced at one of the tapesteries. Eurydice pulled that tapestry aside to reveal a flight of stairs leading upward. "The back way," she said.

"So why didn't we go *in* that way as well?" said Lugorix. "We could have avoided that damn tiger."

"Because I didn't know this way existed," said Eurydice. She picked up another map, one that showed an outline of the palace. "But I do now."

Then she took out a dagger and slashed the Librarian's throat.

"Did you have to do that?" asked Matthias as the man bled out.

"Otherwise they'll know what we took," she said—and led the way up the stairs. They were cramped and winding, but Lugorix didn't care: at least they were returning to the surface. The shouting behind them faded a little, drowned out by something else. Something that was echoing from up above, a hollow rhythmic thumping that seemed to somehow reverberate through the walls. Lugorix and Matthias looked at each other.

"Sounds like drumming," said Matthias.

Lugorix nodded. The noise sounded akin to the booming noise made by an oarmaster as he beat out the rhythm for a galley. Only it was far louder. Especially when they opened the door at the top of the stairs and came out into a corridor. Lugorix shut the stairway door behind them, noticed that it was concealed from this side. He glanced at Eurydice.

"Which way?" he said.

"There," said Eurydice, gesturing to the left. "Back to the ships."

But Matthias shook his head. "I want to see what that drumming is," he said.

"I don't think you really do," said Eurydice.

Lugorix knew that she was probably right. But he also knew that Matthias wasn't going to take no for an answer. Because really, all of them knew exactly what that drumming was all about.

Especially now that it was punctuated by a shrill screaming.

"Fuck this," said Matthias. He raced down the corridor, toward the screaming, and it was all Lugorix could do to keep up. Eurydice ran after them, yelling at them to stop being idiots. But it was way too late for that.

The screaming subsided as Matthias and Lugorix rounded a corner into a section of the corridor whose walls were lined with arrow-slits. Each of those slits was glowing with a strange light. Lugorix peered out one of them.

And wished he hadn't.

He was looking out at one of the citadel's many courtyards. Only this was no ordinary courtyard. A vast metal idol with jagged teeth and green eyes dominated half of it. Flames licked up from a pit in front of that idol. Carthaginian soldiers stood at attention while priests dragged a struggling Athenian toward that pit. Lugorix caught a glimpse of Hasdrubal and Perdiccas watching the spectacle from a private box set over the courtyard. Hasdrubal had the expression of a man about to blow his load. Perdiccas' face was grim. But he said nothing—rendered no protest as the priests reached the edge and pushed the Athenian in. Screams filled the air once more. The odor of burning flesh assailed Lugorix's nostrils. Matthias turned from the window as Eurydice came running up.

"They're barbarians," was all she said.

"No man should have to die that way," said Lugorix.

"Not if we have anything to say about it," muttered Matthias.

Eurydice looked at him, realization slowly dawning on her face. "What are you suggesting?"

"Not a suggestion," said Lugorix. "We're going to free the prisoners."

"That's not a good idea," said Eurydice.

"Nothing's good about letting my countrymen roast to death." Matthias' face was quivering with rage. "I'll be damned if I'm going to stand by and let that happen."

"You've got to be reasonable," said Eurydice.

"Oh? Why's that?"

"Because we've got the *key to the lost treasures of the ancients here,*" snarled Eurydice. "Which may be the only thing standing between Alexander and his conquest of the *entire fucking world.* So how about you get a grip on yourself and get a sense of proportion before we lose—" She broke off as more screaming filled the air. Another Athenian had been hurled into the pit. Matthias whirled to face Eurydice.

"We either do this or we're not coming," he said.

"This will be the death of us," said Eurydice quietly.

"So be it," replied Lugorix. "Now show us the way."

Eurydice nodded. She consulted her map, then turned and led them back along the corridor, past the concealed door and back the other way. Lugorix was all too conscious of just how conspicuous they were, given that they were out of the secret warrens and into the main concourses of the citadel. And unlike back at the palace of Agathocles, they weren't in disguise. Sooner or later they were going to run into somebody.

It turned out to be sooner. They weren't even out of the corridor when the concealed door from the library popped open and a squad of soldiers came through—along with several dogs who immediately started howling when they saw the three intruders whose scent they'd been pursuing. The soldiers began yelling in Phoenician as they released the dogs. Lugorix led the way around a corner, threw open a door as Matthias unslung his bow. As Eurydice rushed past him, Matthias fired an arrow into the mouth of the first dog just as it came round the corner. Then he slammed the door and threw the bar.

Lugorix looked around, was relieved to see this wasn't a dead-end, that there were two exits. The room itself was filled with what looked to be supplies for the nearby temple: wood, coal, rope, vats of oil and pitch. There were a series of thumps as the remaining dogs hurled themselves against the door—followed by the unmistakable sound of soldiers breaking the door down. Pieces of wood flew across the room as the door started to bulge inward.

"That way," said Eurydice, pointing to the leftmost of the exits. "Takes us back to the harbor."

"And the prisoners?" said Matthias.

"I'll show you where we can do a detour." The hammering intensified. "Now can we please leave?"

"First we're going to delay these pricks," said Matthias. He grabbed some of the rope—turned to Lugorix, but the Gaul was already on it, turning over the nearest vat of pitch and spilling it across the floor. As he did so, he heard a clicking next to his ear. Eurydice had taken out a tinderbox and was striking iron onto flint, setting fire to the map of the palace.

"Don't we need that?" he asked.

"Already memorized it."

Lugorix nodded—picked up a second barrel of pitch and began pouring it out behind them as they got the hell out of there. Twenty yards along the new corridor, and Eurydice tossed the burning scroll onto the trail of oil. A tongue of flame hissed away down the corridor as they all started running—and came into a kitchen filled with servants preparing food, all of whom fled screaming as the two mercenaries looked around.

"Get down," said Eurydice.

They hurled themselves onto the floor just as a huge explosion blew down the corridor. Pieces of cutlery and food were flung through the air. More explosions followed, punctuated by screaming.

"That'll buy us some time," said a soot-covered Matthias as they staggered to their feet and out of the kitchen. Eurydice proceeded to lead them through a series of passages that apparently were earmarked for the palace servants; Lugorix got glimpses of the harbor out the occasional window. They were getting closer.

"Where's this damn detour?" said Matthias.

"Right there," replied Eurydice—pointing at the wall. Matthias knelt, began groping for its edges or handles. But then Lugorix shoved him aside.

"Allow me," he said, swinging Skullseeker down onto the door, crumpling it inward. He drew back his boot, kicked in what was left. Then ducked to enter a low-roofed corridor.

"That way," said Eurydice, gesturing to one end where a flight of stairs led up into darkness. The three of them set off, rapidly finding themselves back in the same kind of passages through which they'd originally entered the citadel.

Only now they were much noisier. Shouts echoed along them. Someone was putting the prisoners in lockdown. It wasn't hard to guess the reason why. Lugorix and Matthias charged round a corner to find two Carthaginian soldiers looking down on the mass of Athenian prisoners, darts at the ready. Their backs were to the three who'd just arrived.

"Hi there," said Eurydice.

The men whirled round—just as Matthias and Lugorix proceeded to shove them hard—they reeled backward, lost their footing, tumbled into the room below. An enormous cheer went up from the Athenians, who swarmed the two hapless soldiers—punching, kicking and rending. That was when Carthaginians on the other platforms started hurling darts.

"Let's get them," said Eurydice. She and Lugorix sprinted away down the corridor while Matthias opened up on the Carthaginians. He was considerably outnumbered—until Lugorix and Eurydice hit each of the other platforms in rapid succession. The only one who saw it coming was the last

Carthaginian, but Matthias shot him even as he was about to hurl a dart at the oncoming Eurydice. Matthias then dropped the rope down to the Athenians. Men wielding the Carthaginans' weapons began clambering up while Lugorix dashed back round to join them. By the time he got there, those prisoners had already poured down the stairs and were flinging open the room's main doors from the other side. Lugorix got a quick glimpse of the Carthaginian guards who'd stood watch there—and who were now in the final throes of being butchered—and then that view was obscured by the hordes of cheering Athenians who charged out into the corridors outside. Lugorix, Matthias and Eurydice looked down at the chaos.

"Happy now?" said Eurydice.

"Ecstatic," said Matthias.

"Let's go," said Lugorix.

This time there were no objections. They headed away from the prison-warehouse, past the gardens, back toward the harbor. From the looks of the view out the apertures and windows, most of the Athenians were concentrating on setting fire to the palace. Lugorix was glad he and Matthias hadn't been appointed the ringleaders of the whole enterprise—and even more glad that Matthias hadn't started giving orders. Holing up in the citadel of Carthage seemed like a really shitty idea. Getting back to the ship was clearly the way to go.

Though some of the Athenians seemed to realize their rescuers had a plan. More than a hundred prisoners were following them down the covert corridors, past the garden-rooms and down the stairs toward the harbor. Lugorix considered telling them to find their own way out, but he figured Matthias would have a problem with that. Which still left a bit of a dilemma.

"There's not room for them all on our ship," he muttered.

"There's not room for *any* of them," said Eurydice. "But there are a lot of ships."

He had a point. The Athenians poured into the room with the murder-holes and set to work with alacrity, dropping ropes down those holes and onto the decks of the ships below. Those ships weren't taken completely by surprise—they were already on alert thanks to the alarms sounding throughout the palace, and were frantically prepping for action. But they were ready to defend the harbor from a naval threat, not from furious former prisoners suddenly falling onto them from above. A ferocious battle developed, as Carthaginian marines rallied against the rain of Athenians, some of whom were literally leaping down to the decks below. In moments, the scene was one of total pandemonium.

"That'll buy us some cover," said Eurydice.

Matthias said nothing—just sprang to the ladder against the wall, began climbing down to the jetty where the *Xerxes* was moored.

Only it wasn't moored there any longer.

The sluice-gate beneath which the *Xerxes* had snuck in had just been stoved in by a ram—and the Carthaginian warship that had done so was backing water, towering over the three who stood on that jetty looking up at it. It was a pentereme—five banks of oars, two masts, and a horde of marines lining the deck. But none of that was as problematic as the man who was standing on the prow: Perdiccas himself. He was flanked by both Macedonian and Carthaginian soldiers, and he looked more than a little surprised as he caught sight of Eurydice, who he obviously recognized.

"What the fuck are *you* doing here?" he yelled.

"Go fuck yourself!" yelled Eurydice. Lugorix would have thought that someone as smart as she was could have come up with a better insult than that, but then again, she was under pressure. They all were now, as Carthaginian archers crowded alongside Perdiccas and took aim at the three who stood on the jetty beneath them.

"Give yourself up," said Perdiccas.

Lugorix hefted his axe, looked the Macedonian general straight in the eye.

"Come and get us," he said.

"Kill the men and bring me the woman," said Perdiccas. The archers drew back their bows—only to suddenly be knocked to the deck as another Carthaginian warship rammed the pentereme hard amidship. It had emerged from the roofed harbor where the pitched battle was raging between the prisoners. At least one of those ships was now under the control of the Athenians—and that ship now backed water in an attempt to vacate the hole it had just created and flood the holds of the pentereme.

But it was stuck.

Either it had embedded itself too deep or there simply weren't enough rowers at the oars to provide the necessary leverage. The pentereme was clearly taking on water, though, slowly sliding to the side, putting ever more strain on the ship that had impaled it.

Not that anyone was waiting around for it to sink. Carthaginian marines leapt from their own ship, dashing across the prow of their assailant and pouring onto its deck, where they were met with Athenians eager to finally come to grips with their tormentors. In short order, the decks of both ships became a scene of absolute mayhem.

"This is the part where we make ourselves scarce," said Eurydice.

There were no objections. She led them away from the ladder, along the stone jetty, away from both the stricken pentereme and the interior harbor where fighting was still taking place on several of the ships. They came out from under the roof and found themselves against the wall of the exterior harbor. Lugorix looked back at the carnage going on across the interior harbor, at the smoke pouring from the palace. More ships were sortieing from the adjacent harbors; these ones seemed to be fully armed and prepped and ready to kill some Athenians. There was no point in sticking around.

"We're sitting ducks here," said Matthias.

Eurydice nodded. She led them through an overflow channel—so narrow and low that once again Lugorix had to crawl, this time through water that sloshed around his hands and knees. He had to wriggle a few times to keep going—and when he emerged he was staring along a promontory that cut along the border of the outer harbor.

"Time to sprint," said Eurydice.

They dashed along the promontory, out into the harbor. The battle that was going on in the interior harbor didn't seem to be a factor here. Or—more likely—the crews were still in the city. The three fugitives kept on running, though Lugorix could see they only had a few hundred more meters before they ran out of room altogether.

That was when three ships emerged from the harbor, rowing at full speed, bearing down on them.

"Shit," said Lugorix.

"We're running out of room," said Matthias.

"Run faster!" yelled Eurydice.

Matthias and Lugorix did so, just as arrows began to sail past them. The ships were vectoring in on their quarry. Lugorix could hear shouting in Phoenician echoing across the water, getting louder. He didn't want to die with an arrow in his back—Taranis would never let him past the gates of death. And being speared in the water would be an even more shameful ending. Meaning he'd have to turn and dare them to come to him. That was the only way he was going to get a clean death. Ahead of him, Matthias reached the end of the promontory and dove in. Eurydice followed suit.

Just as the *Xerxes* surfaced.

The ship broke water barely ten yards past the promontory—Matthias had already covered half the distance to it, with Eurydice not that far behind. But just as Lugorix was about to dive in after them—

"Wait!" screamed a voice. He whirled to see two Athenians running along the promontory toward him. "Hurry up!" screamed Lugorix—and dove in. Because he knew that waiting was the one thing that the *Xerxes* wasn't going to do. He paddled furiously toward the ship as he heard the Athenians leap into the water behind him.

The hatch opened and Barsine appeared on the deck and hurled a rope into the water. Matthias grabbed onto it. The *Xerxes'* engine started up; the ship began powering away from the edge of the promontory, leaving Lugorix swimming frantically to catch up. But it was too late, the boat was drawing away. Matthias had already reached the ship; Eurydice was clambering up the rope. Barsine looked out toward Lugorix—raised a strange-looking device with a hook set into it. There was a loud twang!— the hook came shooting straight toward Lugorix, just missing his head and splashing into the water.

It was only then that Lugorix noticed the rope that had been trailing behind it. It was out of his reach, but one of the Athenians grabbed onto it, seizing it with both hands. Lugorix didn't hesitate; he grabbed onto that Athenian's boot, and the second Athenian grabbed onto *his*—and then all three men were jerked forward, pulled through the water while Matthias and Barsine worked to haul in the rope. The *Xerxes* was steadily outpacing the pursuing Carthaginian triremes, but now siege-engines atop the harbor wall opened fire. Huge rocks sailed through the air and crashed into the water uncomfortably close to the *Xerxes*. Waves slapped against Lugorix's face—he almost lost his grip but locked his legs around the rope for additional purchase and hung on as best he could. He'd almost reached the *Xerxes* now, but the rope stretched over the engine and it wasn't clear how he was going to climb over it. But then the ship turned, and suddenly he was being hauled in toward its side. He put his feet out to brace himself, hit the side, and then walked himself up, following the first Athenian. Moments later, all three men were spluttering onto the deck.

"Never doubted you," said Barsine.

"Get below," said Eurydice's voice from the hatch.

The ship started to dive.

CHAPTER FIFTEEN

The two Athenians were marines. Their names were Xanthippus and Diocles. Xanthippus was a grizzled old veteran; Diocles a young soldier who had never seen combat. Both men were utterly exhausted—they sat on the floor of the *Xerxes'* pilot-room, water dripping off them. The expression on their faces was that of men who refused to accept their surroundings. Lugorix was tempted to feel sorry for them—but then he recollected they might be the only Athenians who had survived the carnage going on back at Carthage. So maybe they were actually the fortunate ones.

All the more so as no one had asked them to any rowing. Lugorix and Matthias had paddled the ship beneath the surface for more than an hour until they'd put Carthage well behind them. Finally Barsine surfaced the *Xerxes* and switched the engines on, whereupon she sent Matthias up top. It was a little frustrating, because Lugorix was burning with questions he couldn't ask—there seemed to be a tacit understanding among everyone that they wouldn't discuss what they'd seen in the Library in front of the Athenians. It was only now that they'd put Carthage behind them that Barsine turned to the two men.

"Were you part of the garrison of Carthage?" she asked.

"No," said Xanthippus. "We were part of the fleet that sailed from Syracuse."

Eurydice sat down on the floor opposite them. "What went wrong?"

"I don't know," said Xanthippus.

"Everything," said Diocles. "That's what went wrong. Everything." He seemed about to continue but then he shook his head and shut up as though someone had clamped his jaws shut.

"You need to tell me," said Eurydice gently.

"I can't," said Diocles.

"I can," said Xanthippus. He took a deep breath. "I've sailed from one end of the Empire to the other thrice over, and I've spent as much time on ships as I have on land. But I've never seen a storm like the one that hit us when we were half a day from Carthage. The sky turned purple and red and the rain came down so hard it swept men into the sea. There was a huge wave; it capsized all the ships and horse-transports. Horses swimming for their lives and going under, making a noise I never want to hear again… lightning tore off our masts and we lost contact with the rest of the fleet. And then there was a huge wave. Our ship foundered shortly thereafter. We clung to driftwood, somehow ended up on the African coast."

"And then the Carthagianians found us," said Diocles.

"After all we'd been through, I was thanking the gods for it," said Xanthippus. "We've heard what Berbers can do to a man. But sometimes the ones who call themselves civilized are worse than any barbarian."

Lugorix wasn't sure about that, but he said nothing. For a long while, no one did. Finally—

"Where are you taking us anyway?" asked Xanthippus.

"We're going west," said Barsine. "Through the Pillars of Hercules."

"You must be joking."

"Do you hear me laughing?"

"You should be, because you can't go that way."

"Why not?"

"You'll fall off the edge of the world. There's nothing beyond there save Abyss."

"I have reason to disagree."

Xanthippus looked at them like they were all totally crazy. Lugorix wasn't sure he was wrong. Xanthippus met his eyes, then shook his head. "What do you think the Pillars are, anyway?" he asked.

"You tell me," said Barsine.

"They're the two monsters that Hercules battled. Scylla and Charbydis, right?"

"I think you might have your myths mixed up."

"I don't care. They're monsters, and we're not going near them. Besides, haven't you heard about what's out *past* those Pillars?" It seemed to Lugorix that if the Pillars really *were* monsters, no one would get past them anyway, but Xanthippus wasn't waiting for an answer. He just kept going: "No one's gotten more than three days west and returned to tell the tale. There's something out there and it's not pretty! There's talk of whirlpools and monsters and boiling seas and—"

"Damn right," said Diocles. "You need to turn around right now."

"We can't do that."

"Well, we can't go on," said Xanthippus.

"We *won't* go on," said Diocles.

There was a long silence. Finally—

"OK," said Barsine. "What would you suggest we do with you then?"

Xanthippus was only too happy to tell her.

The Romans were a strange lot, Eumenes thought.

They only ruled the central part of Italy, but they carried themselves with the arrogance of a people who had already conquered a mighty empire. Or maybe arrogance wasn't the right word—perhaps a better one was *assurance*. As though they were guaranteed to some day rule many peoples beside those who currently did them homage. Which at this point meant the Samnites, the Etruscans, the Rutuli, and a few others. Not enough for anyone outside of Italy to give two shits about. But if you wanted to march down the length of the peninsula—well, that was a different story. You would have to deal with the Romans.

Which was why Eumenes had ridden into their city that morning as a *legatus*: an ambassador on behalf of the Macedonian king whose army was encamped fifty miles north of the city. As the representative of a foreign invader, Eumenes wasn't surprised to see that the Roman people weren't too happy to see him. Soldiers held a jeering mob back as it pressed forward, screaming oaths and throwing enough rocks to keep Eumenes' two shieldbearers on their toes. The lack of discipline and order was a sight to behold. Had he not seen the Roman legions gathered up in full battle order in front of the city, Eumenes might have wondered how in the name of all the gods this people had ever conquered anything at all.

But even if he hadn't seen the legions, he'd have ceased wondering when he arrived at what the Romans called their *Senate*. It was a word that meant *council of old men,* and it certainly lived up to its billing. No one in that chamber seemed to be less than eighty years old, and yet somehow all of them seemed to be wise beyond their years. Eumenes was ushered in just as another speaker was finishing up. That speaker wasn't a Senator. He was another legatus, like Eumenes.

Only he was Athenian.

He was finishing up a rather eloquent speech rallying the Senators to join Athens against the cause of Alexander—or at the very least to block Alexander from passing through Roman territory to the boot of Italy and on to the island of Sicily. Neither the speaker nor the Senators seemed to be in any doubt that Syracuse was Alexander's ultimate destination. It was the only thing south of here worth all the trouble. But Eumenes had to hand it to Alexander for being able to keep his objective a secret for so long. Once Syracuse fell into his hands the remnants of the Athenian Empire would lie in ruins, and the granaries of Italy would be lost to Athens, just like those of Africa already had been. It might even be possible to starve Athens out at that point; at the very least, the days of Athenian glory would be well and truly over. Eumenes listened impassively as the speaker wound up into a peroration asking Rome to defend its own sovereignty and reminding everybody of all the great things that Athens had done for Rome.

From the sound of it, it wasn't much. *We tried to turn your city into an economic dependency of ours* was tough to spin. And Eumenes felt the speaker could use a few tips regarding his style. The Athenian Assembly was a very different audience than the Roman Senate. When the echoes of the speaker's final impassioned plea had died away the low droning of the Latin translator continued for another ten seconds. After which there was what could only be described as an awkward silence.

"Er, um, thank you," said the speaker. No one said anything. He shuffled off, giving Eumenes a dirty look as he did so. Eumenes stood up and cleared his throat. It had taken him exactly two weeks to learn Latin—his record so far.

"Senators," he said. "My thanks for receiving me as an ambassador to your august city. I come before you to—"

"Stop," said one of the Senators.

Eumenes stopped.

"We've heard enough speeches for the day," said the Senator. A murmur of assent went round the chamber, followed by some scattered clapping.

"What would you prefer instead?" asked Eumenes.

"We'd prefer to ask you questions," said another Senator. There was more clapping this time. It occurred to Eumenes that the Senators might dislike the Macedonians even more than they disliked the Athenians. After all, the latter weren't trying to invade them. Still, all he could do was grin and bear it. He smiled the smile of the well-practiced diplomat.

"Of course," he said.

"Your king, Alexander—we hear he is not the legitimate king of Macedonia."

Uh-oh, thought Eumenes. "You are misinformed, my lords."

"Conscript Fathers."

What kind of title is that? "Conscript Fathers," repeated Eumenes. "Your pardon. My king"—*shit*—"my *kings* rule Macedonia jointly."

"We heard the father reprimanded the son."

What father doesn't? "I fear your reports are misinformed. Kings Philip and Alexander are the very picture of harmony. And they are of one mind on Macedonian policy. Including the policy that sends me to your doorstep." Sure enough, the next Senator swallowed the bait and changed the subject:

"Why *did* you bring your army into Italy?"

Because we could. "We have no quarrel with the Roman people, Conscript Fathers. Our war is with Athens, but Athens controls the southern reaches of Italy and we need to pass through your territory to bring our war to—"

"You misunderstand," said the Senator.

"Then I ask for your pardon and clarification."

"Why didn't your king send you *before* he crossed the Alps and brought his soldiers to the edge of our territory?"

"Originally my king intended to venture on into Iberia, but the pleas of the oppressed people of Syracuse so moved him that he had a change of heart at the last moment." That was a load of crap, of course, but it was better than saying that Alexander was so paranoid he hadn't even told his closest advisers what he intended to do until the last moment. Even now Eumenes and Hephaestion were the only ones beside the king to know that the real game underway went far beyond mere questions of conquest and empire. During the review of the weapons, Hephaestion had taken Eumenes aside and confided his concerns about the king's *mental stability.* Those were his exact words. Eumenes had thought that Alexander had

ceased to venture away from the camp at night—certainly the sentries reported nothing—but now it turned out that he was doing it *every evening,*
sneaking back in past the sentries every morning like he was on a one-
man commando raid. And when he was in bed, he muttered to himself in
arcane languages that Hephaestion couldn't understand. Eumenes didn't
know what he found more shocking—the information itself or the fact
that Hephaestion was so disturbed he was confiding in him. It was all he
could do to stay focused in this stupid Senate chamber and deal with the
situation at hand. Another Senator stood up.

"So what is it you want?" he asked.

"Permission for our army to pass through."

"With your weapons?"

And for the first time in the cross-examination, Eumenes was candid:
"Well, yes. We need those to deal with the Athenians, after all."

"No foreigner may cross the domain of Rome while armed!" yelled a
Senator. Another Senator shouted him down. For a few moments the
chamber was a mass of yelling geriatrics. And then another man shouted
above the din for order. Much to Eumenes' surprise, he got it.

"If that is all that King Alexander requires, then surely this is a request
we can meet." Eumenes hadn't noticed the man previously. He stood at
the back of the chamber, and unlike the Senators, his toga was red rather
than white. Two men flanked him wearing togas of grey; each one carried
a bundle of rods surrounding an axe, tied together with strips of leather.
Eumenes recognized them as the *fasces*—symbols of Roman power. Which
made these the officials known as lictors—which meant that the man who
stood between them was one of the consuls. Eumenes chose his next words
carefully.

"I thank the consul and the Conscript Fathers for their forbearance,
and assure you that the only other things that my king asks of you are but
trivial compared to what you have just so generously granted."

There was a long pause while the implication of those words sank in. The
consul was the first to speak.

"What else does your king want?"

"He wishes to step aside from his army's march to visit the valley of Avernus, south of Naples." A confused murmuring ran through the chamber. A
Senator gave it voice: "Why does your king desire to go there?"

"He is interested in local culture"—*like fuck he is*—"and understands that Avernus is a center of your religious practices."

"Perhaps we can grant that," said the consul. "Perhaps. Does your king want anything else?"

Here it comes. "Indeed he does." He paused, then: "He wishes to enter Rome and inspect the Sibylline Books." The last words of Eumenes' sentence were drowned out by a single collective howl from everyone in the room. It was at least half a minute before the consul was able to calm things down enough for any individual voices to be heard, and during those thirty seconds there were several occasions when Eumenes thought he'd be lucky to escape from the chamber with his life. In theory, envoys to Rome were untouchable; in practice, there were undoubtedly things that would cause that rule to be violated. Whipping out one's dick on the floor of the Senate, for example. Or describing some particularly lurid fantasy regarding the Vestal Virgins. Both of which were probably *slightly* less offensive than a request to consult the most sacred volumes of prophecy the Roman people possessed, but most of the Senators weren't in the mood to quibble. When the consul finally addressed the floor, his words were ice.

"You talk sacrilege, Greek."

"Then I ask for your forgiveness."

"Apollo is the one you should ask. Given that it's his temple that holds the Books. It's he who you have offended."

"In that case, my king asks permission to travel to his temple."

No one bought that for a second. "Your *king* will remain outside the city and await our instructions as to when and by what route he can march his army."

No one gives Alexander instructions. But all Eumenes said was, "My king needs to march now."

"What about the Books? Does he withdraw his request to visit them?"

"Perhaps the Books could visit him?" As the rumbling growl around him swelled toward a roar, Eumenes raised his voice: "I mean only that my king would be willing to consult the books in any place you might choose. In or outside of Rome."

"The books don't leave Rome," said a Senator in a tone that would have won an Olympic award for patrician contempt.

"Why is your king so intent on consulting these books?" yelled another Senator.

"Does he put himself above the priests of Apollo?" asked the consul.

Eumenes judged that he had waited long enough. "Yes," he said. "He does." He expected that to result in another tide of anger, but the chamber slowly faded to silence.

"My king is the Son of Zeus-Ammon and divine in his own right," said Eumenes, his words ringing out in the chamber. He was starting to enjoy himself; the expression on their faces was priceless. "That makes me the emissary of a living god, and I must warn you that should you defy his wishes your fate will be severe."

There was a moment's stunned pause.

"These Macedonians are all insane," said someone.

"You *dare* threaten the Roman Senate?" said the consul.

"I dare more than that," said Eumenes. Suddenly they all heard the noise of absolute bedlam outside the Senate House: explosions, collapsing masonry, screaming people, clashing swords. Eumenes had to give the Senators credit for poise. None of them even moved. Instead more Roman guards raced into the chamber, positioning themselves by the doorways. The consul strode toward Eumenes, flanked by his lictors—who were unravelling their bundles of wood and taking out their axes.

"How did you do it?" asked the consul.

"Do what?" asked Eumenes.

"Get inside our city."

"You invited me in."

"I mean your army," said the consul.

"Army is a bit of an overstatement," said Eumenes. "Most of it's still outside the city destroying yours. No force in the world has yet withstood the direct charge of Alexander's Companion Cavalry, and I doubt yours will be the first, particularly once we've softened them up by lobbing gas and Greek fire into their midst." The noise of the fighting outside was growing louder. "As for the disturbance on your doorstep, that's really the result of your own investments in infrastructure. Such excellent aqueducts, such magnificent sewers. In particular that—what do you call it?—the *Cloaca Maxima*—a nice long underground channel leading outside the city. Of course, I suppose one could always go the other way—"

That did it. Before Eumenes could finish, the consul grabbed an axe from one of his lictors and rushed at him. Eumenes stepped under the sweep of the blade and tripped him. The consul sprawled on the floor of the Senate while his two lictors moved in. Eumenes grabbed the arm of the first man and broke it—seized the rod the man held and smashed him over the head with it—then leaped back out of range of the second man's axe. As the man drew the axe back for a second swing, Eumenes slipped a hidden dagger out of his boot and hurled it into the man's throat. He went down choking. Eumenes stepped over to the consul—who was pulling himself to his hands and knees—and kicked him in the face. He fell back onto the floor and didn't move. Throughout this time, none of the shocked Senators had risen from their seats—but guards were racing down the steps, their weapons drawn and ready to hack Eumenes to bits. He turned to face them, acutely aware there were way too many.

But now more figures entered the chamber. They wore the colors of Macedonia and the Roman guards turned to confront them.

Only to draw back as they realized what they were facing.

Which, of course, was the point. The typical golem was only a slightly better swordsman than the typical soldier—but they were more difficult to kill, and besides, the psychological dividends in utilizing them were undeniable. Being confronted by metal men was enough to give pause even to the elite guards of the Roman Senate. The fact that each golem was covered in shit from its trek through the Cloaca Maxima only added to the surrealism of the situation. But these Roman guards were the elite—and after hesitating for only a moment, they charged the golems. Only a few were left to deal with Eumenes, and he took advantage of the confusion to race past this and leap onto the consul's vacated chair.

"*Stop!*" he yelled. And such was the surrealism of the moment that everyone did. The soldiers backed away from the golems, who stood their ground. For a brief moment, there was utter silence inside the Senate House—except for the noise of the fighting continuing outside. Though even that sounded like it was now beginning to subside. Eumenes raised his voice a few more notches.

"You have lost," he said. "Your army's beaten, we're inside the city, and now Alexander's creatures of sorcery have reached this very chamber. But my king's terms are generous, and they start with the confirmation of your rule of central Italy. He doesn't even ask for tribute—just the granting of the requests I made earlier. Give us that, and we will spare your city, your people and all your works. Defy us, and we will erase the name *Rome* from history."

The Senators began muttering among themselves. But then a voice snarled up from the floor. It was the still-prone consul.

"Take the deal," he hissed.

The Senate did.

"So where *are* we going?" said Lugorix.

It was several days later. They'd left the two Athenian marines on an Iberian beach, along with some weapons and rations. They'd explained to them that there wasn't an Athenian base for thousands of miles, but that just seemed to make the two men all the more eager to get the hell off the boat. Lugorix could relate. Part of him was tempted to go along with them. They were still babbling about the edge of the world and monsters as they waded ashore.

"And they never even thanked us," said Eurydice.

"What about my question?" said Lugorix.

"We deserve some answers," said Matthias.

"Sure you do," said Eurydice. "But we couldn't talk in front of those Athenians. As soon as they started opening their mouths, I knew they'd want to get off at the first available stop. Couple of chickens, is what they were. Why Barsine felt like being so generous to them, I don't know—"

"You're both avoiding the subject," said Lugorix.

"Atlantis," said Matthias.

"Yes," said Barsine, "that's where we're going."

"What's Atlantis?" asked Lugorix.

"A bunch of bullshit," said Matthias before either woman could speak.

"Really?" said Barsine in an amused tone. "Why didn't you say that—"

"—back in that freakshow of a library?" asked Matthias. "We were all a little busy then, weren't we? And I thought this was the part where you levelled with us." He looked at Lugorix. "Atlantis is the kind of thing that the storytellers tell around the campfire when they've got done singing about centaurs and pegasi and can't be arsed to invent anything new. It never happened. So come on, ladies: what are we *really* talking about here?"

"Just that," said Barsine.

"But what the hell *is* Atlantis anyway?" asked Lugorix.

"I just told you," said Matthias.

"Ever heard of Plato?" asked Eurydice. Lugorix looked at her blankly. "He was my father's teacher back in Athens. He wrote of a legendary city that used to rule the world and that was buried thousands of years ago—"

"He wrote a bunch of crap," said Matthias—Eurydice started to reply but he just kept talking over her: *"A bunch of crap* so he could sell a bunch of books. It was a couple of fucking *paragraphs* and it was the most quoted thing in those stupid dialogues. You really want to base your *entire strategy* on that?"

"Of course not," said Eurydice. "Plato never *published* his real work on the subject. He *wanted* people to think it was all a legend. So that the enemies of Greece would never realize the truth that lay behind it."

"So you're saying Plato *didn't* tell the public," said Lugorix. "But he *did* tell Aristotle."

"Actually he didn't," said Eurydice. "He was beginning to doubt my father's loyalties."

"To him?" asked Barsine.

"To Greece."

"Ah."

"My father never saw himself as betraying his people, of course. He'd convinced himself that Macedonia had designs upon neither Greece nor Athens."

"He was naïve," said Matthias. Lugorix braced himself for Eurydice's reaction to that, but she just nodded:

"Of course he was," she said. "Like so many scientists, he existed mainly in his lab and in his head. But he woke up toward the end. And I think part of what made him do so was that he realized the stakes involved."

"When he uncovered the secrets of his teacher," said Barsine.

"Exactly."

"The lost book of Atlantis—"

"Not the book," said Eurydice. "Just fragments."

"That was all?"

"It was enough. To get him on the trail."

"And then Athenian intelligence got on *his* trail," said Barsine.

Eurydice nodded. "And traitors within it tipped off Philip."

"Now *that* I'm not so sure of," said Barsine. "Philip might already have put two and two together. Because as far as I can make out, Athenian intelligence remained loyal to Demosthenes: his shadow outfit that kept reporting to him even when he was out of power. So when I told Demosthenes what I'd found beneath Babylon, he and I realized what I'd have to do."

"Consult with my father," said Eurydice. "And find Atlantis."

"Please tell me there's a limit to this horseshit," said Matthias.

Lugorix frowned, still trying to keep up. "Earlier you told me that we were in search of the Gardens of Hespa-what-the-fuck."

Eurydice smiled grimly. "Call it what you like, it's the same thing."

"It is?" Lugorix was a little skeptical of these shifting stories.

"A lost domain in the far west containing forbidden magick? It's got many names, but that's what it boils down to."

"Okay," said Matthias, "let's say—just for the sake of argument—let's say I bought this. Then in that case why *didn't you just say Atlantis in the first place?*"

Eurydice shrugged. "Atlantis is a term with too much baggage. It automatically strains credulity. You wouldn't have believed us."

"I don't believe you now."

"Point made," said Eurydice. "But if I'd told you earlier, I'll bet you would have jumped ship at first opportunity." Matthias' face went red—but before he could open his mouth Lugorix broke in.

"So where does Alexander fit in to all of this?" he asked.

"Everywhere," said Eurydice. "The Athenian position west of Syracuse is now total shit. Alexander has sacked Massilia and suborned Carthage to revolt. And he's apparently used magick to destroy part of the Athenian fleet."

"Those storms," said Matthias.

"Those storms," she agreed. "I think that's what we saw to the north several days back—that may have been the destruction of any ships that escaped Massilia. But it seems there was another storm—one we didn't see. It hit the fleet coming out from Syracuse and left... not much."

There was a long pause. Behind them, the Iberian coast was fading into mist.

"All this talk of what was going down in the West wasn't just talk," said Eurydice.

Matthias frowned. "What do you think is going on?"

Barsine looked at Eurydice. "Do you have a theory?"

Eurydice shook her head. "I wish I still had a library," she said. "My father had several volumes that might have given us the answer...."

"Or not," said Barsine. "If what's doing this are creations of Alexander's sorcery, they might not be in any book. If they really are demons—"

"They're not demons," said Eurydice. "They're his mind. He's controlling the elements."

"You sure about that?" asked Barsine.

"I'm *sure* of nothing, Persian."

"So maybe you shouldn't be so quick to speculate." Barsine only shrugged; Lugorix was realizing that the closed-doors conversations these two women had been having were far from cordial—he was starting to realize just how much they disagreed about. Which didn't bode well for the future. "How far is it to the Pillars?" he asked.

"Several days," said Barsine. "Let's get below."

"I'll stand watch," said Eurydice.

"I'll join you," said Matthias.

She gave him a dirty look. "I'm not in the mood for company," she replied.

Matthias was, though. So the next watch was him and Lugorix. They stared out at the night-time ocean. They were running parallel to the Iberian coast. To the south, the moon glimmered off gathering clouds.

"Are those coming our way?" said Matthias.

Lugorix studied them. "I don't think so," he said.

"She's driving me nuts."

"I can see that."

"She thinks she's so much smarter than me."

"I suspect she's smarter than everybody," said Lugorix.

"Are you defending her?"

"I'm just calling it like I see it."

"Which doesn't mean going west of the Pillars is a wise thing to do."

"No," said Lugorix, "it doesn't."

"I wonder if those two Athenians had the right idea."

Lugorix said nothing. It was a moot point now. They were along for the ride, and they'd just have to hope that whatever Barsine and Eurydice were plotting wasn't totally crazy. There was no doubt about it, they were in strange waters now. And he was getting more than a little worried about Barsine. She seemed to be driven by something deep within her. Her pregnancy hadn't started to show, but it was undoubtedly at the center of all her calculations. Abruptly he saw a flash of lightning on the horizon.

Then another, much closer.

"Looks like the storm's coming this way," he said. No sooner were the words out of his mouth then it started to rain—at first mere spinkles but within a few minutes it was pouring down. They could hear thunder rolling across the water toward them. The hatch opened and Barsine peered out.

"Shit," she said.

"Tell me about it," said Lugorix.

She climbed back down the ladder. Second later, the ship turned, started running north before the encroaching storm. Matthias and Lugorix gripped onto the rail while weirdly-colored clouds dumped untold amounts of rain on them. The lightning was starting to crash down around them.

"We should probably get below," said Lugorix.

Matthias wasn't arguing. They clambered down to find Barsine and Eurydice debating how far beyond the safety margins they could push the engine throttle. Eveidently they were worried. Nestled amidst the machinery, the amulet was glowing.

"It looks like you may be overdoing it," said Matthias.

Barsine glanced at the amulet. "It's reacting to the storm. Not the motors."

"What?"

"The storm isn't natural," snapped Eurydice. "It's driven by magick."

Lugorix peered out a window. He would have thought that much was obvious. The *Xerxes* was pitching back and forth now, caught in the throes of the waves. He wondered what the plan was to get them out of this one. If this really *was* the storm that had sunk half the Athenian fleet, then there seemed little reason to believe that even a ship of the *Xerxes'* caliber was going to stand much of a chance. Suddenly he felt the floor shudder beneath his feet. They had run aground.

Except they hadn't. The *Xerxes* kept on rumbling forward.

"Uh… what the fuck?" said Matthias.

"We're getting the hell out of this sea," said Eurydice.

"Works for me," said Lugorix.

Matthias was still struggling to keep up. "Aren't we a ship?"

"We *were*," said Barsine.

And it was true. Eurydice hadn't just made the *Xerxes* a more versatile vessel. She'd also configured it so that it could sprout—

"*Wheels,*" said Matthias. "We're on wheels."

"Think of us as a particularly large ox-cart," said Eurydice.

Lugorix was trying not to think at all. It was all a little too weird. They were now rolling along a beach while rain lashed down on them and waves crashed around them. But at least now no one was going to be able to sink them.

"Alexander is conjuring up this storm to stop us," said Barsine. "As long as they continue, we're stuck on land."

"It can't go on indefinitely," said Eurydice.

She was wrong.

Magickal storms did what they wanted, apparently. Or rather, what their creators could pull off. The days passed and the storm kept on throwing itself against them. The lightning dissipated a little, but the ocean still looked like shit. They were staying as far back from it as possible—right where the beach gave way to endless forests of pine. Lugorix and Matthias took turns huddled on top, keeping an eye out for... what? Tribesmen? Macedonians? Magickal creatures? They never saw any. They just trundled westward across the storm-tossed days and nights, all too aware of how slow they were going, all too aware that those behind them would be making haste to close the gap...

Alexander gazed out upon Sicily.

Astride his white horse, atop the most southeastern hill on the peninsula of Bruttium: it was the classic conqueror's pose, so perfect it might have been planned. But for Alexander this kind of thing came naturally. The exhaustion that clouded his face was only visible up close. He didn't turn around as Eumenes and Hephaestion rode up to him.

"So it was blocked," was all he said.

"It was," confirmed Eumenes.

"Despite deploying the black powder," said Hephaestion. "Any more, and we might have collapsed the roof." Eumenes resisted the urge to laugh; Hephaestion had wanted to use a *lot* more, but Eumenes had managed to talk him out of it. Had he not, they'd be giving Alexander much worse news. As it was, there might still be some way past all those rocks and fallen masonry, further into the cave that lay in the crater of Avernus. They would need stronger sorcery. Which right now they didn't have.

"The books were clear," said Alexander. Eumenes never thought he'd heard the word *clear* used to describe the content of the Sibylline Books, but Alexander had felt sure—almost mystically so—of his interpretation of them. "There's a way in from there."

"Doesn't do us any good if we can't get through it," said Eumenes. Part of him was still struggling to keep up with all of this. He'd always prided himself on being the arch-rationalist. But the three months since had un-dermined that faith. Particularly now that Alexander had let him in on the full range of his calculations—had shown him the burnt remnants of the scrolls found in Aristotle's fireplace at Pella, as well as the papyri taken from the temple at the oasis of Siwah. The king exhaled slowly.

"We'll just have to do this the hard way," he said.

"You mean the long way," said Hephaestion.

"I mean both," said Alexander. He stared down at the Straits of Messina, the hazy outline of Sicily visible in the distance. In the wake of Rome's submission, the Athenian position in southern Italy had collapsed rapidly. The city of Tarentum had lynched most of the Athenian officials there, and the garrison had subsequently put to sea rather than fight. Meanwhile Macedonian gold was flowing into Roman coffers, in return for the draft-ing of virtually the entire labor force of central and southern Italy to chop down every tree they could find. Italy would be virtually deforested by the time they were done.

And a bridge would stretch from Italy to Sicily.

It would span a distance of two miles, but it was the only solution the three men had been able to come up with to the problem of the Athenian navy. Eumenes suspected that Alexander had had it in mind all along; then again, if they'd been able to break through to what supposedly lay beneath Avernus, the war might have been won without ever going to Sicily. But it was certain that once the Macedonians got across, the Athenians would have no choice but to fall back into Syracuse and brace for the mother of all sieges. Should the city fall, that would essentially be the end of the Athenian Empire.

And the beginning of so much else. The tellers of tales regarded the island of Ortygia as the birthplace of the divine twins Apollo and Artemis. The god of the Sun and the goddess of the Moon—but what did such myths *really* mean?

"It's not the primary site," said Alexander, still not taking his eyes off the Sicilian coast. "It's a secondary. Same with Avernus. Same with Siwah."

Eumenes nodded tactfully. For Alexander, myths were as literal as his destiny. Hephaestion, on the other hand, had been growing ever more alarmed as Alexander grew ever more distant, ever more in sync with something that only he could hear. If the king wasn't going insane, he had told Eumenes during the trip to Avernus, then *something had been communicating with him* ever since Siwah—some kind of intelligence that spoke very distinctly and very precisely to Alexander and *that had kept speaking to him since inside his head,* and that clearly knew a lot more about him then he did about it. It had promised him dominion over the earth, known and unknown. It had assured him of his divine birthright. And it had given him certain powers—had allowed him to activate previously-untapped portions of his mind....

"It's a function of the bloodline," Hephaestion had said, though that just begged the real question. Eumenes had just nodded. "That's what it must be keying on," added the king's lover. "Why it told him so much more than it ever told any of those backward desert priests who'd been getting rich off it. And it's why we have to get our hands on *her.*"

"How far along is she?" asked Eumenes.

"Four months going on five," said Hephaestion as though he wanted to vomit. Eumenes could only guess what he and Alexander said about the matter behind closed doors. It wasn't that Hephaestion minded Alexander's dalliances with women. And this particular one had been intended to generate a very particular result.

Problem was, Alexander no longer had control of it.

"We should have headed straight for Gibraltar," said Hephaestion.

"We'd never have made it in time," said Eumenes. "An army isn't what's going to catch her."

Hephaestion had nodded. They'd said nothing more of the matter. Eumenes had no doubt that Hephaestion felt uneasy for confiding in him. But the two of them had been forced to cooperate by virtue of sharing responsibility for all the special weapons—and by the necessity of keeping the ship of state on track in what were increasingly surreal waters. What was at the heart of all this? What lay in the far west? How could they stop Barsine from getting there first? With a start, Eumenes found himself once again staring into Alexander's variegated eyes. They bored into him as though they were taking full measure of his worth.

"How soon can you leave?" asked the king.

"I'm ready now," replied Eumenes.

"There's something I need to give you before you go," said Alexander. He drew his sword. "I regret having to do this."

That turned out to be an understatement.

CHAPTER SIXTEEN

At last they were back on the water.

The storm had eventually died out, though not for want of trying. Euryice said she suspected it was simply a matter of range—that Alexander was unable to reach them that far west. But the water near the Pillars was rough enough anyway. The deck was pitching up and down like the time he'd held on to win his village's bull-riding contest. But at least that had stopped. This time he couldn't get off the bull, and it kept on charging in a direction he didn't want to go, toward the edge of the world. Eurydice had told him that was nonsense—there was no *edge*—but he trusted his common sense over her long-winded explanations.

"Look at that," hissed Matthias.

Gripping onto the rails, Lugorix forced himself to look. All he could see were just more waves. "Where?" he asked.

"*There*," hissed Matthias, pointing. Lugorix followed the direction in which he was gesturing—through the swell of waves, out to where the haze of sky met that of sea.

And then he saw it.

Up ahead, two mountains protruded from the ocean, their tops lost in the low-hanging clouds. The coastline stretched away on both sides, leaving a gap between those peaks—a gap toward which they were sailing.

"Here we go," said Matthias. He stepped over to the hatch and called down to the women.

"We see it," said Eurydice rather curtly. Matthias rejoined Lugorix, a wan smile on his face.

"Everything still okay with you two?" asked the Gaul.

"Nothing's ever been *okay* with us," said Matthias.

"Because she wears the pants?"

It took Matthias a moment to realize that was a Gaulish expression—Greeks didn't use pants. His face darkened as he got the joke.

"Very funny," he said.

"But true?"

"I get the feeling she thinks I'm just her plaything."

"Perhaps you are."

Matthias nodded. "Near as I can make out, there's only one person she ever cared about."

"Her father."

"And she's the first to admit he wasn't exactly a great dad."

"So she's not ready for something serious," said Lugorix. "So you take what you can get."

"It's not enough."

It never is, thought Lugorix. But he said nothing—instead just stared at those oncoming mountains. Now they were getting nearer, they looked more like pillars, reaching up toward the roof of some unseen temple. The closer they got, the stranger they seemed. They didn't appear natural at all. He stared through the spray flying off the waves—

"By Taranis," he said.

"I see it," said Matthias.

The peaks were natural enough, but the figures carved into them weren't. On the left was a single gigantic stone warrior. He held a club ten times the size of the *Xerxes* and his face was enclosed by the snarling jaws of a lionskin. Opposite him was a monstrosity: three human heads sprouting from the body of a serpent. The warrior and the monster gazed at each other across the straits, locked in eternal antagonism, forever separated by the narrow body of water that was the gateway to the outer ocean.

"Hercules and Geryon," said Matthias.

"But who the hell carved them?" asked Lugorix.

"Someone who's dead. I hope."

Lugorix started to answer—but his voice trailed away as he suddenly caught sight of something else. Something far more mundane than those rocks.

But far more of a problem.

"Ships," he said.

There were two squadrons of them, each one vectoring from behind one of the Pillars. Their size marked them as five-decker penteremes. Their colors marked them as Carthaginian. It looked like they'd been expecting the *Xerxes.*

"Crap," hissed Matthias. He turned to the hatch just as Eurydice started bellowing at them to get below. Lugorix was right behind his friend as they clambered down to where Eurydice and Barsine were already pulling levers and hauling away on dials—

"Shut the hatch and start rowing," said Barsine.

"Not this again," said Matthias.

Eurydice almost looked amused. "You'd rather stay on the surface?"

Even Lugorix had to admit that wasn't an option. He and Matthias started hauling on the oars while gears cranked around them and the *Xerxes* dove beneath the surface.

And kept diving.

"Uh… what the fuck?" said Lugorix.

"Shut up and keep rowing," said Eurydice as Barsine retracted that strange instrument called a *periscope.* They plunged down while Barsine and Eurydice argued with each other over angles and distances and depths. Lugorix wondered why they hadn't done this during the storm. Perhaps the fact that it was no normal storm meant it created disturbances beneath the water. Or perhaps it was because submerging was just so damn dangerous anyway—all the more so as it was clear that Eurydice and Barsine weren't in agreement on the optimal way to thread the craft through the space between the surface and the seabed that connected Europe with Africa. The central point of contention seemed to revolve around the question of how far out the Pillars jutted beneath the surface.

But it turned out they all had more immediate problems.

A muffled boom resounded in the *Xerxes,* hard enough to make the metal hull clang—and then the whole ship twisted from side to side as though it was a rat being shaken by a dog. Even as that shaking died away, they could hear other explosions out there, though none came anywhere near as close as the first had.

"They're bombing us," said Eurydice.

"How are they doing *that?*" yelled Matthias.

"Black-powder charges, weighted and timed"—but even as Eurydice said the words another explosion washed across them. This one was almost on top of them; Lugorix was knocked forward, hitting his head against the oar and Eurydice was sent sprawling across the cabin. The other two managed to cling to their seats. Lugorix wiped blood from his forehead as Eurydice staggered to her feet—only to be hurled from them again by the jets of water pouring into the cabin.

"Oh crap," said Matthias.

"Air-tank's punctured," muttered Eurydice as she crawled back to where Barsine sat at the controls. "Jettison it." Barsine pulled on the controls; there was a vibration and then a clang as an iron plate slid across the perforated wall. "You two *keep rowing*," she hissed. "Like your life depended on it." Lugorix didn't have any doubts on that score; he and Matthias hauled on the oars while Barsine and Eurydice worked the tiller and let the *Xerxes* drift still deeper. It was terrifying to be in a vehicle that was sinking in such a way, that couldn't see where it was going—even more so when that vehicle was getting shelled by unseen attackers above it. The only consolation was that those attackers couldn't see their quarry either.

But they were about to feel it.

"Suck on this," said Eurydice as she pulled on a switch; the craft shook once more—releasing something else. Had Lugorix been able to follow its trajectory, he would have seen it shoot up through the water like a cork bobbing to the surface, impacting against the underside of one of the warships right above—and tearing that warship in two with a gigantic explosion that sent pieces of it flying almost all the way to shore. No sooner had Eurydice released the weapon then she grabbed the tiller; the *Xerxes* started turning. Barsine looked concerned.

"You sure we're past the Pillars?" she asked.

"We're about to find out."

They kept on turning and they were still alive. The rumbling of the explosions began to fade. But the sea was buffeting the ship from side to side ever harder.

"Ocean," said Eurydice.

"We've made it," said Barsine.

But Lugorix knew damn well it was really just beginning.

The atmosphere aboard the Carthaginian flagship was sufficiently grim that no one dared go near the squadron's commander. Hanno stood alone on the rear-deck, his leopard-skin warding off the wind while the Pillars faded behind them. Not only had the Persian vessel slipped past them, but they'd lost one ship already. That didn't bode well for what lay ahead. All the more so as the stakes were as high as it was possible to get. If Carthage wanted to keep the liberty she'd just won, she wasn't just going to have to fight for it, she was going to have to stay one step ahead of the competition. For now, she was allied with Macedonia, but Hanno was under no illusions as to what that nation really wanted. He'd looked into the eyes of Perdiccas back at Carthage, had known immediately that this was a man not to be trusted. The Macedonians wanted nothing less than total dominion. And if they gained what was reputed to be at the ends of the earth, such dominion would be within their reach...

But not if Hanno had a say in the matter. He'd taken shit from the Athenians for years, and he wasn't about to exchange them for a new set of masters. He was ashamed to admit it, but he'd despaired that Carthage would ever be free; it seemed impossible that anything could ever loosen the grip of Athens. But now the impossible had occurred; now his city would be able to recapture her glory days and resume her place as chief power in the western Mediterranean. And maybe more... Hanno had been briefed at length by the Sufetes on the knowledge that had been uncovered from the secret recesses in the Library. The whole thing was insane, but it wasn't his to question it. He was a soldier. That was why he was in charge of this mission—because he could be relied upon. Should it succeed, he'd be faced with the ultimate temptation. But really, it was no temptation. Betrayal of the city that had given him life wasn't an option.

For Carthage itself, liberation was a little confusing.

It was hard to keep it all straight. The Athenians were gone but the Macedonians had arrived. Not that their army had been allowed inside the city. Well, *some* of their army had: various commanders and engineers were having discussions with the Sufetes who now ruled Carthage. And those Sufetes were largely the same men who had administered Carthage on behalf of Athens. Not *all* of them, of course: a few had been fed to the Baal for opposing the rebellion that threw out Athens. Or at least, *allegedly* opposing...

for in the taverns and ale-houses there were those who whispered that those sacrifices were really just the result of power-plays amidst the Sufetes, with the losers served up to the ever-hungry Moloch. Or maybe it was just a matter of expediency, for how could the exact same group serve Carthage as had served Athens? Even if the gods didn't need a scapegoat, surely the people did.

To be sure, there was ample reason to believe the gods were angry. Yes, they'd blessed the citizens of Carthage with liberation from the eastern overlords under whose yoke they'd choked for almost a century. But there were odd tales afoot. These ones were too dangerous to be told even in the bars; instead, there were whispers in back rooms and beds and alleys that thieves or demons (or maybe it was both) had taken advantage of the revolt of the Athenian prisoners to break into the treasure chambers beneath Carthage and steal a magickal jewel of terrible power. Some kind of amulet… others said that the demon-thieves had actually been caught infiltrating the libraries, but why would a library contain anything a demon would want? It made no sense.

Neither did the Macedonians. Hadn't their kings said they intended to conquer all the known world? So why were the Sufetes even dealing with them? Had Carthage thrown out one batch of invaders only to have a second invasion hanging over her people's heads? But the walls of the city were some of the strongest in the world, and the Macedonian army (most of it anyway) was outside the city, lacking all siege equipment and paying for all the goods it bought like allies rather than enemies. But that army had come across the desert for a reason, and what was that reason if it wasn't going to attack Carthage?

Some said it was here to hitch a ride.

Those were the most disquieting rumors of all: that the fleet now prepping in the harbors of Carthage was going to take the Macedonians on board as passengers. Like any good rumor, it put a new twist on an expected development, for it was only logical that the fleet should be prepping to put to sea to defend Carthage against any Athenian counter-incursion. Only this fleet didn't look like it was going to be doing much defending. Supplies were being loaded for a long voyage, and huge horse-transport barges were being prepped. The citizen-militia had been issued with arms for the first time in a long while, and mercenaries were being hired from the surrounding African territories. All of which felt a lot more like an invasion was about to be launched rather than thwarted. And the Macedonian general Perdiccas had been spotted at the dockyards more than once—indeed, some said that he'd actually been aboard one of the ships during the prison revolt. So if the newly liberated Carthaginian fleet really *was* going to transport the Macedonian army somewhere—well, there weren't too many places it would be going. There were only so many targets.

And if you thought about it, there was really only one.

Farseeker held up to his eyes, Agathocles scanned the artificial peninsula jutting out from Italy—a protuberance that now reached a quarter of the distance across the Straits of Messina to where he stood amidst the hills of Sicily. Other members of the resistance stood around him; they had ridden out here before dawn and would ride back to Syracuse under cover of night. From the looks on their faces they'd come to the same conclusion he had: nothing was going to stop the Macedonians from crossing. The bridge they were building was the cheapest sort imaginable, but that didn't mean it wasn't effective. Near shore, pylons had been sunk into the seabed to support rope and a myriad wooden planks; further out, newly constructed boats had been lashed together to form a causeway over which an army could move. Agathocles could see the tents of that army spreading over every Italian hill in sight—tens of thousands of men and horses and elephants awaiting the moment when they could cross the sea and storm into Sicily.

Nor were there any prizes for guessing where they'd go there when they got there. Agathocles had spent his entire life trying to free his city from Athenian rule, but he was under no illusions about what would happen were Syracuse to fall into Macedonian hands. Athens was an empire that had passed its prime; it was weakened at the core, and it would one day fall. Macedonia was a rising power, and its rulers seemed to have an intensity about them that Athenian democracy had always lacked. If they got their hands on Syracuse, Agathocles had no doubt that he would die long before the city was freed. In fact, he would probably die very soon, as he had a feeling that the Macedonians would root out the resistance organizations in Syracuse with an alacrity that the Athenians had never brought to the task. Even in the wake of the death of Cleon, Athens had still proven unable to clean up the city. Of course, convenient as it was to blame him for the viceroy's death, Agathocles was reasonably sure that they knew he wasn't responsible for it. The rumor-mill said that Macedonian agents had broken into the Ortygia, killed Cleon, and made off with documents and maps vital to Syracuse's defense. Which would make keeping that city out of Macedonian hands all the harder.

"We're on the same side now," said one of his men, jarring Agathocles from his reverie.

"What the hell do you mean?" he growled.

The man pointed at the bridge. "Us and the Athenians."

"We've got the same enemy," said Agathocles. "Don't mean we're on the same side."

But he had to admit the man had a point. It would be best for all concerned if Alexander and his whole army drowned in the Mediterranean. Yet the truth of the matter was that Agathocles and his ragtag band could do nothing to stop that oncoming bridge from reaching their island. That was all up to the Athenians. Who so far had tried to no avail. Their ships had approached the bridge from both directions, only to be driven off by enormous stonethrowers that the Macedonians had built on the hills above the Straits. Two of the Athenian ships had been sunk by giant rocks before the rest pulled away out of range. They could still be seen there now, out toward the horizon, keeping carefully out of range. The harsh reality was that a land-based siege-engine could always be bigger—and thus reach further—than one based on a ship.

But soon the bridge would be out of range of the land-engines, and that was where things would get interesting. To be sure, the Athenian navy was understrength. Severely so, and Agathocles's agents had given him the exact figures. Athens had lost a couple hundred ships in Egypt, and a couple hundred more trying to reinforce Carthage. And there had been another hundred ships at Massilia which no one had heard of since they'd sortied from the burning wreckage of that city. In other words, the navy had been getting its ass kicked, which was all the more disturbing since no one knew exactly what had happened to the ships in the western Mediterranean. There were stories that Poseidon himself had appeared and destroyed those boats, though Agathocles felt safe in dismissing such tales as the product of terrified men who had felt themselves to be invincible upon the water. But *something* was afoot. Something dire.

And that bridge to end all bridges was getting ever closer.

Eumenes stared up at the Pillars of Hercules as the ship sailed between them. As art, it was impressive; as engineering, it was downright scary. And Eumenes knew a thing or two about enginering: as Alexander's chief of logistics, marshalling the resources for such projects was something he was quite familiar with. It seemed impossible that so much rock had been carved so high above the sea, on so precarious a series of precipices, using only iron tools. Then again, if some *other* set of tools had been used—well, that was the part that Eumenes really didn't want to think about.

But now those Pillars were fading behind him as his ships surged out into the Ocean. For the first time in his life, he could see nothing to the west of him. Yet there was definitely *something* out there.

And he was going to be the one to get it for Alexander.

At first he'd been a little taken aback to be the one selected for this mission. Military operations in the Mediterranean were a long way from over, and he'd been in charge of organization and logistics for so long that his absence was going to be more than a little inconvenient for Alexander. But really, there was no other choice. What happened west of here was of paramount importance, yet Alexander couldn't leave his army if he expected to get them across the Straits of Messina and lead them to victory. And as for Hephaestion, well, Alexander would never allow him to leave his side. Besides which—if one were brutally honest, which Eumenes was only within the privacy of his own skull—Alexander probably wouldn't have trusted Hephaestion to carry out this operation anyway. It wasn't that Hephaestion was incompetent—far from it. But as Alexander himself had acknowledged, his expertise lay in traditional modes of warfare, whether that meant facing Persian armies in pitched battle or rooting Afghan insurgents out of caves. Not in dealing with shit that wasn't supposed to exist.

So that left Eumenes. He was in on all the secrets now, and his mind was flexible enough to engage with them. Though that didn't mean he had to like it. He'd liked his world just fine before—he'd known where all the boundaries were, had known what made sense and what didn't. Not anymore. The whole nature of the world was up for grabs. Because he'd passed beyond the boundaries of the known one.

In ships that were admirably suited for the task.

He had no idea where they had come from. Alexander had kept that one to himself. And Eumenes' own inquiries had only turned up possibilities. Aristotle had built them… no, Aristotle had only designed it… nonsense, they'd been recovered wholesale—found at the source of the Nile. No, said someone else, wrong river: when Hephaestion's agents had ventured into India, they'd explored the wreckage of a derelict civilization at the bottom of the Indus River, torn apart seals in dead languages, recovered the contraption in which Eumenes was now riding.

Kalyana wasn't so sure about that one. The sorceror was from India, after all, and he'd never come across anything like these strange vessels. Then again, he was the first to admit that India was a big place, and contained a lot of "weird shit"—his exact words. Such directness was one more reason why he was accompanying Eumenes on this journey into the unknown. He was Eumenes' official Weird Shit Consultant. From the looks of things, there was going to be a lot of it.

But ultimately, Eumenes was a pragmatist. He was less concerned as to his ships' origin than their destination. He knew the twenty Macedonian commandos riding aboard each of them felt the same way—after all, those men believed their leader to be a god. The vessel in which they rode was evidence enough of that. Somewhere in front of them were the Carthaginian ships that had left their blockading position—Eumenes had thought he was going to have to either negotiate or fight his way through them, but they'd split for the west, hot on the trail of something important enough to make them all leave their position in front of the Pillars. That was a move that Eumenes understood. Pursuit was their way of staying in the game. They clearly intended that Carthage should be one of the players. The Persian witch—the one they were undoubtedly chasing—was another. Eumenes—on behalf of Alexander—was a third.

And Eumenes was willing to bet Philip would have something in the game too.

The ship several kilometers to the northeast was a design of Aristotle's, though it was crewed by Byzantine sailors, all of them loyal to Macedonia. Ptolemy sat within, listened to the waters pound against the hull, took stock of the crew going about their tasks while he sat in his cabin and gazed at maps and contemplated possibilities. And prayed too, thanking Zeus for the chance to finally win everything he'd been denied all his life. He'd always known whose son he was, of course, just as he'd always known he had to keep that fact a secret, lest he burn for it. If it ever suited Philip to recognize him formally, then so be it—but Ptolemy had always figured his status would never be anything but an embarrassment to his father. So he learnt early on to hold his tongue.

But then the father had been greviously injured and—while he returned to Pella—his acknowledged son surpassed him in glory. The already strained relations between Philip and Alexander turned to shit. And Philip turned to Ptolemy and made him his spy in Alexander's camp. The irony was that Ptolemy had long since reconciled himself to serving Alexander—after all, he'd grown up with the man, who even as a boy drew people to him with a natural magnetism. Dealing behind the back of someone he'd always idolized didn't sit well with Ptolemy, and the nature of the promises which Philip was making only increased his discomfort. The war with Persia and then Athens placed many in awkward positions, but none more so than Ptolemy, who was caught between two rival rulers to whom he was deeply indebted—a conflict that finally culminated in Philip's throne room.

So when Alexander struck him in that chamber, everything fell into place. Love became hatred before Ptolemy had even hit the floor: a shift that Philip was quick to turn to his advantage. In the wake of Alexander's departure from Pella, he'd explained it all to Ptolemy—told him why he needed eyes and ears and hands in the far west, told him that what was at stake was far more than the fate of the Athenian Empire. This time there were no hints—it was altogether explicit. As was the reward for success—the chance to supplant Alexander as the heir to Macedonia. Sure, Alexander was invincible. Impossible to defeat. Unbeatable.

Until he was beaten.

Fate was a funny thing. When Alexander had returned to Babylon after withdrawing his army from Afghanistan, he'd been laid low with a debilitating fever. For three days he'd hovered on the verge of death. The doctors had despaired. The priests of the city's ziggurats had wailed and offered up their prayers. The people had stopped in the middle of their labors and waited.

But to everybody's surprise, Alexander had recovered.

Yet since that time, Ptolemy had had ample opportunity to contemplate how life and reputation were such fragile things, how the relationship between the two could be so complex. Say Alexander had died? He'd have perished at the height of his power—never having lost a battle, never having failed to conquer. He'd have gone to his grave untarnished. No, the longer Alexander lived, the more likely it was that he'd be handed his first setback. If that defeat came from magick too powerful for him to contend with… then it wouldn't just be his defeat. It would be his death. His father would have to find another heir.

And the name of Ptolemy would live forever.

They were a cork tossed on the swell of Atlantic now, running steady before a rising sea. Lugorix had never seen waves so big. But they seemed to be par for the course out here, stretching up like green hills on all sides. The clouds overhead were so thick it felt like it was halfway to night, though it was still only morning. Still early in his shift.

"I can't sleep," said Matthias as he came on deck. His mood had gotten as black as the weather. This run into the unknown was affecting all of them in different ways. Eurydice most of all. Which had an all-too-predictable result on Matthias' own temper.

"She won't sleep with me anymore," he said.

Lugorix shook his head. Greeks seemed to almost enjoy taking these things to heart. Gauls had a different outlook on things. If one woman refused you, find another. But that was the problem with being on a boat with only two of them. There weren't that many choices. Leaving Lugorix with little choice but to listen to his friend.

"But you're still sharing the same cabin," he said.

"Doesn't mean we're doing anything exciting in there."

That puzzled Lugorix. "Just flip her on her back and—"

"Get my teeth knocked out? All she does is sit in the middle of the cabin with her charts and instruments, scrawling out diagrams and equations that run off the parchment and onto the floor. I think she's going nuts, personally."

"She's a sorceror," said Lugorix. "They're all nuts."

"Even Barsine seems to be getting a little pissed off with her."

"I noticed."

It was hard not to. Barsine and Eurydice were barely talking now, and that was largely because the latter seemed to have nothing to say to or ask the former. Which made a kind of sense, Lugorix reflected. After all, she was the one who knew the science or magick or whatever the fuck it was. Whatever calculations she was making, there was only one person she was debating them with: herself. So Barsine did most of the piloting, and Eurydice occasionally took over from her, but generally just called out the occasional course-correction to her. Leaving Barsine largely in the dark, and the two men completely so.

"Did she tell you anything about those islands we saw?"

"No more than she told the rest of us—that they weren't worth stopping for."

Though the name made them sound otherwise. The *Fortunate Islands*—Lugorix remembered the librarian back at Carthage mentioning them. Tacking before favorable winds, the *Xerxes* had sailed between two of them, close enough to see hills and ruined buildings and… something else. With the farseeker, Lugorix had made out some details: a collection of megaliths more extensive than any he'd ever seen, great rocks arranged in some order that might have made sense to a druid. But whatever was on the Fortunate Islands, Eurydice didn't feel it was going to assist them with their journey.

Either that, or she'd decided they couldn't risk stopping. When they'd surfaced several kilometers west of the Pillars, there was no sign of the Phoenician ships. It was just them and the sea. But two days later, just as Lugorix and Matthias were exchanging watch duties on the cusp of evening, they'd caught a glimpse of two of those ships' masts on the horizon. The *Xerxes* had submerged immediately, and when it resurfaced there was… nothing. Yet Eurydice still seemed to act as though they were being chased. Those Phoenician ships had looked like ordinary wooden warships—how she was thinking they could possibly still be tracking the *Xerxes* was beyond Lugorix. But perhaps they had their means. Perhaps they had sorcery.

And perhaps that sorcery had something to do with the hairy star.

It had appeared for the first time that very night that they'd resurfaced after seeing those masts. Hairy star was the only way to describe it—a large star with tresses of fire trailing behind it. A hairy star. But what was it? What did it signify? It had risen every night since then, ever larger, ever brighter. Eurydice said it meant that things were drawing to a close—that everything was converging. Lugorix had nodded as though she spoke wisdom.

When all she spoke was obvious.

Kometes: the hairy star. So said the astrologers. It lit up the sky to the point where the workers on the bridge no longer needed the light of the torches to labor through the night. But they kept those torches burning anyway. It wasn't just work they needed to coordinate. It was defense. Again and again the Athenian navy had sortied from Syracuse and had tried to approach the bridge from both north and south, only to driven back again and again by unnaturally heavy storms. Many ships had sunk. But there were still enough of them out there to keep those on the bridge on perpetual alert.

The men accompanying Agathocles kept watch around the clock too. They'd retreated further into the hills, were now watching the scene from the woodlands that covered the heights above the Straits. It was actually a surprisingly good command post for Agathocles—he could stay in touch with events back in the city, but he wasn't going to have to rely on messengers to tell him how the Macedonians were faring. Though so far it didn't look like the Athenian navy was going to succeed. They were being kept at bay through all manner of magick. From the looks of things, he'd bet even money that the Macedonian sorcerors had discovered a way to mess with the weather. Which made no sense, but then again, what did these days? Way too many Athenian fleets had been hit by inclement weather to think otherwise. And the Straits themselves had experienced nothing but perfect conditions. Too perfect, really.

Yet even if some of Athens' ships managed to get through, the bridge was practically its own fortress now. Every hundred meters was a platform on which was mounted all the latest siege technology, including long-range bolt throwers the equal of anything in the Athenian fleet. Not to mention flame-throwers for close-quarters work. So far those hadn't been necessary. There seemed no way that Athens was going to be able to stop the oncoming bridge in the Straits.

So they would just have to stop it on the beaches.

Several thousand soldiers and mercenaries had been sent north from Syracuse and were even now assembling on the hills beneath Agathocles' lookout post. Meanwhile stone-throwers of a range far more powerful than anything that could be mounted on a bridge or ship were under construction—or rather, had been stripped from the walls of Syracuse and reassembled a short distance behind the beach to start lacerating the bridge when it got within range. It was a calculated risk, to be sure, but whoever was directing Athenian strategy wasn't an idiot. Even now, they stood a far better chance of stopping the Macedonians on the beaches of Sicily than at the walls of Syracuse. If you were dealing with the world's most powerful land army, your only hope was to use water. The decisive moment was approaching, and everything hung in the balance. Agathocles could see the soldiers of both sides—out on that bridge, down on that beach—pointing at the flaming star overhead, which was now visible in the daytime. A second sun: and Agathocles' men kept asking him what it meant.

He thought about that for a while, and finally told them it heralded the coming liberation of their city. That cheered them to no end, but in his heart he knew that he was lying. He was no soothsayer, but one look at that *kometos* was enough to see its significance went beyond the fate of any one city. This was something cosmic. But if there *was* a chance amidst the maelstrom for Syracuse to seize its destiny, Agathocles intended to be the man to make it happen. The more Athens stripped its defenses in Syracuse, the better. Or so Agathocles kept telling himself—even as he kept looking at that ever-growing bridge, those swarms of men and soldiers upon it, that field of tents that covered every part of Italy he could see. Somewhere amidst those tents was the man who had become the greatest conqueror the world had ever known—the man who had never been stopped. Somehow he would have to be stopped. If the Athenians couldn't do it, Agathocles would.

Or else he'd die trying.

CHAPTER SEVENTEEN

Perdiccas stared out at the waves.

It was the fleet's first night out of Carthage, heading east toward Sicily, and that star was about to rise in the west like some kind of demented sun. The Macedonians were nervous enough already. They'd thought the desert was as bad as it got, but that was before they got out on the ocean. All these theories about Athenian seamanship and shipbuilding and maritime tradition were all very well, but the fact of the matter is that the Macedonians just didn't *like* the ocean. Yet to win this war they were going to have to beat it.

Which is what they were attemping to do now, thanks to Carthage and its newly revitalized fleet. Perdiccas would have liked to take credit for the alliance with the Phoenicians, but that was really due to Alexander and Craterus. Their back-channel diplomacy been a phenomenal success—not only had it helped engineer a coup that substantially weakened Athenian power, but it had also managed to give Macedonia an ally. A *naval* ally, no less.

There was just one problem: ultimately, Macedonia didn't want allies.

She wanted subjects.

Perdiccas stood on the prow of the transport-barge, looking out into the gathering dark. They would need to do it before the comet rose and the light grew too great. Ahead of him he could barely make out the stern of the Carthaginian galley that was towing his vessel, surging up and down as it crashed through the waves. More barges were visible off to each side, each one packed with Macedonian soldiers. Those soldiers were intended for action against Syracuse, which was where this fleet was bound.

But they were to be put to the test much sooner.

Perdiccas signalled the man beside him, who nodded—opened and closed the shutter on the lantern he held in rapid succession. Perdiccas then turned to the other soldiers around him.

"Let's go," he said.

A soldier saluted, handed him a wheeled device about the size of a helmet. Perdiccas slotted it onto the rope that connected the barge with that warship up ahead. Then he gritted his teeth and climbed over the side, gripping the contraption with both hands while looping his feet over the rope, clinging to it a scant few meters above the ocean. One of the soldiers leaned out and adjusted the machine that its inventor, Aristotle, had called a *pulley*.

"Not sure it's working," he said.

"It's working," said Perdiccas, releasing a catch—and suddenly he was being hauled at speed out over the roaring ocean; the last he saw of the barge was a second man climbing over the side to take the place he'd just vacated. Perdiccas could have just ordered someone to lead the assault, too, but the thought of Craterus sneering at him from the afterlife quashed any such notion. Lead by example—that was the code of the Macedonian general. Was not Alexander always in the forefront of any battle? All these thoughts flashed in an instant through Perdiccas' head as he zipped along the rope, the sky overhead and waves all around, their spray flashing across him—and then suddenly he was slowing down, the counterspring deploying as the Carthaginian galley loomed ahead of him. He stretched out his feet and made contact, then scrambled over and onto the deck, drawing his blade as he did so.

Only two men stood at the helm, and they both stared at him as though he were a phantom emerging from the sea. Which wasn't too far from the truth: Perdiccas decapitated the first with a single swipe and stabbed the other through the midriff, holding his mouth shut to stop him from screaming while he lowered him to the deck. Next instant the Macedonian solder who had followed him was climbing over the railing—and reaching into his satchel to pull out iron and flint, striking the one against the other to produce sparks and using those sparks to light the torch carried by the third soldier to arrive. As soon as that torch was flaring, Perdiccas led them forward to the ship's mast, hacking two more men to bits while the torch-wielder set fire to the sails.

Which was like kicking a hornets' nest. All of a sudden all the Carthaginian sailors who had been below deck taking their evening meal came pouring out to deal with the fire. But Perdiccas and his two soldiers weren't waiting around. They faded back toward the stern, crouched behind one of the catapults while they gazed out into a twilight that looked almost like a meadow dotted with fireflies as the sails on warship after warship burnt merrily. And then those fires began to waver and dim. The Carthaginians were good sailors, and ready to deal with any exigency a sea voyage brought. They were getting the fires under control, but the sails were shredded and the ships were drifting dead in the water. They wouldn't stay that way for long, of course. Spare sails could be rigged. Oars could be deployed.

Just not in time.

As soon as the three-man squads had crossed the ropes, the Macedonians aboard the barges had lowered their own oars and started rowing hell for leather. Even as the Carthaginian sailors were thinking they had the situation under control, the barges came surging out of the dark, slamming into the back of the warships, the Macedonian soldiers throwing out grappling hooks and pouring onto the ships.

It was over fast.

Most of the Carthaginians were slaughtered, their bodies thrown overboard to feed the sharks and whatever else cared to dine on them. Of those who remained, most were chained and put to work rowing. A scant few were allowed on deck to perform the other tasks that crewing a ship required. But all such tasks were carried out under the watchful eyes of the Macedonian soldiers. The fleet would continue on to Sicily to play its part in the final battle—but under new management. As for Carthage herself, her time would come.

When her ships returned.

The latest viceroy had arrived from Athens. But the people of Syracuse weren't paying much attention. They were too busy working alongside Athenian soldiers to rig the defenses of Syracuse. Ammunition was being prepped. Siege-engines were being hoisted up all the towers. Sections of the wall that had fallen into disrepair were....

"You've got to be kidding me," said Leosthenes, looking over the list of preparations. He'd only just gotten off the boat from Athens and up into the Ortygia and already the bad news was pouring down like a river of shit. He handed his purple general's cloak to a servant, took a goblet of wine from another. Memnon was busy unfurling the maps of both Syracuse and Sicily.

"That's the problem with having an island in the middle of a maritime empire," he said. He slid some paperweights over the edges of the maps to keep them pinned down, looked up at Leosthenes. "You tend to get complacent. Unprepared for the possibility that an enemy might actually reach you."

"Tell me about it," said Leosthenes. He'd been sent out here in the wake of Hypereides gaining ascendancy on the council. The good news was that Leosthenes had seen the writing on the wall—had chosen the correct side in the duel between the council's two rivals. Phocion was now under house arrest. But just as Leosthenes was congratulating himself on yet another arrow dodged, Hypereides gave him his reward for services rendered.

An appointment to head up the defenses of the west.

Leosthenes still didn't know whether that was a death-sentence, a way of getting him out of the way, or a genuine belief that he was the right man for the job. Maybe all three. It was clear enough that none of the other archons wanted to take the job of taking on Alexander. Either they thought Leosthenes might pull a miracle out of his ass, or they wanted to make sure that someone else got the blame. Not that Cleon had set much of an example. One of Leosthenes' first priorities was to make sure the fortress of the Ortygia was as impregnable as its reputation, since there had been way too many forced entries lately. He scanned the map of the city, looking over its defenses while Memnon took an initial look at those of the island.

"What's this?" asked the old man. He was pointing at the section of the Sicilian coast that the dotted line which denoted Alexander's bridge had nearly reached—at the red squares hastily inscribed along that coast. The lieutenant in charge of the briefing leaned forward.

"We've got five thousand men there," he said. "Waiting to repulse Alexander. As soon as his bridge gets within range."

Leosthenes and Memnon looked at each other in shocked silence. The archon was the first to break it.

"Get those men off that beach," he said. *"Now."*

The lieutenant looked confused. "But sir—this was the defense strategy agreed upon before your arrival. It's the only way to make sure that Alexander—"

"Kills us all," snarled Leosthenes. "Don't you get it, man? Anytime you start talking about the *only way* to fight Alexander, you're as good as *dead*. Now pull those men off the beach before I kill you myself." The red-faced lieutenant saluted—then started for the door.

But it was already too late.

They sailed through that ocean for days and nights and never saw any land the whole time. And all the while that hairy star grew nearer—so close now it could be seen during the day as well, reflecting on the dark water all around. Except sometimes that water wasn't dark. Sometimes it barely even seemed like water: sometimes they were immersed in seaweed that stretched off in all directions like the world's biggest carpet, so thick it might have caught a lesser ship in its tendrils. Yet the *Xerxes* kept on plowing forward, eventually putting that strange otherworldly sea behind it. Now they were back in water, and it was once again getting rougher. Lugorix gripped the rails as the waves slapped against the ship, rolling her from side to side. He barely noticed Matthias come up on the deck behind him.

"What's that?" asked Matthias.

"Ocean," replied Lugorix absently.

"No," said Matthias, "what's *that?*"

This time the urgency in his voice was sufficient to make Lugorix turn around—and follow the direction in which his friend's finger was pointing: *up*, at a forty-five degree angle, off toward where the morning sun was rising from horizon. A dark shape loomed there, considerably smaller than the Moon would be. At first Lugorix thought it was the comet, but that was off to the north. This was something else. And it was steadily gaining height.

"What the fuck *is* that?" asked Lugorix.

"My question precisely."

"And what makes you think I'd have the slightest idea? Get Eurydice up here."

Matthias looked abashed. "She and I aren't exactly on speaking terms these days—"

"Just do it," hissed Lugorix.

Matthias did. He got Barsine while he was at it. The four of them stood on deck and watched the bizarre object for a few more moments. Eurydice trained a farseeker on it.

"Shit," she said.

"Can you clarify that," said Barsine.

"Shit. I think—sorry…I *think* it's inflated animal skins."

"That fucker's an *animal?*" asked Lugorix.

"The skins of them. Filled with, um, lighter-than-air gases so it floats." She adjusted the magnification of the farseeker. "With a basket beneath it." Another adjustment—"and a man in that basket."

That did it. The farseeker was passed around like the hemp-pipe back at the *Dryad's Tits*. When it got to Lugorix, he saw a man with black beard, dark skin, embroidered hair, turquoise garments: unmistakably one of the Phoenicians. And he was holding his own farseeker, staring right back at them. Lugorix resisted the urge to wave.

"Just below him," said Barsine.

Lugorix lowered the farseeker slightly—and now he could see the rope stretching down from the basket. He lowered the farseeker still further, following that rope down across the sky, all the way to where it met horizon.

"Those Carthaginians," said Barsine. "Trying to find out where we are."

"Well, now they know," said Matthias.

"We need to pick up the pace," said Eurydice. She turned to the hatch, climbed below. Matthias followed her like a puppy-dog, leaving Lugorix and Barsine there for a moment.

"What's going on?" he said.

"They're only a few hours behind us." But she wasn't meeting his eyes.

"I mean what *else?*" he asked.

"I need to get below," she said—pushed past him. He must have been more afraid of the answer than he realized, because he didn't even attempt to stand in her way.

"A balloon," said Kalyana.

"A what?" asked Eumenes. They were looking through one of the slits in the turret—studying that object high ahead and to the west. It was the first interesting thing they'd seen for a few days. Eumenes had been starting to think they were on the wrong track….

"Aerial reconnaissance device," said Kalyana. "Filled with gases that give it flotational capabilities—"

"Does it have combat capabilities?"

"Not unless you are rash enough to get below it. They are looking for the Persians."

"Well, they can see us too."

"Yes, but we now know where *they* are as well. And we may presume the lady Barsine is not that far ahead of them, no?" Eumenes nodded. As he watched, several lines of smoke began to curl over the western horizon, rising up below the balloon.

"And now we know they don't just rely on sail," said the Greek.

Kalyana nodded. "They would be most foolish to venture so far west of the Pillars with only that."

Eumenes nodded. He got on his knees, stuck his head through the hatch in the floor—met the eyes of his pilot. "Steam," he said. "Let's do it." The man nodded. Moments later, there was a clanking noise, and a rumbling. Smoke began billowing from the stacks aft and rear. Same with the other two vessels in the squadron—and now suddenly the three ships were surging through the water at what seemed like unholy speeds. Eumenes could hear the cheers of the commandos aboard them echoing across the water, merging with those aboard his own vessel. He wished for a moment that Alexander could be there to watch this. He suddenly realized that Kalyana was staring at him, a half-smile upon his face.

"Earthly glory," he said. "I used to appreciate it too."

"Nothing *earthly* about this," said Eumenes sharply.

Kalyana's smile was now a full one. "And if your men truly understood that, the last thing they would be doing is cheering."

Ptolemy looked up at the balloon, off to the southwest. The Carthaginians now had a bird's eye view of the entire situation—the trade-off being obvious enough: that now everyone knew exactly where they were too. The escalating situation was forcing everyone to show their hands. He stared through the farseeker at the lines of smoke emitted by the still-unseen Carthaginan ships—then swung the farseeker back to the left, looking due south at three more lines of smoke. It was as he suspected—he wasn't the only player trailing in the wake of the Carthaginians. But he had no telltale smoke to reveal his position. His craft was configured so that he didn't need it. Meaning that the Carthaginians knew where he was, but the

Persians and any other pursuers didn't. That would give him a momentary advantage. One that he resolved to make the most of. He signalled to his crew to prep the weapons, rig the ship for action.

They were accelerating now, throttling the *Xerxes* up toward maximum speed. Lugorix gripped the rails, felt the spray dash against his face. The water was shot through with whitecaps now. They kept plowing forward, up and down waves, though it seemed like there was far more of the latter—almost like they were charging downhill. He looked up at that strange floating craft dangling over the horizon behind him.

There was a flash of fire from just below its basket.

For a moment he thought the contraption was going up in flames—*good fucking riddance*—but then he realized that the fire was travelling at high speed…straight toward him, hurtling in on the *Xerxes* like the lightning of the gods.

"Shit," he said. But it was like he was in a dream. No one below him could hear. Not that their hearing would do any good. The flame roared overhead, crashed into the ocean about twenty meters ahead of the *Xerxes*. Eurydice and Matthias scrambled on deck in a hurry to see what was up as the boat pitched up and down in the wake stirred up by the object's impact. The daughter of Aristotle trained her farseeker on the faraway basket.

"Artillery," she said. She handed the farseeker to Lugorix just as another flash lit the sky. Lugorix peered through the device to a platform that had been hoisted up below the basket—a large metal tube was mounted on it, and three Carthaginian soldiers were busy aiming the device at the *Xerxes*. Then that view was obscured by flame as the projectile they'd just fired hurtled in. This one fell just short of the *Xerxes,* sending up spray.

"Two misses," exclaimed Matthias.

"Idiot," snarled Eurydice, "they're bracketing us." Barsine was already disappearing back down the hatch. Moments later, the *Xerxes* suddenly lurched hard to port, turning on an angle that practically had Lugorix retching over the rails. No sooner had his stomach adjusted to that then the *Xerxes* went hard to starboard. He wished Barsine could make up her mind. Another projectile crashed into the ocean—another spray of water, another near-miss. The *Xerxes* continued to pick up speed and it started to occur to Lugorix that there was something wrong with the speed—that they were going *too* fast. Certainly faster than they'd yet managed to go.

Perhaps the *Xerxes* had one final reserve of power it had been saving for this moment. Eurydice had that astrolabe out, was measuring the position of the sun, the comet, the Carthaginian war machine—

"What's going on?" whispered Matthias.

"Shut up and hold on," said Eurydice.

"Looks like they've started the party," said Eumenes, his farseeker never wavering from that balloon. It was getting nearer—not because it was heading toward them, but because they were catching up to the ships to which it was tethered. He swiveled his view onto the horizon, adjusted the focus—swore he could see the merest hint of a mast. He lowered the farseeker, turned to Kalyana.

"This is where it gets interesting," he said.

Ptolemy was having exactly the same thought. He swung the great boat south by southwest, let the sails unfurl as he ran before the wind, closing on the Carthaginian position. He knew they could see him coming, but he was hoping the primary target of that artillery-platform would remain whatever it was chasing—presumably the Persian vessel. Though it seemed stupid to him that they'd be trying to destroy it. If it was up to him, he'd be trying to take them alive. There were so many interesting things they could tell him. So many interesting places they could lead him. But that was the Carthaginians for you—impulsive as all hell. They saw the Atlantic as their domain, and they didn't like anyone muscling in on it... even though it wasn't really *their* domain. Indeed, there was a good reason why no one in their right mind ventured this far west. The place was a deathtrap. It was just getting started.

The *Xerxes* was tacking back and forth, and two more shots from the aerial platform had flown wide. But the price of becoming more difficult to hit was that the Carthaginian squadron was overhauling them, their masts growing closer. And the Carthaginians were letting the balloon-tether play out still further, with the result that the range was getting ever less. Eurydice kept making furious calculations with the astrolabe, calling out course-corrections down to Barsine. Lugorix turned to Matthias.

"We're fucked, aren't we?" he said under his breath.

"I think so," said Matthias.

"Think again," snapped Eurydice, whose hearing was apparently sharp enough to have registered this exchange over the noise of the waves and explosions and engines. She screamed something down to Barsine. There was a clanking and a rumbling and then suddenly to Lugorix's astonishment the entire rear platform of the *Xerxes* slid away—and as it did so, a fearsome looking machine swivelled out of the space within. Most of it consisted of a rather large tube—in fact, it looked a lot like the one hanging from the Carthaginian balloon. Eurydice turned to Lugorix.

"Here's how this works," she said. "This is called a *gun*. Making you the *gunner*." Then, to Matthias—"you're the loader." They stared at her. "And by the way, guns don't kill people, people do, so I suggest you *move your asses and start firing*." She gave them a few more instructions—just enough to get them both in serious trouble, thought Lugorix. Within two minutes he was sitting in a smallish chair sprouting out of the side of a complicated apparatus on the rear of that barrel, staring through a built-in farseeker at the Carthagnian platform while Matthias sweated and sought to keep his balance on the pitching deck as he slotted a heavy and curved piece of ammunition into the maw of the barrel. Eurydice stood on the foredeck, mostly busy with the navigation, but occasionally yelling out instructions or insults down to the men below. Matthias locked the ammo into place; Lugorix was doing his best to line up the balloon in the crosshairs of the farseeker, but the rise and fall of the waves made that a little tough. He waited, trying to time his moment. Another projectile from that balloon lanced toward them, crashed into the water close enough to drench him with spray.

"What the hell are you waiting for?" screeched Eurydice.

You to shut up, thought Lugorix. He pulled what she'd told him was the trigger; there was a hissing noise—and then a flash accompanied by an almighty bang. It took a few moments for the light that had momentarily blinded Lugorix to die, revealing the trail of the projectile streaking away into the sky, shearing in toward the balloon. Straight toward it—

And missing.

"Shit," said Eurydice.

"Well what did you expect," said Matthias, "it's not like we're exactly experienced at this—"

"*So fire again!*" she shrieked.

Lugorix and Matthias set about doing exactly that. But Lugorix couldn't help but notice that the sails on those Carthaginian ships were now becoming visible. There were eight of them, including one that looked to be particularly large. Matthias reloaded, and Lugorix lined up the nearest ship.

"Not the ship," snarled Eurydice, "the balloon—" But Lugorix had already fired. The projectile arced through the sky, hurtled down, missed the ship.

Which promptly exploded anyway.

"Bullseye," said Eumenes. The pieces of the shattered Carthaginian ship fluttered down into the water like leaves falling from a tree. Even as he watched, a second ship detonated. He lowered the farseeker.

"Feed 'em two more barrels," he hollered through the hatch to the crew below. Next moment, the ship shook as two more of the metal-fish were released into the water, humming away, closing in on their targets. The Carthaginians were now clearly visible against the horizon, and were only just waking up to the menace that he and his three ironclad ships posed. From the looks of it, they'd been under fire from Barsine and her ship, but that gang couldn't shoot straight. The real question was what the balloon—or, more precisely, the gun suspended beneath it—was going to do. By now they must be almost on top of the Persians. The Carthaginian ships began to return fire on Eumenes' squadron—balls of iron and ballistae-bolts hissed through the air toward the slit through which the Greek was staring. There was a resounding clang as something hit the hull.

"What is that?" asked Kalyana.

"Our armor doing it's job," replied Eumenes.

"No," said the Indian. *"That."*

He was pointing through another slit, off to the northwest. Eumenes stared—had to shake his head to make sure his eyes weren't playing tricks on him. It looked like a gigantic fountain, shooting water hundreds of feet into the air.

"No idea," said Eumenes. And then—to the crew below—"Can we get someone who knows something about the fucking ocean up here?"

One of the sailors climbed up. From the look of his features, he was probably Italian—presumably another mercenary, hired to crew a ship that must have been blowing his mind every day he was aboard it. He squinted—took a look at the column of water off in the distance.

"Waterspouts," he said. Then, when they had no reaction: "Like a tornado, but on the water."

"So we want to stay clear of it," said Kalyana.

"Not it," said the sailor. "*Them.*"

At first, Eumenes thought the guy just didn't know how to speak Greek. But he took another look—and sure enough, there were several of them now. It wasn't clear whether the others had been behind the first, or whether they were just sprouting out of the ocean in rapid succession.

"Shit," said Kalyana.

The geyser towered above Ptolemy, its outer edges crashing down upon his ship like a waterfall gone mad. It had appeared as if from nowhere; for a few moments, he thought he was screwed—that he was about to be swallowed up by the monstrosity. But his crew was nothing if not resourceful—they quickly realized that the wind from the waterspout was practically at gale-force; a few adjustments to the enormous sails, and suddenly the vessel was veering round and to the south of the waterspout, skittering like a water-strider back onto its southwest course. As he emerged from the waterspout's thunderous spray, he could see the Carthaginian ships a short distance ahead.

Along with that damn balloon.

Not for much longer, he thought.

"Will you fucking *hit it?*" yelled Eurydice.

Lugorix shook his head in frustration and anger. This was one damned thing after the next. Two Carthaginian ships were gone, but that balloon was getting ever closer. It was now at too steep an angle overhead, beyond the elevation of the gun-barrel. But if Lugorix and Matthias couldn't hit the balloon, it was operating under no such constraints. The *Xerxes* had endured three misses in quick succession, each one nearer than before, despite the evasive action Barsine was putting the vessel through. As he watched, a fourth projectile plunged in toward them, looking the whole way down like it was going to nail them, but at the last moment detonating to port.

"Can we surrender?" asked Matthias.

"I don't think that's an option," said Lugorix.

Eurydice scowled, still not wanting to admit defeat. "Both of you get ready to—"

She never finished that sentence. From the northeast, a jet of fire shot through the air, looking for all the world like a fiery gob of spit—and then landing like one too, impacting on the platform that dangled from the balloon's basket. There wasn't even an explosion—the thing just sort of *melted;* what was left of it dripped down toward the ocean. Lugorix could hear the screaming of the flaming human torches who had crewed it all the way down. They impacted less than twenty meters from the *Xerxes,* the fires winking out. Now bereft of tether, the balloon soared off ahead of them, caught in a western wind, picking up speed the whole while.

"Damn," muttered Lugorix.

"Shut up and keep shooting!" yelled Eurydice.

But in truth he and Matthias had never stopped. They'd managed to hit one of the Carthaginian ships—it was burning nicely—but were feeling all too exposed as the rest of them started to come within range. Though the Carthaginians now had more to worry about than just the *Xerxes*—not only had the as-yet-unseen ship to the northeast taken out the platform of the balloon, but it (or maybe still other ships) had managed to destroy three more of the Carthaginian vessels with some still-unseen weapon.

"Torpedoes," said Eurydice. "One of my father's inventions."

"What?"

"Whatever's back there is using torpedoes—uh, they're projectiles that move through the water. Think of them as metal, um… fish. Really fast fish, stuffed with black powder. That's why we're not seeing any shots."

"What the hell *are* we seeing then?" yelled Matthias—he slammed another round of ammunition into place, gestured at the massive foaming pillars that had just risen off to each side.

"I think they're waterspouts," yelled Eurydice.

Lugorix fired—the round roared off, streaked through the air and smashed across the deck of a Carthaginian ship, sweeping soldiers off its deck like they were ninepins and then crashing through the mast, which promptly fell into the sea like a tree downed by a wine-crazed woodsman. But the Carthaginians were doing their best to return the favor: ballistae and catapult bolts shot across the water, and one hit the *Xerxes,* bouncing off the forward deck and just missing Lugorix. Eurydice ducked down behind the rail as the ship lurched to the right and suddenly listed sharply to one side. For a moment Lugorix thought they'd been holed below the waterline. He looked down at the ocean.

Which was sloping away from him.

His eyes rebelled against what he was seeing. It was like the *Xerxes* was at the top of a hill made of water. He was staring down into an endless froth of sea that stretched down into abyss. He heard Matthias screaming above the din.

The same word. Over and over again.

Charybdis.

Eumenes was using that word too—alternating it with various curses. "What does that mean?" said Kalyana, his brow furrowing.

"The whirlpool that almost killed Odysseus," yelled Eumenes. Kalyana looked at him blankly, but Eumenes wasn't interested in explaining the finer points of Greek culture to the sage. What he was interested in, really, was not dying. Which right now was proving to be a bit of a chore.

The Carthaginian ships must have had advance warning thanks to that balloon; most of them were busy maneuvering round the whirlpool's edges even as the balloon climbed crazily out of control—into a waterspout, where it was shredded instantly, pieces of it flying across the sky. On the far side of the whirlpool—due west—he could see a strange looking ship that he assumed was the Persian vessel. It looked a lot like his own ironclads, though it was smaller and had a gun mounted on the back. Two figures were clinging to that gun and it was going to be touch-and-go whether the ship they were riding made it past the vortex.

But right now Eumenes had more pressing problems. The first of his three ships had already plowed too far into the slope of ocean, was getting swept away, running deeper even as he watched its crew leaping off, abandoning ship to no avail. They were well and truly screwed. And Eumenes knew he would be too if he didn't move right now—

"Full power," he heard himself screaming.

But his captain was already on it. The ship's boiler was thumping so hard it seemed like it was about to explode. The rudder was making a noise like it was about to give up the ghost. For long and terrible moments, Eumenes' two boats struggled against the deadly undertow. But then suddenly they were past it, surging forward with renewed power. Far ahead of him, Eumenes could see the Persian ship had escaped as well, several Carthaginian ships in hot pursuit, steam pouring from stacks as they throttled after their prey.

But he could also see another ship veering past the whirlpool's far side. One that didn't look like any of the rest.

"That's not Carthaginian," said Kalyana.

"You got that right," muttered Eumenes.

"What the hell is it?" muttered Lugorix.

"It's called a catamaran," said Eurydice in a tone that said *don't ask me why because this really isn't a good time.* It was enormous, consisting of two ten-decker warships with a two-deck structure laid across the top connecting them. It had turned aside from the northern edge of the whirlpool at the last moment, was now moving on the Carthaginian rear, each of its sails almost as large as any one of those boats, sails that billowed out as the wind intensified. Nor was the catamaran the only vessel in pursuit of the pursuers. Two ironclads had emerged from the vortex's southern extremity, were riding low in the water as they vectored in toward the Carthaginian ships. Waterspouts kept raging to both left and right. Ahead of the *Xerxes* the sky was dark, lit only by the occasional flash of lightning. Rain began to spray across the ship's deck. And just as Matthias and Lugorix began to draw a bead on the closest Carthaginian ship, the prow of the *Xerxes* dipped, and the ship suddenly began sliding down another slope in the water—*another whirlpool,* thought Lugorix. He couldn't even see the other side of this one—it was just one long sheet of whitewater, surging down into the dark lightning-filled clouds that now filled the entire western horizon. It was all he could do to hang on.

"Will someone tell me why we're steering straight into it?" yelled Matthias.

"It's no whirlpool," said Eurydice. "And we've no choice." Lugorix noticed she had taken a rope and was... by Taranis, she was *strapping herself to the fucking rail* as the ship picked up speed—and then she drew a knife, sliced off what was left of that rope and tossed it to him.

"Better get busy," she said.

"Can't we just get below?" said Matthias.

"At some point we're going to need that gun," she said. Lugorix wasn't even arguing, was already strapping himself to the cannon—and as he did the same for Matthias, they saw the Carthaginian ships come over the summit of the crest behind them, start plowing down toward them. The catamaran and those two ironclads weren't too far behind. Eurydice kept on screaming instructions down to Barsine—the ship turned at a sharp enough angle that it almost capsized, but instead continued to pick up speed as the slope it was running down kept on getting steeper.

"What the fuck are we *in?*" yelled Matthias.

"And what are *those?*" said Lugorix.

They were cliffs. Vast ragged cliffs, looming out of the clouds on either side of them. The *Xerxes* turned again, tacking back the other way as it steered between two of the chunks of rock. The ship was pitching up and down so heavily Lugorix saw no point in even trying to fire the cannon. Besides, the elements were doing a far better job then he ever could: as he watched, two of the Carthaginian ships smashed straight into rock, crumpling up like so much paper. Lugorix could barely see the rearmost ships now—just the very faint outline of the catamaran.

But then it lit up as though it had been struck by lightning.

Eumenes saw too late where the gun on the catamaran was: just as he realized that one of the compound ship's prows had slid away to reveal a wicked-looking maw, there was a flash and another gobbet of flame roared in toward him. He froze like a mouse before a snake; the burning mass shot past him and smashed into his second ironclad, sending its turret spinning into the air while what remained of the ship detonated from the inside out. Flying metal banged against the hull of Eumenes' ironclad.

"Must have set off the ammunition," said Kalyana calmly.

"No kidding!" screamed Eumenes. He couldn't remember the last time he'd lost his cool; he consoled himself with the thought that it was likely to be the last. And then, to his crew—*"hard to starboard! Fire torpedoes!"* He and Kalyana were knocked sprawling as the ship did just that—Eumenes found himself unceremoniously dumped on top of the seer, the wind knocked from him as the ship pitched up and down in the ever-growing shitstorm.

"We die standing," declared Kalyana.

Even now, Eumenes was enough of a diplomat to see that was a polite way of saying *get your ass off me.* Eumenes pulled himself painfully to his feet, helped Kalyana up as he stared out into the intensifying maelstrom. There were only three Carthaginian ships left now, one of them decidedly larger than the others—presumably the flagship. It had at least twelve decks and was steering easily past the cliff on which its brethren had just shattered. The Persian ship was nowhere to be seen amidst sheets of water.

Eumenes could barely tell rain from ocean now. The catamaran veered, exposing its flame-gun again—levelling it directly at its Macedonian rival. Eumenes stared right at it. He saw his own death.

And then his torpedoes hit.

Afterward, Ptolemy would thank the gods he'd been in the the catamaran's rightward vessel. The leftward one was instantly holed in two places below the waterline even as the firegun mounted on it discharged into the ocean, which surged in on the rowers, engulfing most of them before they could even begin to scramble for the upper decks. Ptolemy caught a glimpse of sailors streaming out of the gaping holes like beans pouring from a sack. The firegun rolled forward and plunged over the side, vanishing into the water, flame still streaming from it. The catamaran began to lean dangerously, though it was hard to tell how pronounced the list was because the downward rush was so great. Ptolemy staggered through into the bridge where the helmsman was struggling with the tiller. Obviously he wasn't receiving much help from the other side.

"What's the situation?" said Ptolemy.

"We're out of control," said the helmsman.

"So let me drive," said the bastard son of Philip—he grabbed the helmsman and hurled him screaming from the ship. Then, turning to the stunned officers—"Give me someone with balls! Someone who can steer this thing! Get that fucking sail down, by the gods! Get some men out on the hull and cut that fucking deadweight *loose!*" He sounded like a madman. He wondered if that was what he'd become. He half-expected those officers to hurl him from the ship too. But the instinct to obey ran too deep. They were Macedonians first. Only second were they men. The catamaran just missed a cliff and then hurtled onto the side of the biggest wave Ptolemy had ever seen. And only the royal blood that ran through his veins prevented him from shitting in his pants at what lay at the bottom of it.

"Nothing," said Lugorix.

As the clouds ahead of him cleared, he could see the water pouring in sheets off the edge of everything, thundering down into abyss. It was the waterfall to end all waterfalls—and yet with Eurydice navigating and Barsine at the helm, the *Xerxes* was hurtling in toward it at just the right angle, making straight for the one place where the water ran down what looked like a gigantic ramp. All Lugorix could hear was the roar of the falls and the sound of Matthias praying. Next moment they were on that ramp and on either side was... *not a thing*—except for two of the Carthaginian ships, turning over and over as they tumbled into oblivion. But their flagship was a little faster—it skated right along the edge of the waterfall and then veered onto the ramp behind them.

"They went that way," yelled Eumenes, sighting with the farseeker. The rain was so intense he couldn't even make out what had happened to the Persian craft—all he could see was that the Carthaginian flagship had followed it, and he knew whoever was piloting that ship was no idiot. Also, both boats seemed to *slide* from view, while the ones that went over the waterfall everywhere else lurched forward sickeningly before plunging out of sight. That was all Eumenes needed to know about where his only chance for survival lay. And as they hurtled in toward it, they saw all that lay beyond...

"The world is *fucking flat*," said Kalyana as he went down on both knees.

"Let's make sure we stay on it," muttered Eumenes.

The ironclad surged onto the ramp, began hurtling down it.

The ramp was the only way that offered even the slightest hope of living. That much was clear. As was why no one dared to venture too far beyond the Pillars. The crazy stories that sailors told about how the ocean frayed and the world ended were all *true*. But Ptolemy had to admire his new helmsman's pragmatism: the man seemed to be beyond fear as he expertly compensated for the intensifying deadweight represented by the left-hand side of the boat. It wouldn't work for long. Then again, it didn't have to. The crippled catamaran roared onto the ramp, charged down into the unknown.

They were picking up speed. As they accelerated away from the lip of ocean, the full extent of the waterfall pouring from the world's edge became apparent, stretching off on either side of the ramp until it was swallowed up by mist. But up ahead, that mist was dissipating; Lugorix could see pinpricks of light glimmering through it—

"Stars," said Eurydice.

Lugorix nodded. He drew his blade, slashed away the rope, began to crawl along the hull of the *Xerxes,* dragging himself toward the turret. Eurydice was so intent on those stars that she only noticed him as he pulled himself up next to her—she glanced round at him in surprise.

"What are you *doing?*" she asked.

"*Look out,*" he said, pointing past her. She looked back in front of her and then screamed a warning to Barsine, who threw the rudder over, just barely keeping pace with how sharply that unearthly ramp turned to the right. The *Xerxes* smashed into the side of the ramp as it struggled to navigate the bend—and then it was through, rumbling down the second part of the ramp which curled back beneath the first. Lugorix could see the massive support struts and beams that sprouted out from the side of what seemed to be a gigantic rocky wall—the ramp ended in a tunnel set into that wall. They roared in toward it while Lugorix climbed down the ladder into the cabin of the *Xerxes.*

Barsine was sitting at the controls, silently weeping. He put one enormous arm around her shoulder.

"It's alright," he said.

"I wish that were true," she replied.

They surged into the tunnel.

"Shall we fire, sir?"

Eumenes could understand the temptation. That damn Carthaginian twelve-decker was only about two hundred meters ahead, and firing the torpedoes down this ramp would be akin to a turkey shoot. Which was the problem. The last thing they needed was a piece of flaming junk right in their path. And that was assuming the explosions didn't bring down the ramp itself. But now the Carthaginian ship was veering to the side as it negotiated a steep turn in the ramp which curved on itself, back toward the edge of the Earth. It lurched sharply; several of the siege-engines on its deck slid over the side and fell into abyss. And then the Carthaginian ship was onto the ramp's lower section, passing beneath Eumenes' ship as it headed in toward the cliff. Next moment, Eumenes' ship was negotiating the same turn; he heard a clanking as his steersmen shifted gears, switching the propellors into reverse, slowing down the ship just enough to prevent it from going over the edge as the rush of water carried it around the bend and in toward a tunnel set in the rocky wall of Earth. But Eumenes wasn't even really looking at it. His eyes were focused on the curve his ship had just traversed—at what was about to try to follow him—

"This ought to be fun," he said.

Ptolemy's eyes went wide as he saw what the hamstrung catamaran was heading for. He gripped the edge of the beam in front of him, muttered a prayer to the gods, the irony of the gesture all too palpable to him: as though the gods would take pity on anyone mad enough to sail a giant catamaran off the end of the ocean. As they hit the turn on the ramp, there was a terrible grinding *crack,* followed by the even worse noise of wood tearing asunder. The floor bucked under their feet as the rightward boat lurched to the side, remained on the ramp while the leftward one sheared off entirely, smashed over the edge, disintegrating into pieces falling away into nothingness, men turning over and over as they tumbled. Ptolemy caught a glimpse of stars above his head—stars all around—and then the halved-catamaran was rumbling after the other ships, closing in on the maw that led into the bowels of the Earth.

"It's not truly Atlantis, is it?" said Lugorix.

"It's been called that," Barsine replied.

Lugorix shook his head. It was all he needed to hear to understand how totally he'd been deceived. For his own good? For hers? For the world's? He didn't know. The tunnel roof had closed in over their heads. The *Xerxes* was sailing down into the darkness. Barsine switched off the engines. Eurydice was no longer calling out any directions. She couldn't see where they were going. None of them could.

"Shouldn't we be getting some torches up on the deck?" asked Lugorix.

"We don't want to draw attention to ourselves," replied Barsine.

There was something in the way she said it that made it sound like she was more concerned about what was in front of them rather than what was pursuing them. The craft was picking up speed now, the angle of their descent steepening. If there was any kind of barrier or obstacle ahead, the first they were going to know about it was when they smashed into it. But that didn't seem to be worrying Barsine.

"I told you before we even got to the Pillars that Atlantis was just one word for it," she said. "But it's got many others. And nearly all of them are romantic myths. Anything to avoid having to face what really lies at the end of West. Because that's the one thing people can't deal with."

And now Lugorix started to see something out there—the glimmers of phosphorescence very far away, as though he was looking up at an enormous bowl. Other lights burnt on top of what might have been a distant mountain peak—or maybe it was a tower—but those lights were strange: they seemed a little like torches, but unlike torchlight they didn't waver. And if they were fire, then they were an odd color: not so much orange-red as yellow-white. Lugorix had never wanted to be somewhere less.

"What can't people deal with," he heard himself say.

"The thing the Greeks call Hades," she replied.

CHAPTER EIGHTEEN

The decisive moment was approaching.

The bridge was less than a quarter mile to completion—just out of range of the Athenian siege-engines, mounted on the hills around the beach. The crews of all those catapults and ballisatae and trebuchets had fired enough rocks across the last few days to have their range calibrated perfectly—they knew exactly where each missile was going to land and they couldn't wait for the workers atop that bridge to extend it another fifty meters. Nor could the several hundred ships of the Athenian navy that surrounded that bridge on three sides. They kept a wary distance to be sure, held at bay by siege-engines positioned along the length of the bridge—but they had their own machines aboard and were obviously preparing to assault the great structure from all sides in a combined offensive.

Watching the scene from a cave in one of the hills, Agathocles figured it was going to be an interesting fight. That's when he noticed Athenian riders tearing ass into the main camp. Shortly thereafter, his spies brought word that a frenzied argument was underway in the Athenian command tent. Apparently the just-arrived viceroy of Syracuse—one of the archons himself—had commanded that the troops be withdrawn from the beach. And some of those troops were objecting in no uncertain terms.

"It's bullshit," said Xanthippus.

Diocles shrugged. He wasn't in the mood to listen to Xanthippus. Truth be told, he wasn't in the mood to listen to anyone. The higher-ups argued about plans, and then the lower-downs argued about what the higher-ups were going to do, and it didn't really matter. Someone who was neither him nor Xanthippus would make a decision, and then someone would die. Hopefully it wouldn't be him.

"Did you hear what I said?" growled Xanthippus.

"Sure I did," said Diocles. "Didn't realize you needed an answer."

Xanthippus spat noisily. He didn't, of course. Bitching was its own reward. It was the only perk involved in crouching in this trench with a bunch of other soldiers looking out at all those ships and that fucking bridge that came closer with every passing day. If Diocles had had his druthers, they'd still be wandering along the barren Iberian coast—or better yet, wandering deeper into Iberia. Getting off the map and into the wilderness and away from all this mess. The two of them had been lovers since Diocles was sixteen, and ever since then that was all Diocles had wanted to do—run away with the older man, split from everything. But Xanthippus had been in the army. That hadn't meant much back in those days—he was stationed in Athens, he'd had plenty of time to spend with Diocles, and there was no real sense that that time would ever be at an end. The empire had been at its height, halcyon days, with no storm clouds on the horizon. Yet for Diocles it had never been halcyon. Everywhere he looked there were those who weren't fully human under law: women, slaves, foreigners... while those in the assembly shouted and swore and those with the money steered that shouting in any direction they wanted. He didn't know why these things bothered him so much. They didn't seem to bother anyone else.

Certainly not Xanthippus. He believed in Athens, and even when he didn't, he believed it was better than any alternative. And when war came, that alternative got a whole lot worse. Macedonia and its god-kings were a whole new level of trouble. So Diocles enlisted too. Not that he fooled himself for a moment that he was doing so for any other reason than to be with Xanthippus. And so, less than three days after being dropped off in Iberia by that crazy gang in that crazy ship (no point in telling *that* story to anyone), he'd helped his lover light a bonfire when they sighted the sails of an Athenian warship. They didn't know how fortunate they'd been until they reached Sicily, where they found out that in the wake of the fall of Carthage and Massilia there was hardly any Athenian activity west of

Sicily. The Empire had pulled in its extremities like a tortoise just seeking to survive.

But now the pair of them were part of that Empire once again. They were Athenian soldiers, said Xanthippus; they'd sworn an oath on the altar of Athena, and you couldn't break those oaths lightly. In fact, you couldn't break such oaths at all, unless the altar itself shattered. Which it probably would before this all this was over. But in that case their bodies would most likely be in pieces along with it.

"Did you hear that?" said Xanthippus. Diocles was too immersed in his thoughts to register that Xanthippus had even spoken—the man had to shake him by the shoulder to rouse him from his reverie.

"Hear what?" he asked.

"We're moving out," said a third man. "Orders just came on down."

"So they finally made up their minds," said Diocles.

"To obey?" Xanthippus laughed. "Took them long enough."

"And obeying's all we can do"—but the third man trailed off in mid-sentence as a series of thunderous booms suddenly reverberated over the hills. The ground shook as though it was getting smacked by an earthquake. Trails of fire roared over the hills from behind them.

"Macks in the rear!" yelled somebody.

"Holy *shit*," said Xanthippus as those plumes arced above them and rained down on the Athenian fleet, pancaking into ship after ship. Some detonated on the spot, some just caught fire, began to sink as the water rushed through the holes punched in their hulls. From an organizational perspective, the attack came at the absolute worst time imaginable, since the orders had just been given to abandon positions and march away. Everyone was yelling and shouting and screaming and a lot of soldiers were just running off the beach entirely. So much for retreating in an orderly fashion…. Xanthippus stayed where he was, so Diocles did too. Which left them in an excellent position to watch while lines of foaming water suddenly began to radiate out from positions on that great bridge—almost as though very fast fishes were swimming below the surface. As each of those lines touched an Athenian ship, that ship detonated, flinging wood and bodies into the water with unbelievable force. Within thirty seconds, every ship that was visible was on fire. But still those plumes of flame kept hurtling in from over the hills.

Only now they were falling onto the beach.

"We're gone," said Xanthippus. He grabbed Diocles and shoved him out of the trench, scrambling after him as the soldiers on the beach began dying messily. Flame and smoke was everywhere. Someone yelled that the Macks were upon them. And then Diocles saw them: hundreds of men wearing Mack armor and riding on… he had to blink to make sure he was seeing them correctly.

They were camels.

He only recognized them because he'd seen a merchant in Athens selling them once, to grace the gardens of the rich. He hadn't been impressed. They were noisy and they were smelly and and now they were everywhere. Macedonians leapt down off their backs and speared Athenians still blinded by the smoke. An arrow hit Xanthippus in the shoulder and he went down. Diocles dropped to his knees next to him.

"Leave me," he muttered.

Diocles said nothing—just grabbed the larger man and dragged him to his feet before putting his arm around his shoulder and helping him stagger forward. He had no idea what the plan was—get back to the trench? Get chopped to pieces? Stand back to back and fight? He saw some rocks up ahead. He pulled Xanthippus into their lee.

That was when he noticed the cave.

It wasn't much. But under the circumstances it was enough. Diocles helped the wounded Xanthippus inside. The two men crawled deeper.

"That's far enough," said a voice.

Diocles stopped. "There's room for us all to hide," he said.

"Your friend needs medical attention."

"I'll manage," grunted Xanthippus.

"We need to get that arrow out," said the voice.

"For that, you'll need some light," said another.

There was the sound of metal striking flint. In the light of the flame they saw a face—long nose and short dirty hair and unkempt beard. Two other men crouched behind him. None of them looked to be Athenian.

"Who the hell are you guys?" asked Diocles.

"Observers from Syracuse," said the first man.

"Doing what?"

"Watching your fleet get axed," said the second. "Perdiccas landed a fleet on the coast."

"Perdiccas?" Diocles was tired of all these strange names.

"One of the Mack generals. Burnt all his boats on the northern shore. Though we never dreamt he'd get here so quick."

Xanthippus frowned. "You're working with the Macks?"

"We're working with the rats," said the first man, gesturing at the burrow they were in. Everyone started laughing, even Xanthippus. After a moment, Diocles joined in too. It seemed like the polite thing to do.

Matthias clambered down the ladder.

"Eurydice said I was needed down here," he said.

Barsine nodded. "You are. You two can start rowing as though your lives depended on it."

"And while we do that you're going to tell me what this place is," said Matthias as he settled his hands around an oar.

"Hades," said Lugorix. He expected Matthias to freak out, but the man just sighed.

"I was afraid of that," he said—and started rowing, the *Xerxes* moving forward through the dark water. So far that was all Lugorix knew about the terrain they were in, because the *Xerxes* still had no lights. He'd seen that roof overhead and that faraway structure. But as to what was much closer—he just hoped Eurydice and Barsine had some idea what they were doing.

But then suddenly lights flared behind them. Through the rear viewport they could see the Carthaginian warship slide from the ramp and onto the water with a thunderous splash. Soldiers crowded its deck, holding weapons and torches. Several of them drew back on their bows while others lit arrows—the flaming brands shot into the dark. Most of those arrows fell into the waters and snuffed out, but others landed amidst tufts of reeds. One landed on what looked like a sandbar, flickering there. None of them fell close to the *Xerxes*. The Carthaginian ship surged out into the water, smoke pouring from its stack.

"They're looking for us," said Barsine. "Keep rowing."

"You had us manning the guns earlier," said Matthias.

"So I did."

"So you thought there was a chance we might face hostiles right off the ramp?"

"And you can thank all your gods we didn't."

Two hundred meters back, Ptolemy's fractured catamaran flew off the ramp and landed in the water.

The mast was still on fire and that was enough for Ptolemy to know that staying on this ship was a losing proposition. He knew what was about to happen, even if his crew didn't. The Carthaginian ship and its arrows had illuminated enough of the area for him to see the immediate environment—he yelled some orders and the half-destroyed catamaran swerved hard to port, straight toward a sandbar as ballistae aboard the Carthaginian ship began firing at his vessel. Ptolemy hunkered down on the bridge as bolts flew past him.

"Give 'em white heat," he said.

"What about that sandbar?" said the helmsman.

Ptolemy didn't even bother to answer.

"Hard starboard," yelled Eumenes.

He was yelling the words even before the ironclad left the ramp. The last thing he wanted to be was anywhere near either the Carthaginian ship or Ptolemy's. Both were lit up, about as conspicuous as it was possible to be. All the more so as now the side of Ptolemy's ship popped open and that gun of his slid out and blasted a huge jet of flame toward the Carthaginian vessel—which was nearly out of range.

But not quite.

The tip of the flame touched the rear of the Carthaginian ship, which immediately caught fire. Eumenes had to hand it to the Carthaginians for their discipline—bucket-brigades were forming quickly to dash water on the fire. Eumenes ordered his ship's engineers to cut the motors. The sailors on the lowest deck began rowing, the ironclad heading steadily away from the other two vessels.

"Do you mind if I ask where we're going?" said Matthias.

"Away from all that light," said Barsine.

"So we can get out of Hades?"

"So we can go deeper into it."

As she spoke, there was a rush of what sounded like wind. Lugorix looked up through the open hatch to see some of those phosphorescent lights overhead momentarily winking in and out. He thought for a moment that was exactly what they were doing, but then he realized that something was passing between them and the *Xerxes*. Eurydice stuck her head through the hatch, drew one hand across her throat.

"Don't even *talk*," she whispered.

Lugorix wasn't about to. He gritted his teeth and kept his head down and kept rowing. Matthias was doing the same. There was no danger quite like the one they couldn't see. But all of a sudden there was no danger at all that they were going to be overheard.

Thanks to all the screaming.

Carthaginian sailors and soldiers were leaping into the water, tearing at their clothes, waving around wildly with their weapons—and all to no avail. Shadowy forms were swarming around the warship, flapping their wings, looking for all the world like giant—

"*Bats,*" muttered Matthias.

"Shut up," said Lugorix. Whatever they were, they were no ordinary bats. They were hard to make out at this distance, but they had a wingspan of at least a yard and teeth that flashed white in the torchlight. They were swarming the fuck out of all twelve decks of the Carthaginian ship. Lugorix watched in horror as men crawled out of oars-ports and dropped into the water. But the bats were aquatic too—they zipped like spears beneath the surface, dragging screaming men back into the air and ripping them to pieces.

It wasn't just the Phoenician ship they were after, either.

Ptolemy knew he had about thirty seconds. As soon as his ship hit the sandbar, he raced to the prow and hurled one end of a rope over the side. He was still clambering down its length when he heard the commotion from the Carthaginian ship. By the time his men realized he was abandoning them, he was already sprinting along the sandbar, his armor weighing heavily on his back, but it would be suicide to do without it. Behind him he heard the screaming starting. So much for his ship. So much for his crew. It was just him now. He'd just have to make the most of it.

"They're fucked," said Eumenes.

"We are too," said Kalyana. "You have brought us to *Naraka*."

"Um… come again?"

"The underworld that the Buddha spoke of. Is that not this place?"

Eumenes smiled grimly. "We haven't died yet, have we?"

The look on Kalyana's face said he wasn't sure of that one.

The screams had finally stopped. The *Xerxes* kept going, Lugorix and Matthias pulling on the oars, moving steadily away from the slaughter behind them, further into the darkness. Since they were on the surface, Barsine had opened slits in the walls on either side to provide more visibility. As their eyes slowly adjusted, Lugorix realized that the dull glow overhead provided just enough ambient light to steer by. Shadows became visible on either side of the boat—intimations of topography that resolved themselves into clumps of gnarled trees and roots. The *Xerxes* sailed into a narrow channel that soon gave way to more such channels. A shifting, labyrinthine landscape, lit up by that ghostly overhead light....

"The Greeks may know this place as Hades," said Barsine. "But for me it is *Chakat-i-Daitih,* the underworld of which the great Zoroaster spoke, the pit into which Marduk hurled Tiamat. And Lugorix will have heard of *Cernunnos*—"

"That name is not right to speak," said Lugorix quickly.

"—the domain of the Horned One. It may be that all of us are correct."

"You're all wrong," said Eurydice.

Barsine looked at her like she wanted to throw her overboard. "So you have been telling me for weeks now."

"Your gods don't exist. Your religions are a sham. The sooner you get that through your heads, the better off we'll be."

"You persist in regarding this place as some kind of Atlantis," said Barsine.

"I thought *that* was yet another line of bullshit," said Matthias.

"It's actually the only sensible way to view our whereabouts," said Eurydice obstinately. "What we're looking at isn't the fucking *afterlife*. Do you think we'll find Damitra here?" Barsine's face went red. "We won't. And we won't find Lugorix's parents either. Or his sister. None of them. I don't know what happens to souls when bodies die. But they certainly don't end up in this dump. My father was a rationalist who—"

"Your father was a bigot," snarled Barsine.

"Think I don't know that? But he and Plato spent their lives trying to understand the elder civilizations that once ruled the Earth."

Barsine shook her head. "You mean that once *tried*."

"Fragments," said Eumenes as the ironclad navigated through the maze of channels in near-complete silence. All that could be heard was the splash of the oars. "Fragments are all we have. Plato wrote of a mighty power that lay west of the Pillars and whose legions subjugated Europa and Africa."

"Doesn't look like they're doing much subjugating now," said Kalyana.

"According to him, they were defeated by Athens."

"By *Athens?*" Kalyana clearly didn't buy it. "How do you explain such a thing?"

"Plato was Athenian," said Eumenes. "It looked good for him to say that."

Kalyana nodded. "More books he could sell, no?"

"More books, sure. More royalties, more hash, more pussy. But it still left the question of just what *did* happen."

"And you believe you have the answer?"

"I like to think of it as a theory," said Eumenes.

"Plato can only take you so far," said Eurydice. "My father's real break-through came when he discovered the lost tales of the bard Thamyris."

Matthias frowned. "Wasn't he mentioned in the *Iliad?*"

"Yes, and not to his credit. He challenged the Muses to a singing contest: if he won he got to fuck them."

"I take it he didn't?"

"Of course not. He lost big-time, after which they smashed his lyre and blinded him. Typical penalty for *hubris*. But he was most famous for the epic poem *Titanomachy*. Which was eventually written down by one of Homer's students and then later destroyed during the Persian sack of Athens. Or so they thought. But my father got hold of a copy."

"As did I," said Barsine.

Eurydice stared. This was obviously news to her. "How?"

"You said it yourself—my people sacked Athens and made off with the spoils."

"Assholes," muttered Matthias.

Barsine ignored him. "The *Titanomachy* made its way into the hands of the Magi. And then Damitra absconded with it during the war with Alexander."

"And you were going to tell me *when?*" said Eurydice.

Barsine smiled mirthlessly. "Now seems like as good a time as any."

Maybe it was just Lugorix's imagination, but he fancied he could hear the noise of Eurydice grinding her teeth. He figured this to be a productive development. If Eurydice and Barsine were at last leveling with each other, then maybe he and Matthias would finally get some answers.

Assuming the two women didn't kill each other first.

"We ought to have discussed this *weeks ago*," said Eurydice.

Barsine shrugged. "I didn't know whether you were working for the Macedonians."

"At least I wasn't fucking them."

Lugorix had to hand it to Barsine—she had class enough to keep her cool. Sometimes being an aristocrat had its advantages. Then again, they were probably used to having their guards beat the crap out of the peasants when they got uppity. No sense in getting their own hands dirty. Barsine took a deep breath.

"All we needed to cooperate on earlier was getting here," she said softly. "There was no sense in talking about the *alleged layout* of this place until we made it."

"Well now we have," said Matthias. "So how about you two get it together and start talking. What does this *Titanomachy* discuss?"

"The war of the Titans," said Eurydice using that patented *dumb-ass* tone that seemed to be so effective at getting Matthias' goat.

"The war between the Titans and the gods?" said Matthias.

She shrugged. "I don't know for sure."

"Then why the fuck are we even listening to you?" said Matthias. Lugorix could only marvel at how totally their relations had disintegrated to utter shit. That was why you should never start sleeping with someone who you were trying to infiltrate the underworld with. There was no way such a romp could end well. Especially now that Eurydice showed herself to have none of Barsine's restraint. She slapped Matthias hard.

But he just grinned.

"Any more of that and I might stop rowing and start getting excited."

"You're disgusting," said Eurydice.

"Eurydice is correct," said Barsine. For a moment Lugorix thought she was talking about Matthias. But then she clarified: "At least from the standpoint of Greek mythology. According to the legends, the gods overthrew the Titans. But the *Titanomachy* doesn't really distinguish between the two—doesn't rule out whether it was simply a war between two groups of Titans, or perhaps two groups of gods. It just says one group was of Olympus; the other, of the Underworld. So to call them *gods* just means we don't really understand anything about their true nature."

Lugorix frowned. "So we're talking about a war between two large and powerful gangs of assholes," he said.

"And if they were gods, they weren't the kind you *worship*," said Eurydice. "They were the kind you *run from*. It was the Olympians who stopped those who ruled the Underworld from conquering the sunlit lands above."

"So the Olympians won?" asked Lugorix.

"Not exactly," said the daughter of Aristotle.

"The Sibylline Books," said Eumenes. "They're the key to all this."

"The books that Alexander consulted with at Rome?"

"He didn't just consult them," said Eumenes. "He ripped them off."

Kalyana's mouth dropped in a wide open O. "He *stole them?*"

"Alexander's never that crude. He bribed the priests with untold riches to look the other way and allow him to substitute a bunch of nonsense texts that Hephaestion and I cooked up. But the real trick is that Alexander got ahold of the *other* Sibylline books—the ones that were supposed to have been destroyed."

Kalyana frowned. "Destroyed... by who?"

"By the chick who sold them to Rome in the first place." Kalyana raised both eyebrows at that. Eumenes just laughed. It was that crazy: "Dig this: couple of centuries back, the Sibyl of Cumae showed up and offered *nine* sacred books of prophecy to Rome's last king. He asked how much, she named a price, and he said forget it, no way I'm paying that much. Whereupon the old crone *burnt* three of the books, and repeated the same offer for the last six books. And he *still* said fuck off. So then she torched three more and offered him the remaining three at *the same damn price*."

"And this time he paid," said Kalyana.

Eumenes nodded. "And those three books were kept in Rome ever since."

"But she didn't really burn the others," said Kalyana.

"Apparently not. Prophetesses are like magicians—you have to watch their hands. Or maybe she had extra copies. Lot of that going around these days, I hear. Hephaestion and I found the burnt remnants of the six beneath Avernus, near Cumae. Which was supposed to be one of the gates to the underworld. And may well be, but the damn thing's blocked."

"By what?"

"Probably during the War," said Eumenes.

"Which war would that be?"

"*The* war. Between the guys down *here* and the guys up *there*."

Kalyana nodded. "Make sense."

"Really? I'm still trying to wrap my head around it."

Kalyana shrugged. "In Vedic scripture, there is a book called the *Bhaga-vad-Gita* that speaks of a war that shook the universe—a war in which the gods themselves took part. So the Sibylline books, they say this too?"

"The first three were the best three it turned out," said Eumenes. "The king of Rome really should have taken that offer. Anyway, the war pretty much brought the house down. The skies rained blood and the oceans boiled and the continents buckled and someone blew up the land-bridge between Africa and Europe—"

Kalyana's western geography wasn't his strong point, but even so: *"What land-bridge?"*

"Exactly. All that's left now are the Pillars of Gibraltar. Both sides hammered away at the other with terrible magick and weapons until they had nothing left to hammer with. In the end what was left of the Olympians got frozen in the arctic ice on an island called Thule and the Chthonic gods got sealed down here."

Kalyana pondered this—looked out at the fire-streaked gloom through which they were moving. "Do you know where exactly?"

Eumenes grinned mirthlessly. "We're heading there now," he said.

Retreats were never pretty.

Most of the Athenian army had perished on the beach, but those soldiers who survived were busy staggering back to Syracuse, joined by hordes of refugees fleeing the invaders. Just when it seemed like matters couldn't get any worse, Mount Etna—that great volcano on the eastern coast of Sicily—had started rumbling and belching smoke and ashes. It was though the gods themselves were signalling the downfall of Athens. Clouds of grey hung low overhead and all the birds had stopped singing. It was like the world itself was dying.

Maybe it was. The rampaging Macks had massacred the first few villages they'd reached; after that, everybody was on the move, frantically heading for the safety of the island's walled enclaves. The most popular of which was Syracuse. That was where the biggest walls were, after all—that the city was almost certainly Alexander's main target didn't really seem to have occured to most of the refugees.

"It's a deliberate strategy," said Xanthippus. His helmet was lifted half-back, nose-guard against his forehead, the better to march with. He was fortunate to be marching at all. But the three Syracusans had done a good job with the arrow that had struck him—cutting the shaft in two, and carving out the arrowhead with a blade they'd first heated in boiling water. They were clearly soldiers of some kind themselves, however much they denied it. Xanthippus had confided to Diocles that they were probably Syracusan resistance; Diocles had replied that he really didn't give a shit. They'd saved Xanthippus' life, and that was all he cared about. Though if they really *were* Syracusan resistance, he'd have expected them to find some way back to Syracuse that didn't involve marching alongside two Athenian soldiers. Then again, maybe that was the smartest way to do it.

"Of course it's a deliberate strategy," said the long-nosed man—the one who seemed to be the boss of the three Syracusans. "Make sure as many people get herded into Syracuse as possible. There'll be that many more mouths to feed."

Diocles hadn't thought of it that way. But the Syracusan seemed to know what he was talking about. He seemed to have contacts everywhere, too—peasants and woodsmen kept coming up to him and whispering in his ear. It was after one of these encounters that the Syracusan—who called himself Antiphon, though neither Xanthippus nor Diocles believed for a second that was his real name—swore loudly and turned to his companions.

"He's landed," he said.

There was no need to specify who *he* was. But Antiphon then proceeded to tell everyone in earshot all about it, and everyone perked up his ears to listen. He warmed to his audience, waxing poetic about how—with his advance guard already wreaking havoc across the coast of northern Sicily—Alexander himself had ridden across the bridge at the head of his entire army. The king had been flanked by his Companions, with his recently named consort, Hephaestion, at his side. Both wore golden armor, and the king himself sported his customary ram's-head helmet. Behind them were the divisions of the Macedonian phalanx, interspersed by elephants and chariots and metal-men who knew neither fear nor mercy. No sooner had the army reached Sicily then it turned south for Syracuse.

"They're heading this way now," finished Antiphon. A low moan swept through the crowds of refugees, who proceeded to pick up the pace insofar as they could.

"If that volcano erupts while he marches past it, then maybe that would put paid to Alexander," said Diocles.

"It won't erupt," said Xanthippus.

"How do you know?"

"Because nature itself is on the king's side."

Diocles shrugged. It wasn't like he could offer any argument to the contrary. They reached Syracuse shortly thereafter as part of a throng heading through the gates. Diocles found it strange to be back here again—it felt like things had come full circle, since this was where he and Xanthippus had set off from on the journey to Carthage. But that time he hadn't even been allowed off the ship at Syracuse. Now he saw the city from the point of view of the landward defenses. The city sprawled up onto the Epipolae plateau and down to the waterfront, the island-fortress of Ortygia towering up against the sea. The city-walls were bristling with peculiar looking pieces of artillery, and in many places the height of those walls had been extended still further with additional wooden levels. They looked all too precarious to Diocles, and he hoped he wouldn't have to go up on top of them.

But it was to the Ortygia that Antiphon now demanded to be taken. That caused no little mirth for the Athenian guards whom he accosted and considerable consternation for Xanthippus and Diocles, who were forced to admit they knew Antiphon—but not that well, of course… they'd simply met him on the way to Syracuse….

"In a cave," said Antiphon. "Above the beach. While the rest of the army was getting wiped out."

"You're fucking crazy," said Xanthippus as the guards moved in.

"I'm not," said Antiphon in a loud voice. "I'm Agathocles of Syracuse, wanted by the state of Athens for sedition and I have a message for the new viceroy. And these guys"—he pointed to Xanthippus and Diocles—"are my friends."

"Fucking great," said Diocles as the guards grabbed him.

Leosthenes was up to his neck in shit. His order to get the troops off that beach had come too late; worse, there were reports that the captains on the scene had actually *argued* with one another over whether to obey his command. Though at this point mutiny mattered far less to Leosthenes then the realization that he'd already lost the first battle against a king who didn't even know the meaning of the word *defeat*. There was a knock on the door and Memnon entered the room.

"A visitor for you," he said.

"I don't have time," said Leosthenes.

"You do for this one."

"Who is it?"

"Someone with an offer I don't think you're going to be able to refuse."

As usual, Memnon was right.

CHAPTER NINETEEN

Ptolemy was no stranger to running for his life. He had done it many times before. But never quite like this. The sandbar gave way to the most desolate shore he'd ever seen. He struck inland into a wilderness of scrubland that rapidly became some kind of forest. Though not the sort he'd ever seen. The plants scarcely seemed to be alive, and they were virtually overwhelmed by fungus basking in the phospherence which glimmered overhead. He stumbled through those growths until he reached the river he knew had to be there. He could only hope and pray it was the Lethe. He kept off its bank—he felt that would leave him too exposed, so instead he kept the river in sight as he moved through the woods, following a parallel course to the Lethe. It led directly to where he was trying to go—the hub of it all. But there was a long way between here and there.

The noises were making it seem all the longer.

At first he thought it was just those damn bat creatures. He could occasionally hear them fluttering overhead, and the sound sent cold shivers up his spine. But eventually he realized that there were other noises, on the ground around him. Nothing too near—but not nearly far enough away for him to feel remotely comfortable. Especially given the nature of those sounds—strange growls and roars and warbles, and he hated to think of their sources.

But it was when the voices started that he really got the fear. Those voices weren't human. That much was clear from the outset. They howled and shouted in tones that went well beyond the human register—at times deeper, at times shriller than any human voice could be. And the languages they spoke were unrecognizable. Assuming they even *were* languages. Sometimes it was just sounded like fighting. Maybe that was all it was. Moans of agony; howls of triumph… occasionally he heard the clash of blades and caught a glimpse of flame. Sometimes he saw shadows, off in the trees. He had no intention of going near any of it.

But then he saw something ahead of him he recognized all too well.

The *Xerxes* was out of the channels now, back onto what could only be described as a river. But its shores were utterly straight. Beyond those shores, the terrain seemed to consist of nothing but forbidding woods packed with gnarled trees and oversized fungus. Here and there, fires were dimly visible through the trees, along with absolutely unearthly shrieking.

"Why doesn't that attract the attention of those bat creatures?" he asked.

"Sometimes it does," replied Eurydice.

Everyone but Barsine was up top. Matthias had his bow out, was scanning the shore for any movement. Lugorix kept one eye on that shore, but he also didn't trust that water. The *Xerxes'* engine was back on; it was so dark it was difficult to see the smoke emanating from the funnel, but Lugorix still felt uncomfortable about it, given the noises that were emanating from the land. Still, it beat rowing.

"As best I can make out, those bat-things are some kind of automatic defense," said Eurydice in a low voice. "They're largely concentrated on preventing intruders from crossing the River Styx."

Matthias frowned. "Um… River Styx?"

Eumenes looked impatient. "Remember when we got dumped into this place and had to traverse some open water before we ended up in this river? As in, three minutes ago?"

"That open water—*that* was the Styx? Didn't seem like much of a river."

"Semantics," said Eurydice. "The outermost Ocean encircling the world above us—*our* world—a lot of scholars call *that* a river. The Styx is in an analogous position: it encircles the underworld. You don't make landfall without crossing the Styx."

"And what about the other side?" asked Lugorix. "What's encircling the Styx?"

"Nothing but rock. We're in a giant cavern, or hadn't you noticed?"

"Wait a second," said Matthias. "Isn't the Styx supposed to have that weird ferry dude?"

"You mean Charon?"

"Yeah, that's it. Charon. Where's he?"

"As best I can determine, he's indisposed."

Matthias looked puzzled. "What the hell's that supposed to mean?"

"It means he's probably *there*."

She pointed at that strange tower with the bizarre lights atop it. Lugorix couldn't help but notice they were heading straight toward it.

Eumenes was having the one conversation he didn't want to have, but that couldn't be put off any longer. It was one thing to discuss all this with Kalyana, who was impossible to outweird. But the soldiers and crew of the ironclad were a different story. To some extent, Alexander himself had helped lay the groundwork: by couching his own campaigns in mythological terms, he'd prepared them—however unconsciously—for dealing with otherworldly shit. Men who had conquered the world's largest land empire and ventured to the Hindu Kush were at least a little more ready to deal with all this then small-town hicks who had never left their village. But that logic only went so far. At some point, the men needed some answers.

The question was whether they could take them.

"Most of this place's denizens are on the land," said Eumenes, scanning the faces as he did so. Some looked like they were crapping their pants. Some looked ready for anything. Some looked like they'd had a few shots of strong wine, and he really couldn't blame them. "Most of the creatures spend most of their time fighting each other. As long as we stick to the river, we should be okay." No one seemed too convinced. "Think of the Underworld as a gigantic wheel. It's surrounded by the Styx, which you'll be pleased to know we already crossed. There are four other rivers, and they're all straight as arrows—they radiate outward from the center like spokes on a wheel, essentially dividing the land into four quadrants. There's the river Acheron, the river Cocytus, the river Phlegethon, and—"

"Which one are we on?" someone demanded.

"That'd be the Lethe."

"Isn't that the one that makes you forget stuff?" asked someone else.

"Supposedly. I wouldn't drink it, if that's what you're asking. I wouldn't drink *any* of this shit, no matter what river it's in." That drew a chuckle; keep 'em laughing, Eumenes thought, and they'll follow you all the way to—

"How do you know all this anyway?" The laughter stopped instantly. The soldier asking the question was giving Kalyana a dirty look. They were all suspicious of the Indian. Not only did he look different, but he seemed to know a little too much. There were even some whispers that he'd cast a hex on Eumenes, and that was the reason they were down here in the first place. Which was one more reason why Eumenes had decided it was time to level with them...

"We're not the first to come down here," he said, doing his best to project a confidence he really didn't feel. "Orpheus made it down here, didn't he?"

"Orpheus wasn't real," said a soldier.

"Someone should hang you for blasphemy," said Eumenes, and he couched the line in just enough of an am-I-kidding way to have them all on edge. Then he laughed, and managed to draw a few chuckles. And in that moment: "I assure you that the lyremaster Orpheus *was* real. As was the Roman hero Aeneas. Whose explorations formed the basis of a number of books that our glorious leader Alexander liberated from the inner sanctums of Rome itself. So we're not blind down here. Far from it."

"But why are we down here in the first place?" asked someone.

"And what's that thrice-damned *tower thing* we're going toward?" asked another.

"Well," said Eumenes, "it's like this."

Ptolemy didn't like the feeling of being the hunter. Not in this place. It was far safer to assume one was being hunted at all times, and concentrate on that. But he'd almost caught up with his quarry and he had to make his move. The figure was heading through the trees just ahead of him, dodging nimbly round the fungi (who knew what poisons they were extruding?), intent on staying close to the river. Which gave Ptolemy the advantage. He knew where his prey was going. A quick burst of speed round to the side, and then he was in front. The figure stepped out of the trees.

But stopped when he saw Ptolemy.

For one terrible instant Ptolemy thought he'd made a mistake—had forced a confrontation with one of this place's denizens. The man carried a barbed spear that looked like no wound from it would be survivable. He wore leopard-skin over his armor, and his helmet was carved to resemble a lion's open jaws.

But he was human. And Ptolemy knew his language too.

"I'm Macedonian," he said in Phoenician.

For a moment, he thought the Carthaginian was going to try to run him through anyway. But then the man raised his spear.

"So?" he said.

"So we're on the same side," said Ptolemy. "Our kings and your Sufetes have signed a deal to—"

"That's why you destroyed our ships?"

"I daresay you started it." There was a howling noise in the distance. "Look, we haven't got time for this. We'll live longer if we stick together."

"Baal himself came down here at the invitation of Mot," said the man. "Mot tricked him and trapped him in the Underworld." That was the moment that Ptolemy got the surprise of his life as two other men stepped out of the trees. They were nearly naked, wearing loincloths, and they had thin ropes wrapped their heads and waists. Ptolemy recognized them instantly: they were slingers from the Balearic Islands. Which technically was an Athenian possession, but the islands had historic ties with Carthage—ties that apparently had been resumed. These two men would be utterly loyal to the Carthaginian. Their culture trained them from birth as slingers: as soon as Balearic children were old enough to walk, their mothers placed loafs of bread at distances from them and forced them to shoot so that they either learned accuracy or went hungry. All of a sudden, Ptolemy was no longer bargaining with a potential equal—he was talking for his life. His mind raced over what little he knew of Phoenician myth.

"But Baal escaped the Underworld, did he not? Despite Mot's trickery?"

"He did," said the Carthaginian. "But he was a god."

"Then we must survive by unleashing their power," said Ptolemy. "We both came down here for the same thing, no?" The Carthaginian said nothing. "The thing that could make all these deaths worthwhile. You know of what I speak."

"Is there a reason we should not just kill you now and leave you to the demons?"

"There is," said Ptolemy. "I can get us to the Macedonian ironclad. Which is our only hope of making it to the tower."

"That ironclad destroyed my ships," said the Carthaginian.

"A misunderstanding," said Ptolemy. "As I said, did not Alexander come to an arrangement with your Sufetes to help liberate your city? Down here we either stick together, or we are all lost."

The Carthaginian stared at him. The howl sounded, still closer. "We should hurry," said Ptolemy.

"Agreed," said the Carthaginian as though he'd been pondering it up until the last moment. "We work together. You lead the way."

Ptolemy did so, his mind racing the way a mind does when slingers who could hit targets at hundreds of yards range are right behind it.

"What the hell is *that*?" said Lugorix.

Coalescing out of the darkness: it was a bridge, spanning the river up ahead. Torches burnt atop it, though none of those bat-creatures were in sight. There was movement around those torches, though. Eurydice held the farseeker up to her eyes.

"Yikes," she said.

"What is it?" yelled up Barsine.

Lugorix and Matthias could see them now too. They were the stuff of nightmares: giant misshapen insects with animal heads and metal claws. They were cackling and screaming, and even before the *Xerxes* was within range, they were already throwing rocks and burning torches into the water. Matthais drew back his bow and sent an arrow humming through the air, impaling one of the creatures through the head, sending its body falling into the water. But they weren't the only threat in sight...

"Behind us," yelled Lugorix.

Eurydice whirled to see another ship back there in the gloom. Clearly it was one of those which had pursued them down into the underworld, and it had apparently been catching up with them the whole time. But only now was it close enough to be visible.

"Clear the decks," snarled Eurydice.

"Hold your fire," yelled Eumenes. Kalyana nodded agreement: if they destroyed the Persian ship here, there might be no getting around it. Besides, that ship must have been hit by the demons on the bridge; it was already sinking below the surface of the water. Eumenes watched as it disappeared entirely. On the one hand, it was a relief—there was that much less competition now. On the other hand, Alexander would be less than happy that Barsine hadn't been delivered to him alive, her seed intact. Still, there might be other female members of the Persian royal house that could serve his purpose. But right now there was a more immediate problem. They were drawing near the bridge; spears and arrows and claws clanked against the ironclad's armor.

"Burn them," he said.

A hatch popped open on the front of the ironclad. Gears turned levers that compressed a gigantic pair of bellows; fuel ignited and suddenly a huge plume of Greek fire jetted onto the bridge, engulfing the creatures. Their howls filled the air, as did the stench of their burning flesh. Above him he could see the bat-like creatures swooping down, attracted by the flaring light. But they found slim pickings: the ironclad's hatch had already shut, and all the bats had to pick at were the insectoid creatures sizzling and writhing in their death agonies.

And something else... suddenly four figures raced onto the bridge and leapt from it, one of them landing just in front of Eumenes' view-slit. He didn't hesitate—waved an archer forward, who drew back his bow and—

"Eumenes," yelled a familiar voice.

"You are shitting me," muttered Eumenes.

He wasn't. It was Ptolemy. Alexander would have had the archer fire away and good riddance. But Eumenes wasn't Alexander. He and Ptolemy had been friends since they were children—and down in Hades, Macedonian factions scarcely seemed to matter. Besides, Eumenes was the one with the twenty commandos. All this flashed through Eumenes' head in an instant, but he was already ordering his men to unbolt the hatch and stand ready. Ptolemy staggered inside.

Along with three other men.

"Who the hell are these?" asked Eumenes as the sailors threw the door shut and let the bats smack against the metal.

"This is Hanno," said Ptolemy. "The commander of Carthage's expedition to the ends of the earth. You know, the one you helped to wipe out?" Presumably the Carthaginian didn't speak Greek: he bowed, though he still hadn't put away his spear. "And these are his personal slingers," added Ptolemy.

"Great," said Eumenes. "But I don't speak Phoenician."

"I do," said Ptolemy.

"So do I," said Kalyana.

"You can do the translating," said Eumenes. And then, to Ptolemy: "Why did you join up with them anyway?"

Ptolemy pointed through the forward slit... his finger extending a line toward that edifice in the distance toward which this river led—the center of this world beneath the world. Now they were past the bridge, they could see that tower clearly. It reached at least a quarter of the distance to the ceiling of the cavern, those weird lights flickering atop it.

"Because we're going to need every sword," said Ptolemy.

"And even that won't be enough," said Xanthippus.

Diocles wasn't about to disagree. The Macedonian army covered the plains around Syracuse. And it wasn't just the Macedonians either. Men of every nation seemed to be out there: Persians, Italians, Thessalians, barbarians of all stripes. Diocles couldn't see the infamous metal men that were reputed to be animated by Alexander's sorcery, but he had no doubt they were in the mix somewhere. Behind the army were all manner of tents, some of them quite large, many of them presumably the workshops in which the siege-engines that would storm Syracuse were being readied.

"You never know," said Agathocles. "No such thing as a foregone conclusion in war." Diocles noticed that he was accompanied by a man who carried so many spears he looked like a porcupine. Xanthippus narrowed his eyes.

"Think you've got enough spears there, buddy?"

"They're *my* spears," said Agathocles. "And no, I don't."

The men were standing atop a tower on the fortress known as the Circle, midway along the wall that dominated the Epipolae plateau. To the east were the buildings of some of Syracuse's richest districts; to the west, the plateau sloped sharply down toward the plain on which the Macedonian army was gathered. If they were going to take Syracuse, they were going to have to capture the plateau—once they'd done that, they'd have the high ground.

Which was precisely what the Circle was intended to prevent. Per its name, it was a massive circular bulwark anchoring the Syracusan line, towering over the walls on either side by a good twenty yards. While most walls just had arrow-slits, the Circle had artillery-slits: portal after portal behind each of which a ballista was just waiting to go to work. It was easily the most strategic position in the entire Syracusan defenses.

Precisely why Diocles didn't want to be there. It was obviously going to be the number one target for the Macedonians when the shit got underway. Which was exactly why he *was* there, of course: Agathocles' audience with Leosthenes had gone well, but the viceroy had covered his bases with all the guile of an experienced politician. He'd accepted Agathocles' offer of help in return for shared power once Macedonia was repulsed. Part of that meant that Agathocles' resistance network emerged from hiding and took up arms along the walls. But that wasn't all. Agathocles knew he'd need some kind of safeguard against Athenian treachery once the battle had been won, and the solution for that was as obvious to Agathocles as its was distasteful to Leosthenes: arm the populace.

Eventually, the two of them had hashed out an agreement. And so a city militia had been hastily formed, one that contained enough thieves, sailors, club bouncers, mob enforcers and other ne'er-do-wells to make it a force to be reckoned with. Especially since they'd be fighting from behind fixed defenses. As far as Agathocles was concerned, matters would never be the same again: Syracuse would have attained at least a quasi-independence once the Macedonians had been repulsed.

Not that anyone really expected that to happen. The very fact that such extreme measures were being taken was clue enough that the city was about to get steamrolled. To be sure, there were plenty of other clues. The pall of ash drifting over the city from smoldering Mount Etna was one. As were the storms raging less than a mile off the coast, preventing any naval reinforcement from getting through. It made it feel like the gods had taken leave of Athens.

Diocles certainly felt like they'd taken leave of *him*. It had been just his and Xanthippus' luck to show up at Syracuse with the man who was public enemy number one. At that point, nothing they could say made any impression on Leosthenes, who had clearly decided that they couldn't be trusted. Even as he thanked them for their service with honeyed words, he was giving orders for them all to be transferred to the Circle, separated from the rest of Agathocles' men, surrounded by loyal Athenian soldiers, and ready to deal with whatever the Macedonians might throw their way. Agathocles seemed to take those measures in stride. Perhaps he figured that it was a worthwhile concession to make for being able to arm his people. Perhaps he just figured they were all doomed anyway, and they may as well die with their boots on.

Or perhaps he had a scheme to somehow escape from this mess. Diocles certainly hoped so—and that he'd be able to persuade Xanthippus to get out when the time came.

Otherwise they would all perish in fire and shit.

"They're going to parley," said Agathocles suddenly.

Xanthippus looked round. "What?" But Agathocles was already pointing out over the plain, to where the white flag of truce had gone up in the middle of the Macedonian formation. A few more minutes, and then a trumpet sounded from one of the gates of Syracuse. A squadron of horsemen emerged from the city, bearing their own white banner as well as—

"That's Leosthenes' own standard," said Xanthippus. More horsemen broke from the Macedonian line, heading toward the approaching Athenians. Agathocles' eyes narrowed.

"And that's Alexander's," he said.

"This really isn't a good idea," said Memnon.

Leosthenes said nothing. Memnon was almost certainly right, but not for the reasons he probably had in mind. Leosthenes wasn't really worried about backstabbing. Historically, Alexander didn't *do* treachery. The man lived by the strictest of codes; to him honor (or at least what he perceived it to be) was everything. All his life he'd sooner have hacked off his own limbs then violate a flag of truce. And yet there had been disquieting rumors that Alexander was no longer himself. Spies in Italy had sent back reports that the king had been acting strangely—drinking for days at a time, disappearing for nights on end.

But that was precisely why Leosthenes wanted to meet Alexander. He needed to take the measure of his opponent—this man who had never been beaten in battle. The *real* danger in such a meeting was that battle wasn't the only field on which contenders wrestled. Within hours of the parley, every man in Syracuse would know what had been said. If Leosthenes lost the war of words, then that would inevitably be regarded as an omen in the coming fight. Leosthenes reined in his horse as the two entourages approached one another. He and Memnon cantered forward. Two of the Macedonians did likewise, coming straight toward them.

"Here we go," muttered Memnon.

Not for the first time in his life, Leosthenes wished Memnon would shut up. He took a deep breath, forced his heart to be calm as the four men faced each other mere yards in front of their respective entourages. Alexander wore his customary ram's-head helmet; his eyes were curiously multi-hued, and as he met their gaze, Leosthenes experienced the faint shock of recognition. This really was Alexander right in front of him, the most famous warrior of his age and perhaps all ages, the one the vanquished Romans were already calling *Magnus*. As for his companion: judging from his height and red hair, he was the king's consort Hephaestion. Leosthenes had never heard of a man taking another man as consort, but if anyone had earned the right to make his own rules, then that was Alexander. The king raised one hand in greeting; Leosthenes did the same. As he did so, he studied Alexander's expression; the man seemed calm and regal, every inch a king. If there was anything amiss with his mind, it wasn't written on his face.

And his words were direct enough.

"You cannot hope to win," he said.

Leosthenes said nothing.

"You can't," repeated Alexander. "Your only hope was to stop me from crossing to this island. Now that opportunity has passed."

"Did you call me out here to tell me that?" asked Leosthenes.

"I called you out here to tell you of Achilles," said Alexander.

"What about him?" Leosthenes knew the hero of the *Iliad* was Alexander's idol.

"After he killed Hector, he tied his body to the back of his chariot and dragged him three times around the walls of Troy. You have heard this, no?" Leosthenes nodded. "I did the same to your colleague at Gaza, outside Egypt—the Athenian commander. I believe his name was Heron. He defied me, and after I took Gaza, I tied him to the back of my chariot. But unlike Hector, he was still living. At least until some point during my second circuit of what was left of the city's walls."

"Are you trying to threaten me?" asked Leosthenes.

"Of course not," said Alexander. He smiled. "Should you choose to fight, you will die in battle. I have no doubt of that. But if you were to surrender now, you would spare the people of Syracuse great suffering."

Leosthenes nodded gravely. "So what are your terms?"

"Clemency for the people of Syracuse. Free passage for yourself and your men back to Athens."

"For me to report to the people of Athens that I have lost them Syracuse: that would be its own death sentence."

Alexander shrugged. "If you are a true commander, then you care only for your men. This is your one chance to spare them."

"There is one other chance," said Leosthenes. "That of battle. *That* is the chance I will take. Athens bows before no man."

"But I am not a man," said Alexander, and now the smile was something Leosthenes wanted to run from. "I am the Son of Zeus, the reborn Hercules. My Father spoke to me at Siwah, and gave me powers over the celestial sphere itself. Why else do you think your fleets have fallen prey to the lords of lighting? Why does the Earth belch brimstone and blot out your Sun? The end of your era is upon you."

Leosthenes took a deep breath. "That of Athens?"

"That of man. The gods themselves are waking."

"Well, that went well," said Memnon.

Leosthenes had never been so happy to get back within the walls of a city. As he and his entourage rode back through the gate, it swung shut behind them, huge bolts sliding into place, followed by a second and third set of bronze doors slamming and locking.

"At least now we know he's crazy," said Leosthenes.

"You really needed to talk to him to figure that out?"

"I did, yes. Needed to look him in the eyes."

"Never mind the eyes," said Memnon. "I thought he was going to start frothing at the mouth."

"Give him time," muttered Leosthenes. He looked up toward the Epipolae plateau on his left, wondered if the main thrust would be there or whether that would just be a feint. He'd done everything he could to strengthen the Circle—would it be enough? The encounter had left him shaken. If Alexander was insane, so was all his army, for they were prepared to follow him as a god-king. And then there was the even more alarming question: say he *wasn't* nuts? The Earth *was* belching fire. The storms *were* keeping the Athenian fleet at bay—assuming any of it was left. For all Leosthenes knew, Athens itself had been demolished in an earthquake or engulfed in gigantic waves. He had received no word from the capital in weeks.

Nor would he get any now. They were well and truly under siege. The noose was complete. And Leosthenes had made his choice. The city's fate would depend on his ability to defend it. It occurred to him that perhaps that was unfair. Why should the people of Syracuse die because Athens wouldn't surrender their city to Macedonia? Then again, it was the people of Syracuse who were now lining the walls to defend themselves. They weren't like those of Egypt—they weren't prepared to welcome Alexander as a liberator. Perhaps it was because they knew damn well that if he ever got into the city, they wouldn't be able to get him out. Or perhaps it was all bullshit: when the full weight of the Macedonian attack got underway, they'd throw in the towel and throw the Athenians to the wolves and beg for mercy. Certainly Leosthenes knew he'd already given away the crown jewel in Athens' empire. The people of Syracuse were armed; there was no going back on that now. If the Macedonians were to be repulsed, Syracusans would effectively control their own city.

Of course, that was a rather big *if*. Ahead of Leosthenes, the Ortygia loomed, indomitable, undefeated. As he rode up the causeway toward the gates, he turned to Memnon.

"It'll kick off any moment," he said.

Memnon just nodded.

"So I guess the viceroy didn't take the terms," said Diocles.

"You think?" said Xanthippus sarcastically.

"The king would have offered to spare Syracuse," said Agathocles. "So Leosthenes' coming to terms with our people in advance was a deft move on his part."

"You mean on *your* part," said Xanthippus.

Agathocles shrugged. "We saw eye to eye," he said. "That was enough."

Xanthippus spat over the edge of the battlements. "Has it occurred to you that you might have been better off throwing in your lot with Alexander?" he asked.

"Of course," said Agathocles.

"And?"

"And I trust weapons more than I trust words. This way the people are armed. Alexander would never have done that."

"But now he's liable to massacre all of you."

Agathocles gestured out at the Macedonian army. "The price of peace would have been enslavement. I'm not an idiot: I know all about Alexander. As much as the viceroy does, in fact."

Veteran that he was, Xanthippus took umbrage at that. "The viceroy's one of *the archons of the city*. How would rebel scum like you know as much as—"

"Because the Athenian council leaks like a sieve," said Agathocles. "That's how. The Macedonians aren't the only ones with spies in Athens. Add to that the fact that the Athenians have plenty of spies in Pella and maybe just as many in the Macedonian camp, and that means *I* know all about what happened to Alexander at Siwah. In his mind, that's all that counts."

But now Xanthippus just looked bored. "I know, I know. We've all heard that one. He thinks he's—"

"Don't you get it?" hissed Agathocles. *"He doesn't just think."*

As one, the Macedonian siege machines began firing.

CHAPTER TWENTY

"Periscope up," said Eurydice—but Barsine was already on it. The *Xerxes* was scarcely past the bridge beneath which it had submerged, but for all Lugorix knew they were sinking for real now... that all he and Matthias were doing was just propelling the craft to the bottom of this river. They'd been hit by a lot of shit hurled from that bridge. But Barsine claimed that nothing vital had been touched.

"What the hell *were* those things on the bridge?" Matthias asked, pulling on the oars.

"Does it matter?"

"I think it does."

"Can we just agree to call them demons?" asked Barsine. As she said that, she slotted the cylinder she called a *periscope* up into the ceiling and projected the images it displayed along the walls. It wasn't pretty. That infernal tower was coming ever closer—the river Lethe ran from a giant archway in its base, across the plain of Hades toward them. Barsine swivelled the periscope round to the shore where—

"Shit," said Matthias.

Lugorix was thinking the same thing. In the distance, a portion of the forest had caught fire. Creatures that looked like crosses between men and bears were running from the flaming woods, only to be ridden down and speared by other creatures that looked to be some bastard offspring of men and horses.

"They're *centaurs*," said Matthias.

"They're servants without masters," said Barsine.

"What do you mean by that?" asked Matthias.

"How many times do I have to explain it? The masters are all in *there*." She gestured at the approaching tower. "Imprisoned or asleep or just resting."

"How do you know?"

"Because otherwise they'd be *laying down the law out here*," said Eurydice. "Instead of letting their servants fight it out."

"In rather squalid anarchy," added Barsine.

Matthias snorted. "That's just a theory," he said.

"Of course it's *just a fucking theory*. But there's no doubt that anarchy has reigned in Hell for a *long* time. No one has united the realm of Hades because no one's had the strength to. Hercules was the last to come down here, and the place was a zoo then too. Otherwise he'd never have made it out. As far as we can tell, the lords of Hell—the Chthonic gods, the Titans, whatever you want to call them—have been inactive for thousands of years."

"And if they *hadn't* been, do you think this place would confine them?" asked Eurydice. She pulled on some levers; gears turned, and the ship began slowing down—Lugorix and Matthias were still rowing just as hard but apparently the fins on the outside of the craft were no longer moving as quickly. They were hewing close to the shore now, Lugorix noticed. The ship was shaking as more waves rocked against it. A shadow fell across the wall—and then they saw it slicing past them: the Macedonian ironclad. Its engines were at full power as it surged on ahead. It was at least three times the size of the *Xerxes,* and had two steam-funnels, as well as grey-metal hatches all along its length. But in the dim light no one aboard it seemed to notice the periscope just off to their side.

"They think we're dead," said Eurydice.

"Let's hope so," said Barsine as she pulled on more of those levers. They began speeding up, getting in behind the ironclad, moving into its wake.

"Are we going to attack 'em?" asked Matthias. Lugorix wondered what he was proposing to attack them *with,* but Eurydice just grinned.

"Why should we?" she said. "Last thing we want to do now is call attention to ourselves."

Lugorix laughed. It made sense to him. "You're saying that whatever the defenses of that tower are, they're going to be keying on *them,* not *us*."

"Exactly," said Barsine.

"Sure," said Matthias, "but *why the fuck are we even going in there in the first place?*"

"Because," said Eurydice, "they've got something worth the stealing."

"And when we get it?" asked Ptolemy.

Eumenes nodded. He understood the question perfectly—knew that Ptolemy wasn't really asking what to *do* with it. He was asking who would *control* it. The two Macedonians had sequestered themselves in the forward observation chamber and barred the door. Kalyana was giving Hanno and his slingers a tour of the ship while pumping him for info. Because Hanno had to have *some* kind of info—surely he hadn't come down here blind? At any rate, that gave the agents of Philip and Alexander some privacy while they tried to come to a meeting of the minds. Eumenes looked at Ptolemy's aquiline face, saw in those eyes the same thing that filled his own head: raw calculation.

"We need to get our hands on it first," he said simply.

"Right," said Ptolemy, making one of those half-shrugs of his. They were on the same page: if by some miracle they weren't killed by what was in the Tower—if they actually got what they'd come all this way for—then there'd be no splitting the difference. Ptolemy and Eumenes were both servants of the Macedonian Empire, but they were still bound to different masters. If Ptolemy got near Alexander, then the king would kill him, probably quite slowly. If Eumenes got near Philip, he would have to either betray Alexander or die. Which meant that if the Tower failed to kill either Ptolemy or Eumenes, at some point one of them would have to slay the other. There was no getting around it. But until that point, they were stronger working together. Years of surviving in the shark-tank known as the Macedonian court meant that such realities could go unspoken. The playing-field was very simple now. In theory Eumenes had the advantage, since he was the one who the soldiers reported to. Then again, Eumenes was Greek. As always, that was his weakness—the factor that might allow Ptolemy to suborn the loyalty of his crew and soldiers. So taking Ptolemy on board the ship was a gamble, to say the least. Then again, so was coming downstairs into Hades…

"What maps are you using?" asked Eumenes.

"I was following the Carthaginian ships," said Ptolemy. "Who were following the Persians—"

"I'm not talking about how you *got in*. I meant *once you got here*. What are you using?"

"Some scraps that Philip lifted from Aristotle's lab. Before the old man split. What about you?"

"Same. Some of Aristotle's notes."

"Which ones?"

"You missed some of the shit in the fireplace."

Ptolemy looked disgusted with himself. "Tell me it wasn't worth *too* much."

"It had its uses," said Eumenes. He watched as several crocodile-men ran along the shore and hurled themselves into the water, their tails thrashing as they swam toward the ironclad. There was the distinct sound of one of the ship's gun's whirring; next moment, Greek fire poured over them. The smell of a particularly foul roast meat drifted through the cabin. "Though not so much for trying to piece together whatever we're going to find in that Tower," he added. "For that I've mostly been relying on the Sibylline Books and some of the scrolls that Alexander took from Siwah."

Ptolemy's eyes narrowed. "So what *did* happen there?"

"The oracle told him what he wanted to hear."

"Of course he did," said Ptolemy. "We're down in the pits of *hell*, so how about you level with me?"

"Sounds like you already know most of it," said Eumenes evenly.

"Enough to know just how crazy the man really is."

"He's not crazy," said Eumenes. And then, off Ptolemy's look: "He's not."

"Then what is he?"

"He's hearing voices."

"So there you go. He's crazy."

"But say he isn't?"

"How would he not be?"

"Say the voices are real?"

"Then I'd have to say you're crazy too."

"And let's say those voices gave him powers over, oh I don't know—how about some of the elements? Like, say, the currents of the sea and the winds of the air?"

Ptolemy took a deep breath. "You've seen this?"

"The Athenian fleet has."

"So you're telling me—what? …he really *is* the son of Zeus?"

"Honestly, at this point I'm not sure how productive labels are."

"Spoken like an oh-so-pragmatic Greek."

"You think we should just fall to our knees in wonder and throw reason out the window?"

"I'm more interested in what *you* think," said Ptolemy.

"The Earth is flat."

"That seems hard to deny at this point."

"The Earth is flat," repeated Eumenes. Off on the shore there was an explosion, followed by some truly hair-raising shrieking. "There's been a debate about whether it's round or flat, and now that debate's settled."

"Fine. Granted. Will you please tell me where you're going with this?"

"Kalyana was the one who pointed it out to me. If the Earth was flat, and the Sun were far away—"

"How far away?"

"Far enough so that the rays of the sun are in effect *parallel* to someone on Earth. Hundreds of thousands of miles. Maybe millions."

Ptolemy looked skeptical. "Is the universe even that big?"

"Wait till you see where I'm going with this. If the Earth was flat—"

"Which it is."

"—and the Sun *were* that far away, then shadows of the same-sized objects would be the same size no matter where you were on any given north-south line. Which they fucking *aren't*. So the Sun is close. *Very* close. Only a few thousand miles away."

Ptolemy frowned. He was struggling to keep up with this. "If it's so close, wouldn't it appear to change size as it crosses the heavens?"

"It should."

"So then how do you explain—"

"Either we're missing something, or... well, Kalyana thinks the atmosphere's distorting it, magnifying it the further it gets away from the observer. I don't know if he's right. But what we're starting to think is that the celestial sphere *isn't that far overhead*. It probably includes the sun, the stars, the Moon, the planets, anything we can see up there. And *we don't know what that sphere is made of*. We don't know what intelligence or *machinery* is behind it. But somehow the operators of that machinery—*or that machinery itself*—is in touch with Alexander."

Ptolemy mulled this over. "Is it possible that machinery is in the Tower?"

"I daresay it's more than possible."

Just as Ptolemy was about to reply, there was a loud rapping on the door. "Sir? You're needed on the bridge." Eumenes swung the door open—and walked out, following the sailor who had summoned him.

But then he turned.

"What do you think you're doing?" he asked Ptolemy.

"Me?" Ptolemy hadn't moved. "Oh, I thought I'd stay here and keep an eye on things."

"How about you come with me to the bridge so we can keep an eye on each other?"

Ptolemy shrugged, the ghost of a smile on his face. "Works for me," he said.

The bridge was crowded. Several members of the crew were there, along with Kalyana. The Tower loomed large in the observation window. Now that it was so close, it seemed like it was hewn from a single rock. The lights atop the tower were flickering on and off like flashes of lightning. The ironclad was closing in on the archway from which the river Lethe ran—above that archway was a single round window-opening. As Ptolemy inspected the gears and levers, Eumenes took Kalyana aside.

"Where's the Carthaginian?"

"He's with two marines and a sailor who speaks Phoenician. We're getting him new armor, since his is so beaten up."

"Never mind his armor," said Eumenes. "What did you *learn* from him?"

"That he knows what we are after. And he wants it to."

"But he'll join forces until we've got our hands on it?"

"Presumably," said Kalyana. "But I would not turn your back on him."

Eumenes smiled grimly. "Does he have anything that passes for a map of Hades?"

Kalyana nodded. "Quite a detailed one from the sound of it. Though they lost it when the ship went down. He keeps saying that the lowest level is death."

"Like we needed him to tell us that." Eumenes turned to a member of his bridge-crew. "Full throttle," he said. "Keep an eye on that archway." Sailors adjusted controls; a rumbling went through the craft as the ironclad plowed into the whitewater rapids that were surging out of that arch. But suddenly another sailor rushed onto the bridge. Eumenes recognized him—he was the one who spoke Phoenician.

"Aren't you supposed to be with the Carthaginian?" he asked.

"Sir, sorry sir. But I was just talking with him about the Persian ship."

"What about it? It sunk. No longer a problem—"

"Sir, he said it had underwater capacity."

All conversation on the bridge stopped. Eumenes turned to Kalyana. "You should have found that out," he said calmly.

"Hanno and I were talking about Hell, not—"

But Eumenes was already talking over him, giving orders. "Get more men onto the rear-observation platform. Anything they see in the water that's the *slightest bit weird,* we'll use the Greek fire. Now *move.*"

As sailors raced from the room, the Carthaginian entered, bedecked in a splendid Macedonian cuirass, the two slingers behind him, seemingly content to remain half-naked. Eumenes glanced at him: "And someone ask this guy *what else that ship can do.*" Kalyana began talking in Phoenician but the Carthaginian wasn't listening—he was just looking at the edifice that towered over them and babbling in his own language. They'd almost reached the tower's arch.

"What's he saying?" asked Eumenes.

"Same thing he told me earlier," replied Kalyana. "The lowermost level is death." Understanding suddenly dawned in his eyes but Eumenes was already yelling the order: "Reverse full speed! *Reverse full speed!*"

That was the moment the *Xerxes* rammed the ironclad.

Once they'd gotten close enough to the tower, Barsine and Eurydice had decided that there weren't going to be any automatic defenses and there was thus no point in using the ironclad as a stalking horse. So they hit the ironclad from the side, the *Xerxes'* ram slicing straight through the weak point between two of the metal plates, smashing into the hybrid wooden-metal framework behind them. Within moments, the *Xerxes* had thoroughly embedded itself in the side of the ironclad; water rushed in and the ship started to list just as Lugorix, Matthias, Barsine and Eurydice scrambled out of the hatch and onto the platform of the *Xerxes.*

It was only now that they were right next to it that Lugorix truly realized just how much bigger the ironclad was—twice the height and three times the width, lined with gunnery and observation slits. But the ship was in trouble, and he could hear pandemonium within. Matthias clambered up next to him and aimed a crossbow that Eurydice had radically modified at the archway overhead, at the window above it, lining it up—

"Do it," hissed Lugorix.

Matthias fired. The bolt shot upward, its spikes burying itself between the keystones of the arch. Eurydice grabbed Matthias; Barsine grabbed Lugorix; both men grabbed onto the rope and then Matthias pulled the second lever attached to the trigger; next moment, they were all hauled upward as the miniature flywheels that lined the crossbow began spinning, the stricken ironclad-*Xerxes* combo dropping away from them, its forward momentum carrying it inside the archway and out of sight.

"Sucks to be them," said Eurydice.

"How about we focus on *us?*" asked Barsine as they reached the upper portion of the archway. Lugorix placed one foot on a keystone, reached out toward the window. His hands closed around the edge. He levered himself around and onto the sill, found himsef staring into a tunnel leading into the tower's interior. He reached out his hand, grabbed that of Barsine, helped her inside, then did the same for Matthias and then for Eurydice. They stared into the darkness of the tunnel.

"A light would help," said Eurydice.

"You sure about that?" asked Matthias. "After those damn creatures earlier—"

"Those are outside the tower," said Barsine. She fumbled with something—and suddenly the blueish light of Damitra's amulet filled the tunnel.

"Guess the *Xerxes* won't be needing that anymore," said Eurydice.

"None of those bastards down there will be needing anything again," said Barsine.

The ironclad's throttle was on maximum now, as the ship desperately tried to make some kind of landfall before it went under. Because go under it clearly would: the Persian ship had embedded itself below the waterline and the list to the side was becoming ever more critical, the helmsman compensating at an ever greater angle to keep the ship going straight. And now soldiers were on top of the ironclad, looking for survivors from the Persian ship's crew; with them were sailors with torches. In the flickering light, Eumenes could make out a vast and cavernous chamber: the carved vaults of the ceiling sweeping overhead, with platform-jetties at each corner, each one with stairs winding up into darkness. Eumenes pointed at one of the jetties; the ship slowly turned toward it.

But then the black-powder bomb in the nose of the *Xerxes* detonated.

It had been Eurydice's idea, of course. Barsine had hated the idea of assembling a live hi-ex device on her ship, but Eurydice had convinced her that once they lit the fuse they'd have at least a few minutes. The force of the blast tore what was left of the front of the *Xerxes* to pieces, ripping more of the ironclad's side away, almost breaking that ship's spine and knocking everybody on board off their feet. Just as Eumenes regained his, the ironclad smashed into the corner of the room, the engines still going as they shoved the nose of the ship ever further forward onto the platform—

"Shut it off!" he screamed. One of the sailors who'd been thrown against the controls managed to do do just that. The clanking of the engines died away; the ironclad was now tilting at a thirty degree angle and sinking rapidly, sliding back off the platform. Eumenes had no idea how deep the water was in this place and he had zero intention of finding out. He threw open the top hatch. In short order he and Kalyana and Ptolemy and Hanno and the slingers were up on the sloping roof of the ironclad, along with about fifteen of the commandos. The others were either still below deck, or had been knocked into the water.

And the men down in that water were curiously passive. They just *lay* there, as though they weren't even trying to swim. None of them were shouting for help. Several were already drifting under. Eumenes caught a glimpse of one of those blank faces and then he understood.

This was, after all, the river Lethe.

"Their minds have been *wiped*," said Ptolemy.

It wasn't like anyone was planning to take a dip in the first place but now they knew the full penalty for doing so. Struggling to keep his balance, Eumenes led the others along the roof of the ironclad toward the stairway in the corner. Two sailors lost their footing, slid into the water—their screams cut off even as they hit. The water must be working on touch alone, thought Eumenes. It would be hard for this to get any worse.

He had rarely been more wrong.

Suddenly something enormous erupted from the water, something that dwarfed the ironclad, a leviathan-like grey-green scaled body from which were unfurling way too many... at first Eumenes thought they were snakes.

But then he realized they were necks.

Several of them were swooping in toward him.

It was then that he made the decision that would save his life. The natural response was to get out of there as fast as possible—just start running up those stairs. But Eumenes realized that the necks were easily narrow enough to follow. And maybe they were long enough too…

"Phalanx," he yelled to those who had made it to the platform. Those who hadn't were getting plucked straight off the sinking ship by those snake-necks—or pulled straight out of the water. Either way, they were being devoured wholesale. The hell of it was that it was only when they were being eaten did those who had been mindwiped scream. Eumenes' commandos turned on the stairs, clustered around him, locking shields as the first of the necks came at them. It wasn't much of a phalanx. It wasn't intended to be—they only had a small number of men, and they certainly hadn't brought their *sarissae*. But they would fight together. The first of the necks came darting in.

And at last Eumenes saw what the heads were.

He froze for a moment in his tracks but fortunately the soldier being targeted didn't—in fact, he was the only among them who was beyond any such emotion, and now he lashed out with his sword and severed the head from the neck with a single adroit swipe. The head hit the stone floor and rolled into the water; the neck thrashed about, blood spraying. But there were many more necks behind that and the creature itself was now pulling itself toward the mini-phalanx—which started to retreat, Eumenes anchoring the left and Ptolemy the right, up the stairs, weapons out and shields locked the entire way. The slingers remained in the rear, flinging rocks over the heads of the Macedonians with good effect, scoring direct hits on two of the heads. The last glimpse Eumenes had of the ironclad was of it settling onto the side, crewmembers abandoning it out the side-portals only to be consumed almost immediately by the monstrosity.

"Any idea what the fuck it is?" said Ptolemy.

"Does it matter?" muttered Eumenes.

"I am thinking it is the guardian," replied Kalyana.

Master of the obvious, thought Eumenes. They had just reached the top of the flight of stairs when the necks came at them again. Eumenes was starting to realize that one of the key advantages to being in a phalanx was not being one of the guys in the front row. They were the ones doing most of the fighting, and so far their shields were holding up. But then a neck darted low and bit a commando's leg off beneath the knee. He fell forward screaming, and in the next instant all the necks were fighting over his still-twitching body. Eumenes stepped into the gap he'd left, took advantage of the distraction—

"There's a door behind us," he snarled. "Everyone through."

They backed through. As the heads finished eating, two of the soldiers slid the stone door shut. The heads began hammering against the other side, but they weren't getting through.

"Not that way, at any rate," said Ptolemy.

Eumenes nodded. As usual, the two of them were on the same page. They had to assume this creature could reach any portion of this tower. But right now, there was only one way to go.

"Upward," muttered Barsine.

"You okay?" said Lugorix.

"Not feeling... so good."

Not that any of them were. The narrow tunnel had given way to a wider corridor lined with carvings that ranked among the more disturbing Lugorix had ever seen. Creatures of all descriptions consumed each other and humans; some of those humans were laid on altar-blocks, their hearts being ripped from them by jackal-headed priests. It was enough to make anyone a little queasy. They could hear noises emanating from somewhere below—screams and shouting conveyed by some corridor or air-vent. It sounded like combat. Perhaps the crew of the ironclad were giving a good accounting for themselves.

Problem was, the noise was getting closer.

They reached a door sealed and covered with runes. Eurydice said she thought those were runes of warning, but Barsine was adamant: there was a staircase on the other side that led to the upper chambers to which they were trying to get. So Matthias sliced away the seals with his *xiphos* and Lugorix opened the door to reveal a circular stairwell.

And a giant snake coming up it.

"Shit!" yelled Matthias, leaping back.

"I'm on it," said Lugorix. He raised Skullseeker, stepped forward as the monstrosity sidled up the stairs toward him. He couldn't see its head and fangs amidst the shadows, but he really didn't need to—all he had to do was time his blow. Which meant waiting for it strike. It moved in steadily.

Then suddenly darted forward with unbelievable speed, aiming straight at his chest—but Lugorix was already stepping to the side and swinging his axe, shearing through flesh and bone. With a gurgling cry, the head of the creature bounced at his feet. He looked down at it.

"Taranis save us," he said.

It was human.

Not only that, but it was beautiful—the most beautiful face he'd ever seen, the face of a young man in the flower of his years, a mop of curly blond hair constrasting horribly with the blood pouring from that head's severed base. And then the mouth opened limply in death and Lugorix could see row after row of razor-sharp teeth within. The others stared over his shoulder—at the gorgeous face, at the monstrous trunk of a neck. Then Lugorix kicked the head down the stairs.

"Let's go," he said.

They started up. Lugorix was helping Barsine as they did so—she had an arm around his shoulder, and was clearly in some distress, looking pale and dizzy. Lugorix put that down to what they'd just seen.

"Got the feeling there's going to be more of those things," he said.

"Let me confirm it for you," said Eurydice. "That thing's the hydra."

Matthias frowned. "The *what?*"

"Or the monster Cerberus, who Orpheus snuck past. Or Geryon, who Hercules subdued. Ever wonder why so many of the creatures described in the myths of Hell have got multiple heads? *Because it's the same animal we're talking about.* And I don't know if it can regrow them, but I'll bet it has a shitload more. *So how about we pick up the pace?*"

There were no objections.

As long as you were the one on the walls, there was something to be said for siege warfare. Particularly atop the Epipolae, where the Macedonians' siege-engines couldn't reach. The defenders had been destroying the Macks all morning—or rather, they'd been destroying the Mack allies. Xanthippus said the same thing had happened outside the walls of Athens: that the Macks had been exceedingly reluctant to commit their own forces, but quite generous in committing everybody else's. Bodies were strewn all around the walls of Syracuse. The steep slopes of the Epipolae plateau had been a particularly effective slaughterhouse. The ballistae and catapults had done most of the work, but they'd been joined by some innovations that supposedly came straight from the drawing board of Aristotle himself. Pride of place was given to something called a steam-gun, which hissed and clanked and shot metal bolts further than any ballista. There were two of them atop one of the towers of the Circle and Diocles could feel the heat on his face every time one of them fired.

But even that wasn't quite as impressive as the aptly-named crusher, which dumped rounded boulders from the walls along the Epipolae, letting them bounce down from the plateau, leaving gore in their wake as they smashed everything in their path. Throughout the first morning of the siege, the men on the walls barely had recourse to their own weapons. The archers had fun picking off the attackers who got closest, and Agathocles even nailed a couple with some well-chucked spears. But mostly it was just Xanthippus making wisecracks as bodies piled up around the walls. As midday approached, there was a brief respite as the attack of the Macedonian allies ceased and everyone still alive took time for lunch. Diocles asked his lover how he could be so jocular about the whole thing. Xanthippus wiped the sweat from his brow; reached out and touched the young man's cheek.

"Because this won't last," he said.

He was right, of course. Shortly after noon, there was an almighty hammering from the Macedonian camp—the noise of a colossal steam engine, one that put to shame those that powered the guns near Diocles. Then it was joined by a second almost next to it; the men on the walls watched as two parallel plumes of steam rose into the air, soaring upward until they were lost in the grey overhead. Moments later, a sound that might have been the blasting of Vulcan's own forge filled the air.

"Uh-oh," said Agathocles.

"What is it?" asked Diocles.

Xanthippus said nothing, but Diocles noticed that his face had gone pale. Everyone was staring out at the Macedonian camp—at the forest of tents and makeshift buildings that stretched off as far as the eye could see. Something was rising from that camp, something that had been built from the felled forests of Italy, that had been transported in great pieces across the bridge to Sicily where it had been assembled, hidden amidst the tents and banners until it was time to use the largest engines Alexander had to haul its top into the air while its base was held steady on blocks and the summit of the edifice was raised toward the heavens like some malignant relative of the colossus that was said to have been erected at Babel: a fifty-story high siege tower whose name the watching men of Syracuse didn't know but it was the *Helepolis,* the City Taker, and take Syracuse it would before the day was out, for so the king had commanded. There was the noise of scores more engines cranking up—and then those motors joined with hundreds of mules and horses inside the Helepolis and the entire structure began clanking forward toward the Epipolae plateau.

"Fuck *me,*" said Agathocles.

Leosthenes was on the battlements of the Ortgyia when Memnon found him. The old man was out of breath from having run up too many flights of stairs.

"You would not believe what's crawling up the Epipolae," he said.

Leosthenes looked out over the city. He couldn't see the far side of the plateau, though plumes of smoke were rising from beyond it. He'd figured that's where the main assault would come, and that when it did, the best place for him would be at the Circle, commanding the main defenses from there. The danger was that there'd be a sneak assault on the Ortygia while that was going on. But that was a chance he'd have to take. He'd purged the fortress of men he didn't trust, had installed his handpicked officers in charge of the defenses. That was all he could do. It was time to ride like hell for the Epipolae, and take every last one of the reserve troops with him. He turned, met Memnon's eyes.

"Tell me as we go," he said.

Perdiccas felt like a god. He stood on the roof of the largest siege-engine ever built, climbing steadily toward the walls of the last Western fortress to hold out against Alexander. The standard procedure for this kind of thing would be to build a gigantic ramp but the engineers of the Helepolis had gone one better: they'd constructed the floor of the machine so that its base was divided into sixty-four separate hydraulic lifts. The base remained entirely flat until the Helepolis reached the plateau's foothills; at that point it began to shift through a myriad permutations as the siege-machine slowly hauled itself toward the summit of the plateau. Halfway up there was a reverberating groan of metal, followed by a fearsome crack: one of the lifts had broken. As Alexander and the entire Macedonian army watched, the structure tilted about five degrees—then steadied itself as back-up lifts deployed.

Perdiccas never even broke a sweat. As far as he was concerned, this was a damn sight better than crawling through endless desert or getting tossed like a bloody cork on the sea. And now Alexander had seen fit to reward his loyalty with the ultimate honor, promoting him to marshal and entrusting him with spearheading the destruction of Syracuse's defenses. Archers, javelineers and artillery crammed the rooftop, along with each of the ten levels below the roof; all the levels below that were filled with battle-hardened soldiers and revved-up golems ready to charge onto the battlements of Syracuse. As Perdiccas rose past the rim of the plateau, the walls of Syracuse slowly came into view. It took the Helepolis the better part of an hour to crank itself up onto the plateau's summit, but once it had done so, it was finally back on level ground. Ahead were the city's walls; in their center was the Circle fortress. Perdiccas picked up one end of the speaking tube that slotted through the roof and went all the way down to the level of the engineers, right above the base.

"Sir," said a voice.

Perdiccas lowered his helmet's faceplate. "Flatten them."

CHAPTER TWENTY-ONE

The stairway ended in a larger corridor with still more carvings. Most of them seemed to involve the hydra. Endlessly intertwined necks stretched down the corridor, endless number of achingly beautiful heads. Eurydice mentioned more details about the myth of Hercules's fight with Geryon, who was supposed to have had three heads, one of a man, one of a monster, the other of a maiden. Lugorix wondered if that meant the creature downstairs had other types of heads. He fervently hoped that wasn't the case.

"This place is designed for a predator," said Barsine. She was leaning against the wall whenever Lugorix wasn't supporting her; there was clearly something wrong with her. "There may be doors here and there, but I'm sure that thing's necks can get anywhere they like—"

"Quiet," said Lugorix. He could hear something up ahead. "Sounds like water," he said.

"More like a waterfall," said Eurydice.

She was right. The corridor widened still further; the roof above them grew still higher. Spray drifted against their faces; Lugorix had heard enough of the river Lethe for that to make him anxious, but there didn't seem to any adverse effects. And there wasn't much they could do about it in any case. The walls kept widening and the ceiling kept getting higher until finally it was no longer visible. All they could see above them was some kind of mist, dimly reflecting the blue glow from Barsine's amulet.

A few hundred meters more, and one of the walls ended.

They were in an enormous chamber, though apparently still within the tower. A huge waterfall tumbled from the mist above, plunged into the cavern below. The place was dimly lit by light from some indeterminate source. Stone bridges spanned that cavern at several levels—Lugorix could see at least three bridges a few levels down, and two further up. The corridor they'd been following—now more of a cliff's ledge—ended in just such a bridge; the other end of that bridge was next to the waterfall.

"That must be what's powering the rivers," said Matthias.

"Sure," said Eurydice, "but what's powering *it?*"

There was only one way to find out. They started out across the bridge—Barsine grew dizzy again halfway over, and Lugorix had to help her keep her balance. The stones were slippery, and all of a sudden she lost her footing. He went to one knee to keep her upright.

But that was what saved his life.

The rock which flew straight past the place where his head had just been was quickly followed by another, but by now they were all ducking. Sure enough, three bridges below them were the Macedonians. There were at least ten of them, but the real problem was the slingers. Matthias drew his bow and fired an arrow, but it bounced off a soldier's shield. That was when one of the Macedonians caught sight of Barsine.

"Barsine," he yelled.

"Eumenes," she yelled back. "Still serving as your master's errand-boy?"

"Alexander promises to spare you should you surrender. He has nothing but love for you—"

"He doesn't give a rat's ass about me!" she yelled down at him. "All he cares about is his precious baby!"

"So you're still with child?" Relief was palpable in his voice.

"We need to move," said Eurydice, grasping Barsine's hand. But she pulled away, leaned back out—

"Is that Ptolemy down there too?"

The Macedonian in question smiled. "An honor to see you, my princess," he said sardonically.

"Who's calling the shots?" yelled Barsine, and suddenly she swayed as though the exchange was physically draining her. "You or Eumenes? *Philip or Alexander?*"

But there was no reply: because that was the moment when several of the hydra's heads rose from the gloom below and suddenly the Macedonians were in the thick of combat, locking shields as they fought their way off the bridge. Lugorix figured that was a good time to get the hell out of there; Matthias and Eurydice led the way while he helped Barsine. By the time they reached the end of the bridge he was practically carrying her.

"Don't know what's… wrong with me," she said.

"Relax," he said, "it's going to be all right."

"Don't count on it," said Eurydice—she was gesturing at what hadn't been visible until they got close to the waterfall: a ladder, disappearing into the mist and spray above them. Lugorix grasped its rungs and—

"No," said Matthias, "you need to carry Barsine. I'll go first."

Lugorix nodded in acknowlegement. Matthias started climbing as Eurydice helped Barsine onto Lugorix's back. She grasped her hands together around her neck, riding piggyback as he began to climb. Eurydice brought up the rear. They were all going as fast as they could—for all they knew, the Macedonians had already gotten onto this very ladder or were ascending another one nearby. They climbed into a darkening mist lit only by Barsine's amulet. The noise of combat below subsided; all they could hear was the rush of the waterfall close at hand.

"You holding on okay?" Lugorix asked.

"Yes," said Barsine. "But it hurts."

"Where?"

"Belly."

Lugorix figured that to be the worst news possible. Yet all he could tell her was to hold on. Strangely, it almost felt like she was getting lighter— was she dying? Was her soul taking flight from her body?

But then he realized that *he* was getting lighter too.

"Is it just me," said Eurydice, "or is it—"

"It's not just you," said Matthias. Lugorix noticed the noise of the waterfall was subsiding as well. He wished he could see what was going on.

"Gravity," said Eurydice. *"The gravity's changing."*

Indeed it was. It was getting weaker and they were climbing faster—to the point where Lugorix felt like he was floating, as though Barsine might actually start to drift away. He kept on climbing, ready to grab her if that happened. But then suddenly the gravity was growing stronger again.

In the other direction.

"Okay," said Matthias, "this is weird."

"Just keep climbing," said Eurydice.

"But we're fucking upside down."

Lugorix was already working on that. He grabbed onto Barsine with one hand while he reached the other hand past his feet and managed to turn himself around, holding onto Barsine while he did so. And then he kept on... *descending* was the best word for it, although it had been *up* a few moments ago. The reverse tug of gravity began to intensify and within a few more rungs it was back to normal proportions, only now entirely the other way. The mist was growing lighter too. But there were still no visual points of reference, no hint that the natural axis of absolutely everything had turned upside down in the space of only a few rungs.

"Um... any idea what's going on here?" said Matthias. Lugorix could see that neither he nor Eurydice had flipped themselves around. They were both climbing, head downward—hardly convenient, but then nothing about this was.

"Gravity is each object seeking its natural balance," said Eurydice. "That's what my father said—"

"Screw your father," said Matthias. "There's nothing *natural* about this."

Apparently Eurydice was far too freaked out to take umbrage. "There's a platform down there," she said.

She was right. The ladder descended to a long wooden platform. As they alighted on it, Eurydice's eyes went wide: she had just seen Barsine's ashen face.

"Are you *okay?*" she asked.

"What does it look like?" said Lugorix.

"I'm... fine," muttered Barsine.

"Hey guys," said Matthias, *"where the fuck are we?"*

That wasn't clear, though other ladders and platforms were visible in the distance. Strangely, although they were presumably still in the tower, the overall space around them seemed to be far wider than the tower itself. Lugorix had no idea how that was possible.

"The center must be above us," said Eurydice, pointing back the way they'd come.

"What?"

"The center of balance. The summit of those waterfalls. Maybe all that water is condensing out of all that mist. I don't know. All I know is—"

"There's something else below us," said Matthias.

Lugorix looked over the edge of the platform. It took him a few moments to decide that his friend was right. There *was* something down there in the mist—in fact, it was almost indistinguishable from mist, shimmering here and there, practically transparent. But it wasn't mist. It was something else. Not that far below them either…

"What *is* that?" he heard himself asking.

"Need to… get closer," said Barsine.

Matthias pointed. "That's the only ladder down from this platform."

But even as he said that, they heard noises above them—the Macks yelling back and forth to each other. Like they were still dealing with those snakes. Even as they closed in on their quarry…

"We need to climb down," said Barsine.

But as Lugorix looked at the ladder, he noticed something. "It ends in midair," he said. "Too far above whatever's down there."

"But it gets us closer," said Barsine. "We need to get *closer*."

Lugorix shrugged. He bent down, got onto the ladder when—

"No," said Barsine. "I'm going with you."

"You *can't*," said Eurydice. "Don't you realize you're sick?"

"Can't be helped," replied Barsine. She was practically doubling over now in pain.

"Listen to me," snarled Eurydice. "It sounds like you're *miscarrying*. For pity's sake, lay down and let me tend to—"

"I *can't*," Barsine said. And then, to Lugorix: "In the name of any love you may bear me, *get me down this ladder*."

"Don't do it," said Eurydice.

"Shut up," said Lugorix as he bent down and helped the stricken Barsine onto his back. Then he began to climb down the ladder. Eurydice shrugged, turned away. Matthias had his bow out, was scanning the mist and ladders above for the first sign of those Macks. Lugorix rapidly descended, Barsine clinging to his back—maybe a hundred rungs or so.

After which there was only air. Lugorix held onto the lowest set of rungs, struggling to control his vertigo, staring down at whatever it was that was shimmering in the mist. Now that he was closer—maybe only about ten yards above it—he could see it was somehow reflecting the light…

"It's a *mirror*," said Barsine.

Lugorix realized she was right. It *was* a mirror—or a series of them fixed together—as though each one was the facet of some great gemstone. Its dimensions were hard to tell. It seemed to run parallel with most of the platform. But—and now he was squinting—were its edges falling away off in the distance?

That was when he noticed something else—something right on the surface of those mirrors.

"Moving pictures," he said. "Like the ones when the *Xerxes* is submerged."

"What?" said Barsine—she turned her head to see.

"But they're not reflections," said Lugorix.

And the surface below them obviously wasn't just a mirror either. Now it looked like they were gazing into water—a shimmering pool of water, with *images* appearing and fading away on that surface. Lugorix wanted nothing more than to get away from it. It took all his willpower not to climb back up the ladder. He was directly above some kind of witches' scrying device—one of their magick cauldrons, perhaps. It occurred to him that maybe it was Barsine who was the real witch—or at least Damitra's apprentice. But he glanced back at her, couldn't help but notice that she seemed as astonished as he was. He started to say something, but Barsine motioned him to be quiet.

So he just clung onto those rungs and stared.

The image was of a city that Lugorix recognized: Syracuse. Only some of the buildings he knew weren't there, and there were others he didn't recognize. Athenian soldiers were being paraded through its streets, their hands bound in captivity, flanked by Syracusan soldiers. But their uniforms and weapons were somehow… off. And they were accompanied by *Spartan* soldiers too.

"Their uniforms are from a century ago," said Barsine.

"But Athens *conquered* Syracuse," said Lugorix. "This is the—"

"—other way round. Yes."

The image faded, to be replaced by another: that of generals and retainers clustering around a man laying in a luxuriant bed. The room might have been a palace. The man might have been a king. And he seemed to have just died—mourners were wailing, and slaves were wiping the last beads of sweat from his brow.

And now sweat was running down Barsine's too.

"That's *Alexander,*" she said. Her voice was shaking. "Back at Babylon."

"Maybe it's prophecy?" said Lugorix.

"You don't understand," she said. "He took ill, in just this way. *But he lived.*"

"What?"

"This is something *that didn't happen*."

No sooner had she said that then she began convulsing—foaming at the mouth, clutching her hands around his neck, muttering deliriously to herself. In a near-panic, Lugorix started to climb back up the ladder. There was nothing else he could do.

But that was when he heard the repeated twanging of Matthias' bow.

"They're *here*," yelled Eurydice. Lugorix quickened his climb.

Yet as he did so, a voice sounded right next to his ear. It was speaking his name. It was using Barsine's mouth.

But it wasn't her.

"We have them," said Ptolemy.

Eumenes certainly hoped so. The Persians only had one archer, but he was a serious pain in the ass. He'd already wounded one soldier and killed another, and neither of the slingers had adequate armor to have a hope of withstanding his arrows. Hanno assured him that on normal terrain that wasn't such a huge problem—they just had shieldbearers stand in front of them—but on these ladders, none of the Macedonians could effectively perform that role. The only real way to approach the platform where the Persians seemed to be trapped was to climb face downward, shield out, and hope you could maneuver that shield against any angle the archer might be able to get. That was what Eumenes' soldiers were trying to do now.

Problem was, the hydra was behind them. At least several heads were only a few hundred yards back—Eumenes' initial fear that they were for all practical purposes indefinitely long had proved to be true. The only piece of good news was those heads continued to prove vulnerable to the slingers' rocks. They'd already nailed four of them, smashing those beautiful faces into mushy pulp, after which the necks on which they were attached withdrew. Eumenes thanked the gods—did thanking the gods even make sense any more?—that he'd never seen more than a fraction of the bulk of the hydra's body, which presumably was still just sitting there in the waters beneath the tower. Hell, it never even needed to *move*—all it needed to do was send out its undulating heads. Kalyana had suggested that it might actually be a type of *plant*, one that automatically went into accelerated-growth mode in the event of intruders.

Not that Eumenes gave a shit about that. He was much more concerned about whether those heads might be coming in from multiple directions—

like from the flanks, for instance. Anything was possible, especially with the weird-ass gravity of this place. Even Kalyana had no idea what *that* was all about. The Vedic scholars had always believed that objects naturally tend to fall toward the center of the universe. So the idea that gravity could suddenly reverse itself made no sense.

"Unless we've *reached* the center of the universe," said Eumenes.

"I had hoped it would be a cleaner place than this," muttered Kalyana.

"What the hell did you do with Barsine?" said Lugorix. He was as comfortable with the notion of possession as any superstitious tribesman. Possession he could deal with. What he couldn't deal with was having its arms draped around his neck. Every instinct within him wanted to climb like crazy for the platform above. But those arms had tightened onto his windpipe, along with a single word from Barsine's own:

"Stop."

So he stopped. He couldn't tell how he knew that it was no longer Barsine's voice. There was almost no difference. Perhaps it was slightly deeper. Perhaps it was slightly higher. Perhaps that was the problem—there was a curious ambiguity to it that made it tough to pin down—an odd factor that just didn't sound fully human. He twisted his head to look at Barsine's face but it wasn't like her eyes were glowing red or her tongue was lolling out or anything dramatic. There was just a curious absence—as though Barsine was no longer home. To be replaced by an undeniable *presence* that sent chills up Lugorix's spine.

"What did you do with her?" he asked.

"I need you to climb down to the last rung," said the voice.

Lugorix clambered on down. "What did you do with Barsine?" he repeated, looking down at nothing below save mist and mirror.

"Now I need you to jump," said the voice.

"Are you nuts? The fall will kill us both—*aarrgh.*" This as the grip on his neck tightened. "Just do it," said the voice.

"Did you already kill her?" Barsine's grip tightened still further. Lugorix let go one of his hands, and grabbed her arms. Under normal circumstances, he should have been able to pull her hands away from his throat and release the pressure. Clearly these weren't normal circumstances. Her grip was like iron. But all of a sudden the grip relaxed.

"No," said the voice, "I didn't kill her."

Lugorix took a deep breath. *"Because she's your fucking mother?"*

The arms of Barsine grabbed his own and pulled him off the rung. He and Barsine plunged more than thirty feet—and suddenly slowed down about ten feet above the transluscent surface as the gravity simply gave out, cushioning their fall—but not totally, for its pull resumed just below that. They hit the surface—Lugorix grabbed Barsine by both arms—only to be shoved aside by her.

"You're going to do what I say," she said. "Take your axe and smash"—she looked around the curved surface at their endless reflections, seemed to be picking out a certain point—"smash *that* mirror there."

"Hey," yelled Matthias, "what's going on down there?"

"Just jump," shouted Lugorix. "Otherwise the Macks will kill you anyway."

There wasn't much doubt about that. Lugorix could see the first of the Macedonian soldiers coming down out of the mist, climbing downward like a monkey, his shield facing Matthias, daring him to try something. Matthias fired off a single shot—the arrow hit the shield and stuck there quivering. Then he grasped the ladder and started climbing down, Eurydice following behind him. They reached the ladder's bottom, stared down at Lugorix and Barsine.

"You want us to *jump?*" yelled Eurydice.

"I don't really care what you do," yelled Barsine—and when projected, her voice was so strange that Lugorix had no doubt that Matthias and Eurydice were realizing something was up. And then, to Lugorix: *"Now smash that mirror."*

But as Lugorix raised his axe to do that, something humanoid plunged past the platform and struck the sphere. Unlike he and Barsine, it didn't sprawl when it hit. It landed on its feet.

It was a golem.

He hadn't realized the Macedonians had brought one down here—and neither did Barsine from the look of shock on her face. It had the helmet of a hoplite but its eyes were dark. Its mouth was expressionless, and its body was as metal as the broadsword it held—a Thracian *rhompaia,* good for both cutting and stabbing. Which it now proceeded to do, heading toward Lugorix with a speed easily the equal of any man. He got his axe up just in time, tried to use its size to keep the thing at a distance while he gauged its reactions. They were quick: he had to use his axe's hilt to forestall a particularly swift blow. But the golem had overextended itself—and now

Lugorix swung Skullseeker forward in an arc, slicing straight through the golem's neck, sending its head sliding away down the curve of mirror, scores of tiny gears streaming out behind it.

But the headless golem kept on coming.

"Shit," said Lugorix. An arrow bounced off its back as Matthias unleashed from above—but it had no effect, and the Greek had to turn his attention back onto the other Macedonians clambering down toward the platform. They were running out of time. And the golem was still very much in the fight, its blade darting in and almost getting under Lugorix's guard. There was only one way to deal with this kind of thing and Lugorix knew it. He feinted to the right, then cut left—and chopped off its sword-arm in a single mighty stroke.

Only to find the golem lunging for his neck.

It wasn't the move Lugorix expected and before he knew it those metal fingers had closed on his windpipe. He couldn't believe it: in less than a minute two different sets of hands had tried to choke him. But these fingers felt like they were severing his neck already. He kicked out with his legs, trying to use his bulk against it, but instead its weight bore him over backward—and then he was on his back while the creature crushed out his life. He heard Barsine yelling something at him—saw something fly through the air toward him. He reached out with one hand and caught it.

It was Damitra's amulet—and as he touched it to the golem there was a flare of blue light and a hissing. Electric sparks ran over the golem, and Lugorix was practically blinded by the acrid smoke as a rattling noise rose from the golem's severed neck. It twitched once more, like a living creature.

Then it was still.

Lugorix pulled himself to his feet. He could hear shouting overhead. Barsine pointed for the third time at the mirror. Lugorix raised his axe.

And this time let it fall where she wanted.

"Sir!" yelled one of the soldiers below Eumenes. "The archer's gone!"

"They've abandoned the platform!" yelled someone else.

"Where did they go?" yelled Eumenes.

No one had a good answer for that. Overzealous machine that it was, the single golem he had in his force had leapt down there, missing the platform altogether, dropping out of sight. Had it seen something ordinary men couldn't? Sometimes golems were useful. Sometimes they did dumb things and got themselves destroyed in stupid ways. Eumenes could have sworn he'd heard swordplay subsequent to its fall. And now that he could see the platform with his own eyes, it was empty.

It smelt like an ambush. He watched in trepidation as two of the soldiers clambered down. He only had seven of them left—in addition to Hanno, his two slingers, Kalyana, and Ptolemy. Which hopefully still left them with the upper hand against the Persians. But not against that monster above them—as he watched, a slinger whirled, sent a rock spinning upward to crack against a descending head, which shattered like an egg. But the only real way to beat it was to stay ahead of it—or somehow find a structure or door past which it couldn't go. Ptolemy scrambled down the ladder onto the platform, looked around.

"There's a single ladder down!" yelled a soldier.

Eumenes and Ptolemy raced over. Looked over the edge.

"Holy *shit,*" said Ptolemy.

By the time Leosthenes reached the upper slopes of the Epipolae, the full weight of the Macedonian attack was underway. The sky was covered with smoke and flame. Trailed by several hundred Athenian cavalry, Leosthenes rode hell for leather toward the western wall, straight through the city's wealthiest districts. Anyone still in those houses was as stupid as they were rich, which was a shitty combination when you got down to it. You had all the money you wanted, yet you were dumb as rocks. Leosthenes knew a lot of people like that. Maybe he was one of them. He'd turned down more bribes to turn the city over to the Macedonians then he could count—not just the kind of money that he'd had all his life, but money for ten lifetimes over. The sort of money that only a king could give. But no amount of wealth could compensate for the loss of his honor. He would defend Syracuse, whatever the cost might be. Yet any illusions he might have been under as to that cost were swept away as the western wall and the Circle fortress came into sight.

Along with the *thing* that towered over them.

It was every bit as impressive as he'd expected: the largest siege tower he'd ever seen, and he could only guess what kind of engineering had allowed it to get to the top of the plateau so quickly. The artillery of the wall was pounding away at it, but the only siege-pieces that seemed to be doing much damage were those steam-guns: as Leosthenes watched, one of them scored a direct hit (it was hard to miss at that range), knocking a slab of the tower's metal armor clean off. But then more than a score of hatches opened on the tower and all manner of flame and metal poured down onto the steam-gun, disintegrating not just it but the battlements on which it sat. Pieces of rock rained down—and then Leosthenes lost sight of the siege-tower for a few moments as he led his force through the eastern gates of the Circle. In doing so, he found himself riding down soldiers trying to flee. Those behind them turned, dove to the side while he screamed at them:

"Penalty for desertion is *death!* But this is your lucky day, because you've just received *amnesty!* As long as you turn around and *follow me right now!*" His words probably weren't as motivating as the scores of cavalry riding in behind him; those horsemen left the would-be deserters with little choice then to turn around and get back into the fight. Leosthenes spurred his horse through the other pair of gates and into the Circle's courtyard. To his surprise, the siege-tower was reversing away from the western wall.

And then he understood why.

"It's coming *back,*" yelled Diocles.

"Of course it is," shouted Agathocles.

Xanthippus said nothing. He just watched as though hypnotized while the gigantic Helepolis ceased reversing and switched its engines into full-throttle again, plowing toward the Circle's wall. That wall had already withstood one impact, and it was highly doubtful it would withstand another. The first such blow had nearly knocked them all off—had sent cracks spiderwebbing through stone, pieces of rock falling into the court-yard below. Missiles of every description were raining down from the tower upon the hapless defenders on the battlements. As the Helepolis thundered in toward the wall, Agathocles suddenly seemed to snap out of it. He reached down to his dead spear-bearer, grabbed a bunch of spears, slung them on his back and—

"Follow me," he said as he started sprinting away toward the nearest tower. To Diocles' astonishment, Xanthippus just seized his lover's hand and followed the Syracusan outlaw. Maybe Xanthippus no longer believed in honor. Then again, maybe honor meant living for a few more minutes. Diocles wasn't about to argue. They reached the tower—it was one of those that had housed one of the steam-guns, so there wasn't much left of its upper levels. But amidst the rubble they could clearly see the flight of stairs going downward. Agathocles took them them two at a time, Xanthippus and Diocles doing their best to keep up. Agathocles was shouting something but he couldn't be heard over the steadily increasing rumbling that felt like it was going to shake all of them apart. The stairway was vibrating so badly they were practically falling down it. They tumbled to the bottom, picked themselves up, raced out of the tower and along a culvert that bordered the western wall.

Just as that wall exploded inward.

One moment it was there, the next it just…*wasn't*. Dust was everywhere, so thick Diocles was coughing and choking and almost blinded. But Xanthippus was still holding his hand, still leading him onward as the world crumbled around them. Diocles could hear the insanely loud clanking of the siege-engine towering above them; he couldn't see it, but he expected to get run over at any moment. But then Xanthippus led him down a flight of stairs and into one of the underground passages beneath the Circle. Only then did Agathocles glance back to see the two soldiers were still behind them. Above them there was a noise like the ocean itself crashing down.

"This way," said Agathocles. Diocles didn't ask him how he knew the layout of the Athenian fortress; keeping tabs on the Athenian defenses seemed to be a specialty for the man. He led the other two quickly along the corridor, turned left, then right, then up another set of stairs, through a door and into—

"Thank *fuck*," said Xanthippus. They were outside the Circle—which was crumbling into pieces before their eyes. Dead men and horses were everywhere. The impossibly huge outline of the Helepolis was dimly visible amidst all the dust and falling masonry. A man stood right in front of them trying to pull another man free of wreckage. He turned as they reached him.

It was Leosthenes.

"Viceroy," said Agathocles, "what a pleasant surprise—"

"Shut up and help me get this rock off Memnon," snapped Leosthenes. Diocles wasn't sure who Memnon was, but Xanthippus didn't hesitate; he leaned forward and helped Leosthenes push the rock off. But the old man who lay beneath was obviously dead, half his body crushed. Leosthenes blinked like someone who was seizing control of his emotions; he leaned down, closed the old man's eyes, then looked back up at the three of them. In the background, the Helepolis was reversing one more time, undoubtedly so it could steamroll straight through the rubble and into the city that lay beyond. Beyond that, the Macedonian phalanx could be seen in the distance, cheering as they advanced triumphantly toward the gaping hole in the western wall. Leosthenes stared up at the Helepolis.

"We need to stop that bastard," he said.

"Any ideas as to how?" said Agathocles.

"I'm down to exactly one," said the viceroy.

A single swipe with the axe was all it took. Suddenly unbroken mirror had become shards of glass flying through the air, revealing an opening within—black tinged with a fiery light. Lugorix was about to peer inside when Matthias landed a few yards from him. Eurydice wasn't so precise—she landed toward the edge of the sphere, began to slide. Matthias reached out and grabbed her, helped her up.

"Thanks," she said—and then, to Lugorix: "What's up with Barsine?"

"She's possessed by her own baby," said Lugorix.

"Got it," said Eurydice. "So.... either she's gone crazy or you have?"

"Where *is* Barsine anyway?" asked Matthias.

There was only one answer to that. Lugorix whirled, realizing that she'd gone through the opening while the other two were hitting the surface. He bent down, stuck his head in.

"What do you see?" asked Eurydice impatiently.

It was impossible to describe. Rungs led down through what seemed to be a tunnel surrounded by fire. But he could feel no burning—could sense no heat. And he could hear the Macks shouting above them. Either they'd reached the platform or they were about to. Lugorix grabbed those rungs and started climbing down through the tube, doing his best to ignore the flames seemed to be raging right in front of his face. Were they real? Was he looking at more of those moving pictures? Or was there *really* fire mere inches away from him his face? It was like descending into a volcano. He finally started to accept that he really was in Hell.

But then suddenly he was out of it: through a trapdoor and onto another platform. Barsine was standing there. Ten seconds later, Matthias and Eurydice were too.

And during those ten seconds, all Lugorix had done was stare at what lay all around him.

CHAPTER TWENTY-TWO

The platform was suspended just below a concave ceiling that curved away in all directions. They were inside the enormous sphere they'd just been on the exterior of. That much made sense. That was basically all that did.

It was mostly empty space—mostly dark, too—and yet it was clearly some vast machine, several miles across, a webwork of gears and clanking steam-pipes, all of it in motion. Rungs and ramps were dimly illuminated by glowing orbs that shone through the black, rattling along metal rails that curved down toward something a long way below, a faraway disc that was a combination of green and blue and brown. It seemed oddly familiar to Lugorix—it took him a moment to place it—but Matthias beat him to it.

"It's like that map," he said. "From Demosthenes' study. *That's what it's like.* It's meant to be—Fates protect us, it's meant to be the…"

"Earth," Lugorix finished for him. Fuck, maybe it *was* the Earth, maybe they'd somehow been transported to far, far above it. After everything that had gone down, it seemed anything was possible. And as Lugorix took in the rumbling network of gears that powered those orbs—"planets," whispered an awestruck Eurydice—he realized that the blackness of the ceiling was actually nothing of the kind—that it was shot through with a myriad pinpricks of light. The fact that he knew they were lit by the vast furnace built into the attic of that ceiling in no way detracted from his wonder at what were very obviously intended to be stars. In some faraway portion of himself, he became aware that Barsine—or whatever was inside her—had

begun to speak.

"This is a mechanical universe," she said, her words flat, without emotion. "A faithful replica of the real one, fueled by the furnace in its ceiling and driven by steam and fire. Like the real universe, it contains interlocking sets of spheres. That of the stars. Those of the planets. And the interior consists of the Earth, the Moon"—she pointed at a grey gleaming orb near the disc—"and the Sun. Which you can't see right now, because it's intended to be night."

"Very pretty," said Matthias, "but what's the point?"

"The point is it's a fucking *computer*," said Eurydice. She used a word that Lugorix had never heard before. "A *calculator-of-worlds*," she added. "Right?"

"More than that," said Barsine. "A controller of them."

Before anyone had time to react to that, they heard the thud of Macedonian boots landing on the roof of the structure above them.

Eumenes hated it when there was only one way to enter a place. Too easy for anyone inside to defend. His soldiers smashed away at the mirrors for a few minutes, but all they found beneath them was iron. Finally he bowed to the inevitable and sent his men inside, down the ladder, through the tunnel of fire, and onto the platform.

Which blew everybody's minds, of course.

Even having some idea of what to expect, Eumenes was still struggling to hold onto his sanity. Kalyana and he had talked about the various possibilities, but talk was one thing and seeing was quite another. There wasn't time to gawk either: Barsine's group had a head-start, and they were making the most of it. Eumenes could see them, ant-like, far below, riding the outermost orb, the orb that was intended to represent the planet known as...."*Kronos,*" muttered Kalyana, as it swung away into abyss. How they'd reached it so quickly baffled him for a moment, until he saw an almost-impossibly long ramp folding back into the bottom of the platform on which he stood, the other half of that ramp retracting into the Kronos-orb below.

"They must have just *slid* along it," he muttered. "Perfect timing—"

"Can *we* control those ramps?" said Ptolemy.

Kalyana looked around, studying the ceiling. "There might be something better," he said—and cautiously led the way along the network of platforms, followed by the others. Eumenes and Ptolemy were right behind them, with the six remaining Macedonian soldiers keeping a wary eye on Hanno and his two slingers. One of those slingers stepped to the platform's edge, whirled his sling so rapidly it was impossible to even see the moment when the stone spun away, whipping after the receding simulacrum of Kronos… which was technically way out of range, but then again gravity seemed to be in full effect within this place, all of it pulling toward that earth-disc far below. The slinger watched as the stone shot off into the dark—stared after it, then shook his head in disappointment. He'd missed, but Eumenes was damned if he could see by how far.

And right now he had more pressing priorities to deal with anyway—like following Kalyana as he reached the end of one of the platforms, climbed up a set of stairs to the very ceiling of the celestial firmament itself—and slid back a trapdoor. Eumenes flinched involuntarily, half-expecting to see fire pouring from the opening thus revealed. Having just climbed in here through that tube he knew that the rafters of this place was one big furnace. But instead of flames he saw something far stranger.

Six of them, in fact.

"Those look like *carts*," said Ptolemy.

"They are," said Kalyana. "Now we must all get in."

It took only a few minutes to do so, and yet all that time Eumenes was conscious that Barsine and her motley crew were moving ever further away—getting ever closer to the place they were all trying to get to. It was still far below them, but their lead was increasing with every second. But the contraptions on the ceiling were simple enough to work. One got in, strapped oneself in—that was important, because you'd be upside down for most of the time. You used one handle to set the thing in motion, another handle to stop it. As for steering—

"The whole ceiling is cris-crossed with rails," said Kalyana.

"And you knew this how?" said Ptolemy.

"Our texts speak of servants moving across the sacred ceiling of the gods. And—how should I put it?—seeing a stairway to nowhere raised my suspicions."

Eumenes shrugged. He didn't really care how Kalyana knew it, just as long as it worked. Kalyana pulled himself up into the first of the carts, strapped himself in while Eumenes and Ptolemy did the same. Hanno and his two slingers climbed into a second cart; the six soldiers took two more of the vehicles.

"Here we go," said Kalyana—he pulled on one of the levers and next moment the cart began to move upside down along the ceiling, over the platform—slowly at first, the other three carts following. Eumenes looked down past that platform, was relieved to see that Kronos's long orbit had barely taken it an eighth of the distance around the sphere. But then he noticed that the orb below it—that of the largest planet, Zeus—had stopped and was *reversing* toward Kronos, the gap between them closing with every passing second....

"They're controlling them," he breathed.

Kalyana nodded. "Those two planets, they cannot intersect, but they are going to try a jump from one to the other. I wonder if..."

But Eumenes was no longer listening. He'd just noticed something else—something far closer. And way more disturbing.

"Speed up," he hissed to Kalyana.

"What?"

"That's a fucking bomb."

Eumenes had to give the sage credit: he didn't ask any questions, didn't even glance at the black-powder device that had started hissing and sputtering above the end of the platform, attached to the underside of the firmament itself—instead he just pushed the lever onto maximum and the car shot away, along the side of the firmament. Following its lead, the other three cars sped up too.

And then the bomb detonated.

Even from the vantage point of Kronos, it was quite a sight: a quick flaring as the device that Eurydice had planted blew—and then, before the detonation reached their ears, an enormous gout of fire sprayed out from the ceiling, huge chunks of that firmament falling away, along with pieces of that platform.

As well as one of those railcars. It fell in toward the four who clung to the top of Kronos, tumbled past them close enough so they could see the the three screaming Macedonian soldiers inside before it hit one of the gear-shafts lower down. The car stuck there. The bodies kept falling.

"That's gotta hurt," said Matthias.

"They met the fate their actions brought them," said the voice of Barsine. "They trespassed on the roof of heaven."

"How exactly is it that *they're* trespassing and *we're* not?" said Eurydice sardonically.

"Because I am the seed of those who ruled here," said Barsine. "My mother is a daughter of Persia, my father a son of Macedonia."

"So I'm *really* supposed to go along with this?" said Eurydice. "You *really* want me to believe that I'm talking to the unborn child of the woman who calls herself Barsine?"

"You are a scientist, are you not?"—it was Barsine's voice, but it just *wasn't*. "How else do you explain my command over this machine we find ourselves in? How else could I deploy its ramps and gears with the power of my presence?" She pointed at the Earth-disc, still far below, but close enough so they could make out the continents amidst the encompassing World-Ocean. A languid hand gestured at different areas on those continents in turn, her voice as hollow as the space they were speeding through.

"After the War, with the mutual destruction of the Olympians and the Chthonics, each side put in motion plans to use the ape-children of the Earth to some day re-awaken themselves and their machinery. This was done through the seeding of royal bloodlines—the code of the *genetikos*. There were several royal houses. The Egyptians were once the foremost— they built Pyramids and other works that might have allowed them to rule all the Earth—but they grew decadent and crumbled before the weight of foreign invaders. The Phoenicians scattered to the seas. The Achaemenids of Persia dominated central Asia until they were undone by the Argeads of Macedonia, who—centuries before—had fled Argos after civil war. They are thus both Greek and Macedonian, and today they are almost certainly the most powerful, even if hate has always existed between their line's fathers and sons. Further to the East were the Vedic princes, who destroyed each other amidst internecine feuding—and had Alexander been so bold as to press on into northern India, he might have discovered even more than he and his henchmen did. And on the far east of Asia are the Han people, who even now rule a territory as large as Alexander, though they are divided into several warring states. If any of them have plans to insert themselves into this contest, I know not. Same with the remaining two houses." She gestured across the eastern edge of ocean, at another long chunk of land, running north to south. Lugorix narrowed his eyes, realized that a slender isthmus at the top of Asia was a land-bridge to still another continent at the very eastern edge of the disc. The entity behind Barsine's eyes saw his puzzlement, smiled.

"The fourth continent—Furthest Asia—contains two more peoples, the Toltecs in the north and the Nazcas in the south. Both possess powerful magicks but I regret to say I know very little of their activities. They may already be far ahead of us."

"Who's *us*?" muttered Eurydice. She was clearly trying to keep up with everything around her. She'd already admitted during the descent to Kronos that she'd made a very small such device once—a replicator of the heavens that she'd called an *Antikythera,* as that was the island in the Aegean she'd been working on at the time. But that had been only a few finger-spans across, rather than scores of miles. So now she was listening to Barsine while she stared at the fire erupting from the ceiling of heaven—and at the three surviving railcars as they raced further down the firmament, keeping pace with Kronos as it clanked along its orbit. But lower down was the orb of Zeus, rumbling in toward them...

"Isn't it obvious?" said the voice of Barsine. "The whole name of the game right now is to get off the disc of the world—*the real one,* the one that's far above us—and into the *actual* machinery that controls the cosmos. And I daresay we have made much progress. After all, here we are in the center of the Underworld, moving toward the heart of the ancillary computer."

Eurydice looked like she'd been slapped in the face. "There's another? One more vital than this?"

"Of course."

"Fuck's sake: *where?*"

"In the real celestial sphere. Far overhead."

"Then—"

"I don't know how to get there. But rest assured I intend to find out—"

"But you don't even know how to use *this* computer to manipulate the world above."

"Because it's latent," said Barsine. "It's turned off."

"Looks pretty active to me."

"*Mostly* latent, then."

"Now you're splitting hairs. Alexander seems to have already attained at least some control over it. Those storms—"

"I'm not sure *how* he's doing that. A telepathic"—Lugorix didn't understand the word, but he recognized it as a compound of the Greek terms for *distant* and *experience*—"link with one or both of the computers, maybe—

but it's partial, and it's only over certain elements."

Eurydice looked like she wanted to throw Barsine straight off the orb of Kronos. "But *how does controlling this machinery control the universe in the first place?* Why should a machine—"

"*What the hell do you think the universe is?*" demanded Barsine.

Throughout this exchange, Matthias' gaze kept flicking back and forth from woman to woman, his mouth open, his brain left far behind. But Lugorix was concerned with more practical matters. Like the cracks that continued to grow along the ceiling far above. More fire kept on licking through, spreading along the roof of the dome. The Macedonians who had fallen into the gear-shaft seemed to have jammed that apparatus completely; as Lugorix watched, it disintegrated altogether, pieces of it flying into still more gear-shafts that in turn broke or splintered—a chain reaction that kept gathering pace, until suddenly Lugorix noticed the rail on which Zeus was rising toward them start to *bend* out of alignment, under ever greater pressure. He cleared his throat.

"Hey guys," he said, "I think we might have a problem."

Matthias suddenly seemed to snap out of his trance—he pointed up at the fiery hole at the summit of the orb above.

"You're right about that," he said. Lugorix abruptly realized that it wasn't just flames coming through anymore.

It was also scores upon scores of necks.

"That fucking hydra," breathed Lugorix.

"This is getting tricky," said Matthias.

All the way to heaven: that's how high the Helepolis seemed to tower. In truth it was only about four times the height of the Leviathans that Alexander had employed at Athens. But no one on the ground was in the mood to quibble. The siege-tower smashed its way through what was left of the Circle fortress—and then poured on the steam, crunching through the monuments and mansions of Syracuse's wealthiest districts. It seemed like the whole city beyond that was on fire. Flame and smoke was everywhere. Those who were still stupid enough to be cowering in the buildings and basements came running out like swarms of insects to be crushed or shot. In the windows that lined the Helepolis, the archers were having good sport. Diocles could hear them yelling and joking to each other as they nailed everything in sight. The fact that he was so close to that monster scared him absolutely shitless.

But it couldn't be helped. Leosthenes and Agathocles had a plan. Which was ironic, the two men who ought to have been enemies cooperating in one last desperate attempt to save Syracuse. And Xanthippus, with his accursed sense of duty, was going to die helping them.

Which meant that Diocles would too. The four of them were making their way along the third level of the city's four-level aqueduct, up to their waists in water and shit and hoping that the Helepolis wasn't about to change direction any more than it had already done. It was right outside, moving parallel to the aqueduct, which ran down across the heights of the plateau and then down its eastern side and into the city. That was essentially the route the Helepolis intended to follow—and as far as Diocles could see there was absolutely nothing to stop it from steamrollering its way all the way into inner Syracuse, straight up to the Harbor, after which it would undoubtedly find a way to get across to the Ortygia and destroy the final citadel of Athenian resistance. He could see it through the aqueduct's archways as it rumbled past them—and then that view was obscured by smoke as hails of flame-bolts fired by the defenders of Syracuse struck the front of the Helepolis, lodging there, burning themselves out against the metal-armor. Ahead of him, Leosthenes had stopped and taken a bizarre-looking weapon out of his satchel.

"Where'd you get that?" said Agathocles.

"From Aristotle's workshop," said Leosthenes. "Where all the good shit comes from."

"Too bad you idiots couldn't hang onto him."

"Treason's a dodgy thing," said the viceroy. The device he was setting up was some kind of large crossbow, except the bolt itself looked for all the world like a grappling hook.

"That one there," said Agathocles, gesturing through the smoke at the nearest arrow-slit as the enormous machinery clanked past.

"It's occupied," said Xanthippus. Agathocles nodded, removed a dart-thrower from his belt—whipped it forward. The dart shot across the space between them and the Helepolis and smacked an archer right in the face. He dropped.

"Not anymore," said Agathocles. Leosthenes nodded, aimed the grappling hook and fired. It flew straight into that window and stuck fast. The rope hung there, suspended.

"Oh shit," said Diocles as he realized where this was going.

"Now there's something you don't see every day," said Ptolemy.

Eumenes couldn't take his eyes off it. None of them could—save for Kalyana who was too busy driving. With a noise that literally shook the artificial universe, the rails along which Zeus was riding had just snapped— and now the huge planetary orb was sailing into space, straight toward the star-encrusted firmament.

"It's coming straight for us," said Eumenes—and now Kalyana *did* look up and acted immediately, sending the railcar ripping down another rail altogether, desperately veering away from the incoming course of the orb. The cars bearing the Carthaginians and the Macedonian soldiers saw the problem as well—the Carthaginians shot off at an angle, still running parallel with the orb of Kronos. The Macedonians went the other way.

It just happened to be the wrong one.

The giant sphere cannoned straight into them and just kept going, leaving a Zeus-sized hole in the firmament from which flame immediately began pouring. So great was the heat that Eumenes could feel it wash across him as the railcar continued speeding down the concave side. Earth was getting ever closer, though the firmament and the terrestrial disc didn't intersect—there was a wide gulf between them even at their closest point. But the competition was in even worse shape. Kalyana gestured up at Kronos, high overhead, where the tiny figures of the four who rode it could still be seen—and whose plan to make the leap down to Zeus was no longer an option.

"No offense to them," said Kalyana, "but they are fucked."

Lugorix was thinking the same thing. They were still stuck on the outermost planet, and the amount of wreckage now piling up in the Zeus-orbit had made any kind of move there basically impossible. Just to make matters worse, the Balearic slingers on the wall of the firmament were getting pretty good at using gravity to augment their shots. Rocks were zinging past, and the four who clung to Kronos had no way to shield themselves. They were right on the top of the orb, otherwise they'd slide right off—and there were no crevasses or or pits to hide in, as planetary bodies were perfect by definition.

Which made Lugorix feel like ever more of a sitting duck. It was only a matter of time before they got nailed. Matthias had tried to get a few shots off with his bow, but he was firing against the pull of gravity, and the arrows got nowhere near the Carthaginians. But even though the situation was rapidly coming apart at the seams, the entity within Barsine didn't seem worried.

"Eurydice," it said. "How many of those bombs do you have left?"

"That'd be one," said Aristotle's daughter. "We used one on the *Xerxes,* one on the roof overhead, so we're down to our last—"

"Give it to me." Eurydice handed it over, albeit reluctantly. As she did so, another stone from one of the slingers just missed her hand—she almost dropped the bomb but Barsine reached out with unnatural speed and grabbed the device. She then smeared on the egg-honey mixture they'd used to adhere the previous bomb to the firmament overhead before adjusting the device's wick and lighting it. As she held it, she looked around slowly—at the Earth far below, at the planetary orbs above that, at the flame jetting in from the ceiling, at all those heads of the hydra reaching down toward them. She seemed to be lost in thought. And all the while that wick was burning down.

"Would you mind getting rid of that thing?" said Eurydice. Barsine looked at her as though genuinely surprised—then in a single fluid motion she threw the bomb directly behind them, right onto Kronos's rail. For a moment Lugorix watched that bomb recede. But only for a moment.

And then it detonated.

Instantly the rail snapped. As it did so, Lugorix suddenly felt Kronos shift beneath him—and suddenly his heart flew into his mouth as the portion of the rail they were on bent under the weight of the planetary orb… which in turn slowed, stopped, and then slid backward, the rail bending still further as they rolled straight toward the severed end.

"Oh shit," said Lugorix.

"Everyone hold on," said Barsine.

They plunged off into space.

"Think that'll work?" asked Ptolemy as they watched the orb of Kronos tumble away toward the inner solar system.

"Not a chance," said Eumenes. He could now see hydra-necks coming in through the second hole, the one that the wayward Zeus had created. Apparently fire was no problem for them. That meant two places where the dome was breached.

Suddenly there were a whole lot more.

A short distance behind where Eumenes was: several of the artificial stars past which the Carthaginian railcar was riding suddenly blew open—the furnace windows shattering as hydra-necks crashed through and seized the hapless occupants of the railcar. The two slingers were caught immediately; Hanno was knocked from the railcar altogether and tumbled away. A hydra-neck darted after him, but wasn't going to catch up with him in time—until its tongue shot out and grabbed him. Eumenes could hear him screaming as he was drawn back to the hydra's maw.

"We need to get off this ceiling fast," said Ptolemy, eyeing the still-extant stars around them.

"I am working on that very problem," said Kalyana.

They hurtled through the solar system, and worlds reeled past them. They shot through the wreckage of Zeus' orbit, in between the gears and rails and ramps hanging in all directions, and plunged ever further downward. They weren't falling as fast as Lugorix would have thought—Barsine said that was because they were travelling through something called *aether*—but they were still going down way too quickly for comfort. The disc of Earth grew as they veered in toward it. Lugorix could see the orbs of the inner planets getting ever closer. They were heading for one in particular—much smaller than either Zeus or Kronos, and colored dark-red.

"Get ready!" yelled Barsine, and it was the most emotion they'd heard from that voice since she'd been possessed by the thing within her. Next moment they just missed that red planet and struck the rail on which it was riding, bouncing for a moment... and then the grooves of gears clicked into place as they slid along its orbit, heading in the opposite direction—but no longer falling.

"Welcome to Ares," said Barsine.

Leosthenes scrambled over the rope first, followed by Agathocles—the two of them disappearing into the window of the Helepolis, that rope slowly growing tauter as the Helepolis kept on cranking forward.

"Now you go," said Xanthippus to Diocles.

"I'm not sure I can," said Diocles.

"I'll be right behind you. *Now go.*"

And Diocles did. He couldn't face being shamed in Xanthippus' eyes, and there were only seconds anyway. Not only was the rope on the point of snapping but the Helepolis was about to brush up against the aqueduct a little further down. So he banished all thought and fear from his mind, grabbed onto the rope—almost slipped, but then locked his legs around it while he pulled ahead with his arms. What probably saved him is that he didn't look down—though looking up was bad enough, for he was staring all the way along the Helepolis, its topmost battlements set against the darkened sky. And then the rough hands of Agathocles and Leosthenes were grabbing him and dragging him through the window, pulling him onto the floor next to the body of the dead archer. It took a moment for Diocles to realize he wasn't dead too. But then he leapt to his feet—just in time to see Xanthippus pulling himself through the window. Next moment there was a gigantic crashing noise: a mere fraction of the sound the whole of the siege-tower was making, but all too loud in that window as the Helepolis began to scrape the aqueduct. Bricks started falling past the room into which the four men had just climbed. Outside the window Diocles watched as the entire aqueduct swayed, then collapsed amidst clouds of choking dust. Then he felt the floor tilt beneath him as the Helepolis began to move down the far, eastern side of the plateau.

"Next stop central Syracuse," breathed Agathocles.

"We'd better make this quick," said Leosthenes.

Which was precisely what Eumenes was thinking as Kalyana accelerated the railcar still further, somehow pushing it way beyond whatever its safety margins were. Next moment, Kalyana hauled on the levers; Eumenes felt a jolt.

Next moment they fell away from the firmament.

Eumenes figured they'd come off the rails altogether, were tumbling down toward oblivion. Beside him Ptolemy was muttering prayers and curses all in the same breath. But then he realized that they were still on a rail—a very slender one, practically impossible to see against all the others that filled this chamber, for it was far narrower than any of the planetary ones and it led in a completely different direction from any of them, past the orbits and gears of Ares and through an opening in the almost-invisible crystal sphere of the Sun, past the orbits of Aphrodite and Hermes—and straight in toward the Earth. They plummeted down toward the disc, which swelled with every passing second. It was all Eumenes could do to catch his breath enough to ask the obvious question.

"What are we on?" he yelled.

"It is the route of a hairy star," said Kalyana. "You remember it, no?"

Eumenes remembered all right, but not in his wildest nightmares did he imagine he'd be riding along the path of one, particularly not in some enormous simulation of the universe so far beneath the real one. They streaked in over the edge of the terrestrial disc, right above the hemisphere that stretched above it, containing air and roiling patterns of weather. Then blue of ocean was replaced by the green and brown of continents: there was a long one running north to south that he'd never even *heard* of, and then they were over Asia. He was stunned to see just how much land there was to the east of the furthest extent of Alexander's march—and then they were cruising in above the mountains of the Himalayas and the Hindu Kush where he and Hephaestion had spent so much time in search of the lost treasures of the ancients… the ancients whose world he was even now penetrating straight to the heart of. He wondered if they had populated the disc beneath him with miniature creatures or automata, or if they'd simply left it barren, uninhabited, the only intelligence in here that of the machine itself. He wondered how that machine worked in the first place—how it was controlled, what it controlled (was it *really* the entire world above?—was the *whole universe* simply a huge machine?—were there worlds beyond even it—unseen worlds past the cosmic fire that ringed the universe, that *contained* the universe, nothing but machine encompassing machine encompassing machine?)—and then they were sweeping out above the Mediterranean, over the Pillars of Hercules, past the Fortunate Islands, dropping ever closer to the Ocean. Which was when Eumenes suddenly realized that Kalyana had screwed this one up, that they were going to smash straight into the hemisphere of air—he was close enough to that hemisphere to see the engines and pipes stacked along it that controlled its atmosphere and weather—but then he realized the ramp extended past it, just missed the edge of the disc and continued onward.

Except now they were switching onto yet another ramp and rising up again, the western edge of the Earth dropping away beneath them, nothing but abyss below them.

And nothing but the Moon in front of them.

"Brace yourself," said Kalyana.

Then they were off, battling their way out into the Helepolis, killing everyone who tried to stop them and sneaking right past all those who didn't notice. And there were a lot who didn't: most of the crew were working the siege-engines and firing out the arrow-slits at the mass of targets below—and there was so much smoke and so much noise that most of them never even bothered to turn around.

Not that the intruders were staying in the high-trafficked areas. Leosthenes led the way; apparently he'd seen the plans for this monstrosity, either through Athenian intelligence or because Aristotle had taken it with him when he fled Pella. The place was a veritable maze of catwalks and stairs and ladders. In short order they made their way off the level they'd boarded at and up some rungs onto the next. There was a gap in the floor ahead of them: Diocles suddenly found himself looking out into a vast hollow space, a hole cut through several levels. At each level, hundreds of men were turning gigantic capstans, while rising through the entirety of the open space were enormous clanking engines and whirling gears that hissed and spat as conveyor belts of buckets dumped water to cool them.

"This way," said Leosthenes. He headed toward an entirely different conveyor belt, one that stretched along one of the exterior walls, rising from a small hole in the floor and through the ceiling. Stone and metal bolts were stacked neatly into each bucket on the belt; Diocles realized this was part of the internal transport system for ammunition. They all grabbed onto rungs and started getting hauled upward—through three levels and then jumping off to run down another passage that ended in one of the corner rooms, domimated by a large window. Protruding through that window was one of the largest weapons that Diocles had ever seen—an enormous barrel to which was attached a metallic sphere fed by bellows. Just as the group reached the room, several crew were hauling on chains to work the bellows; Diocles watched as fire poured out the far end of the barrel, shooting out in an arc and splashing down upon the city far below.

"Kill them," said Agathocles.

They did. Quickly. The room ran red with blood, the screams unheard over the roaring of the machine in which they were all riding. Yet even as he was gutting unarmed gunners and crew, Diocles found himself staring past them as they begged for mercy—staring at Syracuse like he'd never seen it, sprawling down the eastern side of the plateau all the way toward the Great Harbor. As that slope grew steeper, the floor beneath them was levelling out, as though the Helepolis was so sophisticated that it could somehow adjust its own incline. The butchery done, Diocles glanced around to see Leosthenes shoving a torch up against the wooden portion of the bellows, which quickly caught fire. Next moment they were all running back the way they came, back to that ammunition-belt, clambering back onto it and rising higher into the structure. They'd gone only a few more levels when there was a thunderous boom beneath them. Fire shot past one of the windows outside; the entire edifice shook. Diocles whooped in triumph. But Agathocles just laughed.

"What's so funny?" Diocles demanded.

"That'd be you," said Leosthenes, not unkindly. "This machine has at least a *hundred guys* dedicated purely to fire-fighting operations. They'll clean up the mess we just made and they'll be quick about it."

"What are we making for?" asked Diocles. "The command room?"

"Hell no," said Leosthenes. "Too well defended."

"But we've at least got a diversion going," said Agathocles.

"And not much time to use it," said Xanthippus.

They didn't have *any* time at all. They were already sliding down ramps from the orbit of Ares to that of the Sun, but they weren't going to make it. Because the Macedonians had pulled a fast one on them—they'd known about the secret rails that no planet would ever traverse. *The hairy star—* that's what Eurydice had said as they watched the railcar soar down across the Earth—and then on another rail altogether, up toward the Moon. The hairy star. It had beaten them. It meant they had lost.

"And how come you didn't know about it?" demanded Eurydice.

Barsine shrugged. "I never claimed to have perfect knowledge of this place," said the thing inside her.

"Then how the fuck do they?"

"They shouldn't. There's some other factor at play here."

Eurydice looked like she wanted to strangle her. "Maybe one of these other *royal bloodlines* you keep yammering about?"

Barsine said nothing—just led the way off the ramp and onto the Sun's orbit. Though it was a lot more than just an orbit. It was a crystalline sphere, stretching out in all directions, practically translucent, the glow of Sun just visible from behind the disc of Earth, since it was night up here. Lugorix glanced up at Ares high above them, was startled to see those fucking *snakes* already reaching down to its orbit, past all the wreckage that littered the orbits above. They were like some kind of cosmic infection—they would fill up this place until they had consumed all flesh. He suddenly became aware that Barsine was tapping him on the shoulder. He whirled around. She gestured at the sphere upon which they were standing, and for a moment—just a moment—he thought he saw the real Barsine flickering behind those eyes.

"I need your axe again," she said.

CHAPTER TWENTY-THREE

Eumenes gritted his teeth as the Moon filled his vision, covered with patterns of dancing shadow and dappled light, patterns that co-alesced into... what? Some said it was the face of an old man, some said an old woman, and some could see her faithful dog from the years of her youth right there beside her, while still others said there was a trickster rabbit in there, a rabbit with a human face and a mind cleverer than any man had any right to be.

All of which caused problems for sorcerors and scientists alike (whatever they were in the mood to call themselves). Celestial bodies were supposed to be perfect, and yet the Moon was very evidently not. Aristotle had said it partook in the corruption of the Earth itself—was marred by the weight of the four elements—and that was why it looked so unlike any of the objects above it. But certainly the builders of the machine that had operated through eons beneath the core of Earth had taken care to render their Moon faithfully. It had unique standing. Not just because of its imperfection...

"This is it," said Ptolemy as the rail veered in toward the Moon, curv-ing in amidst those lunar valleys. The rail led straight in to one valley in particular. Its sides closed in around them—and then so did the roof. They came to a halt in a gigantic cave.

And then they saw the thing that lay inside it.

The blaze-battling operation inside the Helepolis must have been getting things under control, because the smoke that had been billowing up the stairs was starting to die out. Still, it had bought the intruders some time—they'd gotten up four more levels on that vertical ammunition belt and then made their way along a catwalk that led right above a series of ballistaes, all of them lined up along the front of the Helepolis and flinging rocks out ahead of them as fast as their gunners could pull the projectiles off the ammo belts and reload. Diocles noticed that they were now within range of central Syracuse—that the sky was practically black with projectiles chucked by the Helepolis, crashing down upon the heart of the city. But the defenders were still trying to give as good as they were getting: streaks of fire and balls of stone kept ripping in toward them, crashing against the structure. It was hard to miss. But doing some real damage was another matter altogether. Perhaps the great machine's armor had been penetrated in some places, but the single best way to hurt those aboard was to get a lucky shot through one of the portals through which the gunnery teams were firing. Diocles couldn't help but notice that some of the ballistaes over which they were climbing were smashed, along with the bodies of those who been manning them. He saw his own fate in that torn and crumpled flesh—and then the view of Syracuse outside swayed as the Helepolis began traversing down the steepest portion of the Epipolae plateau's slopes. But the siege-tower stabilized itself once more, continued its relentless progress. The catwalk ended in a hatch. Leosthenes kicked it open.

Lugorix smashed his axe into the sphere of Sun. Cracks spiderwebbed out from where Skullseeker's blade was buried—then he pulled back the axe and raised it high above his head for another blow.

"This seems like a terrible idea," said Matthias.

"No one's interested in your opinion," said Eurydice.

That wasn't quite true. Lugorix was. But he knew better than to make an argument of it. He smashed the axe down again; the cracks he'd already created got wider and spawned their own cracks, rippling out around the four who stood there. Far below he could see orbs that had been pointed out to him as Aphrodite and Hermes: the only planets which were closer to Earth than the Sun itself.

But it was the Moon that everybody was interested in. Barsine had explained the plan for getting there, and it was the shittiest that Lugorix had ever heard. That he was the one setting it in motion endeared him to the scheme not in the slightest. But if it came down to certain death by falling versus getting chewed to bits by the maws of those things that were sidling down toward them, that had left Ares behind, getting ever closer… for a moment he permitted himself a look at all those myriad teeth and eyes—it was the eyes that were the worst, they looked so human. But no human face was ever so hypnotic…

"Finish this," hissed Barsine.

The next blow from his axe did just that.

"What in the name of all the *gods?"* breathed Ptolemy.

"Exactly," said Eumenes softly. "The gods."

Anyone else would have trouble claiming ownership. The machine was several times the length of Eumenes' ironclad, though it wasn't much taller: it stood barely two ship's masts in height. It sat atop a series of low wheels and was the shape of a crescent moon, its extremities sweeping back from the men who stared at it, so graceful it looked almost more organic than mechanic. Eumenes was reminded of some great bird. But this bird had a ramp that led up into its belly.

"We have made it," said Kalyana as he led them up that ramp.

"Made what," said Ptolemy.

"Like you need to ask," said Eumenes—even as he ducked to avoid the dagger that Ptolemy was hurling at his head. It missed by inches, clattering against the wall behind them. Both men drew their swords while Kalyana backed out of the way, deeper into the room they'd just arrived at. It was lined with rows of windows and crammed with banks of lights—there were things that looked like levers and gears and dials amidst them, but they weren't of a sort that Eumenes had ever seen. And right now he didn't really have time to study them because he was too busy fending off Ptolemy. Sparks flew in front of his face as their two blades clashed together, each searching for an opening, each seeking to deny the other. Ptolemy and Eumenes had fought together for years, and not just side by side either. They had been matched in the ring since they were boys—were among that chosen group of youths who were Alexander's own sparring partners, and as such were the only men alive to have ever managed to have broken past the king's guard. So now they fought as they'd never fought before—no holds barred, no practice moves, each seeking to slit the other's throat, penetrate the other's chest, disembowel the other as they battled with the *xiphos* in the dance could only have one ending.

And finally Eumenes achieved it.

He feinted at Ptolemy's neck—but then struck low, slashing his leg with a stroke that brought the larger man to his knee, then kicked him in the face hard enough to send teeth flying. Ptolemy was on the ground, blood streaming from his mouth. Eumenes stepped in toward him, raised his sword.

Something sliced through his back.

Right through his spine—he dropped, both legs paralyzed in a single instant by the blade that Kalyana had just used on him. Though really it looked like more of a whip—Kalyana pulled back his hand, snapping the bending blade back in toward him, letting it wrap around his wrist, back beneath his cloak...

"An *urumi*," said Kalyana in a manner that was almost apologetic. "My people know it as the coiled sword."

"I thought you were... no warrior," muttered Eumenes. His back was sticky with blood.

"The stakes are too high to allow me such luxury," said Kalyana.

"Which allowed us to come to an arrangement," said Ptolemy. He pulled himself painfully to his feet, standing on one leg while he tore strips of cloth from his cloak to bandage his other. But all the while he was grinning down at Eumenes.

"*Fuck,*" said Eumenes. "He's been working for *you*."

"And now it's time to go to work," said Kalyana.

At first Diocles thought he was looking out into the engine-room of the Helepolis. But he'd already seen that room, near the base of the structure. This was something else—an enormous shaft that cut down toward the lower levels, filled with a whole network of pulleys and gears to which were attached huge rectangle-shaped stones that rose or fell depending on the minute adjustments that members of the crew were making. The entire system groaned and creaked, obviously under enormous strain. In a flash, Diocles understood: the stones were counterweights. They were the Helepolis' brakes—the mechanisms which allowed the Helepolis to descend steep slopes without losing control.

Which of course was why Leosthenes had led them to this room.

"Somehow I knew I'd find you here," said a voice.

They looked up—a man wearing the uniform of a Macedonian general stood on a platform on the other side of the room. Leosthenes seemed to recognize him.

"Perdiccas," he said. "So nice to see you again."

For just a moment, the universe was nothing but shards of light—all those countless pieces of heliosphere as they shattered all around like some vast sea of glass crumbling. Lugorix barely had time to swing Skullseeker's straps over his shoulder and do exactly what Barsine had told them all to do: grab onto one of those shards.

And fall.

He had both hands on it, was suspended below it as it dropped. But it was descending nowhere near as fast as he would have thought. To his astonishment, it was doing exactly what Barsine had said it would—wafting down like a leaf caught in an autumn gust, slow enough to make him wonder if he was actually going to survive, fast enough to outpace all those terrible heads above. Below him he could see Matthias and Eurydice clinging to a larger shard; even further below them was Barsine, shifting her body back and forth as though she was being buffeted by some kind of wind. It seemed to Lugorix that he could literally see the waves that wind was making, ripples in the substance through which they were all plunging. But that was why she'd been so emphatic that they had to follow her—she'd said the aether got thicker the closer one got to the terrestrial sphere, and that if one knew how, one could ride its waves as though they were really some kind of liquid. *Stay in my wake and you'll survive,* she said, and they were all trying to do just that as she twisted and turned like an acrobat, riding the aetheric currents past Aphrodite, shining out green amidst the darkness—and then past Hermes, an orange hue set against the backdrop of the Earth. Then for the first time Lugorix saw the Moon from above—nothing on it he recognized, no man in the moon, nothing that formed any pattern, just pock-marks, endless fields of them as though they contained all the universe's distemper…

"The ancients built to last," said Kalyana.

Eumenes could only writhe on the floor as the Indian sage went about his work—turning dials, pulling levers, shifting knobs. A humming noise filled the room, rose steadily in volume, accompanied by a vibration that rumbled through the place.

"Shall I?" said Ptolemy.

"By all means," replied Kalyana.

Ptolemy sat down at one of the chairs that stood on a raised dias up against the forward windows, wedged in between banks of instruments. There was a whirring as what might have been a miniature version of one of Aristotle's lenses descended from the ceiling, suspended on a slender metal arm. Ptolemy pulled the lens toward him, stared through it out at the lunar cavern that lay outside the window. A hatch slid open in the chair's armrest. A slab rose from that hatch. It contained an indentation shaped exactly like a human hand.

"Keyed to the bloodline," muttered Eumenes.

"Yes," said Kalyana. "Which Ptolemy partakes in. How did *you* think to bypass it?"

Eumenes grimaced. "Alexander gave me one of his fingers."

Ptolemy was aghast. "*Cut it off* and *gave* it to you?" But Kalyana just nodded. "Exceedingly generous of him," he said. "Then again, I'm sure he was exceedingly anxious to possess this chariot."

"Chariot," said Eumenes. "Is that what you know it as?"

Kalyana looked like he was choosing his words carefully. "For me, it is the chariot of Krishna. For you perhaps it is the wing that gave Hermes flight. For Ptolemy—"

"It's power," said Ptolemy. "Just that. Nothing more."

"Spoken like a pragmatic Macedonian," said Kalyana. "I think that's why I enjoyed our conversations so much, Eumenes. You have all the imagination and wonder of your people, so why do you serve another?"

Because... he was the only one who could unite us. Because he alone recognized my abilities. Because I thought a man could resist the ultimate temptation and still remain a man. Because.... "Why do you?" was all he said.

"Because *I'm* the one with the bloodline and I was willing to negotiate," said Ptolemy, cutting in. "Unlike Alexander—"

"*Because he thinks you'll be easier to control then me,*" said Eumenes. He looked at Kalyana. "True? You need the bloodline to fly this damn ship and this is how you get it."

"Actually," said Kalyana, "all I need is blood."

His blade flashed so quickly Ptolemy barely had time to scream.

"You guys have *met?*" asked Agathocles.

"Once," said Perdiccas. His face had a weatherbeaten quality to it. He looked like the consummate senior soldier. Even Diocles had heard of him—he was supposed to have survived an impossible march through the African desert and then somehow tricked the untrickable Phoenicians and taken their fleet from under their noses, subsequent to which he'd been promoted to be one of Alexander's two chief marshals, second only to the king's own consort, Hephaestion himself. Now he stood on a platform in the midst of chugging machinery, looking down at them, archers beside him, a wry smile on his face. The situation was all the more surreal for the crew of the braking room ignoring the conversation taking place around them.

"We were introduced during one of those sham negotiations between Macedonia and Athens," said Leosthenes. "Before the Macks launched their legions at Persia. That's what I think it must have been about, really—talks for the benefit of Persian spies so they would think Macedonia's main focus at the time was Athens. Philip was offering us—oh, I don't know—something involving trade routes through the Hellespont. Greater access to the Black Sea granaries. Some bullshit like that."

"You're being unkind," said Perdiccas, but his smile didn't waver.

"I'm being accurate," said Leosthenes. "It wasn't a serious offer."

"But the one I made to you more recently was."

Leosthenes shrugged. "I need more out of life then gold."

"You mean you already *have* gold."

"Probably not anymore."

"No," said Perdiccas, "and now it's too late. Same for you Agathocles. That *is* you, isn't it? I'm sure you wouldn't have sent a proxy with your city about to perish. We offered you the lordship of all Syracuse—"

"Under your dominion," spat Agathocles.

"But you've got to serve someone," said Perdiccas. "There's no getting around that. Even Alexander is in thrall to visions and voices. Both of you were offered the sky by Macedonia, and now you're going to get just enough earth to bury you in. It didn't have to be money either. Didn't have to be power. Where's your imagination?"

"I got your imagination right here," said Agathocles.

There was a deafening explosion.

The Moon filled Lugorix's vision now, the most barren terrain he had ever seen: a maze of mountains and canyons and sheets of rock, and he could only wonder as to the desolation of the real thing. It was hard to tell the size of what was down there—he kept thinking he was right above it, but it kept on getting closer. He held on as hard as he could to the shard to which he was clinging, hoping that Barsine would somehow be able to engineer a soft landing. They were heading in toward one valley in particular. There seemed to be something moving within its depths.

"I take no pleasure in causing such pain," said Kalyana.

He was certainly inflicting enough of it, though. Most of Ptolemy's skin was gone, and the outer layers of his flesh were quickly following—a strand of narrow meat that Kalyana had fed directly into the ship's gears, which were whirling ever faster, almost as though they were an animal that gained energy with the meat they were consuming. The hell of it was that Ptolemy was still alive, restraints binding him to the chair while he kept on screaming in agony, though very soon he would lack a mouth to do so.

"The bloodlines weren't intended to make those who possessed them masters," said Kalyana as he ministered to the writhing Ptolemy. "Quite the contrary, really. Those of the *genetikos* are tools. And need to be treated as such."

"So what does that make you?" demanded Eumenes from his position on the floor. He'd thought getting his spine slashed was as bad as it could get, but now he was almost happy to have lost half his nerve-endings. And his hands were still capable of motion. Perhaps even still capable of reaching the dagger at his belt....

"I'm the one who does what's necessary," said Kalyana. "Alexander's advance guard penetrated to the very threshold of India. His outriders crossed the Indus. I labor under no illusions as to what will happen to my land when the king returns East with fresh troops and fertile magicks. And if Alexander possesses this chariot, his subjugation of the world will be speedy indeed." Kalyana's *urumi* flashed again, and at last Ptolemy's screams stopped. Eumenes felt the floor shudder beneath his feet as the craft began to roll across the floor of the cave. Kalyana shoved Ptolemy's limp body aside, sat down at the controls.

"And what about me?" asked Eumenes. "Why am I still alive?"

"You had the king's ear. You have the king's secrets."

"I'll be damned if I'll give them to you."

"I am not so sure of that," said Kalyana evenly. "You have seen Alexander's true nature. You have seen what he hopes to become. I am thinking you are a man who is just waking up." He pulled more levers; the rumbling of the engines grew to a roar and the ship began to pick up speed, heading toward the cave mouth. Eumenes' hands tightened around the hilt of his dagger. He wondered if he should hurl it now. But he knew he'd only get one chance. And Kalyana was almost entirely protected by the back of the chair. So for now Eumenes did the thing he'd always been so good at.

Play for time.

"How is it you were the one charged with championing your people?" he asked. "The Vedic nations. Of all the warriors, scholars, princes—"

"There are no princes left," said Kalyana. "No true ones anyway." He nodded at Ptolemy as the volume of the craft reached fever-pitch. "Perhaps that is for the best. If you want to master the universe, then first you must master yourself. So I walked the paths of my mind for years until at last I came to the end of all roads. And then your king came East seeking answers and I stepped forward to provide them."

"You've done all this *on your own initiative?*" Eumenes couldn't believe what he was hearing. "No one gave you orders?"

Kalyana shrugged. "Who would dare it?" One of his hands shoved the largest of the levers forward; the other grasped something that looked half a wheel and pulled back on it. Suddenly the floor beneath Eumenes was tilting and the valley was dropping past the windows as they roared out of the moon-that-was-no-moon and off into the aether.

Only to see something falling straight in toward them.

The hand-sized canister which Agathocles had hurled was divided into three sections. One contained quicklime, another sulphur, the third water—and when the fragile seals partitioning them shattered as the bomb hit one of the counterweights a few stories down, the resultant explosion sent sheets of fire tearing back up the chamber. A deadly chain-reaction ensued. Huge weights fell past, their ropes trailing into abyss. Leosthenes leapt onto the pulleys and platforms, moving in toward Perdicccas, whose archers were already firing. But Agathocles began hurling spears in rapid succession—impaling two of the archers, while the others ran for cover.

There was plenty of that to be had. Smoke was everywhere and severed counterweights were crashing down into the shaft below. Those of the crew who hadn't been instantly crushed were doing their best to get out of there. One came running right at Diocles; he wasn't sure what he was supposed to do so he just let the man keep going. Indeed, he was running himself now—following Xanthippus as he raced along a catwalk, closing in on Perdiccas from the opposite direction as Leosthenes. The Macedonian general saw them coming, drew his sword with a snarl sharper than most blades. All the while they were all doing their best to hang on as the Helepolis swayed back and forth, the view of Syracuse shifting in the windows. Then came a snapping noise that sounded like the Gordian knot itself fragmenting: Agathocles lost his footing, tumbled away into space, the Helepolis picking up speed as it trundled down the Epipolae plateau, rocking ever more precariously from side to side.

"Who's driving now, bitch?" said Leosthenes as he reached Perdiccas.

Their blades clashed with a clang that sounded above all the bedlam.

At first Lugorix thought the thing rising toward them was some piece of the Moon with a volition all its own. It even looked like the Moon did when it was waxing—just the sliver of some great disc, curving back on both sides. But it was there that the resemblance ended: fire poured from its rear as it gained speed, heading straight at them. It was the gods' own chariot. It could be nothing else. Lugorix had the briefest glimpse of what might have been a hatch still open in its belly, a ramp retracting into that opening, the hatch sliding shut.

But just before it did so, Barsine accelerated toward it, plunged inside it.

If she expected everyone to follow her, she was disappointed—as soon as she vanished within, the craft banked sharply, leaving the three above tumbling in toward the Moon, gaining speed as they did so. Meaning they were officially screwed. Even if they survived the impact with the faux Moon, they'd be unable to get off it—left there to await the attention of all those terrible heads as they closed in from above. So Lugorix did the one thing he could do—the one thing he didn't want to do.

Use Damitra's amulet.

He had nothing else that even remotely resembled an ace in the hole. So now he held out the amulet with one hand while he clutched the shard of sunsphere in the other—instantly the amulet glowed its familiar blue and then began *pushing* him backward, propelling him onto the course of the still-swerving vehicle below him as he in turn pulled Eurydice and Matthias after him, all of them caught in the ambient undertow of the amulet. Then the chariot was filling his vision, coming straight at him. He got a quick glimpse of Eurydice and Matthias hitting the leftward side. But right ahead of him were the thing's forward windows. He stuck out his boots, crashed on through.

The Helepolis was totally out of control. All the counterweights had crashed deeper into the structure or had fallen off altogether and from the way the behemoth was lurching it was a wonder that it hadn't toppled over yet as it careened down the Epipolae's slope, flattening everything in its path. Explosions sounded from deep within as the steam engines trying to hold the monster steady blew in rapid succession. Hundreds upon hundreds of men were trying to abandon the doomed vehicle—leaping from it regardless of the height lest they suffer certain death in what was guaranteed to be the mother of all wrecks. But for those still fighting inside the demolished brake-room, fleeing wasn't an option. Diocles was only a few paces behind Xanthippus as he closed on Perdiccas, who realized that he'd only have a moment or two more to deal with Leosthenes before the newcomers reached him. The general feinted with his sword—and then in a single stroke pulled out the dart he'd concealed on his weapon's hilt and hurled it into Leosthenes' left eye. The viceroy didn't even make a sound—just crumpled backward, the penetration of his brain killing him before he hit the floor. Even as he fell, Xanthippus was leaping to take his place—but Perdiccas anticipated the move to perfection, met him with the blade of his sword, a blow that partially hacked through Xanthippus' armor and knocked him to the ground. Diocles suddenly found himself standing over his wounded lover, battling the Macedonian general. If he survived the next few blows, it was only because he didn't even try to attack—just held his ground and parried the swipes of a man who'd seen more battles than a year had days, who'd fought at Alexander's side, and who was now laughing at him as the Helepolis kept gaining speed.

"I've already won," he said. "The phalanx is moving up behind us. Don't you get it, boy? The defenses are in ruins. *My machine has done its job.*"

The walls began ripping away around them.

Lugorix tumbled through into the chariot; crashed over a chair and hit the floor, losing his grip on the amulet. Something metallic flashed at his head—there was nowhere to duck; instinctually he held up the sunshard as a shield, which shattered as the weapon smacked into it and danced away. It was a bending blade that looked to be a cross between a sword and a whip, held by a much older man whose skin was as dark as his beard was white. Lugorix rolled along the floor, away from him—and then leaped to his feet and swung Skullseeker, parrying the next few blows from the sword-whip. As he did so, he saw three bodies huddled against the far wall. One might have been a man once. Another was a man he'd seen earlier: the Macedonian leader Eumenes.

The third was Barsine.

She was bleeding from the mouth and had slash wounds along her chest and legs. She was trying to talk, but wasn't really accomplishing too much.

"You've killed her," said Lugorix, swiping at the old man's head, who ducked back with unnatural speed. Through the leftward window the Gaul could see that Eurydice and Matthias were still out there—still hanging on and unable to do much else as the chariot soared upward.

"She killed herself," said the man. "When she was impregnated with the seed of Alexander"—and then without looking round, the man whipped the curved sword behind him, blocking a dagger that the prone Eumenes had suddenly hurled at him, sending that dagger ricocheting straight back into Eumene's leg—who glanced down at it, a wry smile on his face.

"Damn you Kalyana," he said.

"It seems we might not be continuing our conversation after all," said the old man.

"That's for sure," said Lugorix. He stepped forward with Skullseeker, putting all his force into the swing—a blow capable of shearing through metal and bone and anything else it needed to. But the curved sword connected first, whipping round his axe and holding on as though it was a rope—and all of sudden Lugorix was in a tug-of-war, clutching onto his axe as the man pulled backward, the blade tightening its grip further. Lugorix had the strength but somehow that didn't matter. He felt like a great fish being reeled in by a tiny string. One move and he could snap it. But he couldn't find that move...

"You should let go of your axe," said Kalyana. "It will be less painful that way."

"Less painful for you," said Lugorix. He noticed Barsine was trying to pull herself across the floor even as the tug on his axe intensified. Then the whole chariot shuddered—he and Kalyana were knocked against the instrument panel. To his horror, Lugorix lost his grip on Skullseeker entirely; hurling himself to the side, he tried to get past both weapons and deal with Kalyana directly, even though he knew there was no way the man would let him face anything but steel....

But Kalyana was no longer inside the chariot.

It happened almost too fast to see: a hydra-head shot through the cockpit window and grabbed the Indian, pulling him straight out into space in a single motion, the axe and his whip-sword both falling from his grip as they smashed against the window-frame. Kalyana never screamed, and the expression on his face never changed as he was hauled away, other hydra-heads tearing off pieces of him as they fought for the fresh meat. Lugorix steadied himself against an instrument panel—he could see several more hydra-necks entwined around the right-hand wing of the chariot. They were pulling the entire craft off course even as more hydra-heads reached in toward it. Off on the left, Matthias and Eurydice were still hanging on, but they wouldn't be doing so for much longer. Lugorix looked desperately around—saw the amulet lying at the back of the craft. He stumbled in toward it—

"That's no longer needed," said Barsine.

As though summoning one final reserve of strength, she pulled herself into the chair and slapped her hand down onto an armrest in which (Lugorix only now noticed) the outline of a handprint was clearly visible. Next instant that handprint glowed; the ship's engines grew thunderous. Wisps of smoke curled up from the hydra-necks coiled around the right wing. They writhed like paper curling in heat.

"Help your friends," muttered Barsine.

Lugorix grabbed the blade of Skullseeker, extended the handle out to where Matthias was. Eurydice seized the Greek's hand as the Gaul pulled them both in. Barsine lolled in the chair, looking more dead than alive, staring at her hand implanted in the incandescent armrest as though it wasn't her hand. Then she raised her head and gazed out at the hundreds of hydra-necks snaking in toward the craft.

"They faced me once before," she said.

Her whole body shook as the chariot spat fire.

The jagged remnants of the exterior wall framed Perdiccas against the onrushing sprawl of central Syracuse: plume of helmet waving, sword weaving, pieces of the accelerating Helepolis falling past him as he systematically broke down Diocles' guard. Another blow, and Diocles' *xiphos* flew from his hand. Perdiccas drew his sword back one more time—

And Agathocles ran his last spear straight through him.

Perdiccas staggered back, dropping his sword, grabbing at the spearshaft, the spearhead protruding from his back. He seemed to be trying to tug it out. To the extent he succeeded, he died faster. He muttered something about Macedonia and glory and then stopped breathing as Agathocles pulled himself up onto the platform, still clinging onto the rope that he'd grabbed a few stories down. He knelt over the prone Xanthippus, looked at the blood that was pooling under his cuirass.

"How is he?" he asked.

"I'll live," muttered Xanthippus.

"No we won't," said Diocles.

There was no way they could. Every part of the Helepolis that had allowed it to retain control was shattered. All the brakes were gone. The engines were blown. Half the wheels had fallen off. Most of the lower levels were in flames. The shrieks of the trapped and the dying were almost louder than the howl of breaking metal as the structure kept on hurtling downhill. The top ten stories had already fallen off—and then the next ten followed, hundreds of pieces flying out behind what was left. Now there was nothing above the men on the platform save sky. Up ahead, the Epipolae ended in a steep escarpment, below which was the central city itself. Diocles knelt beside Xanthippus, holding his hands, cradling him. They were going to die, but they were going to die together. All the shouting and crashing around him began to fade away.

Then there was only silence.

So this was what it was like to be dead.

Except he wasn't: Diocles looked up to see that he was still on the top of what was left of the Helepolis as it raced downhill. But he was staring out at everything through a weird purple light. It took him a moment to see the source of that light: an amulet that Agathocles was holding, the orb of its illumination enveloping the three men.

"What in the name of Hades is *that?*" asked Xanthippus.

"Something I was really hoping I wouldn't have to use," replied Agathocles. The Helepolis reached the escarpment and flew off into space. For just the briefest of instants Diocles could see the whole central city laid out before him as though in a dream—and then they were tumbling down toward it, the indigo orb they were in just one piece amidst an avalanche of debris from the Helepolis as what was left of the structure disintegrated. Wood and metal and bodies flew everywhere as they crashed through into the city's lower Neapolis district, a hail of shit smashing through roof-tops and walls and people. But the purple orb never stopped—it just kept *bouncing,* like a children's ball, the three men inside it huddled together as they hit the roof of the temple of Apollo and careened over another wall and into the hippodrome beyond it. They rolled along a chariot raceway, slowing down, finally coming to a halt against a wall where they lay in a heap.

Agathocles flicked something on the amulet and the light switched off. He pulled himself slowly to his feet, looking up at the rows of benches stretching all around them.

"Mind explaining what just happened?" said Xanthippus as Diocles cradled him.

Agathocles nodded. He stared around at the burning city, looking like he was about to weep. "It's what *didn't* happen," he said. "From the moment Aristotle reached Syracuse, my whole goal was to loot his lab and kidnap him," he said. "The only way to save my city: I made one run myself, and another through proxies. The first yielded me *this*"—he pocketed the amulet—"while the second brought me nothing but the news that Aristo-tle was dead at the hands of Macedonian agents."

Diocles was scarcely listening. He was too busy removing Xanthippus' cuirass and tearing off strips of his own tunic, bandaging the wound. It didn't seem to be deep but it was right next to where the arrow had struck him back on the beach. There was plenty of blood.

"You'll want to get some wine on that," said Agathocles.

"I could use some wine elsewhere too," said Xanthippus, grimacing with pain as Diocles wrapped the makeshift bandage. "So Aristotle made that thing of yours?"

"I doubt it," said the Syracusan. "I think it's a piece of ancient magick. From what I've learnt, there're several of them, one for each of the colors of the rainbow, and each of them have different effects. I'd hoped to collect more, use them to stop Macedonia."

"Too late for that," said Xanthippus. He gestured up above the arena, up along the trail of wreckage that the runaway Helepolis had left, all the way to the very top of the Epipolae. Steel glinted all along those heights.

Along with the banners of Alexander the Great.

"The Macedonian phalanx," breathed Diocles.

But Agathocles was looking in the other direction—staring up above the city, an odd expression on his face. The clouds were clearing. The sun was coming through.

"What?" said Diocles.

A vast screaming filled the sky.

CHAPTER TWENTY-FOUR

The chariot turned out to be crammed with guns of every descrip-tion, crowded all along the length of what Lugorix was coming to think of as the wings. He'd have expected nothing less but he was still in awe as the hydra's heads disintegrated before the roar of the craft's weaponry: rays of light, beams of fire, and thousands of tiny iron balls tore through the necks and sent their flesh falling down in pieces, splattering against the chariot, some of it sailing through the open window where it slapped against the back of the wall against which everyone except Barsine was huddling. She looked like total shit. Her head was lolling from side to side as she sent the craft roaring past what was left of the planets, the Earth-disc dwindling beneath them as they hurtled in toward one of the holes in the vast sphere's shell. The same one they'd come in, in fact. But there was something peculiar about it. It took Lugorix a moment to figure out what.

"Where did all the fires go?" he asked.

"Cauterized," said Barsine. "Automated processes to wall off further damage."

"Not like we haven't done enough already," said Eurydice. They swept through the hole in the ceiling and out into mist. They could see nothing, though Lugorix could feel the craft banking sharply, the occasional plat-form and ladder reeling past, way too close. And then they were completely surrounded by mist, getting ever darker. As though her life was linked to that light, Barsine began to slide from the chair.

"Hold me up," she murmured—but Lugorix was already leaping forward, grabbing her shoulders, steadying her in the seat, keeping her hand pressed against that glowing armrest. To his horror, that hand was icy cold.

"My mother is dead," her voice said with suddenly renewed strength. "I'm sorry. The shock of direct interface with the chariot finished her."

"You mean *you* finished her," said Eurydice from the back wall where she and Matthias clung to each other. It was tough to tell which of them looked more freaked out amidst the vehicle's headlong rush. Lugorix grabbed Barsine and shook her.

"Come back," he said. *"Please."*

"I said she's gone," her voice said. "I'm all that's left."

"I don't even know who you are," said Lugorix dully.

"Don't you *get* it?" said Eumenes. "The one who battles the hydra?"

"Hercules reborn," said Eurydice and her voice had gone all hollow.

"I haven't even *been* born," said the voice, no longer sounding female, no longer sounding anything at all. "This place feels familiar, but I can't tell if that's because I've been here before or simply because of what runs in my blood." The mist outside was almost entirely black now—then suddenly they roared out of the top of the tower whose base they'd entered all that time ago, its lights falling away beneath them. They seemed to Lugorix to be the same type of yellow-white illumination as that which winked amidst the levers of the chariot. The tower fell away as they soared toward the vault of the underworld.

But the floor of that underworld was changing rapidly.

The tower they'd just left was shaking—and then toppling. The ground was crumbling all across that great space, collapsing as though into a sinkhole. The rivers were draining away, becoming waterfalls that poured away into darkness—revealing something impossibly huge beneath all that collapsing surface, something with giant gnarled branches sprouting up from around a vast trunk which could only be described as a—

"Tree," breathed Eurydice.

"That's what holds up the Earth," said Barsine's son—for Lugorix could no longer think of it as Barsine. His mind was so far gone he could no longer really think at all.

"But what holds up the tree?" said Eurydice.

"No one's ever gone down to find out," said Hercules.

"Not even you?"

"Not when the gods are down there."

"That's where the rulers of Hades sleep?"

"Not anymore. *They're waking up.*"

And maybe it was true. There seemed to be some kind of huge, sinuous *movement* in those depths, as well as a glowing that was altogether different from that of the phosphorescent forests that had just tumbled away into nothing. It seemed almost like the embers of some great fire. Lugorix was happy that the chariot was steadily gaining height, climbing up toward the ceiling. But Eumenes didn't seem pleased at all.

"*You* did it," he said to the thing at the chariot's controls. "*You* woke them up. That was the whole point of your coming down here, wasn't it?"

"You keep on assuming that I have the answers," said Hercules. "I don't. When my mother's body boarded this craft, your friend was ready. You saw what happened: he used the ship's internal defenses to batter the life out of her and almost kill me too. So don't make the mistake of thinking I've got some kind of masterplan. I'm making this up as I go: I became aware of myself about *half an hour ago*—came to full consciousness inside my dying mother, absorbed her own consciousness as I did so."

"Thus does your own blood condemn you," said Eumenes.

"Spare me," said Hercules.

"Too many have already done so. It's like Kalyana said: those with the *genetikos* were intended to be tools of the those who created them. So don't try to—"

"I'm not," said Hercules. "I probably *am* the tool of those stirring below. Do you think I'm a fool? Turning on this chariot has activated something that lay latent. So now the Chthonic gods themselves are coming back to life, to take charge of the machinery that kept watch over them while they slept. But as to how long they will take to wake—neither you nor I know for sure." Barsine's right hand reached out, turned a dial—and suddenly the chariot went vertical, flinging everybody back to the wall. Only Lugorix held onto the flight-chair, held onto Barsine while they burned up a shaft just barely wide enough to accommodate the vehicle. He buried his face in her hair while rock streaked past, tried not to listen while that mouth kept talking:

"But if it *was* all their trap, then so be it. I don't *feel* loyalty to them, that's for sure. Not like my father. He really *does* think the gods are talking to him, that he exists to be their loyal servant."

"And what about you?" muttered Eumenes. "What do you intend to do?"

"What my mother wanted," said Hercules.

They soared out into the world above.

Rising away from a cratered mountain—roaring above the greenery of adjacent coasts facing each other across a sea of sun-polished blue… Lugorix didn't recognize any of it. But Eurydice did.

"We're over Sicily," she said.

Eumenes nodded. "We just got spat out of Mount Etna."

"Had to emerge somewhere," said Hercules as blood ran from his mother's mouth. "There are many portals between this world and the one below. They cause no end of trouble." Barsine's dead hands tightened on the controls; the craft swung about, describing a long turn as it descended toward a long line spanning Italy and Sicily. Just as they got close enough to see it was a bridge of boats and ramps, flame ripped from the chariot again, long streaks of light that seared in toward several points along the bridge. There were a series of monstrous explosions. The biggest two occurred on land: huge clouds of fire rising up above the boot of Italy and the edge of Sicily.

"So much for the Macedonian supply-lines," said Hercules. The chariot's engines surged as it hurtled down the Sicilian coast, running due south.

"We're heading for Syracuse," said Eurydice, understanding.

"Yes. At the hour of Alexander's triumph."

"And you know this how?"

"He's my father." Part of Lugorix wanted to sweep Barsine's head off with Skullseeker. Part of him didn't dare harm the god-child she'd created in tandem with the man she'd known such terrible passion with. "He knows I'm coming for him and yet there is nothing he can do. His stranglehold on the elements is broken and his bid to conquer the world is at end." As he said this, they saw plumes of smoke in the air ahead of them. Syracuse was fast approaching. The chariot accelerated, dipping in low toward the plateau that dominated the city. Lugorix caught a glimpse of the Macedonian army covering that rock, swarming down into the town.

Then the chariot opened up with all its weapons.

They circled back twice more, mercilessly gunning down the invaders, raining down liquid fire on elephants and men and golems as the invincible phalanx broke and fled. It wasn't like the Macedonians didn't try.

Rocks and projectiles of every description hit the craft but nothing made a dent. The chariot veered back over the Macedonian camp and destroyed it with a single bomb while the surviving defenders of Syracuse cheered and cheered. When it was over, they roared away, gaining height, climbing out over Italy, over Europe, rising ever higher. The real disc of Earth lay below now. Yet Lugorix still found himself wondering if it was really any different from the one he'd already seen, save in size. Above them was only Sun and sky—but now he knew that the daytime blaze of that Sun blotted out all that cosmic machinery overhead.

"That's where we're going now," said Hercules as though reading his mind.

"Why?" Lugorix wasn't following. "We've done what you wanted to do."

"I've only just *started*. You saw what's going on down there. The war between Macedonia and Athens is over. But the real war is just beginning. The Plutonian gods are awakening. Which means someone needs to get the Olympians into the game fast. Or else rise up into the heavens and take charge of their machinery."

"We saw how well *that* worked downstairs," said Eurydice sardonically.

"But he's right," said Eumenes with the tone of someone making up their mind at long last. "We don't have a choice. We need to find their calculator-of-worlds and switch it on so that we can...." His voice trailed off.

"Yes?" said Eurydice—and then they all saw it, another flame in the sky, a ball of fire rising up toward them out of the heart of Italy, closing on them with insane speeds. Eurydice's face went white.

"Avernus," she said. *"Another of those gates"*—and then the fireball hit the chariot. There was a deafening bang and this time Lugorix was hurled across the craft. For a moment there was nothing outside the windows save flame. The roar of engine shredded away into a high-pitch whining that intensified as the craft plummeted. Lugorix hauled himself back to the chair to which the body of Barsine was somehow still clinging, her hand gripping that armrest but no longer resting on the imprint.

"I need you to hold my hand there," muttered the mouth of the woman he'd loved like no other. He reached out and did just that, grabbing onto the back of her chair as the machine stabilized slightly. But nowhere near enough—it was more of a controlled dive now, the Earth still rushing up toward them. At the last moment, the mind of Hercules or the body of Barsine or his own hope or just plain luck managed to even the thing out. They just missed a range of mountains, soared back up into the air. Ahead of them were endless plains of grass. Off to the right was a body of water...a giant lake of some kind...

"The Black Sea," said Eumenes.

But they were moving past it, leaving it behind as they descended. Barsine's body gripped the controls, throwing her whole weight into it, leaning this way and that as though the force of her physical exertions could somehow maintain control. But they kept getting ever lower. Endless green-brown became tractless steppes, nothing in all directions. They were racing just above the ground now.

"Get ready," said Barsine—and this time it *was* her voice.

They hit.

And bounced back into the air, still throttling forward. And down again. And then back up—skipping through a vast plain of grassland. Each time they impacted more of the chariot broke apart and more of what remained caught fire and all the while all Lugorix could do was cradle Barsine's broken body, trying to somehow shield the living baby within. Smoke filled his vision and noise filled his brain and finally he could see nothing and hear nothing save the tearing of metal and the roar of engines as what was left disintegrated, the craft sliding toward a halt. Even before it stopped, he was climbing out the front window, choking against the smoke as he leapt onto the wing, ran down it and jumped into the grass. He set Barsine down, then turned back to the shattered chariot. There wasn't much left of it—but he waded back into that smoke to see if he could save anyone else. Yet even as he did so, Eurydice emerged, her face ash-black, Eumenes riding piggy-back on her shoulders while she carried Matthias in her arms.

He was dead.

There was no doubt about it. His neck was broken, his head at an unnatural angle. Eurydice was weeping, staggering, and it was all Lugorix could do to get through to her that they had to keep moving away from the chariot lest its remnants explode. He took the limp Matthias from her, led her over to where he'd placed Barsine, put his friend down beside the dead princess. And then he was kneeling beside him, holding his hands, closing his eyes, wishing him good fortune in the afterlife. But inside, he just felt hollow. He gradually became aware that Eumenes was speaking to him.

"We need to operate right now," said the Greek.

Lugorix didn't understand, but Eurydice did. She drew her knife and bent over Barsine. Three strokes of the blade and the noise of a baby's crying filled the air. She lifted him out and held him for a moment—then handed him to Lugorix.

"She wanted you to keep him safe," she said.

Lugorix gripped the baby that had called itself Hercules—that might yet call itself Hercules again. It looked like a normal baby—which was surprising given that Barsine hadn't made it past the sixth month of pregnancy. But holding it felt anything but normal. It felt like it was his own child. And as he stared into its eyes, he realized they were odd: one was brown, the other blue. Unlike those of regular newborn babies, they were already focusing—staring up at him as though imploring.

"It doesn't have access to adult vocal chords anymore," said Eumenes.

"He's going to have to grow up fast," said Eurydice.

Lugorix held the baby close. He looked at the splintered, flaming chariot—and then at the blackened trail that vehicle had scorched through the grasslands, a line of smoke leading back to the horizon. Then he looked down at the baby again.

"We all do," he said softly.

THREE MONTHS LATER

Frigid mountain air blew through the evening streets of the Macedonian capital. Pella in the dead of winter was about as unappetizing a place as could be imagined. People huddled indoors around their fires and no one went out without a good excuse.

That was fine by the man who'd just entered the western gates. He wasn't there to attract attention. He was nothing special. He looked exhausted and bedraggled and wore the dirty, tattered uniform of a veteran soldier. There were certainly enough like him right now. And there were so many more who wouldn't be returning. The war in the West had been lost, the army destroyed, most of the bodies too charred to even identify.

Alexander's among them.

It seemed incredible that the king who never been beaten was gone. But even more incredible were the stories told by the survivors—of how a great burning bird of the gods had descended from the skies and poured flame down upon the entire army as thousands watched from downtown

Syracuse. The bird had then climbed toward the Sun and vanished in its glare. It had subsequently been seen by witnesses over Italy, who had reported it being hit by a sudden eruption from the crater of Avernus that had been unlike any other volcanic eruption they'd ever seen: a single bolt of lava shooting for miles into the sky that struck the bird and sent it streaking off wounded, metal feathers falling for miles, smoke and fire trailing behind it as it vanished northeast, into the heart of Europa. What had happened there, no one knew. There were rumors that the bird had crashed into the steppes north of the Black Sea. Macedonian cavalry had galloped north from the naval bases on the coast. But what they found, only the king knew.

And there was only one king now. He sat in his palace and no one saw him. Earlier in the year all the talk around the campfires was whether he had one son or two, but now he had none. He had lost one in Sicily, the other (so it was rumored) in the far west, at the world's edge. He had no flesh to call his own anymore. Save his own…

He still had a kingdom, though. Not just Macedonia either: the East was still his; Persia showed no signs of shaking off his yoke, and he showed no signs of coming to terms with Athens. That city had held onto at least some of its empire—had kept at some portion of its navy, had regained Carthage and struck a deal with Syracuse. Now the world waited to see what would happen next.

Nor was it simply about kings and empires anymore. It was something more. First the hairy star; then the storms; then the burning bird. And now the tremors in the Earth. The autumn had been bad. The winter promised to be worse. It seemed the ground shook every few days now. Strange portents had been seen. Oracles said the gods were displeased. Priests kept to themselves. Peasants kept to their villages at night. They were said to fear monsters that had crawled up from the underworld and that roamed the woods around them. No one of any repute had seen one. Still, it made people nervous. It made it easier for the man to skulk through Pella. He was no monster. He may have been missing a finger, but no one would notice that. No one would care. He was just one of the crowd.

Now he was one of the king's guards. He knew a brothel where some of them cavorted. He knew a back door. He never even used the front—just went straight into one of the rooms and relieved the client within of his uniform and his life. The girl too. By the time they found the bodies none of this would matter. Ten minutes later he was riding with a score of other guards across the promontory that led to the palace, escorting a train of wagons carrying supplies. Five minutes after that he was moving through the darkened, draft-filled halls. He didn't need any credentials now. He was at one with the shadows of the flickering braziers. He blended right in—walked past sentry-posts and guards and he was just darkness flitting on the wall.

Getting into the throne room was a little more difficult. There were no guards inside, but there were plenty of traps. Fortunately he knew most of them. And those that didn't, he was able to deduce. He knew too much of the mind of the man who had set them. In short order he was climbing across the vaulted ceiling that overlooked the throne room—and then sliding down one of the lion-emblazoned banners that hung from the arches. From the bottom of the banner it was twenty feet to the floor. The man dropped to it as lithely as a cat.

Then he approached the throne. It was the only thing in that huge chamber that wasn't entirely in darkness. Torches surrounded the giant chair, their light making the tree from which it had been carved look all the more misshapen.

Same with the man who sat in it. If anything, Philip had gotten even fatter. It would have been impossible for him to get uglier. He stared at the figure closing on his throne and didn't seem in the least surprised.

"You took your time getting here," he said—and raised a wine goblet in mock-toast.

The figure stopped, threw back his hood. "It wasn't easy," he replied.

"Neither was being defeated, I'm sure."

Alexander nodded. He'd seen it in the mirror: his face looked five years older. He felt at least ten. "Hephaestion is dead," he said dully.

"Dead?" asked Philip. "Or just keeping a low profile?"

"He was burnt across half his body. I held him as he died."

"That must have been touching."

"I never"—Alexander stopped for a moment. Then: "I never imagined defeat would be so hard."

"You mean you thought you'd never be defeated."

"It wasn't a fair fight."

Philip laughed. *"Fair?* That word means nothing. You knew the stakes. You failed to master them."

"So did you."

"Ptolemy—"

"—met the same fate as Eumenes."

"You should have gone yourself," said Philip.

"I would have lost my army."

"You *did* lose your army."

Alexander nodded. Almost like a chastised child. Then—"How many soldiers do we have left?"

"*I* have thirty thousand," said Philip. "And twice as many allied units."

"Enough to hold onto Persia."

"Enough to continue to fight Athens."

"Which you don't intend to do."

"Who knows?" The king slurped wine. "But they're no longer the real enemy. The folks you stirred up downstairs are."

"They won't be up here for a while."

"We don't know that, do we?" Philip's voice dripped sarcasm. "They could be here in a hundred years. They could be here next Tuesday. My guess: we don't have much time. Tell me, do you still hear the voices?"

"No. They've gone silent."

Laughter: "Because they got what they needed from you. Someone dumb enough and powerful enough to switch the lights back on."

"If we had been able to secure the chariot—"

"They never intended for mortals to have it."

"What they *intend* and what they've *gotten* may be two different things. There was a lot of fighting downstairs. A lot of damage. I think whatever... *apparatus* was communicating with me wasn't unscathed. Look at the weather. It's now out of control. And it used to be under *my* control."

"Only partially," said Philip. "Only to the extent their machinery allowed it. So you could stir up some waves and conjure up some clouds? So what?"

"So I still retain some powers over the elements. Some residue."

Philip's eyes narrowed. "Did you acquire one of the amulets?"

"I can only wish."

"*You're* not the one with the powers. It's *them*. That's the way they intended it."

"I disagree. I still have the—"

"*Fuck* your bloodline."

Alexander shrugged. "It's yours too."

"It's also your *son's*. Who you let slip from your control."

"I'll get him back."

Philip practically dropped his wine-glass. *"He's still alive?"*

"I know it for a fact."

"So in other words: you've fucked up totally."

"I admit there have been setbacks."

Philip threw back his head and laughed. "Name one thing that's gone right."

"I know who my father really is now."

The laughter stopped as quickly as it had started. A welter of emotions crossed the cragged face. "So you're... you understand that what happened at Siwah was a sham?"

"Yes."

"And that Zeus was a lie."

Alexander shook his head. "The voice that claimed to be Zeus... maybe. The real Zeus... never."

"I don't follow."

"Zeus is *Olympian*. Not Plutonian. He rules in the heavens above."

"And you've spoken with him how many times?"

"I don't need to speak with him to know I'm his son."

"So you really *are* still crazy."

Alexander shrugged. "A strange word to use after everything that's happened."

"Nonetheless: an accurate one."

"How so?"

"You need to put aside this childish obsession with sucking the dicks of superbeings."

"And suck yours instead?"

"I said don't be childish," snapped Philip. "You truly think those above will bear you any more love than those below?"

"It's not love I'm interested in. It's finding a way to kick the Plutonians back down to Hell when they show up." A long pause, then: "I *accept* what I couldn't before. I truly do. Your seed was put into my mother without interference—without acceleration of the bloodline. But that just means that ultimately Zeus is father of us *both*—the one who set all this in motion."

"Too simplistic a theory," said Philip. "There were a lot of cooks in the kitchen, and they weren't all on the same side either."

"Nonetheless. The only way for me to salvage this situation is to get upstairs—get to the All-Father's side—"

"And take his place," said Philip. "No? You step inside his machinery, you take charge of his magicks—if you could do that, you wouldn't just be the one who ruled the world. You'd rule the *universe*."

"Is there any other ambition worth having now?" asked Alexander. "There are god only knows how many other gods downstairs waking up, plotting—among themselves, against each other, against all of us. There are at least *seven* other bloodline-houses that might have bred players capable of climbing into the gears of the celestial sphere. So what the hell else are we supposed to do but *get moving?*"

"Work together," said Philip. "That's what." Alexander said nothing. "You know I'm right. You may have come back here thinking you were going to try to kill me, but I'm sitting in this throne and you know what it's capable of. Same way you know that the reason we failed was that we didn't work together. Our men worked at cross-purposes. That can't happen again."

"It won't," said Alexander.

His multi-hued eyes *shone;* suddenly Philip was illuminated as though from within—every bone in his body glowing with white-heat, his whole skeleton incandescent for a single instant. He screamed and writhed—and gripped the arm-rests of the chair, which sent a hail of missiles flying at Alexander: arrows and spears and iron-balls, all of them flying in from every corner of the room, every single one of them somehow missing as Alexander just stood there, as Philip's screaming ceased and his fat melted and his body set fire to his throne.

The doors to the throne room flew open. Guards poured into the room—only to stop as they saw who stood beside the flaming pyre.

"I'm king now," said Alexander.

There was a stunned pause.

"The only one," he added.

No one was arguing. More soldiers entered the great chamber—and still more. The word spread quickly; they filled that throne room up. In Persia, Alexander's subjects had bowed before him with *proskynesis*. But Macedonians crawled before no man. So now they proclaimed him king by acclamation, in the tradition of their army. He had been king for months by his own proclamation, but he wasn't about to refuse the direct ratification of his father's forces. After all, now they were his.

Then that army parted as an old man entered the room. He stooped and used a stick to steady his walking. But he walked steadily enough as he went right up to Alexander and kissed him on both cheeks. His eyes were wet with tears.

"My king," he said.

Alexander embraced him. "Thank you for rendering that throne useless."

"It was straightforward enough."

"Getting inside his head was not."

The old man shrugged, lowered his voice so that only Alexander could hear. "He thought I had returned to his side in both body and spirit. The prodigal philosopher. He used the threat of his assassins to convince me that I'd be safer in Pella. But this city is still the same cage it always was."

"Now that he is dead, that will change."

"It had better. You need me, Alexander."

"It took me too long to realize that. Do you still have qualms about my deeds?"

"Not when I've seen the decadence to which Athens has sunk with my own eyes. They are nothing but mob now."

"They were never anything else," said Alexander. "There is not a man among them whom money does not move. It blinds them—even as it makes them see what we want them to see. A poisoned sorceror, for instance."

"There are many types of poisons," said Aristotle. "And the kind that merely seems to kill can be more useful than one that actually does the job."

Alexander looked at him almost ruefully: "Yet you could have been of so much more help. You watched the game, but did not play it."

"I needed to understand its nature."

"Your daughter showed no such caution."

The old man nodded. "I taught her too much. She tampered with my work rooms. Read a few too many of my scrolls. Refused to confine herself to the tasks I'd appointed her. And now she is almost certainly dead on account of it."

"If she is still alive, you will bring her to heel."

"We'll bring all creation to heel," said Aristotle. Alexander took his hand and turned back to the troops who filled the hall. Beside him, the body of the old king kept burning, smoke pouring from the blackened throne and past the lion-banners, rising through the atrium skylights far overhead, out toward the starry orb above. Alexander held up Aristotle's hand.

"I'd like you to meet my new chancellor," he said.

APPENDIX:
BUILDING A WORLD THAT WASN'T

Alternate history—"counterfactual history," as historians like to call it—is a tricky business. The world you envision is a combination of stuff that happened and stuff that, well, *didn't*, with the latter category encompassing a spectrum that runs from the it-really-could-have-been-that-way, to the kinda-unlikely, to the downright impossible. Nonetheless, one starts with an understanding of the past as it occurred, and a few notes on that might be in order to help readers unravel the world of *Pillars*.

On Alexander the Great:

The more he recedes in history, the more he towers over it. After the death of his father, few expected the untried boy who became king of Macedonia to survive, yet in just over a decade he conquered an empire the size of which still boggles the imagination more than two millennia later. Alexander has lost none of his ability to captivate and charm during that time—but that's all the more reason for us to be careful.

What I found particularly interesting in penning this manuscript is just how far the view of Alexander in fiction has diverged from the scholarly consensus of him. Much of the literature—SF or otherwise—has followed in the footsteps of W.W. Tarn's vision of Alexander, a Victorian scholar who saw in the king echoes of the British Empire's self-styled "civilizing" mission, and who thus painted a picture of an Alexander who was not just a near-perfect ruler, but also the very best of men. Tarn's most notable influence was of course upon the peerless Mary Renault,[1] but his shadow has fallen upon many other writers, all of them quick to explain away every single act of the king's that might give his admirers the slightest pause.[2]

---

1 Jeanne Reames, "Beyond Renault", downloaded from http://myweb.unomaha.edu/~mreames/Beyond_Renault/renault.html
2 A tendency examined by Nicholas Nicastro in the introduction to his novel *Empire of Ashes*.

Yet from a scholarly point of view, Tarn's view of Alexander has long been a dead letter. Ernst Badian of Harvard University saw to that when he demolished Tarn in a series of revolutionary articles, portraying Alexander as a ruthless manipulator who excelled at *realpolitik*, a king whose ability to wreak slaughter on the battlefield was equalled only by his skill at orchestrating intrigue behind it. To quote Badian himself:

> No aspect of the career of Alexander the Great should be more important and constructive to the historian than the series of executions and assassinations by which he partly crushed and partly anticipated the opposition of Macedonian nobles to his person and policy. Yet no aspect has, on the whole, been less studied in modern times....This procedure is part of an attitude towards Alexander the Great of which Tarn was the most distinguished (though by no means the only) exponent, an attitude which has made the serious study of Alexander's reign from the point of view of political history not only impossible, but (to many students) almost inconceivable. Yet there is no plausible reason why the autocracy of Alexander the Great should not be as susceptible of political analysis as that of Augustus or Napoleon, for the grim and bloody struggle for power that went on almost unremittingly at his court is amply documented even in our inadequate sources.[3]

Badian also wrote at length on the trajectory of Alexander's megalomania, the other part of the key to understanding the king, though I'll be the first to admit that *Pillars* takes more than a few liberties in articulating a metaphysic that frames that megalomania in a rather different light. Indeed, it's only in recent years that Tarn's grip on the world-view of Alexander novelists seems to have loosened, and a more balanced view of Alexander has begun to come to the fore.[4]

On the Geopolitical Gameboard:

The question of what would have happened had Alexander turned West might just be the oldest alternate history of all, since the Roman historian Livy devoted a portion of his ninth volume to how Rome would have fared had the Macedonian Empire invaded Italy. Writing at the height of Rome's

---

3   Badian, Ernst, "The Death of Parmenio", *Transactions and Proceedings of the American Philological Association*, Vol. 91 (1960), pp. 324-338.
4   See, for example, Nicastro's *Empire of Ashes* and Annabel Lyon's *The Golden Mean*.

power, Livy was anxious to reassure his audience that Alexander would have met his match against their forefathers; his attempt to do this by naming a long list of unknown Roman generals who he believed could have taken on the champ rings less than totally convincing. Nonetheless, Livy was onto something when he observed that "Alexander died young....before he had time to experience any change of fortune." We can only say what might have been.

More recently, Arnold Toynbee's *Some Problems of Greek History* concludes with three fascinating essays that explore various permutations of Alexander and/or Philip living and potentially turning west. In some ways, Philip II remains one of those unfortunate characters of history, a man who might have been hailed as great in his own right, had it not been for the son who came after him. Yet it was Philip who built Macedonia into a superpower capable of taking on the world—and imagining the ongoing struggle between him and his son carrying over into a post-Persian mileau made for some intriguing speculation.

Of course, the West that Alexander would have ventured into was decidedly different than the world that he confronts in *Pillars*. The minor tweak is that Rome had dealt with the Samnites and consolidated central Italy; the big change is that Athens had won the Peloponnesian War—and not only that, had established an empire across much of the Mediterreanean basin. This isn't as unlikely as it might sound, since the whole rationale for the Syracusan Expedition was to open up the West to Athens in an attempt to bring unparalleled forces to bear against Sparta.[5] Peter Green's *Armada from Athens* devotes his fascinating second chapter ("Wheat, Timber, Gold") to documenting the history of Athens' longstanding interest in exploiting the resources of the West; wondering what might have happened had she harnessed them to create the empire featured in *Pillars* first occurred to me while reading Green's volume some years back. It remained only to envision Alcibiades himself as the founder of the *real* Athenian Empire, and then to sketch out a period of low-intensity conflict between Athens and Persia as backdrop to the latter's abrupt destruction at the hands of Alexander.[6] (The real problem with *Pillars*, of course, is that in such a scenario, a sensible Athens would never have allowed Macedonia

---

5   Interestingly, Thucydides himself never says the Syracusan Expedition was a *mistake* per se; he just takes issue with how it was carried out. Given it became one of the biggest military blunders of all time, this nuance on his part is worth noting.

6   Let's not forget that Periclean Athens had more than a passing interest in relieving Persia of Egypt, launching an expedition against that province only a few years before the outbreak of the Peloponnesian War.

to attain great power status in the first place; one is left to assume exceptionally poor leadership on the part of Athens, though in my defense it must be said that it woudn't be the first empire to be steered by such).

On the Technology:

I've always felt that steampunk was way too cool to be left to the stodgy old Victorians, but the really intriguing thing about the ancient world is just how much steampunk was in it already. Most people have no idea that the steam engine itself was invented in the first century A.D. by Heron of Alexandria; the problem was it was never put to any practical use. The question of the conditions sufficient and/or necessary for the "take-off" phase of industrialization is far too complex an issue to be dealt with here, and it may well be that the slave-based economies of the ancient world lacked the prerequisites for such industrialization by definition (who needs labor-saving devices when one has all the slaves one needs?).[7]

But one sure can have a lot of fun with what they came up with. With the exception of the really crazy stuff (like golems capable of combat), virtually every piece of technology in the book had its roots in some ancient prototype. If you want to get your mind blown (and who doesn't), check out Michael Lahanas' excellent website http://www.mlahanas.de/Greeks/Greeks.htm for a comprehensive list of ancient Greek technology, along with lots of cool references and pictures. To be sure, much of the tech on that list (Archimedes' steam-gun notwithstanding) is more gearpunk[8] than steampunk… but the sheer extent of that capability is something that we're only just now waking up to. When the Antikyhera wreck was first discovered, historians initially scoffed at the idea that the device contained within—which essentially functioned as an analog computer, mirroring the heavens with more than thirty distinct gears—was in fact from the ancient world. Had the device not been uncovered in that wreck, we would have had no way of suspecting it had ever been invented. And when we consider that more than ninety percent of classical learning was lost in the Dark Ages, we can only wonder at what we'll never find. As always, time has the last word.

---

7   Readers interested in exploring the question further ought to once again consult Peter Green, specifically chapter 27 of his *From Alexander to Actium*, chapter 27, "Technological Developments", which speculates at length on factors that straitjacketed the classical economies.
8   Or clockpunk. Whatever.

With special thanks to:

Kristen Dawson

Mark Williams

Brian De Groodt

Erin Sheley

Marc Haimes

Peter Watts

Howard Morhaim

Tom Doyle

Gail Carriger

Mike Brotherton

Nicola Griffith

Kelley Eskridge

Aiden Thompson

Erin Cashier

Ilona Gordon

Jeremy Lassen

Jason Williams

Ross Lockhart

Jenny Rappaport

Simran Khalsa

The Beasts

ABOUT THE AUTHOR

David Constantine resides in Los Angeles with his not-so-loyal army of cats. Learn more about the War of Athens and Macedonia at www.thepillarsofhercules.com.